I0761604

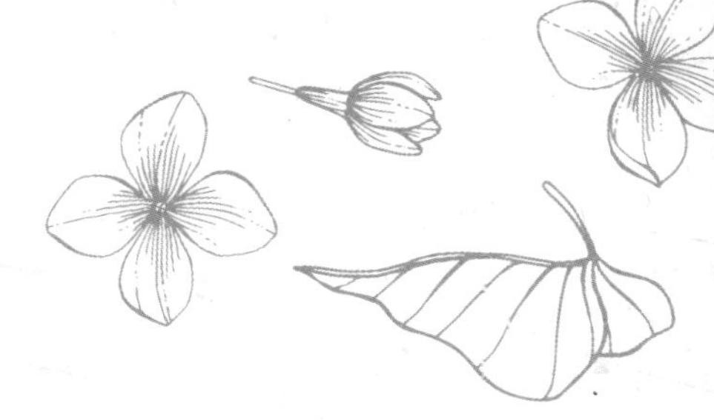

Lila and the Winds of War

Sayuri Ueda

YEN ON
New York

Lila and the Winds of War

Sayuri Ueda

Translation by Michael Blaskowsky † Cover art by Haruko Mimura

This book is a work of fiction. Names, characters, places, and incidents are the product of the author's imagination or are used fictitiously. Any resemblance to actual events, locales, or persons, living or dead, is coincidental.

Yen On
150 West 30th Street, 6th Floor
New York, NY 10001

Visit us at yenpress.com † facebook.com/yenpress † twitter.com/yenpress † yenpress.tumblr.com † instagram.com/yenpress

First Yen On Edition: November 2025
Edited by Yen On Editorial: Christopher Fox
Designed by Yen Press Design: Eddy Mingki

Yen On is an imprint of Yen Press, LLC.
The Yen On name and logo are trademarks of Yen Press, LLC.

The publisher is not responsible for websites (or their content) that are not owned by the publisher.

Library of Congress Control Number: 2025025265

ISBNs: 979-8-8554-0283-4 (hardcover)
979-8-8554-0284-1 (ebook)

1 3 5 7 9 10 8 6 4 2

HJM

Printed in South Korea

Lila and the Winds of War

Sayuri Ueda

CONTENTS

CAST OF CHARACTERS

Count George Silvestri
A Romanian nobleman with a mysterious past.

Jörg Huber
A young German man sent to the Western Front at the outbreak of World War I.
A soldier for the German Empire.

Lila
A Polish girl living with Count George Silvestri.

Xandra (Alexandra Nastase)
A doctor. She lives with Count George Silvestri and runs both the hospital and the inn.

Milos Krasić
A werewolf hidden within the Serbian Army.
He was once a member of the hajduks,
a group of Serbian brigands.

Nil
A monster of nothingness.

Fritz Ziegel
A soldier for the German Empire who serves alongside Jörg.
An excellent painter.

Fabrice LeRoy
A soldier in the French Army.

Hubert Duran
A soldier in the French Army and member of Fabrice LeRoy's soccer team.

Christine Duran
Hubert's older sister.

Radosław Kowalski
Lila's father.

Alicja Kowalski
Lila's mother.

Bernadette
A Belgian woman working in a brothel in Paris.

Diana
A German woman living in Berlin.

Elyne
Count Silvestri's wife.

Razvan
The Count's father.

Andrássy Csaba
A close friend of Razvan.
Transylvanian nobleman.

Vlad III
Walachian ruler during the fifteenth century.
Known as Vlad the Impaler.

János Hunyadi
Voivode of Transylvania.

Murad II
Sixth sultan of the Ottoman Empire.

Mehmed II
Seventh sultan of the Ottoman Empire.

Karl Liebknecht
A member of the Social Democratic Party of Germany.

Rosa Luxemburg
A revolutionary and Marxist political theorist.
Liebknecht's comrade.

Colonel Dragutin Dimitrijević
An officer in the Serbian Army. He was believed to be involved in the Sarajevo incident: the plot to assassinate Archduke Franz Ferdinand, the heir to the Austro-Hungarian throne, and his wife, which triggered World War I. (The actual assassin was Gavrilo Princip, a young Bosnian Serb.)

Map of Europe During World War I

Allied powers

Central powers

Neutral countries

*Numbers in parentheses indicate the year in which a country joined the war after it had already begun.

Part 1

I
Half a Body

1

Gray clouds stretched across the sky, so low that it almost seemed you could reach up and touch them from within the depths of the trenches. Even now, it looked as if it would start to drizzle at any moment. He felt horribly small beneath that endless sky. Like a mouse hiding low in a gutter.

Jörg rubbed his hands together and blew on them, his rifle slung across his shoulder. The early-morning air had chilled his fingers, but they were finally beginning to warm up again. The stench of stale water and putrid soil rose incessantly from underneath the duckboards laid out over the ground. Although the smell was better today than when the weather was hot, it was still awful. Yet Jörg had lost any capacity to despise it a long time ago.

As soon as a person joined the army, training camp immediately destroyed their idea of a normal life. The reality of war had exacerbated that effect, shattering the spirit of every soldier. Whether they overcorrected or failed to adapt, in the end, no one could remain sane. A person might one day cry themselves to sleep, praying to return home as soon as possible—only to wake up the next morning thinking it was only natural that the war would go on forever. Huddled for weeks on end at the bottom of a trench, surrounded by wretched odors as they indifferently consumed food and water, snatching moments of peace by showering affection on the cats that caught the ration-thieving trench rats. No one could tell the soldiers on the front line when the war would end. Even Wilhelm II, the emperor of Jörg's homeland—Germany—couldn't say what might happen in the future. The Western Front, the Eastern Front, the Balkan Peninsula—Jörg had no answer for how to douse the flames of war that had spread across the continent.

June 28, 1914. A Bosnian Serb had assassinated the heir to the Austro-Hungarian Empire and his wife during their inspection of Sarajevo, causing Austria-Hungary to declare war against Serbia on July 28. Thus began Europe's Great War—what would eventually become known as World War I.

Each nation in Europe had been faced with the choice of aligning themselves with one of the great powers or defending their own land as a neutral country.

Jörg was a soldier with the German Army. The German Empire had decided to support Austria-Hungary, and the Ottoman Empire and Bulgaria followed suit, forming the alliance of the Central powers.

France and Great Britain had elected to oppose Germany. Russia, who supported Serbia, had joined them, forming a coalition referred to as the Allied powers. Every nation of the Allies had become an enemy to Jörg.

At first, both the Central powers and the Allies believed that the soldiers fighting in this war that had consumed the whole of Europe would "be home before the leaves have fallen from the trees." They confidently declared that it would be decided within four months.

Yet the war raged on.

The middle of December arrived, and still there was no sign of an end to the conflict.

Although the war continued, on Christmas Eve of that year, soldiers from both sides left the trenches to celebrate the birth of Christ, share wine, and even play a friendly game of soccer. Neither side fired a bullet that day. The times allowed for such a moment of peace.

Christmas the following year afforded no such frivolity. Commanding officers on both sides ordered their soldiers to shoot anyone who attempted to repeat the event.

Before arriving at the Western Front, Jörg had lived in a small town in southern Hesse, where he helped out at his father's barbershop. However, his hometown had changed completely with the outbreak of the war.

A belief settled over the villagers that a man's honor demands he do everything possible for his country, so he should voluntarily join the war effort—a stance Jörg also adopted. And so he, too, soon went off to war.

His barber shears were replaced by a rifle in his new life. Jörg's days consisted of felling the enemies that ran through the sights of his M 98 or mowing down Allied soldiers with an MG 08 machine gun. A shiver had gone through his body the first time he killed someone—a French infantryman—but he hadn't felt as guilty as he thought he would. As the fusillade continued, he became absorbed in the world around him and soon began to feel nothing at all.

Exposed to the cacophony of the battlefield, the first thing soldiers lose is their hearing. The bang of rifles firing, the rumble of artillery fire striking the ground, the endless roar of machine guns spitting out rounds—every noise does horrific damage to their ears. Eventually, the only sound they can hear is that of their own breathing, and they become unable to distinguish whether even that is real or a delusion. Meanwhile, they're running into no-man's-land under orders to charge and fighting off enemy soldiers rushing into their trenches. Jörg could remember furiously beating a man with his club, then thrusting his knife into the man's stomach and chest before tearing his throat out with his trench shovel. It was the first time he'd felt as if he was truly broken.

Jörg felt nothing, no matter how terrible the act. After a battle, he returned to being just a normal person. It terrified even himself. He realized that the moment a person killed someone on the battlefield, they also killed themselves. Not only did their soul become numb, but a part of it died, meaning they could never return to the person they had been before taking a life.

And so, soldiers spilled oceans of blood across barren land and heaped up piles of corpses, hoping to push the front line even the slightest bit forward. Yet that way of fighting hardly ever showed results. The vast majority of battles ended in stalemates, with each army returning back to their trenches battered and bruised.

Every aspect of this war differed from those Jörg had heard about from his parents' generation. The amount of gunpowder used, the variety of weaponry, the scale. On top of that, enemy bullets weren't the only things that flew into the trenches. Overused cannons would sometimes misfire, raining fodder on friendly troops, and some days, warplanes even dropped bombs on them. Had he known all of this before enlisting, Jörg wasn't sure he would have joined. It would have been better for him to flee to the US, which hadn't joined the war at that point.

Is there such a thing as a war that never ends? Probably. Not because of the incompetence of generals or the mistakes of politicians and diplomats, but simply because humans will continue to decimate one another...

Jörg leaned over the edge of the trench, feeling it press slightly into his abdomen. His stomach fluttered and twisted in strange ways. Recently, every morning greeted him like this. Because when the light broke, the gunfire started.

Tormented by discomfort, he looked to the sky again and saw an unfamiliar black shape emerge slowly from behind a cloud.

It's big. A bomber?

Was it a Russian plane? A Sikorsky Ilya Muromet that had gotten lost and been blown off course or that was trying to make an emergency landing after taking damage?

No, it's something else.

The black shape was neither warplane nor bomber but had wings like an eagle's. Jörg pushed himself farther out of the trench to get a better look at it, and someone yelled at him to get down. Even a slight movement like that was enough for an enemy sniper to take a shot at him, and a headshot would spell instant death. Still, the shape in the sky intrigued him.

As it passed in front of a gray cloud, Jörg thought it looked more like a bat than an eagle. He could see what appeared to be a membrane between the struts supporting its wings. It must be some new kind of machine.

Suddenly, a deafening noise rained down from the skies. It was less like the whistle of a bomb falling through the air than the shriek of a beast.

Jörg covered his ears. A commotion broke out among the other soldiers. One frightened man tried to escape from the trench, but he was desperately pulled down by a few of his comrades. That sort of thing happened sometimes when they were under heavy gunfire. As everyone was waiting out the barrage in bunkers, one soldier might suddenly stand, pick up his belongings, and announce that he was going home. Thrashing around like an angry bull, he'd fight off anyone who tried to stop him, before eventually being tied up and laid on the ground. What was happening now was no different.

The black shape continued emitting its cacophonous sound for a short while, then disappeared to the west.

They all held their collective breath.

After a time, enemy reconnaissance planes appeared from a different direction.

That's a bad sign.

They needed the cover of the trenches. Jörg leaped down to the duckboard, and his comrades hurriedly followed, as though waking up from a bad dream.

Fritz traded his place in front of a gunport with Hans and walked up to Jörg. "I don't like the look of that."

"Yeah."

"Do you think that's what Baldanders looks like?"

"That thing was smaller. More like the size of a dragon."

They heard the roar of the enemy artillery, and dirt and mud sprayed up into the air where the shells landed. Their own cannons and howitzers set up in the second camp immediately answered back. On the reverse slope directly behind Jörg and his unit, mortar companies and infantrymen began to prepare for a charge from the French Army.

White smoke trailed like clouds, carrying with it the scent of gunpowder. The artillery fire sounded awfully close today—and it was getting steadily closer. A bad feeling settled over Jörg.

Just then, a sandbag went flying in front of his eyes. Dirt and rocks rained down on his head. A huge hole had been blown open in the ground, caving in a part of the trench beside him. Jörg and his company ran like mice being chased by a cat, jumping over the hole in search of safety.

Another shell tore through the space in front of him.

Jörg was flung into the air, losing all sensation of the world around him. As his senses came back, the smell of niter and blood stung his nostrils, and he found himself lying on the ground, unsure of how he'd managed to retain consciousness.

He couldn't hear gunfire. Assuming there hadn't been a pause in the fighting, his eardrums must have burst. Half-buried in mud and wood, he couldn't so much as move a finger. His entire body felt horribly cold and the taste of blood filled his mouth. His heart still beat faintly, deep in his chest, but he felt as weak as an old man ready to breathe his last.

A faint sense of relief washed over Jörg.

He'd never need to make another charge or fire a gun again. If he died, some other young man would take his place and fight in his stead. His job was done. All he wanted to do was rest.

Just then, someone pulled him from the mud and rolled him onto his back so he could breathe easier.

It wasn't a member of his squad who'd saved him. The face that floated in front of Jörg belonged to a stranger. Somehow, the sight reflected in his severely damaged eyes appeared as clear as a warm spring day.

The man conveyed elegance, his aged appearance mixed with the air of nobility. A fashionable cloak unsuited for a battlefield was draped around his shoulders. He dressed well, but he wasn't an officer.

This was a war zone. Civilians couldn't just walk into a place like this. So why was he here?

The green-gray of his eyes evoked a forest of conifers, while his white face and skin almost seemed translucent. It was a paleness that didn't seem to come from any sort of illness, but it gave off the impression that there was something not quite human about him. His long hair was tied at the nape of his neck, and a few strands fell across his collarbone.

The man looked him over from head to toe, murmured, "Well, you'll do," and pressed a finger to Jörg's brow.

The moment the man's finger touched him between the eyebrows, Jörg felt all the strength leave his body. A sense of comfort enveloped him, as if he'd been submerged in warm water.

The murky gray of the overcast sky dissipated before his eyes, leaving in its wake a long trail of iridescent clouds.

They absorbed Jörg, making him one with their prismatic colors.

2

Jörg woke up to the scent of fresh coffee. He found himself lying on a bed, having been moved there at some point. The air was dry and warm, nothing about it even slightly recalling that of the trenches pooled with fetid water.

The room he was in didn't look like a field hospital, but part of a regular home or small inn. Brightly colored wallpaper decorated the walls, and curtains with a geometric pattern had been pushed to either side of a French casement window, through which sunlight streamed. It must be around midday.

The room looked entirely different from the style of his hometown. The furnishings and lights featured prominent curves and seemed delicate enough to break if handled too roughly. Furniture where Jörg had grown up was plain, sturdy, and coated with thick varnish to highlight the natural colors.

He removed the blanket covering him and sat up. Nothing hurt. Jörg moved his hands across his entire body, but it didn't seem as if he had any major injuries.

There wasn't so much as a trace of blood or sweat in the air. Instead, he smelled a fresh, grassy scent and, sniffing cautiously, realized it came from the flowers in the vase at his bedside.

Jörg took slow, careful breaths. His throat and lungs were fine. It seemed there was nothing wrong with his hearing. But rather than being relieved, it just made him feel more unnerved. With everything that had just happened, *something* should hurt. He wondered if perhaps it was his pain receptors that had been damaged.

A wild hunger suddenly overtook him.

The smell of coffee had brought back memories of freshly baked bread.

He got down from the bunk. His legs were steady, and he didn't feel dizzy. Jörg walked toward the door, hoping to get something—anything—in his stomach, even if it was just boiled potatoes and bread.

The moment he reached for the handle, the door cracked open. Jörg peeked out into the hallway to see a girl of eleven or twelve hiding behind the door. She had shiny chestnut hair and a very healthy complexion, and she was wearing a stylish dress with fabric embellishments, the likes of which he would never see in his hometown.

Jörg smiled, adopting the warm demeanor he used when talking to the children that came into his father's barbershop. "Do you mind if I open the door?"

She simply stared up at him silently, her eyes open wide. Had she not understood him?

With few other options, Jörg pushed at the handle.

The girl took her hands off the door and dashed down the hall. Jörg made to go after her, but just then, a voice called out to him from behind.

"How are you, soldier?"

Turning around, he saw an older woman. She looked nothing like the girl, so this probably wasn't her mother or a relative. The lady was taller than Jörg, wearing a blouse with a rectangular neckline and three-quarter-length sleeves over a slim skirt. Her hair was pulled back into a bun, darker than the girl's in color and almost black.

Jörg was relieved to find someone with whom he could communicate. He asked where he was, then followed it up by saying, "This looks like someone's house."

"It's a hospital."

"It's nice for a hospital."

"It also serves as an inn."

"Then are you the doctor's wife?"

"I'm the doctor."

The woman extended her right hand and gently clasped Jörg's, her cool, smooth fingers wrapping around his own. "My name is Alexandra Nastase. But please, call me Xandra. No one addresses me stiffly as Dr. Nastase."

Jörg awkwardly returned the handshake. "I've never met a female doctor before."

"I'm sure you haven't. In most countries, women are primarily nurses."

Xandra led Jörg to the dining room.

"You can walk by yourself, I see. You're young, so your body's responding well to the treatment. Would you like coffee and a croissant?"

"A 'croissant'? What's that?"

"It's a pastry in the shape of a crescent."

"So it's like a *Hörnchen*?"

"Not quite. But it tastes just as good."

The crescent-shaped pastry on the plate was wholly different from the kind Jörg knew. It had a crispy texture, with dough made up of layers like a pie. It tasted strongly of butter, and the thin flakes peeled off to stick irritatingly to the back of his teeth and the roof of his mouth. *Hörnchen* had a lighter flavor and denser centers. They also didn't get this deep-brown color when baked.

It was still good, though. Jörg practically wolfed it down and drained the coffee in a single gulp.

"What side of the border is this?" he asked, to which Xandra casually replied, "The French side."

Did that mean Jörg was a prisoner of war? No—nobody kept their captives in such fine condition. Nothing about his current circumstances made sense.

Xandra spoke before he could ask another question. "The man who brought you here will be back soon, so you can ask him why you're here. What did you do before becoming a soldier?"

"I was a barber."

"Oh, you were? In that case, I should ask you to cut that girl's hair."

Jörg began to say that he would be happy to, but a tightness gripped his chest and the words caught in his throat.

"What's wrong?" Xandra asked.

"I'm sorry, but I'm not sure I'll ever be able to pick up a pair of barber shears again."

"Why not?"

"When I was just a simple barber, a blade was a tool that let me change a person's appearance and bring them joy. But on the front lines, I saw their terrible potential."

"You're scared of them now?"

"Yes."

"You should forget all that."

"No matter how hard I try, I'll never be able to rid myself of those memories. These hands will never forget what it feels like to take another person's life."

Xandra didn't pry any further. "Did you ever want to be something besides a barber?"

Jörg thought for a moment, then spoke softly. "I used to enjoy thinking about women's clothes and jewelry. Arranging dresses and hats in different ways in my mind, then thinking up hairstyles to go with them… I know that must sound strange. It's not the sort of job a man should be fantasizing about."

"Not at all. Those sorts of jobs are becoming much more popular in the cities. Where did you learn about fashion?"

"I never had the chance to go to school, but I enjoyed reading. One of my cousins is clever, and he often let me borrow his books. Eventually, I started going to the library. I didn't even have a girlfriend, but I would spend hours looking through books on clothes and accessories and furiously scribbling in notebooks."

"Well then, I suggest you promptly forget about the war and start thinking about designing beautiful clothes for women. That's where your true life leads."

Is it really okay to forget about the war? Or rather, can *I ever forget it?*

Jörg's heavy heart acted as a counterweight to Xandra's carefree tone.

Try as he might to imagine beautiful things, all that came to mind were the horrific images he'd seen on the battlefield. No matter how hard he tried, he would never be free of that sinister metallic stench or the smell of gunpowder. There was no way those memories would simply fade away.

It was then that a tall man strolled into the dining room.

Jörg stiffened, still gripping his utensils. This was the same man who had been gazing down at him on the battlefield. He wore a cloak today, too, keeping it on even when he sat down in the chair.

The man spoke, sitting at a slight angle with an elbow resting on the armrest. "Very few people who wake up here have such an appetite. You must be quite strong."

"Thank you very much for rescuing me." Jörg set his utensils down on the table before continuing. "I assume I am a prisoner of war, correct? Dr. Nastase informed me that we are in France."

"Please, call her Xandra."

"If I'm being held captive, then I would prefer to address her by her proper title."

The man sneered at what he'd said, but strangely, Jörg didn't feel offended. It was clear from his attitude that he'd reacted that way out of contempt for the rigid formality of the military, a sentiment Jörg knew all too well.

"My name is George Silvestri," he said. "Everybody calls me the Count, though I no longer hold any lands. We're not French, but circumstances have brought us here."

"Where are you from?"

"Romania. When I was young, however, it was called Walachia. What is your name?"

"Jörg Huber. I was deployed to Champagne with the German Army. The trenches were mostly dug by the time I got there, so I fired machine guns on the front line and, when they gave the order, charged into no-man's-land."

"The most treacherous of tasks. And you're so young."

"I couldn't choose where they sent me."

"And are you happy now that you've escaped the front lines?"

"Yes, that goes without saying. But I left my company behind, so I can't feel too happy knowing they're still fighting."

"We have no connection to the military. I helped you because I have a personal favor to ask of you. You met the young girl here, I presume."

"I did."

"Her name is Lila. I would like you to look after her."

"It didn't seem like she can understand German."

"She understands you perfectly. She's just shy."

A strange realization suddenly struck Jörg. Now that he thought about it, he was having no difficulty whatsoever speaking with either Xandra or the Count. They had chosen to speak in a language he could understand even before he told them anything about himself. How and when had they decided on that?

"I'm not a teacher," Jörg protested, but the Count continued, unconcerned.

"You need not educate her. I simply wish for you to protect her when she goes outside, when neither Xandra nor I can accompany her."

"Would there be any danger involved?"

"No. You would just be with her when she goes out shopping or for a walk. All quite uneventful. However, if the event ever does arrive, I do hope you demonstrate your excellence as a soldier."

"You risked going into a war zone just to find someone for a job like that?"

"Soldiers on the verge of death make good servants."

Jörg gazed at the Count, who smiled enigmatically. He couldn't tell where this conversation was headed and wondered what the man would make him do.

"How do you feel?" the Count asked.

"Fine."

"If I'm being perfectly honest with you, that is not your original body.

I extracted half of your soul and imprinted it into a simulacrum, a hollow body of sorts. Hence why you are uninjured and don't feel any pain."

Jörg furrowed his brow in confusion. "…I don't understand."

"Your original body—your corpus—is still in the trenches of Champagne."

"As a corpse?"

"No. It is very much alive."

"That doesn't make sense. Humans only have one soul, in one body. If I'm alive here, then my body on the front must be dead."

"As I said, I put half a soul in each."

"Half a soul…?"

"I divided your soul in two, imprinted one half in a simulacrum, and left the other half in your corpus."

Jörg looked even more perplexed. "If my soul's been cut in half, then shouldn't I have only half my intellect as well?"

"No. That is one of the wonderful things about humans. It's what makes this magic worth using for me as well."

"So having half a soul doesn't significantly impact intelligence…?"

"No."

"Really? Not at all?"

"Persistent, aren't you? If I say it doesn't, then it doesn't."

Jörg squeezed his cutlery tightly, completely bewildered.

The more answers he got, the more confused he became. He even considered the possibility that he'd sustained severe brain damage and was currently in the midst of some bizarre dream.

The Count continued, unperturbed. "Come now, war requires only a portion of your intellect. The full breadth of human intelligence is not needed to shoot a gun or wield a shovel. Did the army not order you to discard your human sensibilities? And you must have faced a number of situations in which you were forced to throw away rational thought, no? Simply put, fighting only requires a body and a tiny spark of life. So utilize your abundant sensitivities in the simulacrum to protect that child for me."

"So you're saying," Jörg muttered, "that right now, I exist both on the battlefield and on the home front, with one of me in each place?"

"That is precisely what I'm saying."

"How in the world is that even possible?"

The Count ignored the question, instead asking, "You don't want to go back to the front lines, do you?"

"But I left my company behind— No, I guess I didn't. Honestly, I think I probably just want to forget everything and never go back..."

Jörg held his head in his hands. He had thought about running away countless times, but every time, he'd desperately managed to resist the impulse, thinking that he couldn't face the people in his town as a deserter. Yet the harder he fought that feeling, the harder it became for him to stay, and he'd found himself crying at the bottom of the trenches.

The Count spoke as though consoling him. "With each wave of fighting, the part of your mind and soul that despised war grew, and eventually, it was large enough that my magic easily convinced it to leave your body."

"Are you saying I—this me, now—*chose* to leave my body?"

"It happens frequently, especially with humans."

"—What do you mean?!"

"People go to war with lofty ambitions, but when they're faced with the harsh realities of the battlefield, they abandon everything and run away. It happens often in regular jobs as well."

"I guess that's true."

"So leave your corpus on the battlefield and use this simulacrum to enjoy a different life here. With us."

"But if I wander around, I might be conscripted again."

"Can anybody conscript a man like you who has lost his nationality? Provided that you don't volunteer, your simulacrum will never see the battlefield."

Jörg stared blankly ahead, and a faint smile appeared at the corners of the Count's mouth. "It's understandable if you don't believe me. Anyone would have to be mad to simply accept what I'm saying."

"But what will happen to the me on the battlefield? Won't he die in the fighting?"

"So long as I'm looking after him, he won't die. He will heal from any major injury, so you need not worry."

"If you're going to such efforts, then why not just transfer my entire soul into the simulacrum? Then you wouldn't need to keep my corpus around, right?"

"A human's physical body and soul are inextricably linked. The body allows the soul and mind to exist, so if you left your corpus behind, your mental state would suffer."

"In what way?"

"Separated from its corpus, a mind gradually deteriorates until it eventually disappears along with the simulacrum. In that way, it would be akin to dying."

This was all just so bizarre.

If his body and mind were connected, then what did that mean for his memories—both those of his corpus on the front lines and his own on the home front?

"What will happen to my memories? My corpus's experiences and my own..."

"The memories are shared, for as long as the body and mind are connected."

"Shared how?"

"The events endured by your corpus will be transferred to your simulacrum, and vice versa. However, you will perceive them as dreams and remember them as such. Regardless of how real a dream may seem, humans understand them for what they are once they wake up, yes? This will be no different."

"Oh, okay. That seems like it'll avoid a lot of confusion. I feel like I wouldn't be able to tell who I really am if our memories were to meld together..."

"You still seem quite exhausted."

"I am."

"Don't push yourself too hard. Consider today an evaluation period, and I will return you to your corpus for the time being."

"What? You're going to return me to my original body?!"

"Yes. I hope you don't think poorly of me, but I'm going to put you back for a while to let what we talked about sink in. I shall visit you again someday soon. I'll come regardless, but things will go faster if you call for me. Simply call out 'Count,' and I will appear wherever you are."

The Count leaned over the table and instructed Jörg to hold out his palm.

Jörg extended his left hand and opened his fist, upon which the Count set a small sprig of flowers. Their petals were as white as snow, and they gave off a sweet scent. "Take these, as proof that today was real and not simply a dream."

"What are they?"

"The British call them lilacs, while the French call them *lilas*. In your homeland, they're called *Flieder*, and in my own, *liliac*. In Romanian, *liliac* is also the word for 'bat.'"

The Count set his hand on top of Jörg's and gently squeezed the white flowers. "Someday we'll have a chance to discuss this further. For now, however, we must part."

A sudden darkness enveloped Jörg.

In that dark space, he saw the same iridescent clouds he had earlier. However, this time, unlike the last, they only got farther away from him.

The stench of blood and mud crept deep inside his nostrils. Jörg cracked his eyes open just as a wave of intense pain ran from his chest to his stomach. He tried to yell but instead inhaled the dirt lodged in his throat, and a wave of panic swept over him, more from the fear of asphyxiation than the pain.

His comrade Fritz was trying to free him from the mud and wooden debris. Fritz asked the other soldiers around him for help, and together they finally pulled Jörg from the hole. Blood ran down the other man's head, enough to make Jörg worry that Fritz might need treatment before he did.

They carried Jörg to the first aid station that had been set up in the trenches. The people who took him were also covered in blood, and they were all examined one by one. Even though Jörg had lost a lot of blood, his mind was clear and he had a regular heartbeat, so his commanding officer decided that he could remain on the front lines. They were set to cycle out and be replaced by the second line in a few days, so he could go with the other soldiers then.

After having his wounds bandaged, Jörg was moved to a bunker to lie down and rest, where he could finally catch his breath. Wounds covered every inch of his body, but he didn't feel as if he was going to die. His body felt oddly light, changed in some obvious yet indescribable way.

Realizing that his left hand was still clenched tight, he slowly opened it. Flowers as white as snow spilled out. Clear of any mud, they looked as fresh as if he had just picked them.

A chill ran down his spine.

Lilacs. *Lilas. Flieder. Liliac.*

The white petals emitted their sweet fragrance.

That man had said that in Romanian, *liliac* was also the word for "bat."

He recalled that black shape he'd seen in the dawn sky above the trenches, its wings reminiscent of that very same creature.

The taste of coffee and croissants intensified in his mouth, chasing the scent of the white flowers.

II
The Leap

1

The wounds Jörg received from the shelling began to close two days later. Looking at him, you would never imagine he'd been on death's door just forty-eight hours ago. Jörg didn't know much about medicine, so he couldn't even begin to imagine what the Count had done to him.

Although his wounds had begun to heal, the uneasiness buried in his chest didn't abate.

My soul's been divided in two, half in my original body and half in a simulacrum…?

Even if he understood the concept, Jörg still had trouble wrapping his head around it. It was easier to think of the whole thing as just some sort of bad dream. And yet his bizarre healing powers indicated that *something* had happened. No bad dream could explain that.

So what does that make me now?

Am I human, or something else?

I wish someone would make it clear to me.

"Simply call out 'Count,' and I will appear wherever you are."

He remembered the man's words, but Jörg couldn't bring himself to call for him so soon.

If they met again, he knew that half of himself would become something that was no longer human. He still wasn't sure whether that was a good thing or not.

Resting in the bunker with nothing to do soon proved boring. The air hung stagnant, and the rats scurrying in the shadows of the equipment bothered Jörg. Even with all of that, however, he wanted to keep resting for a bit longer, so he held his chest as if it still hurt, furrowed his brow, and tried his best to not arouse suspicion.

He smoked along with everyone else during their breaks. Every time he lit one of the rationed cigarettes, he was reminded just how good they tasted after a day spent doing nothing.

Fritz still hadn't taken off the bandages around his head. Other soldiers who had also been caught in the bombardment with Jörg continued to be racked by pain in various parts of their bodies. On the battlefield, soldiers were not only overworked but suffered from poor nutrition, and unsanitary conditions impeded proper healing. The dead lay in mounds across no-man's-land, while filthy water and humid air filled the trenches. Soldiers crawled around fighting in such wretched places while covered in cuts and gunshot wounds. Even a scratch could get infected, leaving it swollen and purple, with extreme cases leading to high fevers and death.

Some men even purposely injured themselves with dirty nails or knives to try to bring about such an infection and escape from the front lines. If all went well, this method could land them a place in a field hospital, but when taken too far, it invited serious diseases that had even killed some men before getting them to a medic.

Rats scrambled through the trenches in search of food, multiplying their numbers by feasting on corpses. When their tempers got the better of them, Jörg and the other men would squash the rats with their clubs and shovels.

One soldier, Paul, who had worked at a general store in his hometown, tied together all the rats he killed with a rope and would often boast about his trophies. Something about this caught the interest of the field photographer, Hoffe, who asked to take a picture of it. Paul gladly accepted and settled himself a short distance away from his line of hanging rats, smiling up at the photographer sitting atop a log staircase.

Drained of life, the rats had been transformed into mere hunks of meat. Hoffe pressed the shutter release, and the hollow, mechanical sound echoed around them. The other soldiers laughed, jokingly wondering where Hoffe would publish such a picture.

The pain from Jörg's injuries quickly faded, but his scars would remain forever. He opened the jacket of his army uniform to reveal marks running diagonally from his navel up over his chest, the scar tissue pale and raised. A sigh escaped him.

Was this the limit of the Count's powers, or had he purposely left these scars so that others wouldn't question why Jörg had gotten away unscathed? If it was the latter, then could Jörg expect to add to these scars every time he faced danger? What would happen if an explosion claimed a hand or a foot? Would it fuse back to his body if he wrapped the wound in gauze and left it to heal? If the severed appendage wasn't recovered, would it grow back, like a lizard's tail? He really hoped that wasn't the case. The thought alone was far too disturbing.

Jörg resumed his duties once it seemed natural for him to have healed enough to leave bed.

The soldiers stationed on the slope in front of him kept watch against potential night assaults, while others sat against the trench walls, rifles in hand. Some of the men in his unit napped, their bodies curled up like dormice, as Jörg stood in front of them by the edge of the trench.

A half moon hung in the western sky, and the occasional flare fell like a shooting star. It reminded him of the Apocalypse of John, Revelation 9:

"And I saw a star fallen from heaven to earth, and he was given the key to the shaft of the bottomless pit. He opened the shaft of the bottomless pit."

The smoke that erupted from that pit blocked out the sun and polluted the air. Locusts granted the power of scorpions crawled from it, coming not to kill humans, but to torment them incessantly.

Jörg freely wandered the realm between fantasy and reality. The sound of a church organ echoed in his mind. Numerous somber songs he'd learned as a boy seemed to fit this horrific situation all too well.

Each time the darkness was chased away, gunfire rang out. They were targeting the soldiers setting up barbed wire.

Soon after arriving on the front line, Jörg had also often been sent out to lay wire accompanied by more experienced soldiers. Any damaged sections left unattended would allow the enemy entry, so someone had to go out and repair it.

They would sneak into no-man's-land under the cover of night to hurriedly nail up more barbed wire, and they couldn't let their guards down for even a second because the enemy would take shots at them as they worked. More than a few of his fellow soldiers had been killed in this way.

But despite their desperate efforts, the enemy would drop bombs on the area, destroying the barbed wire defenses. The cycle continued—nails hammered, wire erected, fortifications destroyed—over and over and over again. It was disheartening work, but they couldn't let up.

Jörg rubbed his numb hands together and watched the blossoming lights dim and fade into the night. It didn't appear that an attack like the other day's was coming, so he would have to look for another opportunity to call the Count.

Those days in the trenches dragged on until, one day, Jörg's battalion received word that the German Army had attacked the fort at Verdun.

Verdun was a city to the east that contained multiple fortresses. The bombardment had begun on the morning of February 21, supported on the ground by the Sixth Infantry Division. At his low rank, Jörg didn't know why the attack was necessary, but he knew that capturing the fortress would involve intense fighting.

The German volley on the French Army lasted until four in the afternoon, after which soldiers rushed the fort without having constructed any trenches. Their long-distance charge surprised the French, allowing the Germans to immediately break through their front line.

However, from that point on, the French continually repelled their attackers.

Various rumors circulated among Jörg's squad, saying that the fighting would reach them any day now, or that the attack was just a precursor to the beginning of their next campaign. The men grew restless, thinking that prolonged fighting at Verdun would see them deployed there as reinforcements, and they desperately wanted to know what was going to happen.

Their sergeant was a bearlike man who simply said "The German Army will be victorious" with the same fervor he always showed. When they asked him how the war would turn out, he'd say, "It'll end someday," but that was as much detail as the sergeant would go into, only twisting his mustache and muttering "We shall be victorious" and "This time for sure." Apparently, both the chief of the German General Staff and the crown prince had been involved in the strategy to attack Verdun, hence why the sergeant assumed the war would be won soon.

Jörg and the other soldiers didn't press the matter. Even if their sergeant told them the war would end tomorrow, they all knew that a bullet could claim any one of them in the next few hours.

The soldiers sipped on their bean soup with bits of fat floating in it and gnawed on pieces of sour rye bread. As they ate, they whispered to one another.

"I hope it all ends at Verdun and none of that reaches here."

The other soldiers all muttered in agreement. They were done with fighting. They had been here since the previous fall, and it was now winter. They didn't want anything to do with a major battle like that.

"The war can't keep going on if we run out of soldiers and bullets. I hope they use them all up over there."

"But they can always just get more men and supplies from other countries. The ones in charge will keep fighting for as long as possible."

"Then this war will never end."

"Everything has its limits. Win or lose, this war will have all been for nothing if it bankrupts the country."

"How long do you think a country has to fight before it goes bankrupt?"

"I don't know. But they have to end it at some point."

"So you're saying it's just a matter of economics?"

"Yeah, probably."

One night, as Jörg was trying to sleep after coming back from his watch, he felt a familiar sensation and looked around.

The scent of sweet flowers greeted him from nearby. Someone breathed gently by his ear, and he heard a whisper like the wind. "How long do you plan on staying here, Jörg?"

The voice sounded surprisingly clear, but no one around him seemed to hear it. Everyone else was either hunched over asleep or looking out over the sandbags.

An invisible person had approached Jörg; he could tell by the movement of the air that it was the Count. His heart hammered as though he'd seen a ghost.

"Please don't interrupt my precious sleep time," Jörg replied in a whisper. "I have to be up soon."

"I kept waiting, but you didn't call. So I came to you instead."

"I appreciate it."

"Hurry back to us. To delicious pastries and coffee."

The talk of food pained him. Not wanting the Count to hear his stomach growl, Jörg curled further over his gun.

The Count continued. "Stay here, and you'll be sent somewhere even worse."

"You mean Verdun?"

"Precisely."

"I know things are bad over there."

"No, you know nothing at all. You'd change your mind if you saw it. Come, turn your attention this way."

Jörg raised his head, lured in by the strange invitation, and felt the boards beneath him vanish. The world around him disappeared, surrounding him in a void. Half of his soul had been plucked from his body.

A cry escaped his lips. "No, don't!"

He instantly felt the sensation of a physical form, accompanied by an intense sense of unease. The discomfort felt like being forced into clothing that didn't fit.

The darkness evaporated, and Jörg took in his surroundings, stupefied.

In a matter of seconds, he'd been taken out of that dark trench and dropped into a midday field. Faint rays of light peered through the overcast sky, but a peculiar heat filled the air around him. Poison gas and bombs had devastated the surrounding trees, leaving behind the jagged edges of torn branches. Jörg grimaced at the stench, a distinctive burning smell intermingled with the fumes of copious amounts of gasoline.

A high-pitched sound split the air, and a breath later, Jörg was rocked by an explosion and thrown to the ground by a powerful blast of wind. Pain raced through his side. He tried to stand but couldn't. His legs wouldn't move. He didn't have the nerve to look at the injury. Even as he gritted his teeth to fight back the pain, the Count's dignified voice still came through clearly.

"What is this? And just when I settled you into a new body. You'll have to transfer to another one."

"Transfer? How?"

"Search for your next target."

"I'm saying I don't know how to do that."

"You don't have to see them directly. Feel the presence of the person you wish to assimilate and match their breathing. The simulacrum's power should then automatically allow you to leap to them. Now try it yourself. I brought you here to practice."

"What happens when I leap?"

"You enter another person's body."

"And how am I supposed to do that?!"

"I showed you just moments ago. Only this time, you'll be doing it by yourself."

"None of this makes any sense!"

"Are you really so inept? Don't worry about how it works; all you have to do is trust your body." The Count let out an exaggerated sigh. "Right now, half of your soul is imprinted in a simulacrum, as it was the other day. I assume you're following me so far?"

"Yes."

"So now use that simulacrum to possess the body of another soldier."

"What do you mean, 'possess'?"

"A simulacrum can do more than just take on human shape. It can shrink to the size of a bullet or become intangible like mist. It is something that cannot be understood using the logic of this world, hence why it has no difficulty entering another person's body so easily. So go on—try it."

"This is complete nonsense. I have no idea what you're talking about."

"Time's up. I'll do it."

The Count uttered a few cryptic words that Jörg couldn't make out, and just like that, Jörg felt the ground underneath him disappear. His disconnected soul hung in space for a few moments before he once again felt the sensation of a new body.

A metal weight pressed down on his back. This soldier was carrying something incredibly heavy, but it wasn't a backpack or barbed wire.

Jörg looked around to see fires raging in all directions.

In front of him, flames danced like living creatures from the hands of a German soldier facing down the enemy. It almost appeared as if he were holding a small dragon spewing a jet of flames toward the French soldiers.

The flames kept the Allied soldiers at bay. It seemed they were still within rifle range, though, because Jörg heard a constant barrage of gunfire splitting the dust-filled air. German soldiers moved in pairs, always accompanied by another soldier with a hand grenade to protect them.

A number of the German soldiers carried large, cylindrical containers on their backs. The man Jörg was possessing must be wearing the same device, based on the leather straps that cut deep into his shoulders. The soldier in front of him carried the nozzle of the long hose extending from Jörg's cylinder in both hands, which sprayed intermittent bursts of fire.

He heard the Count speak again. "It's a flamethrower. Have you ever used one before?"

"No."

The Count's voice didn't seem to be coming to him through the ears of this man; no matter how deafening the sounds around Jörg were, he could still hear it clearly. There must be some sort of special means by which it was being conveyed to him.

The Count continued.

"The container you're carrying is filled with gasoline. When you pull the lever, gasoline flows to the nozzle at the end of the hose, where a device at the tip ignites it. It doesn't emit fire so much as release a stream of burning fuel."

"Is this a new weapon of the German Army?"

"It is. Though there is still some room for improvement."

Jörg gradually felt the emotions of the soldier carrying the tank, like ink seeping into paper. Buried beneath a rush of adrenaline was the fear and panic of not wanting to die. Surprisingly, the man felt almost no animosity toward the French soldiers and, in fact, harbored more hatred for his own army. A strong sense of doubt and dissatisfaction stewed within him regarding the German Army's treatment of front-line soldiers as disposable commodities.

Their squad had made it all the way right in front of Verdun's Fort

Douaumont, and it seemed that one more push was all it would take for the fortress to fall.

Each gust of wind sent the fire from the flamethrower dancing toward the man holding the nozzle, causing the lead soldier to curse as he cut the feed to the fuel. Eventually, he turned to his partner and told him to trade, likely not wanting to suffer any more burns.

The man Jörg was possessing reluctantly lowered the gasoline tank to the ground. He didn't want to stand in front, but it was better than being shot by the enemy while they argued among themselves. He glowered at his fellow soldier, conveying his resentment. However, the extreme stress of the battlefield suppressed such feelings to a bare minimum.

As the man picked up the end of the hose, Jörg sensed a certain hesitance in his movements. He seemed extremely resistant to the idea of burning another person. Yet even so, with the nozzle in his hands, he had no choice but to wield it. A person couldn't carry a gun and the hose at the same time, so choosing not to release the flame was the equivalent of being unarmed.

The hollow sound of an explosion rang out nearby, duller than artillery fire, and Jörg reflexively turned toward it as the man did. He regretted it immediately.

Flames enveloped three German soldiers—a flamethrower team and their attendant—who thrashed around, screaming. They swatted frantically at the fire, which showed no signs of abating. It continued to burn, like a predator devouring its prey.

Jörg could hardly believe that human beings burned so easily. He trembled and fought the urge to vomit as the Count continued to speak. "That's what happens when the tank is shot. The gasoline spills out and catches fire."

"I can't take this!" Jörg yelled, hysterical. "Transfer me to another body. To a soldier somewhere safer."

"Don't be afraid. Even if the soldier you're possessing burns to death, you won't die. You'll simply be expelled from his body along with your simulacrum."

"I don't want that, either. I don't want to be burned alive. I'd still feel it."

"Pain is an illusion. It's all derived from the power of your imagination. You're inhabiting another person's body, so separate yourself from them."

"That's impossible. No matter what I do, I wouldn't be able to stop thinking about the pain. I can't separate my mind from it."

The Count let out an exasperated sigh. "Listen to me. At some point, flamethrowers will come to be used on your front as well. As such, it would be a good idea to gain experience with them now so you can better avoid danger later. Living with burn scars is difficult. Especially on the face."

Black smoke stung Jörg's eyes, and he bit his lip as tears blurred the horrible sight in front of him. His initial anger had swelled, directed toward this man called the Count, who treated other people's lives as mere playthings.

"Neither I nor this man are toys for you to play with. You're not a soldier, so I don't want to hear anything like that from you."

A deep chuckle emanated from the Count. "I have far more experience in war than you. Do not underestimate me."

"Romania is neutral. They haven't joined the war yet."

"I fought my battles a long time ago. Right around the middle of the fifteenth century, so about four hundred and sixty years ago."

That didn't make any sense. Jörg was thoroughly confused, but the Count went on.

"At the time, my homeland of Walachia was fighting the Ottoman Empire. My father and I, retainers to Vlad III of Walachia, fought in many battles. War back then was very different from how it is now. Yet countless men still stifled their reservations and died meaninglessly."

A black fog materialized out of thin air, congealing at a single point in space. No one else seemed to be able to see it. German soldiers ran past without giving it the slightest glance, while the men with the flamethrowers had stopped firing and were slowly making their way toward the fort, hiding in holes in the ground left by the bombardment.

Looking closer, Jörg realized that what he'd assumed to be fog was actually a mass of black particles that moved like flies. The particles gradually grew larger, morphing into a swarm of carrion beetles. These eventually transformed into a flock of thrushes, then a cloud of bats, and finally a murder of ravens, whose piercing cries reverberated through the gunpowder-choked air. The mass changed yet again, settling into the form of a gallant warrior astride a warhorse.

It wasn't a type of cavalryman Jörg recognized. The figure was garbed in armor decorated with ancient-looking designs and wore a large sword at his waist. He held a long spear that Jörg instantly recognized as having come from an earlier time. The German Army's cavalry still carried lances, but they wore normal army garb and used guns instead of swords.

The armored soldier calmly leaped over Jörg's head on his horse. Jörg looked away from this strange sight and tried to steady his erratic breathing. He was thoroughly exhausted and still felt weighed down by the gasoline-filled canister. He might be inhabiting another person's body, but the pain felt horrifically real.

Even though he wasn't looking at the illusion, the Count's voice rang unrelenting in his ears.

"The weapons you use now were not around when I was fighting the Ottoman Empire. Only bows and slings could strike enemies at a distance, and we relied on swords and spears for close combat. The Ottoman Empire first used cannons in their assault on Constantinople, but the weapon was still in its infancy and did not prove very effective. The reason being, at that time, stones were still being used instead of cannonballs. Seeing the way in which you wage war feels like watching people use magic. Massive cannons that don't break no matter how often you fire them, machine guns, poison gas, hand grenades. Those fighter planes are a particularly impressive invention. From high in the sky, they can shoot guns, drop bombs, and take pictures of enemy positions. None of that existed when I was a soldier."

Clutching his head, Jörg cried out, "Are you saying you used magic to come here from the past?"

"Not at all. Due to some minor circumstances—and unrelated to my own intentions—I have been able to continue living for four hundred and sixty years."

"Humans don't live that long."

"No, they don't."

A shudder went down Jörg's spine. He looked up, feeling a powerful gaze on him, to see the Count adorned in dull gray armor looking in his direction. By now, the mass of black fog had resolved itself to display the figure in precise detail.

Dents and scratches covered his chain mail and armor, which had dried blood and mud stuck to the surface. Mud covered his feet. The sword looked rusted from matted gore, with only small patches offering a glimpse at the true color of the steel.

Those green, conifer-forest eyes stared scornfully down at him. The man's hair was the same length as it had been during their previous meeting but was now dark brown—perhaps the reason why he appeared slightly younger.

The Count spoke slowly. "I thought you realized long ago that I am not human."

"It's not exactly as if I made you say it up front."

"I appreciate the sentiment. Putting that aside for the moment, however, I assumed you wanted to win this battle. Was I wrong?"

The Count calmly pointed his sword toward a faint ray of sunlight piercing the lead-colored sky.

"War only means something if you win. You gain nothing if you lose."

"Did you win? Your war from four hundred and sixty years ago?"

A flicker of tension crossed the Count's face, and he slowly lowered his sword. "We lost, unfortunately."

Jörg swallowed.

"Walachia was beaten," continued the Count, "because we were betrayed by a boyar on our side. My father and I battled the Ottoman Empire alongside Vlad III, but no matter how valiantly we fought, we were unable to push back the imperial army. My father eventually died in the fighting, and I became immortal. My motherland changed its name to Romania when it gained independence from the Ottoman Empire in 1878. I followed its course until then but have lived aimlessly ever since. With the independence of my homeland, I lost my purpose in life."

The Count returned his sword to its sheath, looking incredibly lonely despite his valiant appearance. His human form seemed on the verge of crumbling to dust.

Jörg stared silently at him.

He still didn't know what the man wanted. What was his motive for asking Jörg to look after that girl named Lila?

"Soldiers on the verge of death make good servants." That was what the Count had said when he'd saved Jörg. Between being run ragged by his commanding officers in the army or working for the Count, which was the better life? No matter who he served, he didn't think there would be

a normal life waiting for him. But there was still a big difference between the two.

Croissants and coffee were decidedly better than war. Jörg stayed on the battlefield because he didn't know how to escape from the front line and couldn't imagine what he would do after that. If he ran away from the army, he could never return to his hometown. And he wasn't strong enough to live a life of solitude in some unfamiliar land.

Even if he didn't fight, the war would continue. Soldiers on both sides didn't actually have a good reason to wage war against each other. They were forced to carry their countries' mistakes with them onto the battlefield.

In which case, he could rid himself of half of that burden. But *only* half—not all of it. His real body would remain in Champagne.

"So what will you do?" the Count asked. "Stay and continue to fight?"

Jörg vividly remembered the glorious day he had marched away from his hometown. He couldn't deny what he'd felt back then: pure masculine pride. A simple barber's son, he would return home triumphantly as a hero of his nation. Jörg had fantasized about that on more than one occasion. However, he had lost far too much on the battlefield. The time he'd lost was gone forever. The people he'd lost would never return. And since everyone believed that it was better to win a war than to lose one, no one would return home until victory was achieved. That was the true cause of all of this.

The Count chuckled, as though reading Jörg's mind. "Victory and defeat are not your only possible futures. You can choose to remove yourself from the war."

"I have thought along those lines as well."

"There are other fronts it would likely be better for you to fight on."

"Like the Eastern Front? Or the Balkan Peninsula?"

"That's not what I meant."

The Count spread his arms wide like a raven about to take flight, and a heavy sound filled Jörg's ears—the flapping of a sail full of wind. "Stay in Verdun a while longer. I will come for you again in good time. I hope by then you will have made up your mind somewhat."

Another gust of wind sounded, and the Count disappeared in the blink of an eye.

Left alone inside the soldier he was possessing, Jörg found himself still unable to decide what to do. Should he remain in the army as a human or become the servant of an immortal creature? If he had to choose, he wasn't sure which was the better option.

The fighting around Fort Douaumont continued until February 25.

Jörg stayed in the body of the German soldier the entire time.

Once the German Army occupied Fort Douaumont, they announced their success both internally and to the rest of the world as if they had captured every stronghold in the area. Viewing their situation with grave seriousness, the French used motorized transports to send waves of soldiers to Verdun.

Unlike horses, vehicles never tired; they quickly transported people and goods without relying on railroads. They carried wounded soldiers to the back lines and fresh soldiers to the front and consistently delivered weapons and supplies. The French Army had a large fleet of private vehicles at their disposal, including taxis, all of which had provided support from the beginning of the Great War.

Not to be outmatched by the French forces, the German Army concentrated its military strength at Verdun, bringing in a continuous stream of soldiers from other divisions and neighboring areas. The fighting at Verdun lasted longer than anyone expected, descending into a state where no one could stop it.

Neither side achieved any substantial victories. Soldiers on both sides simply threw their lives away.

They had created another field of perpetual war.

2

The soldier Jörg had possessed was named Johann. In talking with his fellow soldiers, Jörg learned that the man had run a bakery in his hometown, where he had a wife and children.

Johann was troubled by his actions on the battlefield, but he had resigned himself to his fate. He was determined never to fight anyone again once the war was over. To that end, he genuinely believed that the best course of action was to throw everything they had at the enemy to force them to surrender as soon as possible.

Once peace returned, the people of Europe would all be neighbors again. Everyone would go back home, and Johann would happily sell his bread to anyone, French and Russian alike. Because that was the duty of a baker.

He hated the war.

Yet right now, fighting was all he could do to stop this thing he so despised.

However, having seen a flamethrower's capabilities in a demonstration right before the Battle of Verdun, he'd felt a deep sense of apprehension when his commanding officer informed his squad that they had been assigned to operate the flamethrowers.

Was it really military equipment? Could it even be called a weapon? It looked more like something you'd use to exterminate pests.

An intense revulsion had welled up inside him.

He didn't want to burn people.

He just wanted to bake delicious bread.

Yet here he was.

When an order is given, all soldiers can do is follow. So Johann had marched for Fort Douaumont with his battalion, harboring discontent. It was on their way there that Jörg had possessed him.

The fortress was a rectangular structure built of concrete, with low observation and artillery turrets. The French Army had concealed themselves underground to fire at their enemies. Johann's unit had orders to first attack the aboveground structures, then work its way inside to secure victory.

Underground passages covered in stone and brick stretched out like a maze. Johann and his squad felt far more nervous fighting here than on an open field. Fortunately, however, the fort contained very few French soldiers, and the fighting proved to be less intense than a field encounter. Before long, the French forces surrendered, and Johann's troops were given some time to rest their tired bodies.

With the fall of Fort Douaumont, the German Army had broken through the third line of the French Army. After a brief respite, they made ready to attack their next target: Fort Vaux, to the south. Once there, the town of Verdun would be within reach.

Leaving behind the exhausted soldiers who had dumped their

equipment and collapsed on the ground, Johann climbed up the slope of the fortress alone. Once he reached an observation turret, he looked back down across the land they'd just traversed.

Thick pillars of smoke still rose into the sky. The intense shelling, poison gas, and flamethrowers had stripped the area of every last leaf and blade of grass. Pine and larch trees must have once grown here in abundance, with holly and hawthorn decorating the landscape in winter. Small flowers of every color must have dotted this soft green expanse—daisies, thistle, and musk mallow. This great plain must have once been filled with field mice and weasels racing through the grass, skylarks dancing in the air, and finches singing cheerfully. However, none of that remained.

Only the torsos of soldiers blown apart by falling bombs sat in the trees, hanging from the branches like laundry left out to dry. With so many bodies scattered across the mud-filled holes and sloping hills, many of them no longer even resembling the shape of a person, it was impossible to tell how many corpses there were.

From the distance came the cries of warhorses that seemed to curse the very world. And it wasn't just one or two he heard, either. They were injured and would never get back up again. Gunshots rang out intermittently, each one further reducing the number of whinnying voices. Dinner tonight would include a bit more fresh meat than usual.

Johann sat and kicked out his legs.

The man's feelings were beginning to seep into Jörg's mind.

I just want to go home. I don't want to be here anymore.

But once I'm home, how can I go back to being a baker? How can I still bake bread with these hands that have burned people? How could I ever let someone eat bread like that?

Will God ever forgive me?

Johann buried his face in his hands.

How many tens of thousands of men did we leave behind?

And we only took one fort. If we do that a few more times, will this war finally end?

Buried deep inside Johann, Jörg froze.

He couldn't bear sharing the emotional torment as well as the physical pain. Johann feared returning to his normal routine of baking bread, just as Jörg was terrified of his barber shears. They both questioned whether they could intrude upon the innocent lives of those who knew nothing of war with hands that had taken the lives of others.

The dead, however, had even been robbed of having a future to worry about.

When Jörg first met Xandra, she'd told him to forget about the war, but even now, something inside him was vehemently opposed to that idea. A fierce struggle raged between his desire to forget everything and the feeling that he always had to remember.

There were too many things he'd seen on the battlefield that had been burned into his mind. And too many reasons not to forget.

Yet even more would fade into oblivion.

3

Jörg stayed in Verdun possessing Johann. He didn't do it because he enjoyed it; he had no other choice. If he concentrated, he should be able to leap into another body, but he just couldn't figure out how. He had been inside Johann for so long now that he occasionally forgot he was in another person's body. Such extended cohabitation had blurred the boundary between himself and this other man.

The Count never once came to get him.

Unable to make any headway, Jörg didn't call for him, either.

The Count had told him to learn how to control his simulacrum, so the fact that he hadn't appeared yet meant he was probably somewhere watching Jörg's progress. Still, he was taking his time.

As his company marched to Fort Vaux, Jörg often heard the sound of flapping wings. Each time, he looked around, curious to see if it had been the Count flying overhead.

Most times, the noise came from a carrier pigeon one of his fellow soldiers had released. Once, as Jörg was watching a bird disappear over the horizon, he saw a German Fokker plane harrying an enemy aircraft with the Tricolore painted on its wings and tail. One second, the planes were fighting high in the sky, and the next, they'd rapidly descended to just above the treetops and flown away at full speed.

Fighter pilots possessed elite skills, and the planes they piloted represented the most state-of-the-art weapons. They engaged the enemy with a visible sense of pride—an attitude that stayed with them even after they left their cockpits.

Jörg wondered if they ever felt sorry for the men fighting below them. Was that respect afforded all pilots, regardless of nationality, ever directed toward the miserable mud-covered soldiers on the ground?

Jörg's heart secretly swelled each time he spied a fighter plane during a march. Enemy planes riddling the ground with machine-gun bullets or raining bombs on the battlefield filled him with a gut-wrenching fear, but seeing a friendly plane do the same to an enemy caused him to cheer with joy. Watching a plane with the Iron Cross and its roundel-clad counterpart bank sharply and try to outmaneuver each other felt like observing two expert combatants compete in a game of wits.

However, a cold feeling would overcome him as soon as one plane began to plummet from the exchange.

The losing aircraft would sink in the sky, a huge plume of smoke billowing from its fuselage. Planes decimated by a salvo of bullets in midair would fall to pieces before even they hit the ground.

Even the sight of a plane falling was beautiful.

Whenever such thoughts crossed his mind, Jörg couldn't help but be reminded that these were sentiments that had been imprinted deep within him. War was glorious. When and where had someone told him that? Who had engraved that idea into his heart? Or had he always been the kind of person who felt that way? Try as he might, he couldn't recall. Anytime he tried to probe deeper, his thoughts would scatter, crumbling to dust.

Which of his thoughts were his own and which had come from other people? Having lived on the battlefield for so long, he no longer knew.

The fighting at Fort Vaux proved more intense than Fort Douaumont. Suppressing their own fear of the fire, the flamethrower squads ran forward, pursuing French soldiers beyond the third line.

When the French Army retreated to the fortress, the German commander ordered a large-scale artillery bombardment. Jörg had considered Champagne a big battle, but it didn't compare to this. The incessant shelling shook the earth beneath his feet all day. From where the soldiers were, it was impossible to determine the state of the target area through the mounds of dirt that flew into the air with each strike.

With the fort firing back as well, the number of shells exchanged was beyond comprehension. Gun smoke drifted across the ground like clouds, and dust worked its way into people's eyes, noses, and throats, causing an endless stream of tears and snot. It is believed that the German Army launched ten thousand shells every day at Fort Vaux in their attempts to completely decimate the area around the stronghold.

When the barrage eased, Johann's squad once again shouldered their flamethrowers and rushed toward the fort. They positioned themselves at the observation turrets' gunports and at the fort's entrances, spewing fire into the building. They burned the French soldiers waiting for them and forced their way inside. Then, when their gasoline ran out, they took up their guns and raced deeper into the fort.

His troop fired their pistols down the dim corridors. The smell of gunpowder and blood numbed even Jörg's thoughts, and the endless echoes of gunshots made Johann's head spin. Leaning against the wall, he slowly made his way forward. But each frantic counterattack forced him back.

It was an even tougher battle than what Johann and his company had already been through, and after five days of intense underground fighting, they still hadn't taken the fort.

The enemy showed no signs of surrender, and the German Army kept up its repeated assaults, growing more frustrated each time. The French weren't going to send reinforcements here, so if the Germans could exterminate all the Allied soldiers inside the fort, the battle would be over.

Johann sent a continuous spray of bullets toward the enemy. A feeling of perpetual monotony had plastered itself inside his skull, and when he looked around, everyone shared the same expression. The dead and the living had all begun to smell the same.

On the sixth day, the enemy forces charged toward them from deep in the underground maze, guns blazing. Running in a straight line through those narrow passageways spelled certain death, but it seemed the French had come to terms with that, because there was no hesitation in their movements.

One man rushed toward Johann, not even stopping when several bullets hit him.

"*Boche!*" he jeered, and in the same moment, Jörg felt a pain as if a scorching piece of metal had been thrust deep inside his stomach.

Johann slumped to the ground, pressing his wound. The man who had stabbed him also collapsed, having used up the last of his strength. French and German soldiers jumbled together in the melee, and combatants toppled to the floor, their noses and heads smashed by the butts of rifles. Blades flashed and flames erupted from muzzles. A nausea-inducing stench filled every corner of the corridor.

A knife was sunk deep into his abdomen. As Johann fought against the intense pain, the man's emotions rushed into Jörg. Thoughts of his village and his family, and even the bitterness of his lost future, swirled through his mind.

He wanted to go home, hug his wife and children, and bake bread again without a care in the world. But he knew he wouldn't be able to ever again.

Johann's heart practically burst with his desire not to die. Jörg couldn't fight such overwhelming emotions and tried desperately to escape, but all he could do was struggle in vain, still unable to control his simulacrum.

A powerful force took hold of Jörg, pulling his simulacrum down toward the ground. The feeling of falling into an unending abyss terrified him, and a scream tore from his lips. Jörg could no longer differentiate whether it was him or Johann making the noise.

Something flashed and separated the two men.

The scenery in front of his eyes changed.

Jörg had suddenly been transported from the frigid, dank corridor of the fort to the bright living room of the inn.

4

Jörg leaned back into the soft couch, looking on the verge of slipping to the floor.

In the blink of an eye, he had leaped from Verdun to this safe location.

It didn't feel like something he'd done by himself; the Count must have transported his simulacrum here as he had before.

The man sat before Jörg wearing the same long cloak as always. He leaned on one armrest, legs crossed, staring at Jörg with his murky green eyes. His expression was as calm as still water, not giving off any particular emotion.

Jörg righted himself on the couch, then wiped his damp cheeks with the back of his hand.

All traces of Johann had disappeared from his body, leaving Jörg feeling completely himself again. He appeared to have been brought to the same inn where he'd first spoken with the Count. The last time he'd visited, Jörg had seen only one bedroom and the dining room, but this room had a similar smell.

"I imagine you've had enough?" the Count said.

Jörg understood precisely what he meant. "Yes," he answered, still looking down at the ground, before adding, "But I have one request."

"What is it?"

"Could you bring my real body here, too?"

"I only want half of you. I have no intention of taking care of your corpus as well."

"Then would you at least move it somewhere a bit safer? I feel bad leaving it on the battlefield."

"I have no obligation to do such a thing."

"Can you really say that, after taking it upon yourself to separate a person's soul from their body?"

"You're upset."

"Of course I am."

A faint smile crossed the Count's face. "At first, I also considered moving your corpus somewhere safe. However, it is beyond my powers."

"How come?"

"Your corpus has a strong desire to stay on the front lines. So long as it feels that way, my magic is powerless. An extraordinary human will repels magic, just like the power of faith."

"But I'm sick of war."

"Do you remember what you said the first time you were here? 'I left my company behind, so I can't feel too happy knowing they're still fighting.'"

He did remember saying that.

"The you here now wants to get as far away from the fighting as possible," explained the Count. "But your corpus in Champagne worries more about what's going to happen to his fellow soldiers than his own safety, and he would never desert them."

If the *"him here now"* had moved to a simulacrum because he wanted to get away from the battlefield, then all that remained in his corpus must be the idealistic part of him from just after he'd left for the war. The mind of an innocent boy who fought out of petty pride and eagerly dreamed of becoming a hero for his nation.

A hollow laugh escaped him. Jörg couldn't believe he'd been so naive once.

Thanks to the Count's magic, he had left that part of himself behind. Or no—he'd done it of his own volition. *He* was the one who'd split himself in half.

"I see...," Jörg said finally. "This is the part of me that broke free, so it makes sense that the me there would want to stay on the battlefield."

"And so, as planned, your corpus shall remain there."

"Thank you."

Breaking away from the inconvenient parts of himself and discarding them would let Jörg live the life he wanted. That said, there was no way things would work out so smoothly. His reckoning would arrive in one form or another. For now, however, he just wanted to rest. He wanted to get away from the war.

The Count reached out and rang a brass bell sitting on a table.

A short while later, Xandra came into the room with the girl—Lila—following her.

Lila's expression remained stern. Hiding behind Xandra, she gripped the woman's skirt tightly. She looked so nervous Jörg felt sorry for her. Even so, her gray-blue eyes were fixed on him as she tried to understand what was going on.

Her chestnut hair hung a little past her shoulders. He could either put it into neat braids or simply trim the ends and let it hang free; either way suited a young girl. Although individual styles and tastes differed, at that age, kids were so active that the most important thing was for their hair not to get in the way.

Xandra turned around to look at Lila and stroked the back of her hand. "Come now, don't be scared. How about you introduce yourself?"

Lila stayed frozen to the spot.

Did something about Jörg frighten her? Did he still give off a soldier's gruffness, even after being transferred into this simulacrum? Or had his soul been tainted in a way that only children could sense, which had permeated this body, too?

"What should she call him?" Xandra asked. "Mr. Huber? Or Jörg?"

"Mr. Huber would be best, I'm sure," replied the Count. "I wish to ensure Lila receives a proper upbringing, so she must learn respect for others."

"Okay then, Mr. Huber it is. Come now, Lila. Say hello."

Even prompted, Lila remained silent. Jörg glanced at Xandra before speaking to the young girl. "Hello. We met once before, but let's start over from the beginning. I'm a barber, so I can give you a nice haircut and arrange your hair into pretty braids. If there's anything special you want, just let me know. I can even buy you hair clips and other ornaments."

"Well, Lila, what do you think?" the Count asked. "Is the nice man scary?"

"Mm-hmm," Lila murmured reluctantly, lowering her eyes.

Even though he had expected that answer, Jörg was still disappointed. But then he remembered how intimidating he'd found the soldiers and policemen in his town when he was young. He hadn't started admiring them until he was a little bigger. If a boy like him had felt that way, it was only natural for a girl her age to be wary of grown men, especially if they were complete strangers.

"I hate Germans," Lila said softly.

Jörg stood there dumbstruck, but the young girl went on.

"Germany destroyed my country. Together with Russia and Austria. I lost my village and my home."

5

At first, Jörg didn't understand what Lila meant when she said Germany had destroyed her country.

Germans had fought and occupied territory all over the continent since the beginning of the Great War. However, he had never heard of them completely destroying an entire nation.

"When did that happen?" he asked the girl.

"One hundred and twenty-one years ago."

“That’s going back a long way.”

“It doesn’t matter if it happened yesterday or long ago,” Lila said, her tone growing sterner. “Because of that, my ancestors lost their home and had to flee to other countries. So imagine how we feel when everyone has their own land and assumes that’s their right… I doubt that’s something you’ve ever thought about, Mr. Huber.”

“Sorry. I didn’t mean it that way. I’m uneducated about these things and know very little about other countries’ histories. Most people in the small town I come from are German.”

“You wouldn’t call that *uneducated* so much as *ignorant*,” the Count chimed in.

“Is there a difference?”

“One is ignorant if they have little interest in other countries and don’t particularly care. It’s nothing to be ashamed of. That sort of thing is bound to happen when people don’t have opportunities to learn. Just because we live in modern society, that doesn’t mean everyone is able to receive a high level of education.”

“Forgive me. So that thing she mentioned…”

“Lila was talking about the Third Partition of Poland.”

“What’s that?”

“The Polish-Lithuanian Commonwealth was located in an area that made it an easy target for neighboring countries. As such, their territory was frequently stolen from them, until finally, in 1795, the remaining land was divided up. That was one hundred and twenty-one years ago. The current German Empire came into existence forty-five years ago; however, the Kingdom of Prussia laid the foundation for Germany. This same kingdom once worked with Austria and Russia to steal Polish territory and eradicate the country of Poland in the Third Partition of Poland all those years ago.”

Jörg’s shoulders slumped with relief. That meant the German Army he knew hadn’t robbed Lila of her homeland.

“I understand,” he replied. “I didn’t attack Poland, though, so I hope you’ll reconsider. I would like to be friends with you in this era, Lila.”

But Lila only pressed her point further. “Germans today are violent and horrible enough. Have you already forgotten what the German Army did in Belgium at the start of the war? They burned a university library and the historical records inside without a care in the world. It seems it's not just different ethnicities Germans hate, but also academia."

Words failed Jörg. Yet again, he had no idea what the young girl was talking about. He looked to the Count for help.

The Count spoke slowly and deliberately. "You do know that Germany attacked Belgium early on in the Great War, don't you?"

"Yes. They said that passing through there made for the shortest route to fight the French."

"Belgium was neutral at the time. They had the right to refuse passage to the German Army, but the Germans forced their way through, hoping to quickly crush the French as soon as the war began so they could turn those troops around and send them east to strike at Russia. Germany couldn't fight off a pincer attack, so their plan was to demolish the Western Front first, then fight along the Eastern Front. They didn't have time to negotiate with Belgium if they wanted that plan to work."

"So they used force?"

"The Germans wouldn't retreat, so Belgium joined the Allied forces, who officially deployed troops to fight back. It turned into a fierce battle. This all happened before you enlisted, when the German Army still used those *Pickelhaube* helmets with the spike on the top."

According to the Count, the German Army had marched relentlessly through villages and towns killing civilians, raiding food from storehouses, and setting fire to houses. The Allies used these events on propaganda flyers to garner support for the war effort, which they distributed far and wide. These flyers depicted the Germans as beasts, accusing them of massacring women and children, and the governments of the Allied powers called for their young men to take up arms and drive back these savage monsters.

The German Army didn't stop advancing until it had completely conquered Belgium. When they entered the town of Leuven, the Germans mistook a salvo from some friendly units as an attack by the Belgians and retaliated by killing two hundred civilians and setting fire to the town. Leuven was reduced to ruins, and the university library burned to the ground. This was the incident to which Lila had been referring when she said that Germans had burned a library and the historical records inside.

The young girl continued to glare at Jörg.

"I like reading. So I understand why you're so angry," he said, weighing his words carefully.

"Don't pretend you know what it's like. Germans are brutes. They even hate our religion."

"I'm Catholic. We might speak different languages, but I read the same Bible you do. Not all Germans are Protestants. And we have Orthodox Christians, too. Once there's peace, we'll all go back to being regular people."

A hint of color rose to Lila's cheeks. But it quickly faded, and she said in a tone as cool as the north wind, "I don't believe that at all."

She moved away from Xandra and put a hand on the doorknob. "Xandra will cut my hair like always, so don't worry about it. I won't be requiring your assistance, Mr. Huber."

"Well, I'm a professional, so feel free to ask me for whatever you want."

"I won't. I'll be fine without you."

Lila left the room, closing the door behind her.

Once she was gone, Jörg turned to face the Count. "It doesn't seem like she needs a hairdresser or a guard."

"Are you offended by what she said?"

"No. Soldiers are easy to hate. But wouldn't it be better if her guard was a French or British soldier? You didn't need to bring a German like me all the way out here."

"That wouldn't be any fun."

"It hardly matters if it's fun or not."

"Hairdressers don't care about what kind of people they serve; they simply find joy in making their customers look good," the Count said. "All you need to do is show Lila that quality. The rest is up to you."

III
The People on the Home Front

1

Xandra gave Jörg one of the corner rooms to use as his bedroom. It was slightly smaller than the first room he'd woken up in and furnished with only a bed, desk, and dresser, but it was enough for one person. It received ample natural light, and standing at the window, Jörg could look down on the inner courtyard.

Four buildings surrounded the courtyard, obstructing his view of the outside world. The space had two stone pathways running through it—one east-west, one north-south—which connected the buildings. They weren't covered by roofs, though, meaning that anyone trying to cross in the rain would get wet. Or maybe this place didn't ever get rain. After all, there was a monster living here, so it wouldn't be strange for the inn to be shielded by some sort of magic.

Flowers of all colors swayed in the flower beds, and shrubs thrived, covered in glossy green leaves. Jörg opened both sides of the casement window, letting the scents of the garden blow softly into the room. He felt out of touch with the seasons. Despite already being June, this sweet smell and gentle breeze belonged to spring.

His thoughts were in disarray.

Masses of his fellow soldiers still fought on the battlefield, yet here he was, having been brought to this verdant paradise.

* * *

Jörg practiced using his simulacrum, and once he got used to it, the Count suggested he take a break until Lila calmed down.

"Like a holiday?" Jörg asked.

"Take some time to recover from the fatigue you've built up on the battlefield. I assume it's been a while since you spent any time with a woman."

"Where would I go?"

"How about your hometown?"

"That wouldn't be a good idea."

"Why not?"

"I wouldn't know what to say if I ran into my parents or friends. They would think I was a deserter."

"Then how about a stroll around a French town? Paris, say."

"In enemy territory?"

"Even now, away from the front lines, you only know French people as soldiers. Lila detests you because she sensed your dependence on such ideas. So why not start by trying to change them?"

"But a German wouldn't be safe there. Also, I don't speak French."

"I can change the appearance of your simulacrum. And your body knows the language, so there's no need to worry about that. Shall we get started? Place a hand on the table. Either one."

"What are you going to do?"

"Affix a seal so you don't get lost."

Jörg did as he was bade and placed his left hand on the edge of the table.

The Count removed a paintbrush and a small bottle from a shelf, then took up a position standing diagonally across from Jörg. He opened the bottle, soaked the tip of the brush in the green liquid, pared away drips on the edge of the bottle, and began to paint a peculiar pattern on the back of Jörg's hand.

He drew two large concentric circles with a triangle and diagonal lines in the center, then added strange text in places. The paint dried quickly, and the color slowly faded. It didn't disappear completely, though, and Jörg could still see it if he squinted. It had seeped underneath his skin.

The Count set down the brush and closed the bottle. "Humans cannot see that design. Even if you rub it or wash it, it won't come off. It can give instructions and rescind them, which you can do any number of times. Come this way. I'll explain how to use it."

The Count guided Jörg into the hall, where they stopped in front of a door.

Jörg's eyes went wide. The same design that had just been drawn on the back of his hand decorated the door panel. But the paint that had been used here was red as blood.

"You can go through this door to Paris."

"You're kidding!"

"Monsters and simulacrums do not obey the rules of space-time and can go wherever, whenever they please. The design on the back of your hand is set for Paris. If you wish to go there, it will react to your simulacrum and transport you automatically."

"What about when I want to come back?"

"There are similar doors around Paris, so simply find one and return."

"How am I supposed to do that?"

"Your simulacrum will search for them without you having to do anything. Keep an eye out for this design, which you'll find inscribed on doors around the city. It won't be just inns and restaurants, either; you'll often find that the door to someone's house or a warehouse has become a portal. The design is always the same color, so as long as you keep your eyes open, I'm sure you won't miss it."

"And if I don't find it?"

"This is the address for the inn here," the Count said, handing Jörg a piece of paper. "You'll have to transfer a few times, but you can get back using taxis and trains. The same design is on the front door of this inn, so you'll know which one it is."

"I don't have any money."

"I can lend you as much as you need. Just be careful of pickpockets."

The Count removed a wallet from his coat pocket and handed it to Jörg. Next, he reached out with a finger and drew a rectangle on the wall next to the door, which transformed into a mirror. "The symbol on the back of your hand contains a spell to make people see your simulacrum as a Frenchman. However, these days, people might assume a healthy young man wandering around the city to be a spy, so you'll pretend to be an injured soldier with a damaged left arm and a face disfigured by shrapnel. Come now, look into the mirror and see your new visage."

The Count had Jörg stand in front of the wall. The unfamiliar face of a young Frenchman stared back at Jörg from deep within the mirror. The injured soldier was out of uniform, wearing civilian clothes, and he had a large reddish-black scar that ran from his left cheek down to his chin.

Jörg tentatively raised his left hand to his cheek. His arm shook when he tried to move it and wouldn't do what he wanted it to, but when he finally managed to trace a finger over the deep scar, the skin was uneven and had patches where it had been stretched taut.

The Count handed Jörg a thin mask to conceal the scar. The artificial material was the same color as his skin, only thicker. He fit it to his face, where it covered his cheek like a mask at a masquerade ball.

With the scar hidden, his guise as a young Frenchman was complete. He was a sophisticated youth who could walk the city freely and looked a little older than Jörg, just around marrying age.

The Count's reflection smiled. "Right now, there's no more fitting role for you than an injured veteran. If anyone asks you about the war, just talk about the things you did to the French Army and switch the sides around. Simple, right?"

His words were as blunt as ever, but Jörg couldn't argue because it was true. He would certainly have an easier time pretending to be a former soldier than someone of another occupation. Speaking with French people, all he needed to do was replace his position in the German Army with that in the French Army, then throw in a few curses and criticisms against the Germans at the end. It shouldn't be all that difficult.

"What about a name?" Jörg asked. "I should have a French-sounding name in case anyone asks."

"Okay then, how about Pierre Arche? It's short and easy to remember."

Jörg rolled the fake name around in his mouth several times before the Count patted him lightly on the back and said, "All right, go on. Enjoy yourself. Don't worry about things here."

"Do I open the door myself?"

"If you don't, then the twin designs won't interlock."

"Where in Paris will I come out?"

"Directly in front of the Arc de Triomphe du Carrousel."

"What about lodgings?"

"Either find a place to stay over there or spend the night at a brothel. If there are no good options, you can always come back here."

"I don't know my way around Paris."

"The simulacrum will take you somewhere."

"But I don't even have a map."

"It will guide you."

Jörg opened the door, revealing a darkness that seemed to suck in his soul. He clutched the handle tightly, hesitant to take that first step, and when he finally tried to move forward, his legs wouldn't budge.

"Always needing me to give you a hand," the Count muttered exasperatedly, before pushing Jörg firmly between the shoulder blades with his fist.

The ground beneath Jörg's feet instantly disappeared, just like when he'd leaped from the German trenches to Verdun. He instinctively shut his eyes, and a pitiful scream escaped his lungs. He wasn't about to enter another person's body, so he waited for his feet to touch down on solid ground.

Soon enough, he felt himself standing on cobblestones.

Jörg opened his eyes and turned to look around.

The air was dry, and a faint breeze carried the scent of vegetation.

A giant stone arch loomed before him. It wasn't the entrance to a building, however—just an arch.

The Count had said he would emerge directly in front of the Arc de Triomphe du Carrousel, meaning this must be it. With a name like the "Triumphal Arch," Jörg assumed armies must pass through it when they returned home victorious after a war. He stood in awe for a while, watching the sunlight bathe the blocky sand-colored arch, before coming to his senses and realizing that the area around him stood deathly quiet. In the middle of the day during such a pleasant time of the year, a place like this should be crowded. But very few people were around.

Jörg left the arch and walked down the boulevard. Tall buildings flanked the wide street, giving the entire city a brilliant white glow. They looked nothing like the black-timber-frame and plaster-wall homes of Jörg's hometown.

He wandered through Paris, making his way down roads lined with chestnut and plane trees. The sensation beneath his feet was almost as if he were floating. It made him think of a small stone skipping low over the surface of a pond, creating ripples in its wake. Right now, he was that stone, his own will overpowered by the movements of the simulacrum.

Horse-drawn carriages passed frequently, as did quite a few automobiles. The lights that ran down the streets weren't gas but the electric ones he'd heard about.

He saw hardly any working-aged men. Many people had prosthetic arms or legs replacing a lost limb, and some wore face coverings like he did. Others wore a piece of cloth that hung from their noses all the way down to their necks, their wounds so severe that not even a mask could conceal them.

Jörg went past countless women wearing mourning dresses. Every time he did, a chill went down the back of his neck. The newspapers on the stands covered the continued fighting at Verdun; the German Army's onslaught kept pushing the French back, but the outcome was still uncertain.

Not a single person turned to look at him, so he knew they must see him as a Frenchman.

But what if something caused the magic to fade? A German in the middle of Paris would attract a crowd eager to beat him to death. The simulacrum wouldn't die, but Jörg shuddered, remembering the pain he'd felt when Johann died at Verdun. He winced at the thought of having to go through that again.

His knees were trembling slightly, but Jörg was already here, so he had no choice but to continue. If anyone discovered his real identity, he'd just run away as fast as he could, and the simulacrum should lead him to a portal home.

Walking grew tiresome, so he stopped in at a café. There, he checked the wallet the Count had given him. Jörg didn't know the first thing about French money, but the simulacrum's knowledge came to him almost immediately. Bills and notes, franks and centimes—there were several different denominations of each. The wallet contained some 1,000-franc and 500-franc notes, along with a little loose change. He could break the notes if needed.

Jörg picked out a table and sat down. His simulacrum called over a waiter and ordered a glass of red wine and a piece of spinach-and-bacon quiche. He cut a bit off with a fork and put it in his mouth, the firm base and soft filling crumbling on top of his tongue. The egg and butter melted together with the bacon fat and the bitterness of the spinach to create an incredible flavor. He used to eat something similar back in his hometown, with onion instead of spinach.

Thoughts of home made him long for a beer. However, the knowledge within his simulacrum informed Jörg that France didn't have beer right now. The red wine paired well with the quiche, but each sip only made him miss beer more.

As he drank his wine, Jörg thought back over Lila's reaction from the other day.

He wasn't disappointed that she had rejected the idea of him as her bodyguard; considering her history, that was a natural reaction for her to have. What bothered him was the Count's carelessness at bringing Lila and him together. He'd done so despite knowing how the young girl felt, and Jörg couldn't tell whether it was just the cruel trick of a monster or an experiment of some sort. The Count remained as inscrutable as always.

Lila had a very mature way of looking at things. She was small but might not be as young as she looked. Had the inn stopped her from aging outwardly? Or had she matured faster than kids in human society because she'd been raised by a monster?

She wasn't Belgian, so her fury at the razing of the Leuven library must be because she loved books. Maybe reading a book on fashion together might bring them a little closer to understanding one another.

2

Jörg paid for his meal and left the café, once again entrusting the simulacrum with his next destination. The markets of Paris still carried food and the daily necessities. There were some glaring vacancies on the shelves, but compared with Germany, they still had plenty.

In Jörg's town, food shortages had begun soon after the start of the war. Food was requisitioned for the war effort, a rationing system was put in place, and ration vouchers were required for bread or meat. Germany relied on imports for many goods, and when the Allied forces cut off those supply lines, things got even tougher.

Paris had ration distribution centers, too. Apparently, it was already impossible to get hold of some items.

Jörg strolled leisurely past posters meant to inspire the French citizens. They featured brave slogans inviting men to join the fight, supportive words for the women protecting the home front, and harsh criticism painting the Germans as beasts.

Poking his head inside a bookstore, Jörg saw stacks of books critical of Germany with bold titles like *J'accuse!* and *People of Germany, Wake Up!* He was surprised to find that the authors weren't French—*Germans* were criticizing Germany. The books had been translated into French and then mass-produced, written by German lawyers and reporters who must be discontent with their government.

He picked one up and scanned the pages, but it quickly gave him a headache, so he closed the book and returned it to the table. Every citizen in every country had the right to criticize their nation, but the arguments and allegations contained within these books were too extreme for Jörg to accept. He felt as if they were being unfairly critical, which made him a little angry.

As evening approached, men and women appeared from the various buildings and began walking down the boulevard and crowding the sidewalks. Jörg wandered over hills and went up and down stairs and eventually found himself leaving the commercial area for a residential district.

He sensed a presence and, glancing up, saw a solitary pigeon flying towards a seven-story apartment building. The window of the attic room sat half-open, and the pigeon flew inside with practiced ease.

Jörg immediately recognized it as a carrier pigeon.

He didn't know why someone would choose to communicate via carrier pigeon in the city, but with restrictions on collection and delivery times at the post office, they were certainly still convenient. Even if the small message cylinders couldn't carry much information.

Lowering his gaze back to street level, his eyes met those of a woman walking toward him. She looked about twenty-five or twenty-six years old. Her dress was old and worn, and she had her hair pulled back into a ponytail. When she noticed Jörg, her pale cheeks drew taut.

"Fabrice?" she exclaimed. "When did you get back to Paris?"

Jörg was even more stunned than the woman, and for a moment, he couldn't speak. It seemed she recognized the face the Count had given him.

He never mentioned anything about that!

"Don't you remember me?" she pressed.

"...My name is Pierre Arche," Jörg said, finally forcing his stiff tongue into motion. "I'm very sorry, but I think you must have mistaken me for someone else."

The woman staggered and slumped against the wall of a building. "You're really not Fabrice LeRoy? Not even his brother or a family member?"

"No, I'm not."

"Maybe you got injured on the battlefield and lost your memory. Do you remember something like that?"

"I'm very sorry, but nothing of the sort happened to me."

The woman covered her mouth with her hands and gave a muttered apology. "Sorry. You look just like him. You could be his twin."

"If you don't mind, would you tell me a bit about him? I might be able to help."

Jörg didn't understand the situation, so he thought it might be a good idea to do a little information gathering. His words were driven more by self-preservation than by kindness, but the woman politely answered him.

"That's very kind of you. My name is Christine Duran. I have a brother, Hubert, who's five years younger than me, and Fabrice was on his soccer team. The two of you look identical."

Fabrice LeRoy had often gone to Christine's house with the other players.

When Europe erupted into war, Fabrice and Hubert had enlisted and been assigned to the same unit. They had both written to Christine frequently, but she hadn't received any word from them since April. She was worried their battalion might have gone to Verdun, the thought of which tore her apart every day.

"I don't know Fabrice. I didn't see him on the front."

"I see. Then where could they be?"

"You would have been notified if they'd died. So don't give up hope."

Christine seemed overwhelmed with grief, and Jörg didn't want to leave her there by herself. He had asked about Fabrice for purely selfish reasons, but now he wanted to provide her with some comfort before leaving. Times were tough both on the front line and behind it. The soldiers longed for home, while their families worried over the state of the battlefield. He knew he couldn't do anything to help her, but he at least wanted to try.

Jörg recalled something the Count had told him:

"Up until now, you've only seen French people as the enemy. Even though, logically, you know they're human beings just like you."

He was right.

Jörg pushed open the large doors of a housing complex and led Christine inside.

He glanced up at the gigantic spiral staircase stretching high above him. Taking Christine's hand, he sat her down on the fifth step from the bottom, then lowered himself to the floor and leaned against the metal railing. "Were you working today?"

"Yes. The army has taken all the men, so us women are working in the factories now."

Munitions factories, textile workshops, and all the other jobs that until recently had only hired men were now relying on women to pitch in. It sounded as though conditions on farms were far worse, however, as women had taken over the backbreaking labor, leaving children to tend the fields.

The same thing was happening in Germany, so Jörg understood the situation well.

According to Christine, an even wider array of jobs was available to women in Great Britain, including train conductor and police officer.

"The women working in England apparently even wear pants. With their uniforms and hats on, they look exactly like men. They're very proud of their work and consider it an honor. Women even shame men in town who haven't already enlisted."

"The world is changing so incredibly fast."

"It is. I get so filthy working at the factory from all the machine oil and paint that I'd wear pants, too, if they provided them."

Christine let out a sigh. Milk and butter would most likely switch to the ration system soon as well. Daily necessities were becoming even harder to acquire.

"Where was Hubert's last letter from?" Jörg asked.

"Artois. The French Army joined up with the British to attack the Germans there. Where did you come from, Mr. Arche?"

"Champagne, so a little south of that."

"Were you at Verdun?"

Jörg considered how to respond, ultimately saying, "For a little while."

"Is that where you picked up your injury?"

"Yes. That place was truly hell."

"I heard Artois was horrible, too. The French suffered a lot of casualties."

"We made good use of the vehicles we had, though. Injured soldiers were immediately driven to the back lines and treated in field hospitals. It worked much better than the Germans' system, since they relied on trains for supplies. If anything happened to Hubert, I'm sure they got him out right away."

In reality, nothing ever went that smoothly on the battlefield. Not a day had gone by since Jörg looked down from the observation tower at Fort Douaumont that he hadn't thought about what he'd seen there. Corpses blown apart by explosions and buried in the mud that covered the barren field. Broken weapons strewn about the ground. Metal helmets riddled with holes. Dying warhorses being shot by soldiers. Even the lucky survivors stared off into the distance with lifeless eyes, thinking that while they had lived through today, their turn to die might very well come tomorrow.

However, it wouldn't help to tell Christine all that. He didn't know how much the French newspapers reported, but there was no need to share any more of the cruelty of war than was necessary.

Christine looked blankly at Jörg. "Are the German soldiers really so savage?"

"No. They're not as bad as people say."

"The German Army used airships to bomb Paris. They moved along the Seine and kept dropping bombs one after the other. It sounded like hundreds of lightning strikes—tore giant holes in the roads, big enough for a taxi or horse-drawn carriage to fall into. I watched from near Notre-Dame Cathedral."

"When war breaks out, nobody has a choice but to become a savage."

"But bombing a city is so cowardly! What if they hit children?"

"Soldiers have no choice but to obey the commands of their superior officers. If they don't, they're either punished or killed."

"That might be true for the German Army, but no one with the Allied forces is that cruel."

Jörg started to argue but then stopped himself. French planes had shot at and dropped bombs on young German men who had just arrived on the front line. The Allies were just as brutal. There was no such thing as a noble army; all those heroic tales of the battlefield were pure fiction. They stirred hearts and spread far and wide, causing nothing but harm.

"I wonder where Fabrice is now," Christine murmured. "Neither I nor his family have received so much as a letter."

Jörg released the railing and stood up in front of her. He clumsily raised his trembling left hand and gently stroked the mask covering his wound.

"See this? The war irreparably damaged my left arm and gave me this large scar on my face. But I'm still alive. Don't give up hope until you know for sure and see it with your own two eyes. That's the only advice I have for you."

3

He had intended to just have a quick chat and leave, but they ended up talking for quite a while. It had been a long time since Jörg had last spoken with a woman his age, and because he looked like someone she knew, Christine stared at him the entire time, so it took a lot of effort for Jörg to suppress his racing emotions.

Christine removed a photograph from her wallet and showed it to him. "This is Hubert, and that's Fabrice. If you see them anywhere, please let me know."

The photograph showed her with the soccer team. Jörg didn't recall ever seeing either of the men. Hubert had his arms crossed and was leaning to the side, a football at his feet and a carefree smile on his face. He was more muscular than Jörg and taller than Christine. Apparently, he was also kind to the neighborhood children. The thought of a man like that heading off to war to slaughter other human beings in the name of his homeland filled Jörg with an unbearable sadness.

Fabrice's appearance, however, surprised him completely. They didn't just look alike—he was identical to the man. The Count must have based this simulacrum off Fabrice.

In which case, this body might contain some of his memories. Surely the Count knew a way to weave someone's memories into a simulacrum. Fabrice's intense longing for home might have seared itself inside this simulacrum, which would explain why it had headed directly for Christine's apartment building.

Jörg committed Hubert's face to memory, then returned the photograph to Christine.

"If I hear anything about their whereabouts, I'll get in touch immediately. Could you write down the address here?"

Christine nodded, and Jörg removed a notepad from his jacket pocket. He passed it to her, and she scribbled down the address with a pencil before saying, "Thank you."

"I guess I should be on my way," Jörg said. "Stay strong and wait for the day when Hubert and Fabrice come back home."

"Thank you for everything. It's dark now, so watch your step."

When Jörg opened the door of the apartment building and stepped outside, an inky blue-black color was already staining the sky.

The city was darker than he'd imagined it would be. Plenty of streetlights dotted the roads, but none were lit. He'd heard that Paris had electricity, but the streetlamps around here were all still gas, so the lamplighter must be running behind schedule.

"Do you need a taxi, sir?" someone called out to him from behind.

He turned to see a friendly-looking man in a flat cap. The man wore a deep-brown jacket with khaki pants and was leaning against a red automobile. When had it arrived? Jörg hadn't heard the sound of an engine or brakes.

The driver slowly opened the car door. "First time in Paris? You look like you're fresh from the front, taking some time for a bit of rest and recuperation."

"You could say that."

"It's easy enough to find places on your own during the day, but at night, it's that much harder. I'll give you a discount. Come on, hop in."

The taxi consisted of a boxy passenger cabin behind a driver's seat protected only by a canvas awning. The driver's seat was wide enough to fit two people side by side, and a vertically sliding window separated the driver and passenger sections. With the window closed, the driver couldn't hear any conversation going on in the passenger cabin, but passengers could open the window to give directions. The driver told him the car was a 1911 Renault AG-1 and boasted about how easily he could steer something this size.

"I thought the taxis in Paris were all being used on the front," commented Jörg.

"That was for the battle at Marne; most of them are back now. There are also some made by new companies."

"Then, could you take me someplace I can relax over a drink?"

"Of course, sir. May I recommend Montparnasse? It's become quite the hot spot for young artists. They'll even paint a caricature of you as a souvenir."

Jörg smiled bitterly and touched the mask covering his wound. "Even with a face like this?"

"Have them draw what you looked like before you got injured. Real artists can draw what the eye can't see. And that place is crawling with all sorts of talented people who'll probably be famous one day."

"What do you mean they'll 'probably' be famous?"

"Most of the really talented artists are fighting right now. Braque, Léger—they and so many others have been sent off to war. If they don't come back, though, that's it. The people who stayed here in France will lead the next generation."

"I see."

"You used to be able to find Picasso in Montmartre and Montparnasse pretty often not too long ago, but I'm not sure about now. Chagall went back to his hometown two years ago, and Utrillo has been hospitalized too many times to count. So when you're in Montparnasse, try to find some budding young talent. Even Japanese artists who've come all the way from the Far East go there, and the stuff by Modigliani is interesting, even though it doesn't sell. He does caricatures to pay the bills, so find a café and ask around. The drawings he does have strangely exaggerated proportions."

"I don't know much about art, so I can't hope to understand anything too complicated."

"If you don't like it, you can just pay them and not accept the painting. That's what everyone does."

Jörg got in and closed the door behind him, and the man climbed into the driver's seat. As soon as he sat down, Jörg felt the vibrations of the engine as the car smoothly took off. It was a pleasant sensation, riding in a car along the paved road.

The dividing window was open, so the driver's voice reached him easily. "The town is so dark because of the lighting restrictions. It's to keep the town safe from nighttime bombing raids."

"I heard the Germans are using airships to bomb the city. Is it dangerous at night, too?"

"The lights here are electric, so normally it's bright as midday at night. Paris before the Great War was such an incredible place. Have you ever heard about the 1900 Paris Exposition?"

"I was a still a young boy back then."

"In that case, you should see it for yourself. This is Paris's belle epoque."

The city steeped in darkness suddenly grew bright, as though someone had cast a spell over it. Light poured from the windows of the buildings, intermingling with that of the streetlights to flood the avenue in a golden glow that illuminated the people enjoying the evening.

Jörg pressed against the window, transfixed by the scene outside. He couldn't see anyone dressed in mourning clothes or disabled veterans in tatters. Instead, young women paraded down the boulevard in wide hats decorated with ribbons or artificial flowers, blouses with puffy sleeves, and long skirts with tightly hemmed waists, accompanied by refined gentlemen in suits and hats. People filled the café terraces. They lost themselves in conversation or relaxed alone, enjoying their coffee, wine, and cigarettes. Merchandise crammed the shelves of the stores and grocers. Passing the displays in the tailors, he saw colorful fabrics, pure-white cotton garments, and finely made woolen clothes. He could hear lively music coming from somewhere—an up-tempo chanson. A velvety voice sang over the band before being drowned out by cheers and applause. He heard the ring of clinking glasses, and the heated excitement of a cabaret caressed his skin. The sweet scents of fruit and perfume tickled his nostrils. The sound of a man and a woman moaning and panting seductively reached him from somewhere close by, causing Jörg to jump in his seat. He looked around, and although he didn't see anyone, he sensed a mysterious presence.

The driver twisted around to look at him, curious to see Jōrg's reaction. "This was Paris before the war. This is the real city. It burst with raw passion, so vulgar it was invigorating. Everyone living here was like a fish hiding in murky water. But large or small, every city is like this, right? And people in the countryside have their own, more honest way of expressing their desires. Rather than believing in some unjustifiable cause, they live every day to the fullest, indulging in desires appropriate to their situation and cherishing those around them…"

"What *are* you?" Jörg's voice turned cold as he asked the question. "You must be another monster if you can show me something like this."

The driver released the steering wheel and turned fully around to face Jörg. He lifted the brim of his flat cap slightly with his thumb and flashed a wide grin. The taxi continued on without the man driving. It didn't hit anything, and although Jörg no longer heard the hum of the engine, the car carried on down the glittering evening road as though it had transformed into some incorporeal object.

"That peculiar pattern on the back of your hand would draw the eye of any monster," the driver said. "Not to mention the fact that it was drawn by Count George Silvestri."

"You know the Count?"

"The Count and I go way back. I'm the one who taught him how to use his powers. When I first met him, he was nothing but a boring immortal. He couldn't use any magic—a useless man doomed to continue cursing his own existence. What I taught him turned him into a respectable monster."

"Are you a sorcerer?"

"Nothing as strict as that. I'm a nameless spirit that doesn't even appear in the magical books of Solomon—a monster of nothingness known as Nil. I manipulate the aether to create physical bodies from thin air. The Count added his own little trick to that magic to make his simulacrums."

Jörg stared dumbstruck at Nil, who continued unfazed. "I was wondering what the Count planned to do with some dull German he picked up on the front lines. You're too ordinary a human to use as a plaything."

The Count had made his simulacrum look like a Frenchman, but Nil could see Jörg's true self. He hadn't guessed any random country but stated outright that Jörg was German. It wasn't just his appearance, either; Nil had immediately picked up on other things about him, too.

"I'm not the Count's plaything," retorted Jörg.

"To monsters, that's all humans ever are. Which makes me wonder what the Count has planned for you."

"Why do you care?"

"I came across someone else in this city with the same design on their hand. A child."

"You did? Here?"

"I don't know anything more. I only saw them from afar."

"Why not try calling out to them?"

"I'm not in the habit of scaring children." It was a surprising comment to hear from Nil. "But I can't overlook it when he uses that mark on an adult like you. Tell me the truth: What did the Count order you to do in Paris?"

"If he did have orders, I wish he'd told me."

The sights flashing by outside the car window had gradually come to a stop. Jörg could more clearly make out the details of the people walking down the street.

He couldn't believe what he saw next: Lila, walking among the crowd. She was wearing a blue sailor-collar blouse and knee-length skirt, with long stockings on her legs and flat shoes on her feet. None of the adults seemed to notice her strolling down the sidewalk alone, and no one spoke to her. She seemed invisible to them, like Jörg and the taxi. In which case, that mustn't be her real body, but a simulacrum.

Jörg leaned out the driver's side window and called her name. Lila immediately turned around and looked at him in surprise. Jörg opened the taxi door, jumped down, and ran over to her. "What are you doing here? Are you alone? Where are the Count and Xandra?"

Lila's expression stiffened, and she took a guarded stance. "Who are you?"

"It's me. Don't you remember?"

"Your voice sounds familiar. But I don't recognize your face."

"Jörg Huber. We met at Xandra's inn."

"Mr. Huber? You look like someone else."

"The Count did this. A German man could never show himself on the streets of Paris."

The young girl narrowed her eyes and stared at Jörg. "Oh, you're right. I can faintly see Mr. Huber inside you."

Jörg knelt down on the pavement. He stole a quick glance at the back of Lila's hand, where a pattern shone faintly beneath her skin. It was identical to the one on his own hand, drawn in that same green paint.

"Do you always come here on your own?" he asked.

"Yes."

"I'm surprised the Count allows it."

"He doesn't know."

"You don't tell him?"

"No."

"So you can use magic, too? Even though you're human?"

"Apparently so. It might be because I've been exposed to magic living at the inn. I drew the pattern myself this time, too. I remembered it from when the Count wrote it on my hand."

"I see. Now I understand why he asked me to look after you. It's too dangerous for you to be walking by yourself at night."

"I don't go anywhere dangerous. I just come to Paris sometimes to see my friends."

"It's quite late at night for a child to be out."

"I meet my friends in their dreams, so it's easier at night."

Nil stepped down from the taxi and called out, "So you two do know each other."

"Would you mind leaving us alone?" Jorge said. "We have our own business to attend to."

"Sorry, but no can do. If that girl also knows the Count, then I've got a whole list of things to go over."

Lila leaned close to Jörg and whispered in his ear. "Who's that?"

"A monster. He said he knows the Count, but I don't trust him."

"Should we run?"

"Probably."

Jörg stood, picking up Lila, and bolted. He didn't think he could beat a monster in a footrace, but if he could find a doorway home, they could go straight back to Xandra's inn.

Jörg ran, trusting his simulacrum to know the way. The illusion of Paris of old didn't obstruct him as Jörg dashed through the images, passing through them like smoke or fog. They seemed to exist on another plane from Jörg and Lila—a world fixed in a different time and space, like the layers of a pie crust.

Jörg didn't know how long he ran before eventually stopping. Even his simulacrum could get tired, and sweat dripped from his brow.

He saw a stone building towering above them. A peculiar font filled the curved arch above the giant door, its letters reading Théâtre du Grand-Guignol. Signboards decorated with eerie paintings flanked the door. It seemed to be a theater that catered to the general public. From the pictures of a bloody, severed head and a skeleton and the provocative headlines, the current play was clearly some kind of horror story.

Jörg set Lila down on the pavement, and the young girl anxiously leaned into him as she glanced at a signboard. The pictures were certainly too much for a girl of eleven.

Silence surrounded the theater; there wasn't a single soul about. Jörg wondered if they weren't in a Paris of the past or present but had actually been swallowed up by an abyss that opened into some unknown space. An illusory world that felt just like the real thing.

As Jörg examined their surroundings, Nil materialized out of thin air. Jörg was breathing heavily, but Nil didn't show even the slightest hint of perspiration, crossing the street toward them with an air of indifference. The theater door didn't have the pattern to return home, but considering his simulacrum had brought them here, Jörg figured there must be one nearby.

He whispered in Lila's ear. "While I talk to him, you look for a door with the red design on it."

Lila's expression drew tight, and she answered "Okay" before darting away.

Nil watched Lila go with a smirk. "The Count has a bad sense of humor if he put a return portal in a place like this."

"What do you mean by that?"

"Behind you stands the greatest house of horrors in Paris. Its goal is to turn events too dangerous for real life into plays so the audience can experience them in a safe environment. In there, people hear stories of actual serial killers, scandalous tales involving men and women driven mad with jealousy, ominous specters, gorgeous women being humiliated and chopped to pieces, fearsome diseases that devastate the human body, and ghosts that foretell dark futures. They also have comedies that make light of human folly. It provides people with an outlet for the frustrations of their everyday lives, letting them cheer, laugh, explore their curiosity, deceive themselves, and scream in terror. This theater is still operating now, but I expect it won't be long before its popularity slumps and it'll be forced to close. Do you know why?"

"How would I?"

"Fiction can no longer match the atrocities of the current war. Whatever cruelties someone might imagine for their play, and no matter how smart and funny they make it, such a work will be powerless before the horrors of modern warfare. As the Great War continues, people will come to see that the tragedies and satires of the theater are nothing more than fiction. The fear and joy they feel during a play will begin to appear paltry compared with the real world. The final days of this theater are not too far off. As long as the curiosity and savagery of humans exists, there will always be customers who search for beauty within cruelty, but it's already too late for it to continue in this form."

"But aren't monsters like you practically fictional yourselves?" Jörg cried out. "Monsters don't have the power to change human society. If you did, then you'd make a world that better suited you."

"Well, we all have our own sensibilities and levels of restraint." Nil grinned. "But we monsters stay faithful to our own curiosities. Once we find someone that interests us, we stay with them until the end. Don't think poorly of us."

A gentle heat laced the stagnant night air. Goose bumps ran down Jörg's neck. His body reacted the same way right before a firefight or bombardment in the trenches. It defied logic, but his body would tremble before his senses detected a threat.

He regretted not bringing some type of talisman to ward off evil. Jörg knew that ash branches and holly leaves worked as protective wards, but he should have asked the Count or Xandra about more effective items. After all, monsters were everywhere.

Unarmed but ready to fight, Jörg heard Lila clamoring noisily somewhere far away. She was calling for help. Jörg frantically scanned the area and caught sight of a massive man who was approaching with Lila under an arm.

He wore a long coat ill-suited for the season and had a rifle slung over one shoulder. The coat was obviously military issue. On his head was a tall hat with no brim and the top cut into a V shape. His clothes belonged to neither the French nor the German Army. Regardless of his country of origin, he looked wholly out of place—as if some sort of impossible person had invaded this impossible space. He appeared human yet gave off the air of a giant rampaging through the wilderness and smelled like a cold, snow-covered forest barren of any vegetation. The stench of decay mingled faintly with that of iron, carried on the breeze alongside the smell of gun oil.

Lila struggled wildly underneath his arm, but she couldn't break free of his strong grip. Seeing Jörg, the man stopped a short distance away, bent down, and set Lila free on the ground. His rugged features betrayed no emotion, displaying neither hostility nor hatred toward Lila.

By the time he straightened up again, his expression had changed completely. He glared intensely at Nil and suddenly grabbed his rifle and fired. In the blink of an eye, he pulled back the bolt to eject the empty casing, loaded another bullet into the chamber, and fired another shot.

Nil winced slightly the moment the bullet struck him, but of course, it wasn't enough to incapacitate him. Not a drop of blood fell from his wound, and it didn't seem to cause Nil any real pain. Instead, the place where the bullet had hit him crumbled, and his flesh began to scatter into black dust. It looked like ants trying to flee from a collapsed nest, or a mysterious string of letters spilling out of his body and falling to the ground.

As his body disappeared, Nil turned to the man and said flatly, "So the Count called you to rescue them, Milos?"

"No," the man called Milos answered, still aiming his rifle at the monster. "I came here for a break, so I simply didn't want anything annoying me."

"Then go somewhere else. Paris is a big city."

"So they say, but I still managed to run into the guy I most wanted to avoid."

Milos fired at Nil a third time, and the monster's collapsing body finally disintegrated.

Although he had lost his human form, Nil's presence still hung heavy in the air. Jörg heard his voice clearly. "I'll back off for tonight, but tell that Count of yours that I'll come by to visit him soon."

"He won't be pleased to see you," Milos replied. "I'm pretty sure Xandra will put up a barrier."

"I didn't say we'd meet at the inn. Next time, don't interfere. Because I won't play nice."

Nil's presence evaporated. As soon as it was gone, Milos turned to face Jörg. "Why would you bring that child to a place like this?"

"We didn't come together," replied Jörg. "We just happened to run into each other in the city."

"That's even worse. You shouldn't be letting a child use simulacrums alone."

"She's better with them than I am. She learned how to draw the design all by herself."

"Don't lie to me."

"I'm not. Don't let appearances deceive you; she already acts like an adult. Anyway, I really appreciate you saving us. Thank you. Are you a monster, too?"

"Can't you tell by looking at me?"

"Well, I thought you might be an exorcist or something. What army do you serve with?"

"The Serbian Army."

An Allied power, huh? So an enemy of Germany. Jörg wondered how this man would treat him if his simulacrum didn't appear French.

"So you know the Count?" Jörg asked.

"If by 'the Count' you mean George Silvestri, then yes, I do."

"Good. Yes, that Count. Even if it was purely by chance, you really did save us. But if you're a monster, then why are you in the army?"

"Long before the Great War began, I fought against the Ottoman Empire to wrest Serbia free from imperial control."

"Serbia gained independence a long time ago."

"The country has been lost again."

"It has?"

Milos frowned. "Perhaps you haven't been reading the papers. If you were on the front lines, you must know what happened in the Balkan Peninsula, right?"

"I was on the Western Front."

"But don't you care about what's happening in other countries? It's an Allied nation."

"Sorry, I haven't been keeping up with the news. What's it like there now?"

"It's pretty rough. It will still take some time for us to strike back."

"How did you end up fighting in the war?"

"I have a duty to humanity."

"A *duty*? That's something I haven't heard from a human mouth in a while."

"It's not?"

"No."

Milos appeared troubled by that, and Jörg felt a tug of affection, seeing the stern man look so pained.

"My human name is Milos Krasić," he said, finally introducing himself. "I'm a werewolf." Milos glanced over to Lila. "Let's get that girl home. I've had enough of the city for one night and there are a few things I want to ask the Count."

4

Lila complained bitterly about going back home without meeting her friends, but they couldn't afford to risk running into another monster. According to Milos, such beings were drawn to one another, so the group would be in real trouble if other monsters sensed their encounter with Nil and flocked here.

With his simulacrum's lame left arm, Jörg couldn't restrain Lila's flailing, so he had no choice but to ask Milos to pick her up again. The young girl thrashed about like a cat in distress, but she was no match for Milos's powerful arms.

They discovered a portal home near the theater. When he saw the diagram clearly drawn in red paint on the door of a bar, a wave of relief swept through Jörg. They could finally return to the inn.

Jörg pushed the door open, and what should have been a loud room reeking of alcohol instead revealed Xandra's tranquil inn. He stood in the hallway, just as he had before he left. He'd felt a faint sense of time passing on the way to Paris, but the trip back had happened instantaneously. Perhaps his simulacrum had acclimated to the speed of the trip, or perhaps it was some strange power at work due to Milos being with them.

When Milos set Lila down in the hallway, she looked even more upset. Jörg tried his best to console her, telling her in a whisper, "You should sneak back to your room. I won't tell the Count."

"Stop trying to make it sound like I owe you."

"That's not what I meant. I just don't want to make this any more complicated than it already is."

Lila glared hard at Jörg but eventually turned on her heel and hurried off toward her room.

Milos strode down the hallway as if he lived there.

"Where are you going?" Jörg asked, following after him.

"To see the Count. He should be in the lounge at this hour."

"You seem to know him well."

"I've been here many times before."

When they arrived at the lounge on the second floor, Milos knocked on the door, then stepped into the room as if he were meeting family.

The Count was sitting in a chair by the fireplace, reading a hefty book. A wine bottle rested on the round table by his side. A few sips of his drink were visible at the bottom of his wineglass, the deep-red liquid looking like something squeezed from a living person.

Xandra sat behind a long table, pen in hand, writing something on a piece of paper. Her usual brilliant smile rose to her face when she saw Jörg and Milos.

"What do you want?" the Count called out, not taking his eyes from the page.

Milos didn't answer but just nodded briefly to Xandra before taking a seat at the end of the table. He set his rifle by his feet, then turned to the Count. "Romania is going to join the war. Probably sometime in August."

"And what about it?"

"It's a chance to help your motherland. Come help."

"Walachia is my homeland; the neighboring territory is no concern of mine. And it's still unclear which side they'll join."

"Surely the Allies for the Slavic people."

"Before the Great War, Romania was allied with Germany and Austria. It's neutral now but may still choose to go over to their side at the eleventh hour."

"They would never. If Romania was going to do that, it would have done its duty and joined the war when it first started. If they're choosing to fight now, they'll do it on the side of the Allies."

"Well, my duties ended when my homeland won its independence from the Ottomans. I have no inclination to do anything more."

"Such indolence!"

"Furthermore, I dislike this 'Greater Serbia' doctrine you hold so dear. Protecting the rights of the Slavic people from the great European powers is certainly a noble cause; however, I cannot abide having Serbia take the helm. Let Romania do as they wish. It doesn't need Serbian politicians meddling."

"Now is not the time to worry over such trivialities. The Slavic people must band together to repel the imperialism running rampant throughout Europe."

"See, it's that earnest determination that I detest. Shouldn't we live our lives with more decorum? I, for one, shall do nothing. I have resolved not to concern myself with the whole affair."

"I met Nil in Paris. He suspects that you're planning to start something."

"He suspects everything," the Count responded wearily, "but I'm afraid he's assumed wrong. I plan to do nothing about this war. I don't want to influence it, and I don't care who wins. I only saved that man because I pitied the thought of him dying on the Western Front. Oh, which reminds me, I haven't undone the spell."

The Count set his book on the table and snapped his fingers.

Jörg was immediately overcome by a sensation like a layer of skin peeling away from his body. His wounds disappeared, and he could move his left arm without any issues.

Milos's face hardened the moment he saw Jörg's true form. "You're German?"

"I'm sorry for not telling you. I had to disguise my simulacrum to go to Paris."

"So you're all on the side of the Central powers?"

"Don't make such base assumptions," the Count cut in. "I have interacted with soldiers from all nations since the fighting began, but he is the only one to have obtained a simulacrum in the most ideal way."

"Even so, you didn't have to help a German."

"Stop discriminating against people based on their nationalities. We were treated the same way in the Balkans for a long time."

Milos was lost for words, and the Count continued. "The Serbian Army suffered great losses from fall last year up until winter. I'm glad to see you got out alive."

"You're bound to lose some days fighting a war."

"Regardless, that was horrific for Serbia. Even with the help of the Montenegrin Army, it ended in utter defeat. You also met up with the refugees and crossed Albania during the winter, did you not? I heard that between the spread of typhus and those who died fighting, Serbia has lost almost thirty percent of its population."

"But we aren't destroyed. We can regain our former strength."

"The soldiers who have fallen back to Corfu certainly still have the will to fight. But it must be quite an inconvenience for the Allies."

"What are you talking about?"

"The Central powers you were supposed to hold back moved south down the Balkan Peninsula, almost to Greece, and that became the Macedonian front. Serbia refusing Austria's ultimatum is what started this war. Don't you find that shameful?"

Milos slammed his fist down on the table. "Are you saying we should have just accepted Austria's annexation of Bosnia and Herzegovina? Should we have sat by quietly and watched them take Albania?"

"Serbia's population before the war was approximately 4.3 million people. Austria had ten times that. Surely you knew from the beginning that you would never survive a direct confrontation, even with Russia's help. And yet you still chose to assassinate the archduke and his wife."

"That's precisely *why* we did it. We couldn't match their army for size, so we had to find another way. If he had ascended the throne, our nationalist movement would have died."

"And that justifies murder? You should have tried finding a solution through diplomacy and politics." The Count gave an exaggerated sigh. "Plenty of people in the Serbian government wanted to avoid war. That's true of Austria as well. They didn't want the Balkan Peninsula razed again over nothing. Serbia should have handed the assassins over to Austria immediately. And it should have made a public announcement that it would not submit to Austria's unjust control."

"You don't need to tell me that. That was the government's decision."

"In that case, Colonel Dimitrijević should have assumed leadership and started transitioning to a republic during the May Coup. Serbia should have rid itself completely of the monarchy then. Letting it remain only invited chaos and sowed the seeds for future problems."

"Excuse me, sorry," Jörg said hesitantly, "but could you give me a bit more background? You're talking about some very unsettling things, and I really don't understand the situation..."

The Count shot Jörg a scornful look and said, "Surely you know the history of neighboring empires interfering in the affairs of Balkan countries. The Austro-Hungarian Empire, Russia, the Ottoman Empire—they all controlled other nations by force. Even my homeland, Walachia—the country now called Romania—felt their heavy hand. As did Milos's motherland of Serbia."

"That much I know."

"All these countries are bonded together through Slavic culture and have opposed any attempt to forcibly interfere. There are several nationalist movements inside the Balkan Peninsula. The Greater Serbia movement we were just talking about is one of them."

Franz Ferdinand, successor to the throne of the Austro-Hungarian Empire—one of the major powers of Europe—had been opposed to war with Serbia. However, he'd also devised a plan called trialism, which would have created a state within his empire for the Slavic people.

Like the Czechs and the Croatians, the Serbians were also considered Slavs. The anti-Austria segment of the Serbian population viewed this plan as an unforgivable level of control and worried that their nation would become a vassal state to Austria if they didn't eliminate the archduke.

It was at that point certain people began to plot his assassination. One such group was the Black Hand, an organization formed by officers from the Army of the Kingdom of Serbia. Its core members played a role in the assassination of King Alexander I and Queen Draga during the May Coup, denouncing Alexander as a bad king who had robbed the people of their rights. These soldiers who toppled the tyrant and installed a new monarch were glorified as heroes and wielded considerable power within the military, Colonel Dimitrijević among them.

A separate group of nationalist young men with connections to the Black Hand had also worked to oppose Austria. One of their number was Gavrilo Princip, the assassin involved in the Sarajevo incident.

Milos spoke up. "If we hadn't done something then, Serbia would have ended up under Austrian control. We'd just rid ourselves of the Ottoman Empire and were about to become slaves to Austria."

"That's conflating a country with an ethnicity," the Count replied coolly. "Slavs are Slavs, no matter where they are. If you wanted to protect your country, you should have done so through politics and diplomacy. People who can only think of assassination and war may be popular, but frankly, they're rather unenlightened."

"You know, you deserve the name 'Count,'" snapped Milos. "Whatever the era, you spend your time in blissful ignorance away from the common man."

"You've been fighting on the front, so your mind has been poisoned by the dark side of humanity. Where's your pride as a werewolf? Have you lost that?"

"I've always been on the side of humanity. I don't know how to live as a werewolf."

The Count laughed loudly. "Says a man who hasn't been able to truly become human after more than two hundred years. Anyway, you should stop fighting. Your time would be better spent going to Prague and examining Mucha's workshop."

"What are you talking about?"

"Six years ago, Mucha started on a work called *The Slav Epic*. He isn't making prints like he did in Paris during the art nouveau period, but he's working with giant canvases and pouring all his passion into them. The whole thing seems like nothing more than a delusional sense of idealism to me, but Mucha's artistic spirit is overwhelming. It's incredible he decided to begin work on such a masterpiece when he's already over fifty. He even went so far as to completely shut himself off from the outside world… Such intense mental fortitude amazes me. Those ambitious paintings are well suited to men like you. Go stand in front of them and rediscover your inner self. You have that same Slavic blood running in your veins, so you should be able to understand the difference between Greater Serbia and Pan-Slavism. Stop for a moment and truly consider the meaning behind those ideas."

Milos rose from his chair without a word. As he shouldered his rifle, Xandra, who had been silent the entire time, called out to him. "If you ever get hurt, know you can always come here. I'll make sure to fix you up."

"I appreciate it. Sorry for always bothering you with this, but while I'm here, would you sell me some more of that medicine? And the one that works on humans, as well."

"Of course. Take whatever you need. I imagine supplies are running low in Corfu."

"Thank you. We have too many sick and injured. I highly doubt there's enough to go around."

"Just use it on those who mean the most to you. There's only so much you can do."

Milos nodded, and Xandra stood up to join him.

"I better go as well, then," she said.

"Of course," the Count replied, as if he wasn't the least bit affected by the argument he'd just been having with Milos. "I leave it in your capable hands."

5

"It seemed like you and Milos don't get along, but that's not actually the case, is it?" Jörg said to the Count once they were alone.

"We've known each other for a very long time," the other man replied. "If you take the foolishness of a human, combine it with the ruthlessness of a werewolf, then add in Milos's unique sense of justice, you get the unbearably distorted personality you just met. He brought it on himself, so he doesn't want to entertain even the slightest of doubts."

"He did seem overly serious. I hope it doesn't surface in a bad way."

"In the fighting last fall, Germany, Austria, and Bulgaria formed an alliance to crush the Serbian Army. However, the Serbians wouldn't admit that they had lost. You could call their determination heroic, but to me, fighting until everyone dies is just irresponsible. If they continue fighting and refuse to retreat even an inch, the country of Serbia will one day be destroyed and wiped from the face of the earth."

"We were told the same thing in the German Army. That we should never retreat, no matter what the circumstances."

"Only humans whose souls are broken in some way can keep fighting until they die. You chose to escape, and that makes you more human by far."

"But back in ancient times when you were a knight, didn't you say the same thing to the men serving underneath you when you faced the Ottoman Empire?"

The Count frowned, then said in a pained voice, "I did. Which is precisely why I can recognize the deceit in those words. Being told to risk your life for your country is nothing but pure sophism, regardless of the purpose behind it."

"Why does Milos care about people anyway? Don't werewolves attack humans?"

"Yes. Werewolves dig up people's graves to drink their blood."

"So he must have some sort of reason."

"Long ago, groups of Balkan bandits resisted the Ottoman Empire. Like Robin Hood and his Merry Men, these bands stole from Ottoman caravans and distributed what they stole to the Slavic people. In Serbia, they called these brigands 'hajduks.' Milos was taken in by a band of hajduks when he was an infant and has lived his life as one ever since. He volunteered for the army after the Serbian independence movement began in earnest."

"Ah, so that's why he cares about humans."

"It's less that he cares about them and more that he believes, one day, he can *become* human. I don't know who put that idea into his head, but it's a fool's dream. How did you meet him, by the way?"

Jörg finally had his first opportunity since arriving back at the inn to tell the Count about his experiences in Paris. He talked of his meeting with Christine, and when he mentioned that his Frenchman disguise was a carbon copy of Fabrice LeRoy, the Count said, "Ah, it seems like it was a little too close to the real person. It's a pain making a body from scratch, so I used the form of someone I've met."

"Is he still alive?"

"I only know what happened to him up until he became of captive of the German Army. He's likely living in a prisoner-of-war camp now."

"Was that after the First Battle of Artois?"

"I believe so."

"How do you know him?"

"I've spoken with many soldiers on the front lines; Fabrice LeRoy was one of them. However, his handling of simulacrums was abysmal and he never showed any improvement."

"I see..."

Jörg touched on his encounter with Nil but mentioned nothing of Lila, as he'd promised her. "Nil called himself a 'monster of nothingness.' What does that mean?"

"It's just as the name implies. He values the idea of nothing over all else. Losing something and being unable to gain anything, everything returning to the void—these are facts that no human can escape during their lifetime. Everyone will experience loss at some point and carry that unbearable feeling with them throughout their lifetime. But sometimes, people with knowledge and power try desperately to resist this. Nil is the one who mocks them. And when he sets his eyes on someone, they end up meeting quite a grisly fate."

"So he believes all our efforts are meaningless because everyone will die someday?"

"Not quite. Nil claims that those who do not accept nothingness will never find true peace. That is where Nil and Milos disagree. Milos wants to make sure that, no matter what happens, his actions achieve something. It's only natural, considering he was raised as a hajduk. Hajduks, outlaws—they have to return to their people with something. They want their efforts to bear fruit, no matter how small."

"Ah, that makes sense. You're saying, to Milos, the concept of nothingness can only be bad."

"Precisely. On a different note, were you able to relax sufficiently in Paris?"

"I would've enjoyed myself a bit more had I not run into Nil. All I did was get a meal and walk around a bit. I missed the chance to visit a bar or a brothel."

The Count motioned for Jörg to get another wineglass down from the shelf. Once he retrieved it, the Count nodded to the bottle on the table and told Jörg to pour himself as large a glass as he liked "to make up for what you couldn't drink in Paris."

The moment Jörg started pouring the liquid, a strong, fruity aroma rose from the glass. He took a sip, letting the drink linger on his tongue as a refreshing scent filled his nose and he tasted the sweetness of vanilla. The distinct bitterness balanced out the intense fruit flavor well without overpowering it, and the liquid slid down his throat as easily as water. It tasted completely different from the wine he'd had in Paris.

"So it *was* wine."

"What do you mean by that?" the Count asked.

"It looks like human blood."

"I would never do something so cruel to you."

The Count poured some more wine into his glass. "It is a bit worrisome having Nil nosing around. Although I'm genuinely not planning anything."

"You really intend to do nothing?"

"Yes."

"Don't you get bored?"

"If you live without a purpose, then you forget who you are. You should exist, but you don't; you're practically dead despite still being alive. It feels as if your sense of self has vanished… Does that make it easier to understand?"

"That's rather philosophical."

"I'm frustrated by the fact that I cannot die, yet it's difficult to get people to understand this feeling. You see…no matter what danger I face, I can't die. Even if I'm shot with a machine gun, or a bomb is dropped right on my head, or I breathe in poison gas, I won't die. It's frustrating."

"Is it really that bad?"

"You would understand if you were to become like this."

Jörg found himself at a loss for a reply, so instead, he changed the subject. "Do you have a talisman that will chase off Nil? If I had something like that, I could handle him myself."

"Those sorts of things won't work on him. All those trinkets that humans believe work on monsters are all fake anyway. Stories about some sort of extraneous object managing to scare them away or someone talking them into leaving have been exaggerated and passed down over the years."

"So I'm helpless against him?"

"There is one thing you can do. I mentioned this once before, but monsters cannot defeat a human will that is so strong it borders on faith. But right now, do you have the power of belief?"

Jörg looked down at the floor. Unlike his corpus, which had refused the Count's invitation through sheer willpower, that was the one thing this Jörg lacked the most.

"Well," the Count continued calmly, "if I get the chance to meet him, I'll tell Nil in no uncertain terms that he is not to come anywhere near us."

6

The next morning, Jörg was eating his breakfast of a baguette with bacon covered in melted cheese and drinking his coffee in the dining room when Lila came in and stood beside him.

It was rare to see her at this time of day.

The young girl had avoided him up until now, even for meals, but Jörg hadn't pushed her. He'd planned on waiting until Lila decided to open up to him, thinking that was the best solution after everything that had happened between them so far.

"It can wait until after you're finished breakfast," Lila said, "but can we talk in the courtyard?"

"Of course. I'll be done soon, so maybe in a few minutes?"

"Thank you. I'll meet you there."

And just like that, Lila left the dining hall. It seemed she'd finished her own breakfast long before him.

Partway down the first-floor hallway, Jörg found the door leading to the courtyard. A rich green color suffused the frosted glass. He pushed the door open and walked outside to see the gentle morning light shining down on a carpet of white clover.

Jörg continued down one of the paths that formed the cross-patterned walkway in the garden, toward the beds of roses and lobelia flowers in full bloom. Lila stood beneath a *Flieder* tree. That was the German word for it, but in French it had the same name as her: *lilas*. Butterflies and honeybees flew back and forth in front of Jörg, and the sweet scent of the violet-red and pure-white blossoms wafted over to him. He remembered having been given a sprig of small flowers the first time he'd met the Count. They'd probably been taken from this courtyard. If so, then lilacs must grow here year-round, bathed in the bright sunlight and ruffled by the cool breeze.

Lila looked at Jörg much more calmly than she had in Paris. "You really didn't tell the Count."

"Of course not."

"I thought you'd tell him straightaway."

"Why?"

"You work for him, don't you?"

"I was only hired as your bodyguard. As soon as I determine there's no reason to guard you, I'll quit."

"But I refused."

"I reserve the right to decide that for myself."

She stared at Jörg. "Mr. Huber, half your soul is still on the battlefield killing people for Germany, right? If so, there's no way I can accept you as my bodyguard."

"Sorry, I understand that must be nauseating to you. But the Count is the one who extracted half my soul and brought it here, so you should really be complaining to him. Either way, the me standing here in front of you is the one who fled the battlefield because he detests war. This isn't the same me who's still on the front lines."

Lila silently reached out to a bush behind her and stroked a white flower. "Can you smell these flowers?"

"I can," replied Jörg.

"Being able to smell and taste properly is a sign that you're starting to adapt to your simulacrum. It's rare for someone to adjust so quickly. But it can also be a dangerous sign."

"Why's that?"

"It shows you're not strongly opposed to turning into something nonhuman. The longer humans stay here, the more they transform into monsters. Be careful."

"What about you?"

"I'm special. The Count used his magic to make sure I don't change."

"If you don't want to become a monster, then why stay here?

"I don't know. I just found myself here one day."

"What do you mean?"

"I lost my old memories. I have no idea how I ended up in this place."

"What about your parents?"

"I think I had a mom and dad. I have a faint recollection of them."

"What about memories of where you lived before?"

"I can only remember that we lived in a city called Lille. It's in northern France, close to Belgium. If you go from Lille toward the sea, there's a port called Dunkirk. A lot of Polish people work in the mines at Lille; I have a feeling my parents did, too."

"If they were regular people, then how did you end up here?"

"I assume the Count brought me after they died."

Jörg pursed his lips. The Count—a monster—wouldn't take in a human child out of the goodness of his heart. He must have had a reason.

"Maybe they got sick," Lila continued. "Or there was an accident. I remember them disappearing, but I don't remember how."

Jörg thought he probably shouldn't carelessly ask Lila about her past. The Count might have used his magic to intentionally lock away Lila's memories of her parents.

"In that case, you shouldn't try to force yourself."

"You're probably right."

"What are your plans for the future?"

"I'm going to leave here someday. A lot of monsters live here, and I don't plan on becoming like them."

"Have you talked with the Count about it?"

"I told him the same thing I just told you, and he said he wouldn't stop me. He only asked me to wait until the war was over."

"So what was that when you left the other day?"

"That was just to get a change of scenery. Besides, I want to know all about the outside world if I'm going to live there someday, and there are things I need to do."

"Like?"

"No one knows if Polish people will have a country to call their own once the war ends. Whether Germany and Austria win or Russia does, countries' borders will probably stay where they are now. If that happens, we'll need to keep waiting. And for us to keep waiting, we're going to need money. I guess you could call it a fund to retake the motherland. Poles scattered throughout Europe will work together, save up money, and then use that money to—"

"Don't you think that's a job for the grown-ups?" Jörg asked, cutting Lila off.

"Grown-ups bicker with their comrades at the drop of a hat. Even with the best plans, people have fallings-out and give up halfway through. That's why it's better for each person to come up with their own plan. And if everyone's goals are the same, those plans will all come together at some point."

"I see."

"Right now—at least on paper—the Kingdom of Poland is a country in a German-occupied part of the Russian Empire. Did you know that?"

"What does that mean?"

"It means it isn't an independent country. Poland is a puppet state in German territory. It was made to force the Polish people living there to assist the German Army, but the government doesn't actually do any work. It's a country in name only, without even a head of state. Why do adults always do such meaningless things? Compared with that, isn't my plan much more realistic?"

"When you put it like that..."

Jörg refocused his gaze on Lila. "Are you still scared of me? Do you still hold a grudge against Germans?"

"Yes." Lila lowered her eyes a little. "I'm sorry, but it's not so easy to rid myself of that fear."

"It's okay. Don't worry about it."

"You're a strange man, Mr. Huber." Lila gave him a faint smile. "You're neither human nor a monster."

"I guess not."

"I don't need a bodyguard, but I admit it's a good opportunity to set the Count's mind at ease. I'm going out again three nights from now, so you can guard me then."

"Hm? Where to?

"The Eiffel Tower. I'll write the symbol to get there on the door, and we'll leave from there at one in the morning."

IV
Jörg's Corpus (1)

1

Lately, it really does feel like half my soul is gone. That day my unit was bombed and I barely escaped with my life, it was as if something broke loose and fell through me, leaving a hole behind. I can clearly sense the outline of that invisible space inside me, like running the tip of your tongue over the cavity left behind after you've had a tooth taken out.

But it doesn't frustrate or sadden me in the least. In fact, I feel free.

All my previous worries now seem so trivial. So long as I keep moving on the battlefield, I think about little else. Maintaining the trenches, killing people with my pistol—as long as I'm moving my body, it's all the same.

Ever since that shelling injury, I've existed in both real life and a dream world. That's the only way to explain this phenomenon I'm currently experiencing. I haven't set foot anywhere except the battlefield, but in my dreams I've talked with a man in a black cloak who calls himself Count Silvestri, spent time at the inn of a beautiful female doctor, and met an adorable young girl named Lila. I've used a flamethrower at Verdun, walked the streets of Paris, and been chased by a mysterious monster named Nil.

All I can do is watch in stunned silence as the changing scenes of my dreams flash past in a blur. There's no time to take a step back and think calmly about any of it; my body just reacts to that world all on its own, doing whatever it needs to do there. It's in my dreams that I learned the word *simulacrum*, which, according to the Count, is where half my soul exists now, adventuring through those strange new lands. Apparently, its memories get transmitted to me, and every so often, my experiences on the battlefield are transferred back to it.

Memories are the only link between these two bodies with such different dispositions.

Right at the beginning, Count Silvestri suggested that I—the me here in this body—also escape the fighting. He offered to help me leave this place and go wherever my heart desired.

I refused immediately.

I'm here fighting for the fatherland. Until we win this war, I can't return home or go anywhere else. But most important of all, I can't abandon my brothers-in-arms.

The Count looked disappointed, but he didn't seem genuinely concerned. He told me to keep doing as I wished, and that if I ever needed help, all I had to do was call him and he'd come immediately. Then he transformed into a giant bat and flew away.

I've been on the battlefield ever since, fighting the Allied forces as always. More new faces have joined our ranks, but whenever I ask about someone I haven't seen in a while, people always just point to the ocean of barbed wire covering no-man's-land.

All these new troops I don't know are young, and some are even university students. It's my job to train them. Those who can't adapt to life on the battlefield die quickly, and even those who can adapt die easily if their luck's bad. I pass on everything I know about how to avoid death here, as well as what to do when we aren't fighting. I teach them how to pass the time in the trenches, about all the diseases they can contract all too easily, and that no matter how depressed they get, the one thing they can never forget is to eat meals. After all that, I let them loose to do as they please.

It's been a while since I went out to lay barbed wire. Once the army attacked Verdun, the fighting here stopped. Neither the German Army nor the French Army does anything; we all just sit here watching the movements of the other side.

Soldiers who don't have to fight are simply good-natured men. They drink coffee, eat their rock-hard rye bread and meager portions of sausage, and smoke cigarettes during their down time. They play with the rat-hunting cats, fawn over the messenger dogs, and watch the signaler's carrier pigeons in their cages to ease their heavy hearts.

The more dexterous soldiers sit on fallen logs, absorbed in making things from empty shell casings and scraps of metal. They cut into it with knives, gently using the tip of the blade to bend and twist the metal, creating miniature warplanes, ships, and dogs. Everyone enjoys these creations and wants one as a memento of the war, trading bread and cigarettes for such works of art.

Just because there's no fighting doesn't mean we spend our days lounging around, though. We dig and maintain trenches and bail the water out from beneath the duckboards. This type of work saps the energy of even the strongest men, but it's a far sight better than running around under a hail of gunfire.

I envy the combat engineers who know how to build things. Aside from charging at the enemy, all I can do is cut people's hair when it gets too long.

Fritz tells me I've changed a little since my injury. He says I used to observe the things around me with a kind of sensitivity, looking as if I was desperately struggling to keep something bottled up inside me. But now that's all disappeared.

"I wonder if you've got a head injury," he mutters worriedly. When Fritz hit his head, he stared blankly into space and felt nothing for several days.

I think it's just that I've gotten used to life on the front. Nothing I see or touch fazes me anymore. Even if I stick my hand into the mud and it breaks through the stomach of a submerged corpse, I treat it like an everyday occurrence. Just a bit of bad luck.

It's not because the fatigue has worn down my soul. In fact, I feel lighter. My heart feels pure when I face the summer sun, and I laugh wholeheartedly at other people's jokes. Many men in the trenches have turned silent from exhaustion or forgotten how to smile, but life has gotten easier for me since half my soul was taken. Honestly, I should have gotten rid of it sooner.

As the season changes and the days warm up, a fetid air settles over the trenches. With no major fighting here at the moment, though, there's no need for us to stay in one particular place, enduring the stench rising from the duckboards and our own bodies.

The repeated construction and destruction of the barbed wire across no-man's-land has turned the area into a sea of interwoven thorns. Even bombs couldn't destroy it at this point. Any time an explosion blows a section free and hurls it through the air, the entire mess only becomes more jumbled, to the point where no one can tell what's been damaged and what remains intact.

When he's off duty, Fritz continues to draw those same strange creatures—monsters, all of them. He shades them in such incredible detail that each one looks like it actually exists somewhere out there in the world.

Fritz's notebook is filled with reptilian bodies and oddly bent legs. Pointed dorsal fins. Giant wings. Sharp claws and fangs that glisten like knives, strong scales that decorate a body like jewels. Hordes of tentacles. Gills and flippers. Beasts like dogs or lions growling with their fur on end, and others that are neither animal nor plant but some sort of eerie creature with their mouths wide open. I once saw something that looked like the figure I saw in the sky that day from the depths of the trench. That black shadow shaped like a dragon or a bat. Fritz hadn't written a name beneath it, but he had made a note of the location and the date he saw it at the bottom of the page.

Fritz doesn't draw people. He never uses other soldiers, officers, field doctors, nurses, gunners, enemy combatants, or POWs as inspiration for his drawings. He doesn't even try to draw any real animals. Not the cats that hunt the trench rats, the brave, smart war dogs and messenger dogs, the horses that so reliably haul our goods, or the carrier pigeons deployed from the front lines. They all seem like good subject matter, but Fritz never bothers with any of them, instead devoting himself to sketching creatures that live in a world away from the field of war.

Fritz used to have a friend in our unit who also liked to draw.

They hadn't known each other long; they'd only met during the war. His name was Norbert Kerner.

Unlike Fritz, Norbert often drew people. As soon as he arrived in the trenches, he began creating detailed sketches of the life of the men on the front lines. He'd drawn the fear-stricken face of a soldier right before he hurled himself into no-man's-land, the profile of a maimed veteran, men relaxing during their downtime, a new recruit brought a faint glimmer of joy by his rations, and the peaceful expression of a middle-aged soldier as he cut up a sausage to share with a cat.

Norbert's bold lines depicted the scenes more vividly than any photograph. Seeing the soldiers' humanity and vulnerability captured in those drawings, you could practically hear the groans of hearts crushed by the battlefield.

Then, one day, an enemy bullet caught Norbert.

Fritz still takes great care of his friend's sketchbook, which Norbert gave to him right before he died. Fritz swore he would take it back to the man's hometown and give it to his family and said he couldn't die until then. Norbert's death is one of the main reasons Fritz doesn't draw people out here. If he filled his notebook with people and then they died, he'd be left holding a record of everyone who'd gone. Pages upon pages of those he hadn't wanted to lose. Fritz once mumbled that it would be too much for him to bear.

That's why Fritz has such deep respect for his friend who, fully aware of this inevitability, continued to draw people right up until his death. And why Fritz immediately knew he couldn't do the same. He couldn't bear the weight of another person's death. If he re-created the battlefield in vivid detail in the pages of his notebook, fear would prevent him from ever looking through it if he made it back home at the end of the war.

So Fritz decided to draw only for himself. He created closed-off worlds, imaginary lands, and fantastical places. Without them, he couldn't survive the extreme cruelty of the real world.

Plenty of soldiers on the front lines could draw. Some volunteers were apparently even professional painters. They'd joined the war to see it from an artist's perspective, hoping to turn their experiences into works of art—or at least that seemed to be what spurred them to enlist. The government also deployed some official painters to depict the soldiers' bravery in battle to show the people back home. This seems archaic in the age of color film, but the brutal honesty of photography sometimes proves too inconvenient for the government.

When I finished listening to Fritz's story, I asked him whether, if he had the chance, he would kill the man who'd shot Norbert.

Fritz stayed silent for a moment, then answered, "If I could. I wouldn't hesitate if it was during a fight."

"How far away could you do it? As far as a rifle shot?"

"Sure."

"What about closer? Pistol range?"

"If I could pull the trigger."

"Close enough to stab him with a knife?"

"Why are you asking these questions?"

"Because I'm the same."

"I see."

"Can you picture the face of the man who shot Norbert?"

Fritz shook his head.

I smiled. "I don't remember the face of the guy who killed my friend, either. But if there were any way to know, I'd happily kill him."

"That's a big 'if'."

"Should the opportunity ever present itself, I'll help you out."

"Really?"

"You want closure, right?"

"Yeah."

Whenever he had a moment, Fritz would open his notebook and run his pencil over the page with single-minded devotion. A typical day during those dull times consisted of me collapsing next to him while he worked, occasionally glancing at him out of the corner of my eye.

Every so often Fritz would flip through the pages and tell me about the monsters. How people would confuse this one for something that actually existed. How interesting it would be if this one were real. How this one was probably some sort of metaphor, and so on.

When he was immersed in these strange worlds, it felt as if his soul had left his body and gone wandering somewhere. He fantasized and frolicked in worlds that were inaccessible to me, recuperating there before returning to reality.

If he couldn't sketch, his heart would shatter. I've come to understand that was one reason people draw.

I, on the other hand, don't have an artistic bone in my body. If I were completely alone out here, I'd be even more broken—and I probably wouldn't even notice. The army is filled with men like that, mindlessly wielding rifles and pretending they're fully functioning humans. The only way to describe it is society gone mad.

* * *

On the front lines, any stretch of peaceful days will abruptly end at some point.

One day, my battalion suddenly receives the command to move out. Our orders are to head north, the complete opposite direction of Verdun, to a place called the Somme. Apparently, we're moving to distance ourselves from the fiercest of the fighting coming our way, but any order to move either means there's fighting currently going on at our destination or there will be soon, so we can't relax.

The dream I had of Verdun keeps replaying in the back of my mind.

I can't imagine a more terrible place. The German and French Armies send scores of soldiers and weapons to Verdun every day, which leaves other places undermanned. Holding on to the unfounded hope that any fighting elsewhere won't be too intense, I shoulder my heavy bags and begin marching down the dirt road.

It doesn't take long for mud to cling to the feet of the soldiers and the freight horses lugging the large cannons. Everyone keeps checking the skies, fearful of a sudden attack from enemy planes. Each group of friendly fighters we see soaring through the sky like a swarm of dragonflies elicits grumbles that we wouldn't have to march if everyone could fly like that.

We set up camp, and even there Fritz's pencil dashes over his notebook. No matter how much he draws, the pictures just keep bursting out from inside him. He tells me that his head would hurt if he didn't let them out. That he can't think of anything else if he doesn't immediately get the monsters out of his head.

"I've been having really bizarre dreams every night since I got hurt by that artillery shell," I say once the work calms down a bit. "How're you feeling?"

"What kind of dreams?" Fritz asks, ignoring my own question.

"Like my soul has been divided in two, and the other part of me is living a separate life on the home front. He's eating good food in Paris and strolling around the town."

"He can eat, even though he's just a soul?"

"He's using some sort of stand-in body. They call it a simulacrum."

"That sounds like something from a Gothic horror novel."

"It's no story; these are my dreams I'm talking about. But it feels so real, I could almost swear I was awake."

"It's actually quite difficult to tell the difference between dreams and real life."

"How so?"

"That blast tossed you through the air, and you hit your head hard. That's probably why you're having a hard time differentiating dreams from reality. But any fictional event that's indistinguishable from real life is as good as reality to the person experiencing it."

"You're saying I've lost my mind?"

"Think about it this way: In a horrific place like this, it's almost impossible to stay sane. Do you have fun in your dreams?"

"The whole thing just flashes by so fast I can't really relax."

"But even that's a kind of break. It's probably similar to how I feel when I'm drawing."

"I can see how drawing helps you, but what does dreaming do for me?"

"Everyone needs to find refuge somewhere in order to survive. True fear comes when we have nowhere to go."

We finally reach our destination just after a huge battle has ended.

Based on what we hear from the Second Army, the fighting here is primarily against the British. The French siphoned off a lot of their troops to Verdun, leaving them with no other option but to ask Great Britain for help, so the two countries have been commanding a joint operation in the region. The French Army only has troops stationed on the southern wing, meaning we've mostly been fighting the British.

The German Army had endured five days of bombardment by the British Army before the preliminary bombing on July 1. The British troops dug tunnels from their encampment all the way to beneath the German position, set large piles of explosives underground, and ignited them—a strategy that had never been seen before. The earth roared, and huge plumes of dirt were tossed high into the air, stunning everyone on the battlefield into silence by the sheer scale of it. The size of the craters alone is enough to take anyone's breath away. The entire area looks like a giant has sunk a hoe deep into the earth and ripped out massive clods of dirt.

On the whole, however, the British attack was scattered, allowing the German Army enough time to move the heavy cannons and machine guns to a safe location.

The British infantry then charged the German camp thirty minutes after a ferocious artillery barrage—far too late by anyone's thinking. Their joint operation with the French backfired, clearly demonstrating that the two nations hadn't been able to devise a cohesive strategy.

Apparently, the British troops had looked totally untrained as they tried to cross no-man's-land. The majority didn't appear to be professional soldiers but conscripts who'd been hastily thrown together into makeshift regiments. The German Army had regrouped during the thirty-minute interval when the ground fighting died down, and they strafed the advancing infantry with machine-gun fire and preventative artillery bombardment. In no time at all, the tragedy of Verdun had repeated itself. In a single day, the British Army had suffered over fifty-seven thousand casualties, a pointless loss of soldiers.

The lackluster British advance produced mountains of mangled corpses. They lie there broiling in the summer sun, getting eaten by rats, and emitting an eye-watering stench that tortures soldiers on both sides.

Yet even after such a crushing blow during that first encounter, the British Army hasn't retreated. Even since we arrived, they've repeatedly launched small- and medium-scale attacks.

Many German soldiers can't stop their bodies from shaking—but it isn't out of fear. Their limbs and necks stiffen unconsciously, then they start shaking uncontrollably. Men stagger when they try to walk in a straight line, and their feet suddenly stop, causing them to fall over where they are. There they stay, unable to get up or even hold onto anything.

Someone who knows about such things whispered in my ear that it isn't their bodies that are broken, but their spirits. That with continued exposure to such harsh environments, everyone will end up like that to some degree or another.

Whenever I see their strange movements, something stirs within me and I have to look away. It's a feeling that's hard to contain, as if I'm looking at something I shouldn't be. I can't bear to think for even a moment that they might represent my future.

I want to forget that, one day, I'll also reach a point of no return. I don't want to think about anything other than the ending I've envisioned for myself. Even though the present has already dragged me so far away from that possibility.

On the other hand, I can't help but smile faintly at the thought that this continued fighting will someday wipe out all the able-bodied men in Europe.

If nothing is capable of ending this war, then the best thing might be to let it expand to a scale beyond anyone's control and eventually explode.

And when that day comes, we might finally realize what we've done and where we went wrong.

2

I haven't been able to sleep since we arrived. I used to pass out the moment I lay down, but now, when I shut my eyes, I can't melt into that darkness.

During these restless nights, I toss and turn, thinking about a Frenchman named Hubert. He's one of the people I know from my dreams—the younger brother of a Parisian woman named Christine. Hubert's face has burned itself vividly into my mind. I don't know what I'll do if I see him on the battlefield. Tell him that I know his sister and that we should stop shooting at each other because she asked me to let her know if he was still alive?

It's impossible.

Unlike that simulacrum, I don't know French. And I doubt Hubert speaks German.

The moment we point our rifles at each other, we'll have to shoot. Have to drive our knives into each other's hearts and tear out one another's throats.

Anger and frustration slowly begin to spread throughout my chest.

Why should I risk my life for this sentimentality that belongs to the other me? I'll pull the trigger, no matter who I come across on the battlefield.

Yet even as that resolve takes hold, I feel something rise up inside me telling me not to be too hasty. Asking me if I've already discarded so much of my humanity. Accusing me of closing my eyes and covering my ears because I don't want to think anymore. Chastising me for blaming everything on the simulacrum just because it annoys me.

I throw off my blanket and get out of bed.

Is the *real* me that simulacrum or the me standing here? No—we first existed as one self, so I shouldn't think of us as two separate beings.

The fact remains that *I'm* the one fighting. I don't want to be on the battlefield letting that simulacrum's moral compass guide me.

I leave the bunker, careful not to wake any of my fellow soldiers.

Thankfully, the bright light of the full moon means it isn't as dark inside the trench as it normally is. I search for a place where no one will go and stop at the first spot I find, resting against a wooden wall made by the engineering corps. After fumbling around in my pocket for my cigarettes and matches, I place a hand-rolled cigarette between my lips and light it.

As I savor the sweet tobacco smoke, a voice calls out to me from the darkness.

"Mind if I join you?"

The paths in the trenches contain a lot of twists and turns to protect us from enemy assaults. It almost sounded like the voice had come from around the corner. The footsteps on the duckboards gradually grow louder, and I catch a whiff of the same brand of tobacco I smoke. I can't tell who it is just by the voice, though, and I have no idea why anyone would go out of their way to talk to me. Still, I stay put and continue to smoke in silence, thinking I can leave if something feels off.

A man appears. He looks to be in his forties and has the same sort of features you'd see anywhere, but his eyes flash in a way that immediately attracts people to him. Not in a flirtatious way, though. It's the sort of charm that would get anyone on his side, regardless of gender.

He wears the uniform on an infantryman and has a rifle slung over his shoulder, just like the rest of us. Officers wouldn't come out here at this hour. They're all in the deeper parts of the trenches, sleeping comfortably on simple, soft beds that grunts like us can only dream of.

He stops in front of me, pinches his cigarette between thumb and forefinger, and removes it from his lips. "Do you remember meeting me in Paris?"

"I think you've got the wrong guy," I tell him.

"Try to remember. I didn't look like this back then."

Moving my cigarette up and down between my lips, I study his face. "Ah." It suddenly comes to me. "You're Nil. The man who called himself the 'monster of the nothingness.'"

He breaks into a smile and opens his arms wide. "So, what do you think? Does this appearance suit me?"

"A soldier's uniform looks the same on everyone."

"Which do you think looks better, this or the taxi driver outfit?"

"You met my simulacrum, not me. Why are you here?"

"I talked with your simulacrum the other day, so I figured I'd talk with the corpus today. The Count's come to the front lines a number of times, hasn't he?"

"Yeah."

"You're two parts of a whole. It's so interesting, that there are subtle differences." Nil stands next to me, leaning against the wall. "How's life here? Enjoying yourself?"

"Honestly, I'm getting a little tired of it."

"You came here to become a hero, though, didn't you?"

"At first. But the moment I got here, I quickly realized that was a delusion."

Sometimes, when we're charging forward under a hail of gunfire, one of the soldiers in our line might suddenly burst into laughter. No one acts surprised, nor do any of us whisper that he's lost his mind. Nobody wants to stay in a place like this forever.

"Then why not run away? Take the Count up on his offer."

"I'm not interested in becoming one of the Count's servants. I'll choose for myself how I live my life."

In the darkness, a faint smile appears on Nil's face. "You know, I prefer this version of you to the other one."

"Thanks."

"Only a physical body can truly experience 'nothing.' It's because you have physical sensations that you know the fear of suddenly losing them, and that gives you a deeper understanding of the meaning behind your existence. Your simulacrum seemed to have trouble with that. The longer he stays with the Count, the less human he becomes."

"So what? It's not like that's going to bother me."

"And that's what I like about you."

Nil leans in slightly, then whispers next to my ear. "This war is far from over. The situation's going to keep changing, so you should prepare yourself for the worst."

"Change how?"

"They'll keep making new weapons and testing them on the front lines. And every time they do, lots of people are going to die."

"I already know that."

"Food supplies will run out. When that happens, the only provisions you'll get will be moldy potatoes."

"That sounds pretty awful."

"It's harder on the home front. Haven't you heard? In many German cities, the government's bungling of food production and management has led to large numbers of people starving to death."

"What?!"

"German farmers had a bad harvest, and add to that the effects of the trade embargo put in place by Great Britain. Last year Germany harvested fifty million tons of potatoes, but people are worried they might not even get a quarter million this year. The government's urging to 'overcome hunger with idealism' doesn't work anymore, either. There was an anti-war protest in Germany on May Day over the food shortages. Some people can't survive without the army's *Gulaschkanone* mobile field kitchens operating as soup kitchens. One hundred thousand people have already died of starvation since last year—and it won't stop there. By the time the war ends, there will likely be more than seven times that many deaths."

The cigarette falls from my mouth at such a horrific thought. I heard what he said but can't even imagine what that would look like. Never in its history has Germany seen seven hundred thousand people die of hunger. The farming villages might be able to secure enough food to keep themselves from starving, but the city relies on being able to buy from rural areas and can't survive without the supplies they provide. Rationing isn't doing enough, and the supply will soon run out.

And Nil doesn't stop there.

"As morale falls, countries everywhere will try all sorts of methods to raise the spirits of the people. For one, they'll probably start letting women fight on the battlefield alongside men."

"If you're talking about field nurses, we already have them."

"These women would be doing a different type of work. Like men, they would put on a uniform and be trained in warfare, then sling a rifle over their shoulder and head off to front."

"That's ridiculous. Women could never fight in war. They don't have a man's strength or stamina."

"Shooting someone doesn't require any special strength; you just pull a trigger. It's simply a matter of accuracy. I'm sure you have trouble with snipers out here. Shooting is something even a woman could do. In fact, with their resilience, women might actually be better at it."

"A woman, shooting at us?"

"Some country is bound to form a unit like that sooner or later. I'm thinking Russia will probably be the first."

"You don't mean someday in the distant future, but now, in this war?"

"I wouldn't be surprised to see it. The Great War would be a huge opportunity for those women and their commanders. The skills they gain and the results they achieve here would no doubt be utilized in earnest for the next war."

The Russian Army is on the Eastern Front, so if that did happen, it wouldn't affect me here on the Western Front. Still, I don't want to think about a future like that.

I hold my head in my hands. "Would I really be able to kill a woman, even if they were fighting for the other side? Will it ever come to that?"

"You guys viciously slaughtered regular civilians in Belgium. Compared with that, why have any reservations about killing women trained as soldiers?"

"Wars are fought by men. How can we drag women into it?"

"Guns don't choose who wields them. That sentimental attitude will get you killed." Nil lets out a throaty chuckle. "Human cruelty knows no bounds. Allied powers, Central powers—they're no different."

"Tell me," I say desperately, grabbing Nil's arm. "How can it be stopped? What can we do to end this war and save our country?"

"Return the culprit at the center of it to *nothing*."

"What do you mean?"

"The man who rules your country, Kaiser Wilhelm II. Return him to nothing."

"You mean remove him from the throne? But how?"

"However you see fit. Assassinate him, get him to abdicate legally—it's all the same. Just remove the person giving everyone orders from their position."

"I'm just a regular person. I don't have that kind of power."

"No, you do. There is only one way for the German people to change the country."

I bite back the word on my lips and stare at Nil. "Revolution?"

"Precisely."

"Start a revolution with the socialists?"

"I'll let you in on a little secret: There are soldiers fighting out here who are socialists, just like anywhere else. They gravitate together naturally, without having been influenced by outside thinkers or any organization, talking among themselves and lamenting the fate of their country. University students and other educated individuals studied and learned enough to consider things like socialism before coming here. And some of the adult soldiers have likely attended a meeting about it, having been invited by a coworker when they were still working. They'll act once discontent over the war has spread. Why don't you try helping them out as well? All you have to do is return the kaiser to nothing, and the war should end."

"How can you talk about something like that so casually?!"

"I'm a monster that values nothing, so I'm only discussing methods that suit my own interests. Whether you agree with me is up to you, but if it bothers you even a little, you should observe your fellow soldiers closely. There are far more people than you may think looking to save Germany from within, both at home and on the battlefield. Of course, the same situation is going on in other countries as well."

Nil runs a finger down my cheek. "Revolution is so much more interesting than war. If you're willing to do something about it, then rise up."

V
Those Gathered at the Eiffel Tower

1

May 1, 1916. May Day.

Since early that morning, workers living in Germany had packed into Potsdamer Platz in the heart of Berlin. People had come from factories all over the city, answering the call of the Spartakusbund—the Spartacus Group—a socialist society within Germany.

The war that was supposed to end by Christmas of its first year didn't show even the slightest sign of stopping. Instead, it looked as if it would only grow—just like the discontent of the German people.

With connections to the arms industry, the wealthy elite welcomed the war. The workers at the bottom, meanwhile, saw their hours increase without any other changes to their everyday lives, doing grueling jobs for low pay. They worked tirelessly, only for the profits to flow into the coffers of capitalists as their wages stayed the same. On top of that, all physically capable men were required to go to the front. The people on the battlefield and at home were crushed in body and spirit, ordered to bleed for the sake of the nation.

However, the German people weren't sheep who would patiently endure such conditions. Citizens who had decided that the only way to bring about change was to speak up and act continued to gather in Potsdamer Platz. Polish and Jewish workers arrived, too. The Great War ravaging Europe had become a pressing issue for people of every ethnicity.

The refreshing early morning air was soon heavy with the anger of the people. The protest leaders hadn't appeared yet, but the crowd's resentment toward the government was more than enough to rile everyone up.

Police sent by the government occupied one corner of the square. But even under the stern gazes of those uniformed men, the number of workers making their way to Potsdamer Platz and the fervor of the crowd didn't diminish. By eight in the morning, the crowd had already swelled to over ten thousand people.

Eventually, an impassioned cheer echoed throughout the square.

The leaders of the Spartacus Group, Karl Liebknecht and Rosa Luxemburg, appeared in the center of the crowd. A branch of Germany's Social Democratic Party, the Spartacus Group contained groundbreaking socialist thinkers. These two people were known as the face of the group, and Luxemburg, a powerful female orator of Jewish-Polish descent, had written incisive critiques on corruption within the government and political parties.

At the time, Liebknecht was forty-four and a member of the Reichstag representing the Social Democratic Party, while Luxemburg was forty-six.

Years of experience had taught the two of them to perfectly control their passion and speak in a way that was supremely effective at spurring the populace to act. They repeatedly voiced their opposition to the fighting in the days leading up to the war, accused the bourgeois of war profiteering, and worked tirelessly to create a society that would spread the nation's wealth among the workers. The government saw them as the most troublesome source of resistance within Germany and considered them traitors to the state. As a result, the entire Spartacus Group was closely monitored by the ruling class.

The two leaders strolled leisurely through the ebullient square. Luxemburg burned with a fervent passion to put an end to the Great War as soon as possible. War was nothing more than an opportunity for the ruling class to grow rich. It only served to bring hardship to the people. Just stopping the war wasn't enough, though. If the great powers of Europe agreed to a ceasefire simply to restore the world to the state it was in before the war, it would amount to no more than a false peace. So long as empires ruled over Europe, no matter how many times war was waged under the banner of ethnic nationalism, the balance of power between nations would stay exactly where it was. Wars would continue to be fought at the convenience of those in power.

Countries had to find a way to break free of the vicious cycle of the rich exploiting workers for low wages and workers accepting those conditions in order to get by. People's lives shouldn't be wasted on war. They had to act to reform society as a whole and bring about an end to warfare. All those elements needed to occur simultaneously within Germany.

Wearing the uniform of a conscript, Liebknecht stopped in the center of the plaza and scanned the crowd. Pain and fatigue distorted the assembled faces, but every set of eyes shone with the longing for a brighter future. He assured himself that this much passion would ensure the revolution's success. Even if it didn't happen in his lifetime, Germany would change from within, born anew from the hands of the workers. The kaiser would be forced to abdicate, imperialism would crumble, and an era where the people ran the government would finally arrive. That reality was already in sight.

Filling his lungs with the May air, Liebknecht fixed his gaze directly ahead and, ignoring the glaring police, yelled:

"Down with the war!"

A cheer swept across the plaza like a surging wave. Everyone stamped their feet, shaking the earth like cannon fire. Liebknecht kept going.

"Down with the government!"

The police immediately rushed at Liebknecht to pull him from the crowd and take him away. Luxemburg pushed her way between them, not flinching when someone grabbed her arm and struck her with a fist. She'd been subjected to such violence countless times throughout her life and was used to it by now. Vicious blows descended on her, but she didn't give in. Liebknecht was her comrade, and at the same time, a far more important presence.

Enraged over the violence shown against Liebknecht and Luxemburg, the crowd raced forward to confront their attackers. As they did, mounted police moved to the fore, using their horses to hold the crowd back.

The horses whinnied sharply, rearing back with their front legs held high. Apparently, the police wouldn't hesitate to trample the gathered masses beneath the hooves of their horses. Their chief had hammered into them the idea that socialists and communists were enemies of the state—a social poison that equated such people with the vilest of criminals so the police wouldn't feel even the smallest tinge of remorse over their actions.

After Liebknecht was seized, police and protesters continued to fight in the square for over two hours. The commotion spread to neighboring towns, and soon skirmishes between citizens and the constabulary had broken out all across the city.

Liebknecht and Luxemburg had expected to be arrested, yet they'd still risked showing their faces in front of people. They embodied the idea that even with society in such a desperate state, an individual could back up what they said with action, trusting that truth to move the hearts of the masses. Their unwavering beliefs and drive made the German government more wary and would eventually lead to accusations that the state had used the Freikorps, Germany's anti-communist volunteer army, to murder the two of them. At this point in time, however, no one could have imagined that such a future might come to pass.

In the wake of the May Day protest, the invigorated Spartacus Group ramped up their activities. They distributed reams of flyers throughout Germany, pushing for an end to the war and the resignation of those in power.

A military tribunal demanded that Liebknecht's inalienable rights as a member of the Reichstag be revoked. The bourgeois parties were all too happy to comply, with Liebknecht's Social Democratic Party the only opposing voice. Rising patriotism had diminished the SDP's standing since the beginning of the war, causing it to lose some of its support from the people, but this one small action of Liebknecht's had drastically revitalized its popularity among the masses. Thinking they needed to use this to their advantage, members of the SDP made statements claiming that "Liebknecht isn't as dangerous as people make him out to be" and "He's just a madman, so let him do what he will." To members of other parties, they would describe him as "all bark and no bite."

On June 28, 1916, Liebknecht was sentenced to two years and six months in prison. Upon hearing this news, fifty-five thousand munition-factory workers went on strike in Berlin, and protests and strikes broke out in other areas. In normal prewar Germany, political strikes were considered impossible and criticized as revolutionary romanticism, but during the war, people struck with brazen enthusiasm. When he received his sentence, Liebknecht confidently proclaimed, "The uniform of any general cannot rival the honor of my prisoner's garb."

The German government retaliated against Liebknecht's sympathizers, arresting hundreds of members of the Spartacus Group and sending thousands of workers to the front lines as punishment for participating in the strikes. Ironically, however, these retaliatory measures resulted in the spread of socialist ideology among the German soldiers who, day in and day out, were exposed to the cruel reality of the war. Socialists persistently advocated their ideas to the soldiers around them: That if the German people overthrew the government and removed the kaiser, the war would end.

July 10, 1916. Rosa Luxemburg was once again arrested and detained by the police. She was first held at a women's detention center in Berlin, then in a cell at the Metropolitan Police Department, before finally being sent to a fortified prison at Wronki, in the province of Posen.

Luxemburg stayed in confinement until right before the Great War ended on November 11, 1918, with letters from friends and a small bird that visited her cell her only connections to the outside world.

2

A huge number of pigs scurried across the paved road, each and every one of them fat and mouthwatering. Jörg gazed after them, wide-eyed.

Right. This is a dream, he reminded himself.

He would never see something like this on the streets in real life.

German men followed the pigs, hammers and butcher's knives in hand. They ran back and forth across the road, corralling the herd. Once they had an animal surrounded, the men tightened their circle and one person swung a hammer down, knocking it unconscious.

They lifted the pig onto a worktable brought in on a cart and tied it down with rope, then thrust a knife into the animal's heart and sliced open its throat.

Blood spurted from the wound like a fountain, collected by a man holding a pitcher. It seemed they were going to make blutwurst. As the men butchered one pig after the next, pork products piled up beside them on the table—sausage, bacon, ham, lard. Another pile was filled with gorgeous cuts of fresh meat. Yet still the pigs continued to come.

By the time the men captured all the animals and deftly transformed them into food, there would be so much that a huge mound would remain even after everyone had taken their share. The leftover sausage and pork would eventually turn black and begin to rot away, the lard would melt and seep into the paving stones, and the organs and bones would dry to dust and be carried off by the wind. Yet the men didn't stop. They worked their hammers and butcher's knives until none remained, then once the final pig had been slaughtered, they all quickly dispersed.

A deathly quiet came over the town. Then the people started to target the dogs and cats. Unlike with the pigs, the townsfolk merely chased them, not looking to end their lives with hammers or knives. The animals were already skin and bones with tattered, faded fur. The only thing that stood out were their wild eyes. They ran frantically throughout the town before finally collapsing from exhaustion, where they lay completely still. The bodies of those cats and dogs, too, soon began to turn black, rot, and become dust in the wind.

The emaciated horses succumbed next. They were as horrifically skinny as the dogs and cats had been and seemed in pain whenever they moved. They didn't carry riders or haul carts. The condition of their disheveled manes and filthy bodies made it clear that no one had cared for them in a long time. Either they had run away from the field of war, or their owners had died and they no longer served any purpose. The horses walked slowly past Jörg as he stood beneath a streetlight. Just a short way down the road, one after the next, their knees buckled from fatigue. None made a sound of any sort; they had already lost the energy to whinny in pain. They lay upon the paving stones, never to rise again.

Eventually, human figures began emerging from the shadows of buildings. This time, it was the women. Regular women who polished windows, cleaned rooms, watered plants, and cooked every day for their families now held carving knives, their eyes glistening as they stared fervidly at the fallen horses.

The animals' long necks drooped on the sidewalk like withered branches, and the women fell upon them as one, thrusting their knives into the corpses. The horses were lean and thin. Though they had but little meat, the women worked their blades feverishly to shave off as much sustenance as possible. Holding blood-covered lumps in both hands, they tossed their spoils into containers they'd brought with them, clutching the meat to their chests. Like with the pigs, others sat ready to receive the steaming rivers of horse blood. Orphans and beggars joined in the work, carving up the horses and taking what they could before disappearing. The people did it for themselves. For their aging parents. For their children. Because if they didn't get every last scrap of meat they could, they would all die.

Above the mutilated horse corpses and the heads of the assembled people, Jörg saw the motivational slogan that filled German newspapers and posters waving in a maniacal dance. *Durchhalten, durchhalten, durchhalten.* Endure, endure, endure. Endure, even if the army takes your husbands and sons. Endure, even if you don't have enough wood or coal to stave off the cold. Endure, even if your food stores run dry. A doctor who worked in Berlin had contributed an article to one of the newspapers that said people shouldn't worry about a lack of food because they were essentially doing fasting therapy, which would actually benefit their health.

The wealthy alone continued to secure sufficient food, and the government purposefully ignored the conditions of the common people, all the while touting this idealistic belief. It was the same story no matter the time period. The poor only ever suffered.

3

In his room, Jörg leaped up from his chair. He had been passing the time after dinner with some light reading and accidentally dozed off.

He looked down to his feet and saw the cover of the book that had slipped from his grasp.

Once his nerves settled, Jörg revisited the unsettling dream he'd had. He hadn't thought the situation on the home front would be so dire, even during the war, but ever since he'd met the Count, things he'd never expected just kept happening. He couldn't say for certain that it didn't mean anything.

Darkness painted the world outside his window. He'd fallen asleep while waiting for his nighttime rendezvous.

He glanced at the clock: ten past one. Lila had likely already left. Hurrying out of his room, he rushed toward the door leading to Paris.

When he arrived at the portal with its mysterious markings, Jörg took a closer look at the door panel. The color in one section shone more vividly than the others. Lila had added a design so they could leap to a park in front of the Eiffel Tower—the Place du Trocadéro. Jörg held a finger against the mark as he pushed the door open. He stepped through to the other side, and when he felt his feet on solid ground again, he was in Paris.

Jörg scanned the area. The blackout orders made the area as dark as his last nighttime visit. Far off in the distance, he saw a faint light being emitted from a giant structure—a metal tower that looked like a capital A. Why would they allow only that to be illuminated? Lighting something that large would create an obvious target for nighttime bombing raids.

A voice called out to him suddenly from the darkness. "The tower's not actually glowing, you know."

Turning around, he saw Lila in a collared red overcoat.

"Those aren't lanterns or electric lights?" Jörg asked.

"No."

"Then what are they?"

"The lights from people's souls. Think of it as a consciousness that's not contained in a simulacrum. People's souls wander around outside in the middle of the night. The more important question, though, is why you came as a German. That's risky, even if it is really dark."

"The Count undid his spell."

"You still have the inscription on the back of your hand, right? So use it. Think of what a French person looks like. Keep that image in your mind, then place your palm over the design and say the word *phantasia*. Words and the power of imagination combine to create incredible power."

"Really?"

"Try it."

Jörg took a deep breath, calmed himself, and pictured Fabrice LeRoy's face. He didn't need to pretend to be injured this time, so he imagined the man without any scars.

Once he had the image in his mind, Jörg whispered, "*Phantasia*."

Immediately, he felt a thin membrane cover his body. It adhered to his skin, merging with his simulacrum.

Lila removed a hand mirror from her pocket and handed it to Jörg. In the darkness, it was surrounded by a white glow. "See for yourself."

Sure enough, he saw the image of Fabrice LeRoy reflected in the mirror—the face of Pierre Arche. Jörg changed the angle, examining himself from all sides. Nothing seemed amiss.

He gave Lila back the hand mirror, and the young girl immediately set off. Jörg quickly followed her. They walked past fountains and water features, heading toward the tower.

"That's the Eiffel Tower," Lila informed Jörg. "It was completed in 1889 and was a big hit at the Paris Exposition that year. It was also a major draw at the Exposition in 1900 and was originally scheduled to be dismantled afterward. But the army realized it could be used as a radio transceiver, so they left it standing. Right now, it's sending out signals to disrupt German radio waves."

"Why does something like that attract souls?"

"You'll see once we get closer."

When they got to the base, Jörg looked up and saw that the tower was actually an incredibly complicated construction of interconnected steel beams. It hadn't been made by stacking stone or brick like a church steeple. Maybe it was because of the construction material, but it seemed to dwarf any of the other huge buildings Jörg knew. It was unbelievably tall. He couldn't even begin to guess how high it was.

The four legs supporting the tower resembled an intricate lace pattern, and the gradual curve of the thick steel girders seemed almost like train tracks that drew the eye along them. The spaces between the beams made him think of chapel windows without the stained glass.

Faint lights hovered near the steel beams, bathing them in a soft glow. Taking a closer look, he noticed that the lights had arms that extended out from them and legs that fluttered in the air. They were souls—and not those of animals or bugs, but people.

"If you listen carefully, you can hear them talking," Lila told him.

Jörg stayed silent and closed his eyes, focusing intently on the sounds in his ears. He only heard the wind at first, but his eardrums soon began to detect words, then voices.

He realized that all the voices belonged to women. There wasn't a single male voice among them. He also heard the clink of teacups and teapots. How was anyone serving tea in a place like this? The smell of black tea and coffee reached him, paired with the decadent aroma of baked goods. Jörg swallowed back the saliva coating his mouth. Could these souls enjoy everyday pleasures like his simulacrum could? Or was everything, including those delicacies, nothing more than an illusion?

The topic of conversation ranged from quick greetings and family news to letters from the front and concerns about what might happen there. A lot of people complained about their daily lives. With the men taken by the army, women were now able to work in offices and factories, but the souls here criticized the government's claims that this signified women's advancement in society.

"Sure, we earn our own money, but they'll get rid of us as soon as the war ends and the men come home."

"Then there's no point to any of it, is there?"

"The advancement of women in society is just an excuse they use."

"We can't let them try to cheat us."

"Do you think some places might let us stay after the war's over?"

"A lot of the men have died, so they'll still need us at the beginning. For a while, at least."

"But if we stay, the men will get angry and start complaining that women stole their jobs."

"Then they never should have started this war in the first place."

"That's right."

"No matter what we say, they don't listen."

"Men do what they want, and women are left to clean up the mess."

"Just like always."

"It never changes."

Jörg had never heard ladies talk like this in his town. Frenchwomen must have very progressive views on society.

As he kept listening, names and places he hadn't heard of came up frequently in conversation. From the pronunciation, they didn't sound like French words, so perhaps not all the women who'd gathered here were French.

Jörg opened his eyes and looked at Lila.

"Isn't it interesting?" she said.

"Very. It sounds like there are people here from lots of different countries."

"They're from all across Europe. Everyone here has been affected by the war in some way, and they all have pent-up anger or resentment. They come searching for a place to vent."

"I never knew women felt so discontent… I guess I never really stopped to think about it."

"When you're fighting on the front lines, it feels like everyone is supporting you," Lila explained. "Army and government officials only spread information that supports that idea, so it's all the soldiers hear. But stop and think about it for a second, and you'll quickly see that's not the case."

"There wasn't ever time to stop and think on the battlefield."

"I know. I feel so bad for you all. Even the smartest man can't think straight when his life's in constant danger."

Lila was as blunt as ever. Jörg didn't know whether she was trying to sympathize with him or scold him, so instead of responding, he simply continued the conversation.

"These people congregate here naturally, do they?"

"They say that when life gets too hard, a person's soul will leave their body. It usually happens when they're asleep. Loose souls roam around outside all night, group together with any other wandering souls they find, then return to their bodies just before sunrise. A person pushed past that point might even lose their soul during the middle of the day. When that happens, they're usually institutionalized."

"The same thing happens to both men and women?"

"Of course. The soul is the first thing to leave when someone finds themselves in an incredibly distressing situation. That's something you have experience with, though, isn't it, Mr. Huber?"

"Yes."

Lila turned to face the tower. "The Eiffel Tower stands out from every angle, and it emits radio waves, so it's easy to find. That makes it a good place for souls to gather."

"I don't hear any men, though."

"Men go elsewhere for their drunken ramblings. They know the women will just laugh at them if they hear them complaining."

The young girl had said it so casually, but the thought terrified Jörg. Would he be okay walking into a place like that?

"Where are the friends you want to meet?" Jörg asked, changing the topic.

"Follow me if you're interested."

Lila leaped lightly off the ground, her red coat gently unfurling like a pair of wings.

Jörg followed after her, his simulacrum lifting effortlessly into the air. He matched Lila's movements as she climbed the tower, deftly jumping from one girder to the next on her toes.

Suddenly, the assembled souls all turned to watch them. Someone had yelled a warning to the crowd: "*A young man's chasing a little girl!*" The air buzzed with sharp cries from all directions, but Jörg ignored their accusations and continued to climb the tower.

Now that he was closer, Jörg could tell for sure that the glowing white souls were shaped like people. Their forms weren't vivid and lifelike but fleeting and uncertain, almost to the point where one might wonder whether they actually existed.

Elderly women, young women, middle-aged women, and small girls—all of them commoners. Not a single person among them wore fancy clothes or elegant jewelry. Their thin, woven garments undoubtedly let in the winter chill. Yet there seemed to be a strange lightness to each face, perhaps because being a soul gave them a brief respite from their physical hardships.

Lila finally stopped once she'd climbed to where the tower narrowed considerably. There, they found a group of women in their late twenties to forties sipping tea with jam and nibbling on butter cookies. They looked as if they were enjoying themselves immensely, but this pleasant scene masked their pitiful situation, as it was only in an illusion where they could enjoy such foods that were unobtainable in their waking lives.

Lila greeted them cheerfully as she joined the circle. The women welcomed her warmly and made space on a girder for her to sit.

Jörg didn't approach any closer, but watched to see how the ladies would react.

When they eventually noticed him, they put their heads close to Lila's and whispered among themselves. Lila spoke at length, explaining the situation.

Thinking he would be able to hear their conversation from where he was, Jörg started to sit down, when a young woman with curly hair stood up and spoke to him. "You can sit over here."

"You don't mind?"

"We're telling you it's okay, so don't worry."

Jörg paused, but the woman kept her gaze locked on him, so he eventually gave in and walked along the steel beam. Standing in front of the women, he thanked them for letting him join. It turned out they already knew his name and nationality. He'd gone to the effort to make himself look like Fabrice LeRoy, but they already knew he was German. Lila must have told them, but she feigned innocence, swinging her legs where she sat on the girder.

The woman with the curly hair was named Bernadette, who said she worked in a brothel in Paris. The group of souls was made up of women from all over Europe and included Germans, Ukrainians, Russians, Belgians, Brits, Jews, Romanians, Serbians, and Turks.

"Lila's our friend," Bernadette told him. "We can talk with anyone when we're souls. We have no problem communicating with other people, regardless of things like age or ethnicity."

"That's very helpful."

"Sadly, though, I lose the ability to speak with them when I return to my body."

"Would you recognize them if you met in real life?"

"Who knows? I've never met anyone here in the real world, and when I wake up, the memories of my dream start to fade."

"What are you discussing today?"

"Food supplies. It's bad everywhere. You're German, right?"

"Yes."

"Things are apparently really bad in Germany right now. Have you heard? People are starving to death in the cities."

"They are?"

"It's much worse in Russia," one young woman chimed in.

Jörg looked at her, and she greeted him with a slight nod. "My name is Hanja. I'm from Ukraine. Nice to meet you."

"It's nice to meet you, too."

"It was hard enough for farmers in Russia before the war started—and now things are even worse! The army took all the food and livestock. They even took the pots and pans to make weapons."

"German farmers also had their goods seized."

"Not on the same scale. Germany has had one hundred thousand people die from starvation since the beginning of the war. My country will soon reach *one million*."

"It's not about the number of people," another woman interrupted. "Everyone's desperate to get their hands on even the smallest morsel of food." She shifted her gaze from Hanja to Jörg. "I'm Diana. I live in Berlin. Nice to meet you."

"Likewise."

"With a war on this scale, there isn't enough food to distribute through citizens' relief teams. And the prisoner-of-war camps must be even worse."

Every country had internment camps for captured enemy soldiers. The Hague Convention protected prisoners of war, but as food shortages intensified, supplies to those places dried up. After all, they were the enemy. Their treatment came second to the needs of the country's own people. Just as French soldiers were held in Germany, German soldiers were kept in captivity in France and Russia, and with the state of things in the Russian Empire, conditions in the camps had to be unimaginable.

"It's hard everywhere, but I don't want to die doing nothing. It's not just my family and relatives in Berlin; it's all my friends there, too. I want them all to have food."

"Yes, but Ukraine has to send food to the Russian Empire first," Hanja countered. "Russia has been stuck fighting Germany since the beginning of the war, so they've burned through their resources. They're in no position to help poorer countries."

"I can understand that. What about the people from France? I'd like to hear what they have to say. Can the French socialists do anything? They were openly against the war before it started, right? They must have considered consolidating international efforts."

A tall woman grimaced, then spoke up. "I'm sorry to say, but we can't expect anything from them, either. Once the war started, French socialists became more closely aligned with loyal nationalists. They said that the defense of the nation came first, declared that they would never ally with Germany and Austria under the rule of an emperor, and cut all ties with them. They should have been working with socialists in other countries to stop the war! I doubt they'll do anything now, even if you ask them for help."

"Then it's up to regular people to rally together and secure routes to distribute food."

"Mm-hmm."

"Can we do this? Just us women?"

"It's like you said earlier: We should start by thinking about how we can help those closest to us," Bernadette answered. "Once those routes are secure, we can find ways to expand that network. We can only transport so much food by ourselves. And there's also the risk that some unscrupulous types might steal it from us."

"People like that have starving families, too, though," Diana commented.

"You can't be so naive. You need to come to terms with the fact that, if you want to save some people, you won't be able to help others. You're not going to become their savior, but need to be painfully aware that you're nothing more than a powerless individual who will have to turn a blind eye to the people you can't save. Once you accept that, I'll find you a person somewhere between Kleinerbrunn and Berlin that trades food from farms on the black market."

"Are there even people out there storing food?"

"In Germany, some villages in the countryside have secret stockpiles hidden from the government, and they sell their goods to people from the city at inflated prices. They usually only sell to the rich, because these days, they're the only ones who can afford to spend that much on food. Talk to those villagers and see if they'll give you a discount. But no one knows how many more years this war is going to last, so it's going to cost a hell of a lot to get a regular supply of food."

"The most important thing is figuring out how to get that money."

"Factory work won't provide enough. People who have a hand in the black market would say you can sell your body to make money."

"I was worried that might be the only option."

"It would be pointless to sleep with people who are poor, though. If you were to do that, you'd have to lure in rich men or officers who can pay handsomely."

"Wait a second," Hanja interrupted. "We shouldn't talk about something like this in front of Lila. To go that far to help our friends and families—"

"—is better than starving to death," Diana finished, cutting Hanja off. "There's food out there somewhere. We just need money and the means to get it."

"You don't know anything about life as a prostitute. It might appear glamorous, but that's all a lie. You can catch diseases, and some customers get violent. You risk your life with that work."

"I know that much."

"You know nothing! Only lowlifes use prostitutes! What if someone kills you before you find your rich man?"

"If you're really that worried, how about you send us some food from Eastern Europe? Even a little would help. Germany can't import goods from anywhere with the British blockade in place. The farms continue to sit idle, and with the winter this year, an unbelievable number of Germans are going to starve to death. We're already at breaking point."

"Then stop the war. If the Central powers surrendered right now, the war would end tomorrow and you could import food again. That's the way you should be thinking about it."

"But none of the countries' governments are working towards stopping the war."

"There must be people out there trying to achieve peace. We just can't see them."

Jörg listened to the women, captivated. Was Germany really in such a bad state? Then that nightmare he'd had was emblematic of what was really going on?

Lila listened quietly as the women talked. She didn't offer her opinion but simply sipped her tea and ate butter cookies. The women completely ignored her as they continued their heated debate. They discussed things that were decidedly unfit to talk about in front of someone as young as Lila, and Jörg thought they must lose some of their reservations when they become souls. He'd always assumed that Lila's mature attitude came from the education the Count provided her, but perhaps the stronger influence came from here.

According to the women, Germany had made a mistake managing food supplies immediately after the war started. The government had butchered a huge number of pigs, thinking that if they reduced the number of livestock to the bare minimum, the grain used as feed could be given to humans. However, grain didn't provide the same amount of nutrition as meat or fat, so the German populace quickly succumbed to malnutrition. A bad harvest compounded with the British blockade caused the situation to become even more dire. For the Allies, on the other hand, the results of the embargo exceeded all expectations. Once they realized how effective this strategy was, they didn't relent, but only tightened their grip even more.

On the front lines, Jörg had struggled with what the army provided as rations. Potatoes and a scant few vegetables could hardly be called food. Neither could a bean soup with trace amounts of pork fat floating at the top, or meager portions of rye bread and sausage. Rations would increase slightly for a while after a big battle. This wasn't a reward for a job well done from their commanding officers, however, but the portions of the soldiers killed in the fighting that were distributed to those who still lived. They were always struggling for supplies on the battlefield, but at least they were never without food. Jörg couldn't believe how much worse it was on the home front.

Just then, he heard a voice above him.

"Why is there a man here?"

Jörg looked up at the night sky glittering with the constellations of early summer and saw the white soul of a woman standing on a steel girder. The wind blowing through the Eiffel Tower made her long hair sway like seaweed in the ocean.

"Go home, boy," she said. "Men aren't allowed here."

"It's fine," Bernadette said, answering for Jörg. "We let him stay. Come down, Camille."

"I'm not sitting next to some man I don't know."

"There's nothing to worry about. He's Lila's bodyguard."

The woman named Camille scrunched up her face, then jumped down from her perch. She didn't join the rest of them but instead descended just a few girders to sit where she could watch over Jörg and the women.

She crossed her arms and glared daggers at the group. "No matter how badly they need money, you can't send girls to work in brothels. There are other ways to secure funds."

"Such as?" Jörg asked.

"Selling information."

"What information, and to whom?"

"Did you serve?"

"Yes, on the Western Front."

"Then it's simple. Sell information to the Allies about the German Army and what the situation's like inside Germany. The best group to sell it to would be Britain's Secret Intelligence Service, the SIS. They'd definitely buy the information and put it to good use. Do that enough times, and you'll make a fortune."

"You're asking me to betray my homeland."

"I am."

"How can you even suggest such a thing?!"

"Do you want to help your country?" Camille retorted. "Or the girls in front of you? It's an easy question."

"Germany's still my home."

"And if they lose, the war's over. Austria's just following Germany's lead."

"I can't betray my comrades on the front line. If I sell military secrets to the enemy, then everyone giving their all on the battlefield will die. Of course I want the war to end, but I can't agree to doing it that way."

"You're just making up pretty excuses. I'm sure you want to save your friends, but you really just don't want to get your hands dirty. There's no place for such naive thinking in war."

Infuriated, Jörg opened his mouth to reply, when another person called out from overhead. This time, it was a man.

"Why not leave it there, you two?"

Following the voice, Jörg saw the Count sitting on a girder, one leg draped over the other.

The women who'd been watching Jörg and Camille's heated exchange began to speak over one another.

"Another man!"

"What is going on tonight?"

The Count stood up, placed a hand on his chest, and gave an elegant bow. "Ladies, please excuse the interruption. Forgive me for causing such a commotion. That man is not only Lila's bodyguard, but a servant of mine. I beg your pardon for his lack of manners."

"What're you putting on airs for, Count?" Camille spat. "Enough with the theatrics. I was just telling this naive boy about how the world works."

"I agree with your idea of selling information to raise money, Camille," the Count said, as if speaking to an old friend. "But great care should be taken in choosing what to reveal to the British. You have to be selective in what you tell them. I won't help you if it results in powerless soldiers on the battlefield being trampled underfoot."

"You're a bat—a bloodsucker, just like your country. You refuse to pick a side, all the while judging the Central and Allied powers."

"Romania will join the war in the summer."

"On which side?"

"I don't know. Milos might know more."

"See? Like I said: a bat."

"I always have been."

Camille muttered to herself as she stood up from the girder. "Well, Mr. Huber, think about it this way. You had no problem killing people on the Western Front. Whether you kill an enemy or an ally, it makes no difference. It's all murder in the end."

"I don't see it that way. Soldiers aren't murderers."

"It's strange. Why would someone like you object to intelligence work?"

"I dislike dirty jobs like that."

Camille laughed loudly. "That's what everyone says. People only ever do it for the money, but they don't want to be called spies and ask the higher-ups in the intelligence service for a military position. You're all so full of yourselves. I can't stand it."

"How many spies are there currently in Europe?"

"Lots, and they're everywhere. Of course, only the best infiltrate enemy lines. Most gather information on enemy movements near borders. Typically, they employ locals—everyday housewives and workers—who carry out simple jobs."

"Housewives?"

"Women like that monitor a fixed location, watching the same spot every day and reporting to intelligence bureaus if anything unusual happens. Things like convoys—their length and location, plus what they're transporting. With just that information, the Allied intelligence bureaus can decipher the state of Central supplies and their movements. Intelligence work is a lot of mundane tasks just like that. Spies running through towns getting into shootouts is something that only happens in plays. Real agents always keep themselves hidden. They blend into everyday life. You couldn't tell them apart from a regular person. Their game is information-gathering; their value is determined by how the data can be analyzed."

Camille raised her right hand above her head in an elegant gesture, and a pigeon appeared in midair, as if conjured by a magician. It flew down to land on Camille's wrist. "This bird isn't real," she said, stroking its back. "You've been on the front lines, so you should know what this is. It's a carrier pigeon. Even now that telegrams are being used, they're still a useful tool for communication on any battlefield. The Germans use them, too, I assume."

"Yes."

Germany used them for more than just communication between the front and the rear lines; they also attached cameras to the birds to photograph enemy positions from the air. Pigeons were incredibly useful as they didn't stand out, unlike airplanes.

"Between the military and civilian carrier pigeon coops, France has around two hundred thousand birds," Camille went on. "There are four hundred carrier pigeon clubs within France. The ten permanent military coops have between two and four hundred birds each at any given time. Civilian coops are run by a carrier pigeon communications network, which has a number of people who work with the intelligence division of the French general staff headquarters. Carrier pigeons in France collect information on the rear lines. This whole collaboration was started by the citizens themselves."

Still consoling the bird, Camille turned the conversation onto Jörg. "Someone like you should be able to gather information better than a pigeon. Not to mention you used to be a soldier. There's no better spy for the British than someone like that."

"You're telling me to work like the pigeons?"

"That's right." Her eyes twinkled brightly. "Or use your talents for the Central powers and give them the upper hand over the Allies. But with Germany's food shortages, the more you help the Central powers, the more German blood gets spilled and the longer this war goes on. So working with the British will end this war sooner. At least that's how I see it."

Jörg was lost for words. Camille simply ignored him and stood up, the illusory pigeon perched on her shoulder.

"Think it over," she urged. "You've heard what the women here have to say. I won't forgive you if you make them suffer. Count, talk it over with the boy, will you?"

Camille leaped lightly off the girder once more and disappeared in midair. Even though she was just a soul, there was something awfully inhuman about her movements.

Jörg turned to the Count. "Just what is that woman?"

The Count's eyes narrowed in amusement as he stared into the empty space where Camille had just vanished. "She's human, but she has one foot in our world. You know a man named Fritz in your unit, correct? The one with a talent for drawing?"

"Yes."

"She's like him. Their artistic abilities allow them to see into the world of monsters."

"So she's a painter?"

"A sculptor. A fellow artist betrayed her, and they had a fierce fight—the result of which was that she was thought to have gone mad and thrown into a hospital. Not a single family member ever visits her. She spends every day staring at the world outside the iron bars of her window. In truth, she's not someone who does well in a place like that. Her artistic drive must still consume her mind like a tempest, but she can no longer express it through her art. Unable to express herself, her soul wandered out of her body just like these other ladies, and she found her way here."

"That poor woman."

"While her situation is undeniably lamentable, don't be so quick to pity her. For Camille, the hospital is simply the endpoint of having lived her life to the fullest."

"Have you never thought to help her?"

"I'll go and get her once her body stops functioning and she exists only as a soul. I admire people like her, who commit themselves fully to life without worrying about destroying themselves. Come now, how about we get going? It will be light soon."

Jörg realized that the stars were beginning to fade. The souls were hurriedly preparing to return home, wishing one another a safe trip, and promising to meet again soon.

Jörg called out to Bernadette. "What brothel can I visit to meet the real you? I'd like to hear more of your story."

"I work at 12 Rue Drucker, in the Second Arrondissement of Paris near Rue Chabanais. It's easy to find; just look for the number under the red light. If you're coming by taxi, all you have to do is tell them the street name and building number, and they'll take you there from anywhere in the city."

"Is it expensive?"

"It's a long-standing establishment, so fairly expensive. Be prepared to open some bottles of champagne. We're a fully licensed brothel. Some *pierreuse* walk the streets nearby, though, so don't let those low-class whores trick you."

As the souls were leaving, the Count looked over to Lila and Jörg. "Now then, I have a *lot* of questions for you both."

"I came by myself," Lila said quickly. "Mr. Huber chose to come on his own."

"That's fine. I'm not blaming anyone. However," the Count said, glancing at Jörg, "why did you not say anything to me before leaving? After the trouble you ran into the other day."

Jörg lowered his head. "I'm sorry. I didn't think about that."

"Useless man. If you can't do anything right, then perhaps I'll turn you into a worm."

"Not a worm," Lila cut in. "That wouldn't be good for anything. At least make him a house mouse or something I can keep as a pet."

"I shall consider it."

A chill ran down Jörg's spine. Even as a joke, it was in bad taste.

"We'll talk more when we get back to the inn," the Count said, turning around with a swish of his cloak.

4

When they returned to the inn, the Count told Lila to go to bed, then stopped Jörg in the hallway.

"Has Lila warmed to you at all?"

"A little, but there's still a long way to go. I'm more interested in the dire situation they were talking about at the Eiffel Tower."

"The food shortages in Germany?"

"You knew about it?"

"There's nothing you can do to help. Your duties are as Lila's bodyguard. Don't think about anything else."

"But—"

"If you don't drop it, I really will turn you into a worm or a mouse."

"Please don't."

"Blockades are a common military tactic. They've been used since time immemorial. Germany handled the situation like fools."

"But if nothing changes, my country will hold out until the bitter end. I can't just abandon it."

"The people will act when it's time. Believe in the power of your fellow countrymen."

After the Count left, Jörg stood in the hallway for a while.

The people of Germany would rise up if the government failed them. But in the meantime, countless people would die.

He didn't go back to his room but walked to the dining hall instead. If he waited a little while, Lila would get up and arrive for breakfast. He wanted to hear her thoughts about the discussion at the Eiffel Tower and if she would ignore the women like the Count did or help them. If they really were her friends, then she should want to lend a hand now, of all times.

As he entered the dining hall, Jörg caught the lingering scent of food and felt a chill in the air. He sat in a chair and collapsed onto the table. The moment his eyes closed, drowsiness overcame him as if he'd fallen to the bottom of a pit.

In his dreams, he met Nil, the monster of nothingness. Nil spoke to him, but he wasn't the one who answered. The voice sounded exactly like his. The two people were deep in conversation, smoking in a trench. It was the middle of the night, and no one else was around.

Listening to them speak, Jörg eventually realized that Nil was talking with his corpus. The experience was being transmitted to him through his dreams.

Irritation swelled inside his old body. It was understandable that he felt frustrated staying on the front lines.

Nil faced him, relating the plight unfolding within Germany. He also spoke about the revolution the socialists were planning. His corpus seemed interested in the socialist movement, planting a new seed of worry inside Jörg.

Socialist speeches always sounded like some sort of fairy tale. They harped on about how the common people weren't learned enough and didn't pay attention to the world around them, which made them compliant with the whims of the wealthy. Studying socialism would let them steer the world in the right direction.

Hearing such talk made the uneducated Jörg uncomfortable. He certainly wasn't knowledgeable about a lot of things. He hadn't gone to university, but simply worked as a barber in his hometown. Someone like him wouldn't see the world the same way as the socialists did. That much he knew.

Still, he didn't care for the impression they gave off, as if they were the enlightened guiding the ignorant. Jörg found it hard to put into words, but something felt off about them. He couldn't ignore that gut feeling.

Be that as it may, there were so many things he couldn't do. For Lila, for Christine in Paris, for the women of the Eiffel Tower, for his own country.

He wanted to turn even one of his aspirations into reality—but he didn't have even the slightest clue as to how to make that happen.

Jörg felt his body begin to sway, and Nil's outline became hazy.

He woke from his dream to find someone hitting him on the shoulder. It was already light inside the room.

Lila was standing in front of him.

"Wake up," she said with her regular brusqueness. "I can't eat with you sleeping there."

"Sorry. What time is it?"

"Ten in the morning. I overslept a little. I'm going to have a big breakfast, but what are you going to have, Mr. Huber?"

"I'm fine with just some bread, sausage, and a coffee."

"Then let's both use the kitchen and try to not get in each other's way."

"Sure."

Jörg had been making his own breakfast ever since Xandra had given him the croissant and coffee when he first arrived. She wasn't family, and she certainly wasn't hired help, so he wasn't going to ask her to make his food for him. And besides, Jörg wanted to eat what he was used to. He liked to think that the food his simulacrum ate would be transmitted to his corpus, so he always made sure to have proper meals.

Jörg cut a slice of rye bread, boiled a sausage, and made a cup of coffee. He even added a little cheese to the food.

Lila, meanwhile, melted some butter in a frying pan, whisked in some flour, and added milk to make a béchamel sauce. She cut two thin slices of square bread, then coated the surface of one slice in the sauce. She put some ham on top, then cheese, and finally topped it off with the other slice of bread. After heating a frying pan on the stove, she dropped a pat of butter in it. Next, she carefully placed her creation in the pan, making sure it didn't fall apart, and it began to give off a decadent smell. Every so often, she pressed the surface of the bread with her spatula, then halfway through flipped it over to cook the other side.

She was a pretty skilled young chef. It seemed that no matter what it was, Lila preferred doing things by herself.

"What's that?" Jörg asked.

"A croque monsieur," Lila replied cheerfully. "They eat it this way in Paris. It's a dish that was designed for men to eat, so it might a bit too much food for a young girl, don't you think?"

"It sure is."

"But this is the best thing when I'm hungry in the morning. I usually have a much lighter breakfast and just eat a sweet pastry."

Going to the Eiffel Tower the night before must have taken a lot out of her. Lila turned off the stove and put the steaming croque monsieur on a plate. She poured some milk into a ceramic cup, set a knife and fork on her tray, and carried everything to the table. Jörg followed her into the dining hall, where he sat down opposite the young girl.

After saying grace, Lila picked up her cutlery with a look of utter joy. Her knife pierced the bread, cheese oozing out accompanied by the smell of ham. She stabbed the bread with her fork, and when she took her first bite, the bread made a pleasant crunch. Lila's smile widened. She continued to cut and devour the croque monsieur, sipping occasionally at her milk.

Jörg hadn't thought she would eat it with such enthusiasm. Lila always acted so detached and mature, he thought she'd act similarly during meals. Still, it was nice to see her enjoying herself.

"Do you find it interesting listening to those sorts of conversations at the Eiffel Tower?" Jörg asked while they ate.

"Of course. Sometimes I ask questions, but I always learn a lot."

She drank her milk, then flashed Jörg a smile. "Really, they're more like teachers than friends. They tell me to call them my friends, though, so I do."

"I see."

"What did you think hearing what they had to say, Mr. Huber?"

"I didn't know things had gotten so bad in Germany. None of the letters I got from home mentioned anything like that."

"Do you want to help?"

"Yes."

"Then you should do what you think is right. It's a problem your country is facing, Mr. Huber."

"The Count stopped me. He said I need to be your bodyguard."

"Can't you just ignore that?"

"Well, if you help those women, then as your bodyguard, I'll be able to help everyone, too."

"Don't get the wrong idea," Lila replied flatly. "I have zero interest in helping Germany. The best way to solve the food shortages is to have the Central powers surrender. If they do that, then Poland will one day return to the Polish."

"Yes, I understand that. But the decision to end the war would take a considerable amount of time and many arduous steps."

"Can I tell you what I think?"

"Please do."

"On June 4, the Austrian Army started fighting the Russians in southwestern Ukraine. Some Polish people also live there. The German Army arrived to help the Austrians, and they did horrible things to the Polish and Ukrainian people. Why should I help a country like that? Even if they're facing hard times."

Jörg didn't respond. There was no way to justify something like that, just like when Lila had brought up the attack on Belgium.

"If you want to help your people, then resign as my bodyguard, Mr. Huber," Lila continued. "You should either work in Berlin to help the citizens or go back to the front lines and help Germany win the war. It's your life. Do with it what you want."

"You're saying I should go back to my corpus? But I just got used to this simulacrum."

"Remember what I said before? If you stay here, you'll become an actual monster. You should rest as much as you can, then leave. While you're still human."

"But I want to see you happy. I want to see that before I go back home."

"You take things way too seriously. None of this is your fault, so there's no point in thinking about any of it. Instead, focus on saving your own soul. That's what you should do when you can no longer see God or hear his voice."

If you can't see the path ahead, then you need to make it yourself. That was essentially what Lila was telling him to do. She had a point, but it was a hard thing to achieve. To forge a new path, you need willpower, stamina, and luck. And sometimes, you need to make sacrifices. That's why people hesitate to do it.

If Jörg was going to do that, what could he sacrifice? What could he offer? And after he surrendered whatever was required of him, could he look back and smile without any regrets?

Lila studied his face. "Do you want to help your countrymen, no matter what?"

"Yes."

"You'll need money to buy vast supplies of food. How do you plan on getting it?"

"I've considered a lot of options, but I haven't come up with a solution yet. Camille's suggestion just doesn't sit right with me."

"Mr. Huber, you really are way too serious."

"Do you think so?"

"If you want to earn money selling information, there's a better way."

"What's that?"

"I'll become a spy and steal information from the German Army. Then I'll sell it to the British and give all the money to you, and you can give it to women in Germany. We'll use simulacrums to become the world's greatest spies."

Jörg looked stunned, then after a moment, he burst out laughing. He'd been wrong to think Lila was so mature. Only a child would dream up such an outlandish idea.

Lila immediately looked upset and puffed out her cheeks. "Why are you laughing?"

"It's just, I really appreciate how hard you thought to come up with all this."

"You don't look very appreciative. You look like you're making fun of me."

"Sorry, I didn't mean to."

"So? What do you think of my plan?"

"I can't do it. No matter the circumstances, I don't want to make money betraying Germany."

"Okay, then what if we make up a story about you getting back information I stole so the higher-ups in the German Army give you a reward for retrieving stolen information? In other words, we scam them. That way, the information doesn't leave Germany, and we still get the money."

Jörg folded his arms and pressed them into his stomach, struggling to hold back a smile. "I wish the German intelligence bureau was that stupid and trusting."

"So it won't work?"

"First of all, if you don't know anything about the army, then you won't know what information is valuable, let alone what the Allies might find useful. Something like that is hard even for me to figure out."

"We could ask Milos."

"Milos?"

"I didn't say I'd do it alone. We should have him help us. He's part of the Serbian Army, so he'll know what sort of information we should be looking for."

The glimmer in Lila's eyes told him she was serious. Those weren't the eyes of an innocent child. Jörg felt like he was looking at a mysterious creature he'd never seen before, whose passion was fueled by her curiosity in the face of this new situation.

Milos and Lila working together spelled trouble. Milos's seriousness and his contempt for the Central powers ran deep, so he would happily help the young girl if it meant dealing a crushing blow to the German Army. If anything, with Milos in charge, Lila might find herself in over her head.

The smile disappeared from Jörg's face. "This is bound to get serious if Milos is involved. He's a staunch supporter of the movement for Greater Serbia."

"Good. That way, it'll be more like real information warfare. We'll definitely be able to fool German intelligence."

"Once he becomes a part of this, it stops being fake. He'll be serious about stealing a lot of intel. And once we hand that information over, people could really start getting killed."

"I have no problem with that, especially if it means the Germans end up losing. Don't forget, I'm Polish, so I have absolutely no obligation whatsoever to be on Germany's side."

Just when Jörg had thought that Lila was beginning to open up to him, she'd distanced herself from him again.

Seeing Jörg fall silent, the young girl continued. "Mr. Huber, you probably don't believe that a child can do much. But war changes people—not just the adults, but the children, too. We can't live as kids with the day-to-day hardships of wartime. We skip our childhood and suddenly become grown-ups. Do you understand what I mean? To you, I may sound like a heartless monster, talking about such cruel things even though I'm still a child. But if that's true, then it was war that did that to me. The winds of war don't distinguish between adults and children. They turn everyone into monsters. I'm sure you understand that as well as I do, Mr. Huber."

5

That afternoon, Jörg walked around the inn searching for the Count. He could have asked Xandra, but she was busy examining patients during the day. Her patients weren't human, and the thought of seeing a monster face-to-face disturbed Jörg, so he searched for the Count on his own.

The Count wasn't in the courtyard or the lounge, and Jörg didn't come across him in any of the building's hallways. Finally, he went to the Count's room. He knocked on the door, and a voice answered from within.

It was the same level tone as always, so Jörg didn't hesitate to enter.

He saw tightly packed bookshelves and a shelf decorated with a porcelain clock. Surprised by the feel of the thick rug under his feet, Jörg hesitantly crossed the room. The Count wasn't inside but on the balcony, drinking wine in a chair beside the small table as he had the other day.

As Jörg stepped out onto the balcony, the brilliant rays of the setting sun blinded him. He admired the view of the landscape surrounding the inn—a sight that was inaccessible from his own room.

He had no idea what town sat below him. It wasn't Paris; he couldn't see any of the buildings he should be able to see from this direction, and the architecture was completely different.

Needless to say, it didn't look anything like Jörg's hometown in Germany, either.

It appeared to have once been a thriving city which, at some point, had been encroached upon by the surrounding vegetation. A section of the wall of a large redbrick building had collapsed, exposing its contents for all the world to see. Only its circular tower remained whole.

Red tiles covered the roofs of the squat houses surrounding the ruins, and the road running through the densely packed buildings ended in large fields. Beyond them lay a line of hills, which faded into far-off mountains that pierced the bottom of the pale-blue sky.

The sunset painted the houses and ruins in orange, making the ancient town appear even older. The dark shapes of thrushes flew out of the densely clustered shrubs in front of Jörg. He could see only a smattering of people walking down the road, most of the residents likely busy preparing dinner.

The Count's profile was calm as he took in the town. He didn't seem sad, simply filled with a serene sense of nostalgia. The wan evening light turned the Count's green eyes and black hair a shade darker and added a faint tinge of red to his porcelain-white skin.

Jörg moved to stand beside the Count.

"What is this place?"

"Târgoviște," the Count replied. "My hometown. Stunning, isn't it?"

"It is."

So this was Walachia. Jörg felt like a squire standing next to an aged general. The Count had lived for over four hundred years, so from his point of view, Jörg must seem no different from a newborn baby. Standing with the Count in the same spot, looking out at the same view, filled Jörg with awe.

"I spoke with Lila," Jörg said, still looking down at the town.

"And?"

"She's more organized than I am. She said that if we want to help the people who are starving, we should work with Milos to collect information, sell intel on the German Army to the British SIS, and use those funds to buy food."

"What did you say to that?"

"I asked her to let me think about it."

"As indecisive as always."

"I can't make up my mind that quickly. Depending on what happens, Lila and I could end up as enemies."

"All you have to do is stay by her side. Who knows what that child will do?"

"What do you mean by that?"

"You heard that Lila used to live with her parents in a French town called Lille?"

"Yes, she told me that herself. It's in France, but a lot of Polish people live there. The town was built on the coal mining industry."

"Her father wasn't a miner. Her mother didn't work there, either. They were both merchants who frequently traveled to Lille. Their job was to bring in things the people needed from outside the town and sell them at prices people could afford. They sold quality items cheap, so everyone loved them."

"Huh, really? I thought they must've lived there."

"However, they sold more than just merchandise."

The Count looked into Jörg's eyes and smiled. "Do you know what's northwest of Lille? Dunkirk and Calais, both port towns. Cross the Strait of Dover, and you'll reach England. Lille is also close to the Belgian border."

"You don't mean…?"

"Indeed. Lila's father provided the British with information about mainland Europe. In his search for a path to Polish independence, he was working as a spy to get the support of Great Britain."

The Count continued, telling Jörg about the day Lila's father had brought his daughter to Xandra's inn…

Late September, 1914. A cold drizzle was falling the night a man came to the inn with a young girl. The two were soaked, mud clinging to their boots, the girl trembling like a puppy abandoned in a field. They hadn't eaten a proper meal in days, and the famished girl's body made her look no older than ten.

The man's name was Radosław Kowalski. He knocked on the front door, announcing that he'd come to speak with Count Silvestri. The door opened almost immediately. Xandra met him at the entrance and saw their sorry state, immediately beckoned them inside, and made them sit in front of the fireplace in the lounge. She helped them take off their overcoats, gave them towels to dry themselves, then left for a while before returning from the kitchen with soup and bread.

The girl attended to her hunger with single-minded devotion before falling into a deep sleep on the sofa, seemingly overcome with relief.

"That's no place to sleep. I'll take her to a room with a bed," Xandra said, and Radosław thanked her.

At the same time that Xandra left with the girl in her arms, the Count entered the parlor, as though replacing them.

"This is quite the unexpected visit."

Radosław stood from the couch. "I'm very sorry."

"Please, sit," the Count said. "Let's talk."

"Something terrible has happened in Belgium."

"I know."

"What do you intend to do?" Radosław asked.

"Nothing."

"Are you waiting for instructions from your homeland?"

"I have no interest in the Kingdom of Romania," replied the Count. "I shall simply watch this war from afar, observing how quickly it ends or how long it continues. That is, unless you came to request something of me."

"I'm here on a matter unrelated to my duties."

"And that is?"

"I'd like to leave my daughter with you for a little while. She's still young. I can't take her anywhere she might get hurt."

"Where's Alicja?"

"She was killed. Because of my ineptitude."

"Were you found out?"

His body trembling faintly, Radosław clasped and unclasped his hands in his lap, trying to keep his frustration contained. "We did well until the start of the war. We could travel anywhere without raising suspicion. But we didn't expect German intelligence to find us so quickly."

"You're on the run now?"

"Yes."

"Where did you blunder?"

"I don't know. The attack came out of the blue. It was all I could do to grab my daughter and run."

In the days leading up to the Great War, diplomats and politicians from every country wanted the most up-to-date information as they decided whether to attempt diplomacy as a means to avoid war or to use force to suppress the aggressors. Radosław and his wife, Alicja, had worked to collect that information, through which they'd met the Count. They had only one objective: contact political figures in Great Britain and France to collect and disseminate classified information in exchange for their help in rebuilding Poland.

"What do you plan to do now?" the Count asked. "If you want to hide yourself, I have any number of rooms I can offer you."

"Thank you, but too many of my comrades are still out there. I have to warn them."

"If you go into hiding, they'll figure out what happened. It would be best not to move around too much."

"I'd go mad doing nothing and spend all my time remembering Alicja's last moments."

"You need to play the long game," advised the Count. "Even after this war ends, Poland won't be handed back to you so easily. Exhausting yourself now will only break you later."

Radosław didn't respond to the Count but simply reiterated, "Will you look after her?"

"This isn't a church. It's not the sort of place where we can look after a child."

"I understand that."

"No, you don't," reinforced the Count. "What will I do with her if you're killed out there? Feed her to a monster?"

"Please, be serious."

"I have no intention of becoming her adoptive father."

"Send her away from here when she grows up. I'll leave money for her room and board. This is the only place that's safe."

The Count rested an elbow on the arm of the chair, settled his chin in his palm, and thought for a moment. "Money isn't enough. You'll have to agree to my conditions."

"I accept, whatever they are. What do you want?"

"Her name and memories."

"What?"

"She has lost her mother, and she may yet lose her father, as well. I won't be able to take care of her if she's lonely and depressed, so I'll erase her memories of you both. And her name. However, erasing every last detail about you two may create inconsistencies with her other memories, so I'll have to leave some traces… But in the future, if you somehow manage to make it through your multitude of troubles, rebuild Poland, and return here, you will be no more than a stranger to her. She'll even forget the face of her mother. In return, I promise to keep her alive. If you can agree to that, then I will look after the child."

Radosław looked stunned but eventually came to a decision. "If it will keep her safe, then she can forget about us. Ensuring her future is the most important thing."

"You've made a deal with a monster. Be careful you don't regret it."

"Never. I can only thank you. What name will you give her?"

The Count's gaze shifted and he pointed to a large vase in the parlor. It didn't hold a single flower. However, when Radosław turned to look at it, a bouquet of bud-covered stems extended from the vase, instantly sprouting white and purple flowers. Their sweet fragrance wafted strongly toward him. Lilacs—also known as *lilas*.

"Your daughter's new name shall be Lila," the Count declared. "Her old name has been lost. Address her by her former name, and she won't know you're talking to her. She is no longer able to recognize you as her father. But she is promised a future."

"Thank you." Radosław rose from his chair. "I should be going already."

"Radek." He turned, hearing the Count address him by his nickname. "Please try not to die."

Radosław smiled brightly at him, then slid his arms into his partially dry coat, adjusted his sleeves, and left the lounge.

Never to return to Xandra's inn again.

6

Once he finished telling the story of his old friend, the Count said to Jörg, "Lila probably saw her mother die right in front of her. And she must have had some terrifying memories from when she was fleeing with her father. Saying that she wants to become a spy might be her way of getting revenge."

Jörg felt the world collapse beneath him. "Was it Germans who killed her parents?" he asked in a trembling voice.

"Most likely. She has an abnormal fear and loathing of German people. Even with her memories sealed away, they might still be influencing her. However, it's not easy to tell if someone is purely German. A lot of

Germans and Russians in Europe have some Polish blood in them. After the Third Partition of Poland, Germany and Russia established policies for reconciliation, Germanization, and Russification of the Polish people. The two countries tried to win over Poles by telling them to forget about Poland and live as Germans or Russians, where they could join unions and become valued members of society."

"But the Polish people would never stand for that."

"No. They were in the depths of despair, and most of them resisted this callous invitation. But in all honestly, it would have made their lives easier. Assimilating into a more powerful ethnic group creates more opportunities in life than having people point you out as a stranger wherever you go. So some people accepted those policies aimed at reconciliation, which naturally led to a period of infighting among Poles. They argued among themselves, one side asking, 'Have you forsaken the reconstruction of our motherland? Are you no longer proud of your heritage?' and the other side claiming, 'We cannot live on dreams. Such archaic thinking is our enemy.' Yet even so, some people decided to give up their roots. Nothing crushes a person like the hardships of life. No one would blame them for making that choice. Did you know the German Army is full of people who have Polish ancestry? They swear allegiance to the same nation that robbed them of their homeland and fight against the Allied powers as if it were the natural thing to do. To them, people like Lila's father are nothing more than impassioned fools obsessed with an outdated sense of ethnic pride."

Jörg looked up at the sky and covered his face with both hands. "And I'm just another person from that country she can never forgive. No matter how well we get along on the surface, I'll never be able to erase the anger and grief in her heart."

...That's right. She'll never forgive Germany for as long as she lives. Even knowing that German soldiers have families, that they experience unspeakable horrors on the front lines, and that they die like dogs there, she'll never feel even the slightest hint of sympathy for them.

"That is why I asked you to be her bodyguard," explained the Count. "When she eventually leaves this inn and goes out into the real world, whatever group killed her parents may still exist. And they could very well try to kill her."

"Why would they?"

"Her father could have entrusted her with a certain piece of intel—or so they might assume."

"Do you really think she has something like that?"

"I highly doubt it. Radosław traded his daughter's memories of him to protect her. A man like that surely wouldn't give his daughter anything that might endanger her in the future. However, his enemies may think otherwise. They might seek to eliminate Lila for fear that she will expose them for their crimes, thus the need for a bodyguard. Whatever Lila ends up doing, she will need someone to protect her for the rest of her life.

"The rest of her life…?"

"Your assignment lasts until Lila grows old and leaves this earth. Hence why I needed someone who would follow through on their word and was able to control simulacrums. This is not a job for a human body of flesh and blood. If you were to die during her lifetime, then I would need to find another bodyguard. Such is my duty due to the promise I made Radosław."

The Count reached for his glass on the table. "That is why I want you to abandon this idea to do something about the German food shortages. It will surely be too much to do while still carrying out your duties as Lila's bodyguard."

"But with what I know, I can't just sit by and do nothing."

"It's impossible. You must choose one."

"I'll look for a way to do both. There must be a way."

"And how will you do that?"

"This body is a simulacrum, so it should be able to do things normal human bodies can't."

"Even with the unique abilities of a simulacrum, you must still abide by the temporal rules of this world. There is too much work and not enough time. You cannot do the impossible."

"So you're saying that even with a simulacrum, so long as I'm human, there's a limit to what I can do?"

"Precisely."

"In that case, I'll become a real monster."

"What?"

"If I become a monster, then I can do anything. Like you."

The Count let out a laugh from deep within his throat. "Be serious."

"I am."

"At least with a simulacrum, you will die one day—but you won't if you become a monster. You'll exist with no connection to your corpus and will be forced to live in your own unique time frame. Monsters live for an extraordinarily long time, sometimes forever. Do you really have what it takes to live for all eternity? Can you bear watching the people around you continue to age and die while you live a life of solitude? If you can't, then don't be so quick to say you'll become a monster."

"I'll be able to protect Lila better as a monster, though. Isn't that what you want?"

"You don't have to go that far. I can find any number of replacement bodyguards."

"I wonder how Lila would feel about that."

"What do you mean?"

"If she saw one bodyguard after another get injured, die, and be replaced in order to protect her, I'm sure she'd say that she doesn't want anyone else dying for her. She'd say that she would rather die fighting herself than live at the cost of another person's life. That's the sort of child she is. A very kind, determined girl."

"That's nothing more than unfounded speculation. What makes you think she would say something like that?"

"Spend enough time with her, and you'd see it the same way. I'm actually more surprised you don't understand."

Seeing the Count purse his lips in dissatisfaction, Jörg pressed his point.

"Please. Turn me into a monster. I'll gladly give up my life as a human to save other people. I would have died on the battlefield if I'd never met you. I don't have a home to return to, so let me live the life I want to live. I'd give up everything to gain the power of a monster if it meant I was able to protect Lila while also saving innocent people. I wouldn't have a single regret."

The Count sneered. "It's a bit naive to call people innocent."

"I'm serious."

"Do you really think the people on the home front are innocent? That they're just poor civilians who have been swept up in a war between nations? You're wrong. It's humans who wage wars. Humans who plan them, humans who shape them, and humans who start them. Simply put, the fact that they weren't able to stop war from breaking out makes people on the home front equally responsible."

"But there are people and political parties in every country that tried to stop the war from happening. And babies and children didn't choose any of this. All they do is suffer because of the decisions of adults."

"What impudence. It is those same adults who raise the children and babies. Kids don't live life removed from grown-ups and the societies they create, so by helping the children, you also inadvertently end up helping the men and women who are currently waging war. Not to mention, there's no guarantee that those children you save will all grow up to become kind, intelligent adults."

"That doesn't mean they should be sacrificed… When I was working as a barber, I cut hair for a lot of families—children included. There were all types of kids: happy kids, lonely kids, shy kids. Kids who were quick to bully others, kids who were targets for bullying, kids who stood up to bullies. Gentle kids, hot-tempered kids, kids who would cry at the drop of a hat. All of them—*all of them*—were good kids. There are kids like that in every city in Germany. And I can't stand the thought of those children getting so thin they look like shriveled cucumbers and dying."

"I can't believe you would say something so ridiculous. They're not even your children."

"I don't see what's wrong about feeling sympathy for other people. I spent years on the battlefield not allowed to feel anything as a human being."

The Count lowered his chin and glanced furtively up at Jörg. "Turning you into a monster is easy: You just need to receive some of their blood. Any monster will do, be it a minor ghost roaming the hills and fields or an intelligent being fully integrated into human society. The blood of stronger monsters will grant you more power."

"So your blood would be the best, then."

"It seems you understand perfectly."

The Count steepled his fingers in front of his chest. "Do you have the courage to drink my blood?"

"I do."

"With this blood, you will become immortal, like me. You will never die, no matter what happens to you. Even if you grow to hate the world and decide to kill yourself. If your body is torn to pieces by an accident or an enemy attack , it will re-form and you will live again. Your life will never end."

"I'm prepared for that. To gain power that defies the rules of this world… I didn't assume it would come without a price."

"One more thing will change. Once you become a monster, your connection to your corpus will disappear, and the magic I cast on it will be gone. That is to say, if your corpus gets injured, it will die like anyone else. Can you accept that?"

"What about outside of war? Say he gets into an accident—will he die?"

"Of course."

Jörg lowered his eyes and sank into silence for a few moments. Even though they were two separate entities now, his corpus was still his body. It would die. Its protection would be lost. With the current state of the war, one bad decision could leave his corpus dead on the battlefield.

Yet all humans die. His body was no exception. That had been true ever since the day he was born. The only question was whether it happened sooner or later.

Jörg nodded. "I understand. I'm okay with that."

"There's one more annoying detail I must tell you about. The blood of another person is mixed into my own. If that blood enters your body, you will be overcome with such fervor that it could drive you mad. It is the radical blood of someone who would sacrifice himself body and soul for his country."

"Whose blood is it?"

"My master's. I live today because of that magic."

It seemed like a complicated situation, but the Count didn't elaborate.

Jörg repeated his earlier request. "Even so, I wish to receive your blood. Please."

"You really are a fool." The Count raised an eyebrow. "You don t understand the slightest thing about the gift that is death, either as a human or as a living creature. Have you not imagined what peace it might bring?"

"I want power," Jörg reiterated. "I hate not being able to do anything as I am now."

"Become a monster and you must give up your faith in God. Can you do that?"

"Of course."

"You don't care about losing God?"

"I lost faith in God on the battlefield. It hasn't returned to me since."

The Count gripped the armrests of his chair and slowly stood up. "Then come here. I shall give you my blood."

Carrying the wine bottle and glass in one hand, the Count returned from the balcony to his room. He set the items down on his desk, opened a drawer, and removed a knife. The Count put it to his palm and drew the knife across the skin in a single swift motion. Red droplets immediately swelled in the center of his palm, forming a trickle of liquid that fell from his hand. He squeezed some of the blood into the wineglass. Once it was so full that Jörg started to worry about the man, the Count topped it off with wine from the bottle, then commanded Jörg to drink it all. Every last drop.

Jörg lifted the cup with shaky hands. He touched it to his lips, then downed the entire glass, being careful not to spill any. He didn't think about it. He knew that if he considered what he was doing even for a second, he would start having second thoughts.

As soon as Jörg swallowed the liquid, his insides began to burn. No longer able to stand, he placed both hands on top of the desk to support himself.

A voice called out to him from within, but he couldn't make out the words. Something was speaking to him deep in his eardrums.

The Count walked around behind Jörg, supporting him. "You should lie down for a little while. You can use my bed."

"I'd prefer to sleep in my own room."

"You'll collapse before you get there. Please, rest here."

The Count laid Jörg on the bed and stared down at him.

His eyes narrowed, and his pupils took on a dark glow.

"Thanks to your foolishness, it seems I'll be able to see something interesting—an experience that is all too rare in my four-hundred-plus years of life. It is sure to be quite the divertisement. 'I'll gladly give up my life as a human to save humans…' That's the first time I've ever heard a human say something like that. I suppose that is the morality of this new era. A flower unable to bear fruit blooming in the soil of the Great War."

The Count pressed a finger to Jörg's forehead. "Sleep now. You shall dream for a long time. That is my gift to you."

Part 2

I
Immortal Blood

Lying on the bed, Jörg found himself immediately transported into a dream. A sudden gust of wind lifted him high into the air. Snow dotted a steep mountain range. A road ran through a valley like the winding trail of a snake. Deciduous and conifer trees lined gentle slopes and foothills, while sheep grazed the fields.

In a corner of cleared land, a city continued to grow. This was Eastern Europe, on the southern side of the Carpathian Mountains, in an area that had once been known as the principality of Walachia. Jörg's perspective gradually drew closer.

As it approached, he began to make out fine details on the fabric and faces of the people on the road. The antiquated clothing and outdated architecture. He knew this place. It was the same town he'd seen from the Count's balcony. This was the Count's homeland, Walachia. It would later join with Moldavia and change its name to the Kingdom of Romania. Since ancient times, it had sat exposed to the threat of attack from the Ottoman Empire to the south while maintaining a tense relationship with the Kingdom of Hungary to the north.

A voice whispered in Jörg's ear that he was seeing the distant past, as far removed from reality as a fairy tale, when George Silvestri was still a young, normal human being. It came from the blood coursing through his veins, telling him to observe everything, savor everything, remember everything.

Jörg saw not with human eyes but from the perspective of a god. He fully understood the values of the time, from the workings of nations and the actions of governments all the way down to the daily lives of the people.

He landed on the ground and took in his surroundings.

The fates of the multitude of people here had started to feel as if they were his own.

In this age, Walachia's neighbor Serbia was a vassal state of the Ottoman Empire, having been crushed in a fierce war.

Walachia and Moldavia had both also fallen under Ottoman control, but unlike Serbia, these two principalities retained autonomous governments.

In exchange, they paid tribute to the empire.

This arrangement began for Walachia in 1415. The payments of several thousand gold ducats, as well as gifts of sheep, wheat, leather, and textiles, placed a heavy burden on the principality.

The empire also demanded hostages. Among them were the boy who would go on to become Vlad III and his younger brother Radu, who were both held in Turkey from 1442.

Vlad was eleven at the time.

This boy would go on to become the Count's future master—but back then, he was powerless.

The sultan of the Ottoman Empire, Murad II, accorded Vlad and Radu great respect, treating them more like guests than hostages. They were taught Turkish, educated in the ways of politics and the military, and instructed on the importance of seeing matters not simply in terms of their own country, but with all of Europe in mind.

Their education aimed to prepare them for a life in government.

Murad knew that having someone aligned with the empire ruling Walachia would create a strong bond between the two countries. Even a nation as mighty as the Ottoman Empire would have a hard time fighting the powers of Europe by itself. Murad expected that Vlad would bring the countries of Eastern Europe into the fold of the Ottoman Empire, resisting any interference from the great nations of Europe.

However, north of Walachia in Transylvania, a territory in the southern region of the Kingdom of Hungary, the voivode János Hunyadi was resolutely committed to resisting Ottoman rule. A major figure during the Battle of Varna, Hunyadi planned to sow fierce anti-Ottoman sentiment in Walachia and establish a faction of the Holy Roman Empire in the region as a safeguard against invasion by the Ottoman Empire.

In 1447, Hunyadi convinced the wealthy boyars of Walachia to inaugurate Vlad III's second cousin, Vladislav II, as voivode of Walachia.

At the time, a number of Walachian boyars had amassed vast fortunes from the revenue of farms and through their role in the national economy. At any given time, eight to twelve of these men served on the administrative council, and while governmental policies were decided by vote, bribery ran rampant within the council, resulting in a handful of families holding the reins of power. Even the voivode couldn't oppose them, as the boyars would quickly dispose of any ruler who conflicted with their interests and replace them with a new one.

The boyars kept careful watch over neighboring countries to better protect their wealth. They accepted Hunyadi's nominee for the position of voivode, having deemed selling their favor to the Kingdom of Hungary to be in their best interests.

Murad II of the Ottoman Empire immediately expressed his disagreement. Ignoring the will of the Walachian nobles, he put forth Vlad, who had spent so many years by his side, as the most suitable candidate for voivode of Walachia.

Skirmishes soon broke out between the Ottoman Empire and the Kingdom of Hungary over the choice of Walachia's governor. The situation devolved into a confrontation at Kosovo between the two powers, with the Ottoman Empire eventually seizing victory. Vladislav II was removed as voivode and replaced by the sixteen-year-old Vlad.

However, not even two months after the Battle of Kosovo, Hunyadi led a contingent of Hungarian forces against Walachia and deposed Vlad. Fearing for his life, Vlad fled to Moldavia, where he sought the help of his uncle Bogdan II. Yet Moldavia also proved dangerous, as not long after, Bogdan II was assassinated during a power struggle. His safety net lost, Vlad found himself standing alongside Bogdan's son Stephen in mute shock.

Staying put meant their deaths. They needed to figure out their next course of action.

That was when a certain idea came to Vlad.

He decided to petition aid from Hunyadi, the leader of the Hungarian Army and the very same person who had ousted Vlad from his post in Walachia.

This seemingly reckless choice was a calculated gamble by Vlad.

Vladislav II had regained his standing following Vlad's deposition, yet he was currently suffering under the thumb of the Ottoman Empire. The situation was also impacting the boyars—a fact Vlad had learned from Bogdan II. Although Vladislav II had been appointed voivode of Walachia at the behest of the Kingdom of Hungary, the relationship between the two nations had become estranged.

Vlad assumed the Kingdom of Hungary was highly discontent with this situation. He had an intimate knowledge of the Ottoman Empire, so Vlad reasoned that if he appealed to Hungary, he could leverage Hunyadi's thirst for information. He might suffer a humiliation or two along the way, but Hunyadi surely wouldn't kill him so long as he could provide what he needed. Vlad would gladly tell Hunyadi what he wanted to know about the empire. He was sick of life at the mercy of the major powers, so now, it was his turn to use them. With Hungary guarding his back, he would take back the position of voivode of Walachia with his own two hands.

Vlad left Moldavia with his cousin Stephen and headed straight for Transylvania. There was no one he trusted more, and this incident would spark a lifelong bond between Vlad and Stephen, the future voivode of Moldavia.

Just as Vlad had expected, Hunyadi welcomed them with open arms. He didn't force them into servitude or abuse them in any way but instead taught this brave boy of sixteen about the Hungarian Army. He had Vlad accompany him into battle and experience real war. Such actions were Hunyadi's tacit declaration of his intent for Vlad to work on behalf of Hungary in the fight against the Ottoman Empire. That is to say, he trusted Vlad as his comrade in arms.

The depth of Hunyadi's trust impressed Vlad. Murad II had been the same way. Truly great rulers generously gave their help to those they trusted, all the while devising ruthless strategies on the world stage.

Vlad thus learned about the politics and militaries of two great nations—knowledge that helped him develop an unyielding sense of self-confidence.

Filled with pride, Vlad came to think that small countries didn't always need to succumb to larger ones. Someday, he would ensure Walachia's liberation from the suzerainty of the Ottoman Empire. That was his duty as voivode.

In 1456, at twenty-four years of age, Vlad regained his position as Vlad III, voivode of Walachia, having gained Hungary's protection through Hunyadi.

The return of this young man with ties to both the Ottoman Empire and Hungary pleased the boyars of the Walachian council. Not to mention, he was only a naive boy in his twenties. They relished the thought of how easily it would be to control him.

The Ottoman envoy pointedly reminded Vlad that he would still need to present tribute and customary gifts to the empire as before, and the voivode obediently agreed. The envoy returned home and recommended that the sultan wait and see how the Walachia situation developed.

However, Vlad wasn't as meek as those around him had assumed. This young man—who'd been tossed around by the great powers, lived fearing for his life in exile, and amassed a wealth of knowledge from his various benefactors—had finally been given an opportunity to spread his wings. No one yet realized that those wings had grown as large as a bird of prey's or a dragon's, tipped with claws sharp enough to rip and tear his enemies to pieces.

Vlad began by purging himself of the boyars who meddled with his government.

His father and brother had both been killed the year before his first reign. Rumors at the time linked the murders to Hunyadi, but having come to know the man personally during his years of exile, Vlad reasoned that he hadn't conceived the plot to assassinate them. The Walachian boyars were those most affected by any issues related to the voivode, so they raised the most suspicion. Vlad needed to crush them and rid himself of the main culprits of his family's murder.

He rooted out the boyars involved in the illicit trade of agricultural products and other goods, arresting them and sentencing each one to death by impalement. This punishment was typically reserved for theft or other similar crimes, so dealing with the culprits in this way incensed the boyars, who became openly hostile toward Vlad.

The relationship between Walachia's voivode and boyars originally served as a way to avoid internal conflict involving succession of the ruler. The system of having many aristocratic families swear fealty to a single voivode had been created to benefit society and enable the voivode to protect the nobility. So long as that balance remained intact, the stability of the country would be maintained.

However, when the aristocrats used this system to secretly amass power and exploit farmers and merchants, the nation was thrown into turmoil and political corruption spread. Vlad intended to rectify this cycle of depravity.

First, he assigned people from lesser aristocratic families despised by the more powerful ones to fill the vacant positions left by the executed boyars. He chose his appointees carefully, selecting retainers for their wise judgment regardless of stature. Naturally, these lower families were grateful to Vlad and became reliable allies.

Next, he restructured the military, creating a standing army controlled directly by the government.

Until then, the Walachian army had relied solely on traditional knights drawn from the retainers of the great aristocratic houses. Their allegiance was first and foremost to the boyars, resulting in an army that could turn on the government at the whim of its masters.

Vlad now commanded an army to resist this threat. He began to recruit powerful fighters—a call that was answered by the likes of talented mercenaries and farmers who still remembered how to wield a blade. They didn't carry the blood of knights, but they were bold and tenacious men with experience on the field of war. Vlad selected the best of the group to create his own personal guard who served to protect him from assassination. His father, brother, and uncle had all been murdered, so it was highly likely that he might suffer a similar fate. He wanted to do everything he could to separate himself from that possibility.

Death would not take him until Walachia grew stronger.

Until he could announce far and wide that no major power would control them.

Until they gained independence and became a powerful nation envied by all the world.

Vlad decisively handled domestic problems that would give any normal person pause, tackling them with unbridled faith in his homeland.

When the Black Death swept through the region, he burned any infected village to ashes, corpses and all, to ensure the disease wouldn't spread. In the wake of these actions, people began to slander Vlad, saying that he enjoyed burning poor peasants alive, but it didn't bother him in the least. He needed to eradicate the disease in order to rebuild the nation and make it stronger.

He didn't mind being called a ruthless tyrant.

Because everything he did, he did for his country.

1462. Six years after Vlad's reinstatement as voivode.

The Ottoman Empire raised the tribute demanded of Walachia to ten thousand gold ducats, which Vlad used as an opportunity to refuse payment for the first time. It was a direct challenge to the Ottoman Empire.

Eleven years earlier, Mudan II had been succeeded by Mehmed II as sultan of the Ottoman Empire. Irritated at the impudence of the "backwater boy" voivode, the new sultan promptly sent an army of elite soldiers to Walachia. Armed with swords and spears and protected by tough armor, these imperial soldiers quickly made their way through the vassal state of Bulgaria and crossed the Danube to attack Walachian land.

Walachia had entered into a full-scale war, but with the superior number and quality of the Ottoman soldiers, they couldn't hope to beat them head-on.

Vlad purposely let the imperial army penetrate deep into his lands, then used the forests and mountains to launch repeated surprise attacks and nighttime raids. He evacuated his people to the mountains and torched the empty towns to ensure the imperial army couldn't raid them for food. The nerves of the imperial soldiers frayed in this unfamiliar land as lack of food and water caused their bodies and minds to deteriorate. Meanwhile, the Walachian army hid in the forests, striking from where their enemy couldn't see and purposely attacking while their opponent slept. After harrying them for a while, the army would retreat to the overrun forests and mountains where the imperial soldiers couldn't pursue them.

The Ottomans began to steal food from one another, disobey orders while blaming the ineptitude of their commanding officers, and flee from battle in great numbers. Eventually, one particular rumor started to spread among their ranks:

"Demonic warriors fight with the Walachian army—a ferocious father and son as wicked as Voivode Vlad himself."

The pair they referred to were the captain of Vlad's personal guard, Razvan, a hero who'd fought in many battles, and his eighteen-year-old son George.

Both had gained their positions through promotions from Vlad and so were fiercely loyal to the voivode. Within the small territory they held, the two were revered by the people as the kindest of souls. Yet when they set foot on the battlefield, they transformed into wild warriors who slaughtered their enemies without mercy.

They commanded their troops from atop their beloved horses, assaulting the imperial army like a tempest. Upon seeing them, the Ottoman soldiers would cower in fear, as if they'd encountered the devil himself. Even the pair's horses seemed ferocious as they mercilessly trampled enemy soldiers and cried out like monsters.

Razvan and his son swung their swords, cutting through the enemy ranks, slashing and stabbing, sending heads flying. The gushing blood painted the surrounding area red. Not even the imperial commander could escape their assault. They cut him down and thrust a spear through his throat before he even had the chance to beg for his life.

Watching Razvan and his son fight, the Walachian soldiers rejoiced in having these Gods of war on their side. While the pair showed their enemies no mercy, they paid careful attention to their allies. They understood the hardships of the lower classes and always showed them kindness, even on the battlefield. They protected fellow soldiers or wounded men who fell behind and led charges from the front of the line. When the soldiers' resolve wavered at the state of the war, father and son would rouse their spirits with impassioned speeches or calm them with logical explanations. They commanded their forces with quick judgments and swift actions, and their soldiers followed them with admiration. Razvan and George were closer and more important to them than Vlad.

Knowing that the Ottoman army was suffering, Vlad struck an additional blow to their morale.

He mobilized a large group of men and marched to a field several miles from Târgoviște, where he impaled twenty thousand imperial soldiers sentenced to death.

When the Ottoman soldiers came to the field and were greeted by this sudden sight, they froze in terror, as if staring into the eyes of a monstrous beast. Row after row of their fellow soldiers' impaled corpses lined the field, covering an area one thousand yards long and almost three thousand yards wide. The stench was horrendous. Flies swarmed, and maggots writhed. The shrill cries of birds pecking at the bodies rose in the air. With some corpses, the stakes pierced their torsos, making them look like food left on twigs by butcher birds. Others had been impaled through the anus, the tips sprouting from their mouths, shoulders, or backs. Groups of crows pecked at eyeballs and decaying flesh, and intestines poured from gutted stomachs like tattered string. Other corpses were torn like filthy rags, hanging half off the spears. Death by impalement wasn't unique to Walachia; it was also a common punishment in the Ottoman Empire. However, no one had ever seen so many people similarly executed at one time. The sight was more than the hearts of those battle-weary soldiers could bear.

Every soldier turned pale and slumped to the ground, vomiting bile.

It wasn't long before the empire began to call the voivode by a new name: Vlad the Impaler. Before they started the campaign, they had derided Vlad as the naive ruler of a backwater principality. After entering Walachian territory, they had despised him as a cruel despot who resorted to petty tricks. Now, their hatred swelled to contempt at his unforgivable actions, and they quickly lost their remaining strength. The cries of disgust at Vlad's cruelty spread throughout the imperial army like wildfire.

Vlad continued to fight bravely, backed by adherents and supporters both within Walachia and abroad. Rumors began to spread that Vlad might even push into Ottoman territory, but the Walachian boyars that had been the target of Vlad's cruel treatment began to side with the Ottoman Empire and interfere with the Walachian army. Radu, Vlad's younger brother, was even involved in these actions.

The tide of the war turned.

Though they fought tenaciously, Vlad's troops began to find victory unattainable as the Ottoman Empire pushed them back.

Realizing that all seemed lost, Vlad decided to temporarily flee the principality for Transylvania. He was seized under the orders of Matthias I, king of Hungary, and incarcerated.

In a cruel twist of fate, Matthias I was the second son of János Hunyadi, whom Vlad had such respect for.

Hunyadi had succumbed to illness many years before. Vlad gave a wry smile, thankful that Hunyadi wasn't around to see him in his current state. Even after the man had dedicated so much to educate him, Vlad hadn't been able to contain the power of the boyars. Yet he only had the one life, so all he could do was keep fighting for as long as he could.

Vlad's imprisonment lasted twelve years.

Throughout that time, his hatred toward the Ottoman Empire never faded.

He disagreed vehemently with anyone who claimed that small nations could survive only through submission to larger countries, that they shouldn't fight back regardless of their opponent, and that they were fated to simply bow their heads and offer tribute.

Even for a small nation, no one but the citizens should be involved in how it's governed.

The aristocrats and government officials in Walachia who offered such murky promises as "one day" and "for now" did nothing more than enslave themselves to a more powerful nation. Their conspiracies crushed those who resisted in the name of justice. That wasn't the way to run a country. They would reform the government, train a proper army, and work for the enrichment of everyone, not just the wealthy. Only then would it be a proper nation. Vlad would make that a reality.

No matter how treacherous the path seemed, no matter how many cursed his name, he would give everything he had to save his motherland.

1476. With the help of Stephen, the voivode of Moldavia, Vlad took back the title of voivode of Walachia for a second time. And this time, he did it without choosing to submit to the empire.

Once more, he gathered his armies and set out for a final confrontation with the Ottoman Empire.

Mehmed II had grown weary of Walachia's stubbornness and waited patiently in the capital for good news. He no longer hated or despised Vlad but simply pitied him, recognizing his actions as those of a zealot. He had spared Vlad in the last battle and not subjected Walachia to his suzerainty, only making them promise to provide tribute and gifts. He had forgiven everything. So why was this man turning his sword against them? If he had just come under the protection of the more powerful country and done as they required, his small nation would open the way to peace. If Vlad didn't understand that, then so be it. He would entertain the man's desire to fight and wipe him from the face of the earth.

The prospect of facing the imperial army imbued the Walachian soldiers with a nervous energy they hadn't felt for many years, but their enthusiasm lacked the same passion—the same spark it had before. Many of the boyars had sided with the Ottoman Empire when Vlad had been deposed and didn't want to lose their current positions of power.

A few people rallied around Vlad to protect him.

Among them were Razvan and his son.

The twelve years had aged Razvan considerably, but he hadn't lost his skill as a commander.

His son George was now thirty-two years old, with a wife and daughter at home.

Even with so few allies, George decided to fight for Vlad. One thing, however, tugged at his conscience: Vlad's conversion to Catholicism.

Before returning to Walachia, Vlad had followed Hungary's lead and sought the support of the Catholic Church as part of his anti-Ottoman strategy. For that, he had abandoned Walachia's Eastern Orthodox Church and converted to Catholicism.

This affront to the Walachian people caused many to lose faith in him. Aristocrats and commoners alike scorned the decision. Discarding the religion he had followed until then amounted to a betrayal on both an emotional and societal level. Vlad couldn't defend himself if accused that he no longer saw Walachians as his people.

While they were preparing for war, George visited the voivode on behalf of his father to ascertain Vlad's true intentions behind his conversion of faith. Had Razvan gone, depending on how the conversation went, there was a chance he would have openly expressed opposition to the voivode's decision. So he sent his son George instead.

Razvan had assumed that having his son talk to Vlad instead of him would minimize the ramifications of any missteps, but George still felt incredibly nervous. The slightest lapse in concentration could endanger his life, even as a trusted and long-standing retainer of the voivode. Recently, Vlad wouldn't hesitate to execute anyone when his anger got the better of him. He had wrapped himself in too many conspiracies. His life was filled with assassinations and treachery, and even though he'd surrounded himself with only those he thought he could trust, his own brother had betrayed him. It wouldn't be unusual if Vlad was suspicious of everyone by now. George hadn't known if the voivode's whims would result in his or his father's impalement.

Yet even so, he had to act.

George hoped to find something, no matter how small, that would help them continue the fight. If he didn't know the voivode's true intentions, then he couldn't lead his troops as effectively.

Vlad immediately granted his request for an audience. He expected much from Razvan and his son and eagerly wanted to hear reports on troop numbers, equipment, and the specifics of their strategies.

This allowed George the opportunity to converse with Vlad in private. Pointing at a map spread out on the table, he suggested various methods for their meager forces to harry the Ottoman army.

Purely in terms of tactics, Walachia had won the last war. Had they not been betrayed, they likely would have been able to drive the Ottoman Empire out of their lands. Stopping the fighting there had been a major mistake. They couldn't employ the same tactics again, and the imperial army would surely advance carefully this time. Even if they ambushed the invaders as they had previously, there was a good chance that the Ottomans would repel them.

George felt that they had to quickly eliminate the enemy commander early on while minimizing losses to the main troops. The longer the fighting went on, the harder it would be for Walachia. They would form an elite assassination squad, which, while their main force made a show of fighting a regular field encounter, would approach by a different route and launch a surprise attack on the commander's location. They would only get the one chance.

George informed Vlad that he intended to lead the squad. His father would draw out the enemy while the younger George led a group of soldiers with high stamina to carry out the plan.

When Vlad asked George what he thought their chances of success were, the young man admitted honestly that they were very low. "However," he added, "considering the difference in the strength between our forces, if this doesn't succeed, then any other fighting is pointless. As it stands now, no other nations around Walachia have shown any indication of helping. The only other option would be to ask Pope Sixtus IV to send troops."

George silently met Vlad's gaze. At times like this, showing any sort of nervous attitude would evoke the voivode's distrust. Even if he had to be a little blunt, he felt it best to speak honestly and wanted the voivode to drop all pretense with him when it came to military matters.

Vlad immediately understood the meaning behind George's words. "You're expecting me to force the pope to take action," he said in a low voice.

"Yes, my liege. I believe that was the reason for your conversion."

Vlad's eyes narrowed slightly.

George continued without pause. "We should use the Catholic Church to beat the Ottoman Empire. If that allows us to win, my liege, then I will have no objections whatsoever regarding your religion. My duty is to serve you to the best of my ability, no matter where that path may take me."

George hoped that Vlad would find it easier to speak openly now. He waited to hear what the man would say.

"...The reason I converted," Vlad said with surprising composure, "was because I wanted to create a blood tie with Hungary and strengthen our relationship with them. Matthias I, who took care of me during my incarceration, has a younger sister. By marrying her, I forged a bond with Hungary's ruling house. She's Catholic, though, so I had to disavow my Eastern Orthodox faith."

George's eyes dimmed. "And your wife, is she in Walachia now?"

"No, I left her at Visegrád in Hungary. The marriage was just for show; she'll not be involved in any affairs of mine. However, as a result, I now have the Holy Roman army at my disposal."

"How long until reinforcements arrive?"

"That will depend on the pope. He certainly won't want the Ottoman Empire to take over Walachia, but he did lose to the imperial army at the siege of Smyrna, so he may be wary. However, if Walachia falls, the Ottoman army will advance into Transylvania."

Vlad gently ran his index finger over the map. "And if they do that, they can then drive their daggers into Hungary's throat. So it's hard to imagine the church will choose not to act."

George breathed a sigh of relief.

The voivode was indeed a calculating man.

He was using the church as a pawn to help him win his war, his conversion nothing more than treating God as a tool to employ. For that, he truly deserved to be called the devil by his enemies. Although he had converted to Catholicism, once peace returned, he could also disavow his religion again and return to the Eastern Orthodox Church. The Orthodox priests might make a face as if they were being forced to swallow a bitter pill, but they wouldn't be able to stop Vlad if that was what he wanted. If the voivode insisted he needed to return to the fold so that people would follow him, the priests would have no choice but to go along with it. After all, he was Walachia's greatest hero. No one would stand against him.

And yet, George also feared Vlad's recklessness actions. Had this war looked to be in their favor or on even terms, he probably wouldn't have sprung this trap.

The situation in Walachia was more precarious than he'd imagined.

Vlad looked up from the map and stared straight at George with a terrible smile.

"Whichever way this war goes, you'd best not betray me, George."

"I would never."

"Tell your father the same."

"Yes, my liege."

"I pray that your men never attack my camp."

"Never. Such a thing is unthinkable."

Just then, George felt a strange tingling down his neck and casually looked around.

They should have been alone in the room, but he'd suddenly sensed a presence and caught the scent given off by a person in a state of stress. Was there an armed guard waiting behind the thick curtains by the window, or inside one of the armoires against the wall, or in a hidden room next door?

The voivode could have arranged to have someone rush in to kill George if he acted suspiciously or went against Vlad's commands. If he sold the information he'd learned here to the enemy, the Walachian army would be crushed overnight.

It was understandable that Vlad was suspicious, but it pained George that the man didn't trust him, as George had had only ever spoken to him with sincerity. He knew that the voivode hadn't been born so mistrusting, but that his paranoia was a result of being constantly surrounded by such awful political machinations. Yet even then, it troubled him.

A voivode should be more generous and open-minded.

He should be adored by his people and love them back. That was how a healthy government should truly work…

How deeply Vlad must have yearned for a respectable government like that.

Yet he would never see it happen.

Even if peace did come to this land, the voivode would die doubting all those around him. Still ardently believing that if he didn't, he wouldn't be able to protect the country or its people.

"Give your blood and your life for Walachia," Vlad declared proudly. "That is the duty of you and your father. I will not permit you any other life but that."

As soon as he returned home, George reported to his father.

Razvan sensed how terrified George was, having witnessed Vlad's ferocity firsthand. "You should escape if you're worried," he said gently, consoling his son. "I'm already old. I'm not afraid to die protecting our lord. But you have so much of your life ahead of you. You wouldn't want Elyne to become a widow and Matea to grow up without her father, would you?"

"I won't run. I'll fight beside you until the end. Elyne knows what it means to be the wife of a warrior."

"This will be a tough battle. You understand that?"

"I do."

"You can choose to survive and keep fighting for the restoration of our motherland. No matter what happens, don't forget that. Remember my words in your time of need."

Father and son shared a long embrace, then prayed to God for success in battle.

After saying goodbye to his father, George went to his bedroom and told his wife Elyne to get their daughter Matea and flee to Transylvania before the fighting with the Ottomans began.

Elyne told George that she wanted to stay. Even she could see that this battle was going to be incredibly hard-fought, but Elyne felt that if she was going to die, she wanted to die in her homeland with her husband.

George wouldn't allow it. "You have to raise Matea," he said. "That is how the blood of Walachia lives on. *That* is the best way for us to fight."

Persuaded by her husband, Elyne reluctantly left Walachia. She went to stay with an old family friend of Razvan's, Andrássy Csaba, and his wife Petra, aristocrats living in Transylvania. There, she and her daughter would be safely hidden.

The Csaba family gave them a warm welcome in Transylvania, and several days after recovering from the fatigue of the journey, Elyne entrusted Matea to the couple and set off for Walachia with a single attendant.

She couldn't bear to abandon her husband.

The attendant Elyne took with her was a conjurer who'd been with her ever since her marriage to George. They had no name but told Elyne to call them Tutore—"protector" in the language of her homeland.

The conjurer hardly ever showed themself to anyone except Elyne. There was no doubt as to their existence in the world, however, having given Matea herbs to cure a fever during the long trip and prepared gifts to the Csaba family.

The conjurer appeared to Elyne as both male and female. They looked old at times, young at others, and had many different guises, from a frail old lady who was nothing but skin and bones like Baba Yaga, to a refined gentleman. They even took the form of a child to play with Matea. Though their appearance changed, the conjurer's personality and mannerisms always stayed the same.

By the time the conjurer guided Elyne back to Walachia, Vlad's army was already retreating.

No one had made it through the battle unscathed. The soldiers fell as they fled, their energy depleted, yet still they were forced to fight off the Ottomans, who had circled around the Walachian army and ambushed them. Razvan bravely wielded his sword and spear to the last, but a group of enemies surrounded him and released a hail of arrows that snatched his final breath. The soldiers of the empire ridiculed him, calling him a porcupine, before severing his head, stuffing it into a leather satchel, and taking it back to camp.

Elsewhere, a heavily wounded George continued to fight as he fell back. His plan to assassinate the enemy commander had come one step short of success before he was forced to retreat to protect his own soldiers.

George swayed on his horse, lacking even the energy to remove the arrow stuck in his back. Forcing his mind back from the brink of unconsciousness, he commanded his troops in the hope of saving as many men as possible. Although he didn't know what had happened to his father, when George heard the far-off victory cry of the approaching imperial army, an uncontrollable stream of tears poured down his face. That cheer told him of his father's passing. Whatever his ultimate fate had been, George knew he had died valiantly like a warrior. Others might make light of Razvan's death, but never his son. *Never.*

The weariness in his soul reached a breaking point.

Overcome with the all-encompassing desire to sleep, he almost fell from his horse on numerous occasions.

Visions burst forth like phantoms, not of his current predicament, but of memories past.

Images of enemy soldiers who, on Vlad's orders, had been left exposed in that field flickered behind his eyelids. It would be his turn now. George didn't want to be impaled while he was still alive. If that was to be his fate, he wanted it to happen after he was dead. Once he died, it didn't matter what they did to him. His soul would leave his body and, with a bittersweet smile, gaze upon the ridiculous sight of his exposed corpse as it ascended the stairs to heaven. There, his father and fallen comrades would be waiting for him.

He had no regrets in life. They'd fought enough. All the blood that had been spilled would, one day, form the foundation for the liberation of his homeland from the empire.

After finally managing to escape from the enemy and secure a place for his remaining troops to set up camp, George was carried into a tent, his condition grave. It was there that Elyne raced to find him. Looking at her husband's deathly pale face, she broke into tears, assuming the worst.

The officers consoled Elyne and told her that now the Walachian army had been annihilated, the war would soon end.

"It was doomed from the start. If both Razvan and George die, the soldiers' spirits will crumble. Some men have already fled. But that's fine;

there's no need for everyone to share our fate. We plan on making one final assault. We're going to assemble all the men and attack, but please, ma'am, don't worry over us."

The officers gave her reassuring smiles, then bowed low to Elyne.

"You should leave here before the next attack. And promise that someday you will see Walachia restored."

Elyne nodded wordlessly.

It didn't matter if they lost. Considering the long-standing conflicts with the neighboring nations, it was probably inevitable that Vlad and these brave men had gone to war. But even now, they must be satisfied with their efforts. Walachia would become a vassal state like Serbia, and the Ottoman sultan would behave even more arrogantly than he had before. But no matter how cruelly the sultan treated them, the people of Walachia would never forget the blood that had been spilled for their nation. The men who had given their lives for the motherland would forever be remembered as heroes, filling the Walachian people with pride to have that blood flowing through their veins.

As she gazed at George lying inside the tent, Elyne could no longer suppress the emotions welling up inside her.

It was time for Elyne, as his wife, to quietly watch him leave this earth.

Time for her to give up on everything.

Yet the more she let herself succumb to despair, the more intensely she felt the urge to help her husband.

She had served him faithfully as the wife of a soldier, with a strong faith and an endless devotion to God's teachings. Every human must die at some point, and defying that fate was the devil's work. She understood that well.

But even so, the desire for her husband not to die toyed with her heart.

Elyne turned to the conjurer standing by her side and asked if there was any way to save her husband's life.

The conjurer replied that no normal way could do so.

Then what were the *abnormal* ways?

"Powerful magic," the conjurer replied. "Not the kind I use for healing, but an extremely potent spell of a different type entirely. However, it comes with risks, and it requires a sacrifice."

"What do I need to offer? Chests of gold? Land with a spring?"

"My freedom will suffice."

"Your freedom?"

"I have served you for a long time, my lady, but I think the time has come to end this arrangement. Once I have finished treating Master George, release me from my duty to protect you. Promise me that, and I shall do everything in my power to save him."

It was such a pure, simple request that Elyne felt moved, and she agreed.

"Very well, I shall begin my preparations," the conjurer said, then left.

Elyne waited in the tent for them to return.

The conjurer returned close to an hour later. "Voivode Vlad has just passed," they announced with a grave expression.

"What?"

"The boyars of Walachia have betrayed him again. They plotted to have the enemy surround Vlad and kill him without mercy. What a shame. He was still so young, only forty-five."

"What were his last words?"

"'I did what had to be done. Someday, the world will see that.'"

"And the Catholic Church? Did they not send any reinforcements?"

"No. Not one."

"Despicable. The voivode even converted to their faith."

"They saw through to the political intentions behind his conversion, so they didn't trust him. The voivode was a little too hasty. Or perhaps he did it knowing full well that, in the worst-case scenario, this would happen. He saw his own life as a resource to be used for his homeland."

"What happened to his body?"

"The corpse was decapitated. They took just his head, most likely to display publicly in Istanbul. The horrors of humanity truly know no bounds."

Elyne covered her mouth with both hands at the horrific ending that had befallen the voivode. She swayed, unsteady on her feet, and the conjurer caught her. "Settle yourself," they whispered in her ear. "This opportunity has allowed me to make the most powerful of restorative elixirs." A small glass bottle glittered in the conjurer's palm. "This concoction contains the blood of Voivode Vlad himself. There is no more potent an elixir."

"The voivode's blood?"

"Yes. I obtained a small quantity when they removed his head."

"How did you manage that?"

"I am a conjurer. People think nothing of me wherever I go."

"Or perhaps you betrayed our lord, too. Maybe you wanted his blood so badly that you arranged for him to fall into their hands. If that is how you got it, then I will never use it."

"My lady, you are a wise and well-educated woman. Yet how much of your knowledge involves matters of magic? None, I assume. Magic is a skill used by commoners, not something employed by the upper classes. But some wishes in this world can only be granted by the skills of such people. Who transforms cows and pigs into luxurious meals? Or tidies and cleans to make manors comfortable? Everyone works behind the scenes to serve others; conjurers are no different."

Elyne gripped the bottle of elixir. She was aware that she didn't know all the workings of this world. She'd never soiled her hands with the dirty jobs of the common people. Once she began questioning things, there would be no end to it.

"Will my husband really get better if he drinks this?" she asked.

"You know of Vlad's vitality. He possessed an extraordinarily strong life force, so restorative medicine made from his blood is of the highest quality. However, it is rare to obtain the blood of someone so exalted. Such people do not generally allow it—unless, that it, they are cut down by a sword or beheaded."

Elyne held the bottle of elixir, her body tense, and the conjurer put their hands over hers.

"Hurry up, now. George will die soon. Do you want that to happen?"

Hearing those words, Elyne felt a flurry deep within her chest.

She knelt down by her husband's side.

The conjurer supported George's torso, holding his head so he could easily drink the elixir.

Elyne removed the lid from the bottle and, little by little, she poured the crimson liquid down her husband's throat until not a drop remained.

The conjurer set George back down again. "Now we wait," they said. "However, we should hurry away from here as soon as possible. Even with Vlad dead, the officers won't surrender. They will happily fight and die for their honor. We cannot get wrapped up in such foolishness. Requisition a few soldiers as guards and return to the Csaba villa in Transylvania."

The magic soon proved to be real. En route to Transylvania, George opened his eyes, then gradually recovered his strength. His pale face regained its color, and his scars disappeared. Seeing what looked for all the world to be an act of God—but knowing it was nothing of the sort—Elyne trembled as a dark feeling overcame her.

When she told George of Vlad's demise, he muttered, "I will not give up. I promised my father. I shall live to see Walachia reborn. Our lord and the soldiers who died would surely wish for that. Will you help me?"

"Yes. Gladly."

Andrássy Csaba of Transylvania welcomed George's procession for a second time. Although they had already received word of the outcome of the war, the Csabas' attitude toward George and his retinue didn't change in the slightest. Now that Walachia was part of the Ottoman Empire, it was entirely possible that Transylvania would also become a vassal state, so the surrounding nations had to maintain a united front and devise ways to resist the Ottomans.

Andrássy asked George to work for him. The villa had enough room to house George and his wife, and Andrássy implored him to stay there, train the Transylvanian troops, and exchange information with Hungary. The scions of the Csaba family had all been killed in past wars, so to Andrássy, George wasn't just family left behind by a close friend, but like a newfound son. To George, the offer was more than he ever could have asked for. He immediately agreed and, beginning the next day, met with Andrássy's retainers and attended meetings where they planned how to resist the Ottoman Empire.

George was still young and had an air of vitality that immediately drew the people of Transylvania to him. He would tie his long hair back and stride through the region in the clothes of a foreign nation, treating each and every person with kindness and impressing them all by being able to retain his pride after the loss of his homeland. Even the veteran Hungarian generals felt inspired the moment they saw George, firmly shaking his hand and passionately declaring that, together, they would fight against Ottoman rule and drive them off.

"As you wish," George would reply, leaning in close to these weathered generals. He would let out a whisper like an exhaled breath, captivating the men. "I look forward to your support, both in public and private matters."

While Elyne felt great relief at the esteem everyone bestowed upon her husband, one aspect of it troubled her. When they looked into George's eyes—the color of a forest enveloped in thick fog—they would open their hearts and swear fealty to him. It was as if George had cast a spell on them. Vlad had possessed the same quality: that innate elegance and grace, so intimidating it frightened enemies and emboldened allies. It seemed this quality had intensified in her husband as he aged. Or perhaps the harshness of war had changed him.

There was a vitality to George that would fool anyone into thinking he'd not just been on the verge of death. He spoke with soldiers and statesmen, visited people to learn new information, and smiled cheerfully at nighttime banquets.

At such events, he sat not only with lords and warriors, but also with their wives and other young women who had just emerged onto the social scene. Everyone approached George, seeking to speak with him. As his wife, Elyne treated them all with courtesy.

However, on multiple occasions during these gatherings, she also saw her husband conversing intimately with female guests in the shadows of the gardens. And sometimes, she spied him using the darkness as his ally to conduct secret trysts.

Elyne was less shocked by the sight than drawn in by the mysterious atmosphere that surrounded it. The actions of her husband and those women appeared as beautiful as the work of a famous painter and, for some unknown reason, felt completely natural. And when George returned to their room following such meetings, he would ravish Elyne with the same—no, *more* passion, so she couldn't complain.

Only one person, their daughter, Matea, began to avoid George. She turned those cold eyes on Elyne, as well. George continued to treat his daughter with the same unwavering kindness he always had, but Matea wouldn't respond to him and started spending more and more time away from the villa. Rumor had it that she spent her days playing with a local shepherd. People knew him as a hardworking, sensible boy, so Elyne gave him some coins to keep Matea safe. The shepherd immediately understood the meaning behind the money and, from that day forth, ceased being Matea's friend and took up the role of her protector.

A few years later, Matea developed a close friendship with a troop of traveling minstrels passing through the area. Disguising herself as a peasant, she hid herself among them and disappeared from Transylvania. The distraught Elyne wanted to send people to bring her back, but George rebuked her, telling her to abandon the idea.

"Matea saw me for what I am," he said listlessly. "We shouldn't drag her back against her will. I'm sure she'll find happiness for herself, so it's best we let her go."

"You're the one who told me to raise her well for the sake of Walachia. Will she really be happy marrying some nobody and raising his children?"

"We have no way of knowing that she'll marry one of the minstrels or if she'll ever have children. She's smart. She probably has all sorts of surprising talents. We should let her do as she pleases. We have no roots until Walachia is freed from Ottoman rule, anyway, so there's very little we can do."

That evening, George made love to Elyne for longer and more passionately than normal, as if to appease her anger. Pleasantly exhausted, Elyne was lulled into a deep sleep, and in her dreams, she met the conjurer for the first time in a long while.

They wore a black coat elegantly embroidered in red and green over tight black pants.

"Are you satisfied with your current life?" the conjurer asked.

"More than satisfied," answered Elyne.

"How is your husband?"

"He has serious discussions with generals and lords daily."

"And with women?"

"He doesn't seem satisfied with just me. I always see him surrounded by beautiful women."

A faint smile rose on the conjurer's face. "You, my lady, are the only person George truly cares for. He engages with others merely for sustenance."

"What do you mean, 'sustenance'?"

"The elixir that courses through his body cannot be satiated with normal food. You would be best to ignore it. He cannot function otherwise."

The conjurer bowed respectfully. "And so, I shall take my leave. You have granted me my freedom as promised, and I shall not appear before you again. Honestly, I can't believe how long I was locked into that contract. It wasn't even you I first signed it with, but your father."

"My father?"

"Yes. He summoned me from the aether to protect you, binding me when you were but an infant. He tricked me into the agreement so I couldn't escape. I cursed my foolishness at the time. But I've had enough of babysitting. I shall return to my original form."

"And what is that?"

"Something that human language cannot describe. Think of me as a spirit—a *pneuma*."

With that, the conjurer vanished like smoke. Only their black coat and pants remained, yet even those eventually faded and crumbled into dust carried away by the wind.

Ten years went by. Twenty. Thirty.

Elyne passed through middle age and became an elderly woman. Finally, she understood why her daughter Matea had run away.

While Elyne had grown old, George hadn't aged a day.

He had always appeared younger than his years. Those men aiming to overthrow the Ottoman Empire were often as rambunctious as young boys, and so she assumed their vitality had rubbed off on her husband.

But George was an extreme case. He wasn't normal. His skin was more supple than the younger Elyne's, unblemished by a single wrinkle or spot, and he'd retained his full head of hair. Matea must have recognized this strangeness herself early on. Frightened at the realization that he wasn't human, she had fled, knowing she couldn't live with a monster.

Assuming George's youth derived from that elixir, Elyne bitterly regretted not drinking some herself. If she had, then she could have stayed young by his side forever. Instead, she would be the only one to grow old as time went by until, one day, when people saw them together, they would think her nothing more than an old maid in the service of a young lord.

She shuddered at the realization.

Perhaps this was the conjurer's revenge. The implication behind what the conjurer had said during their last meeting was that her father had used spirits from the natural world to protect his daughter with magic. He had used that magic to bind Tutore to her. She wasn't sure if he'd known what he was doing or just happened to summon a powerful conjurer.

For the spirit to leave Elyne's service, a certain amount of time had to pass and either Elyne or her father had to give their verbal permission. The spirit had known this and sought a way out. And once it was released, it must have wanted to get a bit of revenge by preventing Elyne from having any of the elixir, knowing that if they both drank it, she and George would stay young forever, together.

Unable to stay silent on the matter, she spoke about it with George.

"So you noticed," George murmured in despair. "The time is soon approaching for the two of us to leave this villa and find someplace else to live. I bought a manor on the border with Hungary. Let's move there. I intend to stay in contact with the various lords of other lands and continue our plans to attack the Ottoman Empire. I already have Andrássy's blessing to leave."

"Then your secret will be kept safe?"

"Of course."

"But the servants will realize."

"Don't worry about that. I won't employ normal humans."

"Who, then? Another conjurer? Spirits?"

"I'll create them myself. I can manipulate the aether to create simulacrums from thin air. I learned the technique from a man I trust."

"When did this happen?"

"You're better off not knowing. I alone will carry the burden of my troubles." George gently drew Elyne close to him. "You are the only one I truly love. No matter how the years age you, I will always stay by your side. Trust me."

In this way, the two of them came to live deep in the forests of northwestern Transylvania, in a place forever covered by mist. A nearby spring provided a steady stream of fresh water, and they didn't have to worry about anyone stumbling upon them.

To anyone's eyes, the servants and maids at the new manor appeared to be ordinary people. They could express normal human reactions and smile cheerfully—but according to George, they were automated puppets imbued with temporary souls. They worked hard and could even do manual labor, so Elyne treated them just like regular servants. Their skin felt warm like that of a human, and she could safely entrust them with any errand, no matter how trivial.

With this manor as his base, George expanded his range of activities. From time to time, he returned to Andrássy's villa to report on the current state of affairs.

Elyne was lonely, but she cherished this peaceful life. No matter how much she aged, her simulacrum servants never let it concern them in the slightest.

Yet even then, if given the opportunity to drink that elixir, Elyne would have done so. However, it required Vlad's blood, which could never be obtained again, so she had no choice but to submit to the whims of time.

Elyne was more determined than she ever had been before, hoping to maintain some of her dignity as she aged.

Older people possess a matured beauty of the accumulated time they've lived, an intelligence that glitters brightly, and a different sort of flexibility from what they had when they were young.

Elyne was determined to take good care of it all.

She didn't just look after her appearance; she also studied and devoted herself to sharpening her mind and had more than enough time to read, so she was never bored. Elyne had the servants keep an eye on the surrounding fields and made preparations to immediately assist with any bad harvests or diseased livestock. She and George didn't supply this help to the area directly, but employed real people they could trust to act on their behalf. George carried out his military affairs covertly, so he didn't want their names to be known even for benevolent acts.

Elyne never involved herself in George's work. Every so often, she would check in with him to make sure her understanding of world affairs was correct—discussions that George happily engaged in. It helped sharpen the theories she learned and gave her the most up-to-date information.

The years continued to pass.

Now old and infirm, Elyne could no longer leave her bed, but George continued to shower her with love. He would always stay with her, talking for as long as she wanted. George explained that because of the elixir, not only did he not age, but he also couldn't die. Having recovered from a lethal state, his body was now immortal.

It shocked Elayne to learn that they wouldn't even share the fate of death, but there was little good her complaining would do her now. She had laughed, thinking that the spirit must enjoy tricking people, and gently run a wrinkled hand over the disheartened George's cheek as he told her.

George had never once blamed her for the results of the elixir. He'd only ever thanked Elyne and told her how grateful he was for saving his life, vowing time and time again that he would always be her husband. Those words and actions comforted her soul. She had taught George that though death may separate them, love would outlast life.

One night, at that time of year when the daffodils are in full bloom, Elyne broke out into a fever and suffered for an entire day.

The next evening, just as she managed to crack her eyes open, a perfectly clear smile rose on her deeply wrinkled face. Her expression shone so brightly that George was at a loss for words.

"Once I am just a soul," she said, "I shall beg God to let me pass between heaven and earth. I'm sorry if you don't see my soul when I visit, but I should be able to see you clearly. So please, forgive me."

"You don't need to worry about me so much," George said, cradling Elyne's cheeks in his hands. "I can take care of myself. I only ask that you let me kiss you one more time."

"Happily. You still treat me like a young lady even though I'm so old."

"Love outlasts life, Elyne."

"Those are my words."

"I know. And it's only meeting you that let me truly understand them."

In Elyne's last moments, George never left her side.

When her soul finally left her body, George cast a protective spell over it. Evil spirits wouldn't impede her journey, allowing Elyne to safely climb the staircase to heaven.

"This is all I can do for you," he murmured. "Good-bye, my love. I hope you're always happy in God's realm, where there's no hatred or war."

George ordered the servants to prepare Elyne's body for burial, wrap it in a white cloth, and place it in a coffin filled with flowers. The whole process would take some time, so he left the manor, alone, to distract himself while he waited.

A full moon shone in the middle of the western sky, and George's body trembled under it, bathed in its light. Unable to withstand the cold that seemed to cut through his body, he fluttered his cloak and transformed into a winged being.

He flew straight up out of the garden looking like a bat—or perhaps a dragon. The moon appeared as if it were right in front of him. George continued flying toward that destination he could never reach, and as he did, formless figures appeared from nowhere, swarming around him in a mockery of his sorrow.

George growled menacingly at the shadows and used his body to knock them out of the air. He swung his arms wide, raking them with his sharp claws. Nothing could stand against his rage. These things that had flocked to George, playfully trying to devour his heart, flew away shrieking and spitting curses.

George collected himself and landed to rest.

He found himself standing in a field in the depths of winter. Breathing heavily, he looked around.

The frozen earth showed no signs of life. It was as if he'd flown all the way to the land of the dead. His breath turned white in the air before melting into the darkness, and the smell of the sky just before snowfall permeated to the back of his nose. He'd been flying for quite a while, but the position of the moon in the sky had hardly changed.

The forest of deciduous yews and their ever-present leaves formed black shapes in the darkness. A pre-snow frost covered the ground.

The reality of his situation finally struck him. The pain in his chest increased, perhaps from breathing in so much cold air. George squeezed his fists tight, lowered his head, and sobbed.

Love outlasts life. It was nothing more than a convenient phrase people told themselves. No matter how deeply you care for someone, what good is love if you can't hold it in your hands? It was no different than a memory. He didn't want a memory—he wanted Elyne.

Just then, he heard someone calling his name from the darkness. George wiped away his tears and raised his head, scanning the area.

"Are you satisfied?"

The voice dripped with a familiar irony.

George focused on one point in the expansive darkness. A man appeared as though materializing from thin air, wrapped in the same long cloak as George.

The man's deathly pale complexion looked even more ghastly in the moonlight. His sleek hair and eyes seemed to melt into the darkness around him, and although a smile graced his thin lips, there was only a faint hint of crimson in them.

"I'm asking if you enjoyed playing your little game of house," the man continued. "But it's about time you came back to your senses."

George furiously grabbed at him, but the man evaded like a wisp of smoke. George hadn't even been able to lay a finger on him.

"I'm grateful to you," George said, his voice shaking. "I had nothing but doubts about my new body, and you taught me magic and how to use it. I was living in anguish, not knowing what to do, and you gave me a new life."

"I appear before all those who call me."

"So we didn't meet by chance? I called you? But I didn't even know your name."

"I instantly recognize the voice of a soul seeking help. Animal, human, it doesn't matter. Cries of anguish are particularly sweet and attract all manner of monsters, just like how you were swarmed now. Humans fear any encounter with a monster, but they're the ones who call them. Regardless, you've learned to control your powers well in such a short period of time. Manipulating the aether, creating simulacrums, and imbuing them with temporary souls—it's almost as if you've been studying under a conjurer since you were young."

"Nil. I know all too well that you're a monster of nothingness. You have no interest whatsoever in the emotions people feel around life and death. After all, humans are born from nothing and to nothing they return. You just watch that cycle from a distance. But I'm different. Even if that elixir means I cannot die, this body still has a human heart—"

"Which will someday vanish," the monster called Nil interjected. "As you live the rest of your days in solitude, the human parts of you will fall away and disappear, one after another. You'll lose your humanity, then your unfeeling monster side will take control. If it didn't happen like that, you would never be able to live for all eternity. The overwhelming sadness would crush you."

"I will not choose to live like that."

"Then how come you didn't let her drink some of your blood? One cup would have been enough. She wouldn't have regained her lost youth, but she would have stopped aging further. Elyne would have remained just as beautiful and been granted eternal life. So why didn't you?"

"You're saying I should have let her experience this torture? This burning will of Voivode Vlad that courses through my veins? Had she drunk my blood and lived forever, she also would have heard his voice whispering in her ear for the rest of her days. His voice commanding her to keep fighting to save the motherland. Those thoughts would consume her night and day. I couldn't let her carry such a burden. It's a voice that only a soldier could endure."

"And what about you? Will you forever follow Vlad's commands?"

"Until Walachia is freed from Ottoman rule."

"And after that?"

"I don't know. Vlad was a deeply mistrusting man. Even after the Ottoman Empire has been driven out, this blood may still worry over Walachia's future. All of Europe is connected. War never ends."

Nil reached out and touched George's cheek. George's body had been chilled by the frigid air—but Nil's fingers were colder. They felt like icicles against his skin. "You have become a monster. Accept it. I can introduce you to many others."

"Don't. I need no such help."

"It might be good to at least get to know them. You don't want them always interfering with you like they did tonight, do you? You may not die, but certain injuries will still cause you to suffer. You could even be beheaded, but you wouldn't die."

"What if someone crushes my head? I can't recover from that, can I?"

"No matter how finely ground your body may be, your blood will flow together, reassemble somewhere, and return you to your original form. Even if those pieces are scattered to the ends of the earth. That is what it means to be immortal."

Shock overcame George, and he gave a frenzied laugh. "I can't believe it. Then all I can do is despair?"

"Despair is a human emotion," Nil continued. "Not one monsters have. That is why I told you to hurry up and become your true monstrous self. If you don't, then it was pointless for me to teach you all that magic. It will be incredibly difficult for you to rid yourself of those human emotions before you chase off the Ottomans completely, however, because doing so will require you to work with humans. You will never fully become a monster so long as you are involved with them. You'll be a monster, but suffer as a human. It would be best to find a compromise somewhere."

The hem of Nil's cloak fluttered, and he melted into the darkness. "I'll check in on you from time to time. If you ever need anything from me, don't hesitate to call."

"You'll come even if I don't."

"I told you earlier. Monsters appear when humans are sad and in turmoil. Such things come across even without words."

1526. Fifty years after the death of Vlad and one year after the death of Elyne.

As a result of Hungary's crushing defeat by the Ottomans at the Battle of Mohács, Transylvania became a semi-independent vassal state of the Ottoman Empire. Following this, the three principalities of Moldavia, Walachia, and Transylvania fell under complete control of the empire for a long time.

Moldavia and Walachia merged into a single principality and regained autonomous rule from the empire in 1861. They eventually seized independence during fighting between the Russian and Ottoman Empires in 1881 and were recognized internationally as the Kingdom of Romania.

Until that time, George moved residences frequently, always working behind the scenes for the independence of his homeland. Each time, he would change his name and appearance.

He finally settled on the name George Silvestri, giving himself the title of count to allow him easier access to the elite of society, government officials, and military personnel.

Moldavia and Walachia had finally gained independence, but Transylvania remained a vassal state. At the start of the Great War, it was still a part of Hungary. When Romania joined the war on the side of the Allies in 1916, they marched troops straight into Transylvania to liberate it from Hungary and take it for the Kingdom of Romania.

However, this invasion incurred horrific losses. The monarchy had deployed barely trained soldiers who lacked proper equipment and charged in using the same tactics they had before the Great War—an attack that could only be described as thoughtless.

George didn't raise a hand to help.

He maintained his position as spectator.

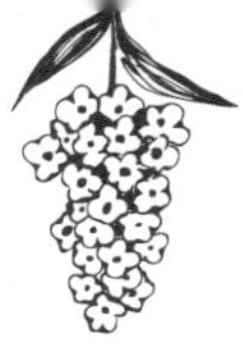

II
Inheritance

It was already bright outside by the time Jörg woke up. He didn't know if he had slept just through the night or for several days.

His body was light, and his head was clear. It felt as if he'd lost one sense but gained a new set of eyes in exchange—eyes that could see a vast host of strange figures.

Monsters filled the Count's room, wandering around and keeping close watch over Jörg. A new monster had been born, so they'd come to satisfy their curiosity.

Some monsters looked human, and some didn't. Some appeared as beasts, or birds, or fish. Some were covered in fur or had two curving horns. Some left trails of wet slime behind wherever they went. Some cackled violently like monstrous birds, or looked at him with dancing eyes that changed color, or were formed of twirling air like wisps of smoke that never took a fixed shape, or had bodies that shimmered like jewels or stars in the night sky. Each one looked satisfied in their own form. They enjoyed their freedom. None seemed to harbor any animosity toward him, but neither did they seem overly friendly. If anything, they seemed to watch him with a kind of sympathy.

Jörg stayed still, not saying anything. It seemed like the smart thing to do.

The Count sat in his chair, reading a letter. He didn't seem to pay any attention to the monsters. When Jörg sat up, the man set the letter on the table and looked toward him.

"I take it you now understand our history. Since ancient times, Europe has seen one group attack another without end. The war between the Ottoman Empire and Walachia was just one example. Smaller countries being absorbed by larger ones, territories whose borders change with every battle—these tragedies repeat themselves indefinitely. That is the natural outcome when countries share the same landmass. Wars do not start from nothing. The long history layered upon this land dictates what shape each era will take. It's meaningless to say that wars only start under certain circumstances; anybody who goes about their everyday life in a time of peace is unknowingly creating the conditions for the next major conflict."

So just by living, we're all shaping the next war?

Jörg released the deep breath he'd been holding in. If that was true, then what hope was there for humanity on this planet?

"Humans are the ones who start wars," continued the Count. "Humans are also the ones who stop them. Everyone has come to believe that. As such, governments and diplomacy have only refined that process. But the Great War is incapable of being stopped, even if people try. This war will not cease so long as nations keep pouring in resources and people from colonies, and as long as they continuously create new weapons to deploy on the front lines, overjoyed to see them succeed. This war doesn't have a clear enemy whose defeat will quickly end the fighting. Do you understand? Right now, you're fighting against that very situation, searching all by yourself for a way to end the war."

"I understand. That's why I asked to be given your blood."

"The blood of Vlad must be urging you on, too. Be careful. His blood will do more than help you; it will consume you with an unbridled passion."

"Is it really that overpowering?"

"It's calmed considerably from what it once was. The Kingdom of Romania gaining independence resolved a large portion of its lingering regrets, but it will burn strongly again given the opportunity. To be honest, I feel it stir with every repeated skirmish in Europe."

"If that's the case, then I'm grateful," Jörg said. "I think I would have given up on my own. I'm just a simple barber; I don't have the perspective needed to lead a nation. But if this blood gives me that… From what I saw, Voivode Vlad didn't seem like a bad person at heart. He may have gotten carried away while he was alive, but as the source of this magic, it feels like he's a little more flexible."

"Do not dismiss Vlad's temperament lightly. He was no ordinary man."

"Isn't there any way to suppress the ferocity of his blood?"

The monsters filling the room all laughed loudly. Jörg heard them repeat how impossible that would be. A voice that sounded like an echo inside a cave said that Vlad's passion was ferocious and unable to be contained by anyone.

The Count frowned, then waved a hand as if he were shooing a fly, ordering the monsters to be quiet. Once they were silent, he addressed Jörg again.

"The best way to suppress Voivode Vlad's blood is to do nothing. Humans are hot-tempered and give in to their passions easily. They march off to war at the drop of a hat. Your best strategy is to devote yourself to a more carefree life. Relax, stay at home, enjoy a dull life of luxury, and you'll be able to soothe Vlad's blood. Go with the flow, like a jellyfish. Now that you're a monster, the worst thing to do would be to dedicate yourself to a cause."

Jörg had thought the Count was a relaxed person by his very nature, so he was more than a little surprised to discover the truth. He thought the man's good upbringing and social class exuded a peculiar listlessness, but the Count was telling him otherwise: It was all a tactic to control the madness inside him.

Living a relaxed, subdued life to hold back the ancient raging blood? That wasn't the lifestyle Jörg had imagined. Thinking about the incredible effort it would require, Jörg felt the chasm between him and the Count shrink ever so slightly. But he held his tongue. Thinking about it from the Count's point of view, he was sure the man wouldn't like being pitied by a servant like Jörg.

Whether or not he knew what Jörg was thinking, the Count continued.

"There is one other important issue. Now that you're a real monster, your body cannot survive on normal food alone. You will have to obtain sustenance from human beings. If you do not, then you won't be able to use your powers."

"How do I do that?"

"Simply by touching them. You can draw sustenance from anyone regardless of sex or age, so take it from whomever you like. After a while, you will be able to absorb it simply by being near your target. You can do the same on the battlefield."

"What do you mean?"

"Once a battle is over, you can sustain yourself on dying soldiers left in no-man's-land."

Jorg pictured it in his mind: In the light of the setting sun, a man encased in a black cloak leans over a fallen soldier like a priest attending to his deathbed. Muttering what sounds like a spell, he takes sustenance from the dying soldier. When the soldier passes on, he searches out someone else, working his way across the expanse. An overabundance of nourishment covers the land like a thick mist that surely must attract other monsters.

"It's like being the God of death," Jörg whispered.

"Yes, in a way."

Jörg stayed silent for a while before saying, "Then do you mind if I go to Paris one more time?"

"Where do you wish to go?"

"The brothel where Bernadette works. It seemed like she wanted to tell me something."

"That would be a fine place to draw sustenance from humans. While you're at it, you should talk to some of the other customers. I assume Allied soldiers will be there."

"Okay. But there's one problem."

"Which is?"

"It costs money, going to a brothel."

"I will lend you some."

"But I don't have any way to pay you back."

"There are many ways for you to repay me. It doesn't have to be money, either; you could continue working as my servant forever."

"No, thank you. I want to live my own life."

Truth be told, Jörg had been worrying about money for a while. Even as a monster, he would need funds to stay connected with human society. He had no idea how the Count made his own money.

"We can work that out later. I take it this means you have enough money that you can lend it out to people?" Jörg asked.

"Of course."

"But you don't work, and you don't own any land. So do you have some sort of ancient, highly pure gold coins or bars?"

The Count nodded. "That, and there have been many extraordinary opportunities for investment in Europe over these hundreds of years. I have made good use of them to increase my fortune to where it is today."

"Do you think I can also learn how to invest?"

"All you need is the will."

"But during war, stocks and bonds—"

"Rise and fall like normal. Perhaps you would like me to buy you some stock in railroads."

"Please. I'd also like to learn how to start a company. I think running a business would be the best way to make money and pay off my debt in full. But I don't know anything about how to do that."

"It's a good idea; however, you should wait until after the war. Your earnings will change dramatically based on which nation you establish yourself in. Countries can fall into a spiral of inflation after a war, which could bankrupt you in an instant. It would be best for you to study business for now, while you wait for the right time."

"I understand."

"It would also be best not to tell Lila that you have become a monster."

"Okay."

"She's a clever girl, so she'll figure it out sooner rather than later, but there's no need for you to tell her now. You can simply explain that you've improved your control of simulacrums."

"She'll hate me once she realizes."

"It doesn't matter if she hates you; you will still protect her. As promised. Speaking of which, what have you decided to do about the intelligence work? Have you come to a decision?"

"I'll do it."

"Which side are you going to help?"

"I'll help both, while also forsaking both."

"Oh?"

"I won't ally with any country. I'm only doing this for my own benefit."

The Count clapped his hands together theatrically. "Wonderful!" he said, sounding delighted. "The words of someone who has become a true monster. *That* is why you are worthy of inheriting my blood."

Part 3

I
The Night Flower

1

Jörg adopted the appearance of Pierre Arche once more, changed his clothes, donned a tie, and headed to Paris through the usual door of Xandra's inn. He didn't need to disguise himself as a wounded soldier this time, so he could move unimpeded.

He passed through the portal and was greeted by the facade of the Comédie-Française. After hailing a taxi, he told the driver to take him to 12 Rue Drucker in the Second Arrondissement. The driver responded amiably, hopping down from his seat and opening the door to the passenger cabin.

When Jörg sat down inside, the driver asked him if he was returning from the war—the same question Nil had also asked him.

"Yeah. My body's all beat up. I'm here to rest my bones."

"How was Verdun? Is it true what they said in the newspapers?"

Jörg winced. "It was worse."

"I thought as much."

"If you don't want to be conscripted by the army, you should leave and go to a neutral country as soon as possible," he told the man. "You can drive a car, so you shouldn't have any trouble finding work wherever you go."

"Thank you, sir. You've given me something to think about."

When the taxi pulled up to the brothel, Jörg paid his fare and a bit extra on top. The driver thanked him and gave him a smile that said he understood what Jörg was getting at and wouldn't say a word to anyone.

Jörg watched the taxi drive away, then looked up at the building. The number twelve shone from a red lantern hanging from the upper part of the building, just as Bernadette had said. It was a plain brick building with dark curtains drawn over every window concealing what went on inside. The lighting restrictions meant that not even a sliver of light slipped outside, and no one stood in the street trying to lure in customers. The place was so quiet that anyone would simply pass by it if they didn't know it was a brothel.

Jörg walked up to the door, rang the bell, and waited for an answer.

He heard the sound of a latch, and the door cracked open. A middle-aged woman appeared in the gap, no doubt the madame of the brothel.

Jörg spoke to her, feigning nervousness. "Someone at a bar on Rue de Rohan told me about your establishment. It's my first time here. May I come in?"

When he mentioned the name of the bar and the owner, the madame smiled affectionately. "Please, come in," she said, opening the door wide.

Thick, floor-length drapes created a screen on the other side of the door, and passing through them, Jörg emerged into a spacious reception room.

The lights were dim, so he couldn't see anyone except the madame. She wore a purple jacket over a blouse covered with fabric embellishments on the collar, all complemented by a long skirt. The madame seemed both warm and rigidly stern, but her gracious manners would assuage the nerves of any first-time customer under her care.

The two of them climbed a staircase to a landing between the first and second floors. A hallway with doors running down both sides led away from the top of the stairs, and the madame guided Jörg to the closest room.

"Pick whichever girl you like," she said. "And as many as you'd like."

"As many—?"

"It's free to look, so take your time."

The door opened, and Jörg gawked at the sight unveiled to him. It appeared for all the world like the greenroom of a theater. The women looked like dancers getting dressed and waiting for their turn to appear onstage—or at least, that was Jörg's impression of it.

There were only ten women in the room, all of them lounging about in lingerie. Their sheer gowns were open from their shoulders to their bosoms, tight bustiers highlighted their curves, and garter belts held up long stockings. They were wearing shoes that made their exposed waists look even more alluring. The scent of powder and perfume tickled his nose. A few women lounged on a sofa and one sat cross-legged in a chair, while others stood in the corner absorbed in conversation. One woman was nodding off peacefully. It seemed even in a profession like this, where work started at night, people got sleepy when the sun went down. So they napped until customers arrived.

The madame called out, and the women turned to look at Jörg. He felt as if a flock of colorful birds had all fixed their gazes on him.

"Come now, go in," the madame told him cheerfully. "Don't be shy."

Jörg nodded and walked slowly down the carpet. He scanned the women as he passed them. Most were around twenty, but some clearly seemed younger than eighteen, while others looked closer to thirty. They had a wide array of hair colors and skin tones, with one woman even appearing to have come from India.

Some cast him disinterested looks, and some proudly stuck out their chests. One girl kept her mouth clamped shut, visibly shaking from fright.

Based on the attention paid to their skin and hair, how plump their bodies were, the quality of their perfume, and the design of the lingerie among other things, this place seemed to be doing good business. After a long while, Jörg finally recognized Bernadette. He hadn't noticed her at first under her thick makeup.

Bernadette was sitting on one side of a love seat, using rollers secured in place with hairpins to curl her hair in cute ringlets—a common style among the women. When Jörg asked her name, she coquettishly replied "Bernadette." She sounded so incredibly different from the impassioned woman he'd heard speak at the Eiffel Tower.

Jörg took Bernadette's hand and turned to the madame. "I'll take her."

She nodded and escorted the pair out of the room.

From there, Bernadette took Jörg to a different room on the same floor.

When the door opened, he saw a salon far larger than the one he'd previously seen. The brightly lit space held sofas and tables populated by men and women. They chatted and drank, and a number of people seemed to be absorbed in some sort of game using tarot cards. Half of the room was partitioned off into smaller areas by curtains, behind which men and women carried out more private engagements. However, the most intimate acts were forbidden here.

Jörg scanned the room, but he didn't see any young men like him—just affluent-looking middle-aged men or older gentlemen with gray hair. They had their arms draped around the women, who pressed their chests up against the men and whispered softly in their ears.

Based on the quality of the customers and the women, it might almost be called a normal salon gathering—so long as you didn't imagine the events to come. Here, men and women could enjoy each other's company, work up their excitement, then retire to the second floor if they came to a mutual understanding. Bernadette told him it was perfectly fine to end things here if he didn't feel like taking things any further. Judging by the bottles of liquor lined up on the tables, the salon seemed to bring in very good money for the brothel.

They settled into a sofa, and Bernadette ordered mint liqueur and champagne from the waitress. The madame came up to the pair, chatted briefly with Jörg, and sat in a nearby seat.

They didn't have to wait long before the waitress returned with the glasses and bottle. Bernadette took her glass of mint liqueur, and Jörg, a flute of champagne. The waitress poured another glass for the madame, then one for herself, and the four of them formed a circle, clinking their glasses to the madame's cheer of "Santé!"

The madame and the waitress departed after that, leaving Jörg and Bernadette alone.

Jörg leaned in close and whispered in her ear. "After we have a bit to drink, I'd like to head straight upstairs. The rooms there are private, right?"

"But I've only just started on my first drink," Bernadette said with a smile. "The night is long; there's no need to rush."

"I'll have them bring up as many drinks as you want. You can even fill the bath with champagne."

"Really?"

"Order two more bottles."

The private rooms on the second floor were crimson, decorated in patterns that evoked an earlier time. Beneath the dim lighting, the red color appeared deeper, almost maroon.

The canopied bed was so gaudy Jörg could only imagine it was a joke. Thick curtains hung over the windows, closed tight to prevent any light from leaking outside, and a porcelain-lined bathtub sat in the room, wide enough to easily hold two adults.

The brothels in the busier areas of Jörg's hometown and the cities he'd frequented during his leave from the front line had all had much smaller, plainer rooms. He usually had sex soon after choosing a girl, as places like this had strict time limits. The women went from one man to the next in quick succession, giving Jörg and the other patrons a fleeting taste of pleasure like leaving a cheap bar after just one drink.

Bernadette set the bottles of champagne down on the table. "You must have been quite surprised downstairs. Places like this have their own specific way of doing things."

"Isn't every brothel in Paris like this? Or is this one unique?"

"People have recently been favoring places where they can get a quick lay, then leave. It takes more time and costs more here, and we're required to learn about our customers so we can accommodate their tastes. It's a fair amount of work."

"It is a lot nicer than the brothels that just throw you out as soon as you're done. This is the first time I've been in a place like this."

"You mean the first time you've been to a brothel? Or are you comparing it with the other places you've been to?"

"The latter."

"I see. Well, then you'll fit in perfectly in a place like this. The men who visit here are searching for a woman who doesn't exist in the real world. There's no need to feel embarrassed, and with enough time and money, we can make any of our customers' dreams and fantasies come true in exactly the way they imagine them. Anything, that is, as long as it's not violent."

Bernadette began unlacing her bustier, but Jörg calmly stopped her.

"Wait. There's something I want to ask you first."

"Oh?"

"You were at the Eiffel Tower in the middle of the night, weren't you? Talking with German and Ukrainian girls. One of them was a young girl named Lila."

Bernadette's fingers stopped moving behind her back. She stared at Jörg in disbelief. "Who are you?"

"I'm the man who was there as Lila's bodyguard."

"Really? You're Mr. Huber?"

"I am."

"You don't look German at all. You look like a born and bred Frenchman."

Jörg told her the lie he had prepared. "My mother was French, and my father was German. His work took us between the two countries when I was young. In France, I go by Pierre Arche, so you can call me that here."

"Which side do support in the war?"

"Neither. I'm frustrated because I'm not strong enough to help either side—I guess is how I'd explain it. I was hired by my master to protect Lila."

"So you don't hold allegiance to any country?"

"No."

Bernadette sat down on the edge of the bed and stared at Jörg. She looked less like she believed him and more as if she was staring at something inexplicable.

Jörg pulled a chair out from the table and turned it around so the back faced forward. He straddled it like a horse, placing his hands on top of the chair back and hunching over. "Let's pick up where we left off at the Eiffel Tower."

"So you didn't come here for sex?"

"No."

"You're quite the motivated man."

"Thank you. Now then, what is it you want most?"

"Freedom. I wanted to meet someone who would make that possible. You called that man who was with you the Count, so obviously he has money. I thought a man like that might take me away from this brothel."

"You want to leave here?"

"Of course."

"Why?"

"The way brothels operate, working girls like us can't leave. We trade worrying over food and shelter for a debt to the madame that we can never repay, no matter how long we work. All the clothes and jewelry we wear for our customers we buy from her, not from a store, which she sells to us for several times more than anybody else would. She makes up all sorts of excuses to make us buy them from her."

"If you know all that, then why would you tell Diana she should work in a brothel?"

"There are exceptions with every job. If a prostitute is going to become wealthy, it'll be because a rich man takes a liking to her. Then she can become his mistress, which is like being a high-class escort. But chances like that don't come by very often. To be an escort, you have to be more than just pretty; you have to be educated, too. You need to be able to talk with men about academics, art, and society. That said, a lot of men like the new girls when they just start out. Some old men are happy simply lying down next to them. All I told Diana was that she should try to aim for something like that."

"But it's incredibly rare for that to happen, right?"

"Well, yeah."

"So it's a gamble. A really dangerous one."

Bernadette laughed. "We women at the Eiffel Tower are friends, but we're not close enough to bear responsibility for each other's lives. That girl's German, and I'm Belgian."

Jörg's breath caught in his throat.

"What, you thought I was born in France because I speak French and work in a French brothel?" Bernadette asked.

"Yes."

"I'm from southern Belgium. We speak French there."

"So you must still hate Germans..."

"I don't think Diana deserves to be unhappy, but it annoys me when she acts like a victim. The German economy collapsed because of the war. If the citizens stood up to the government and put an end to the fighting, they could start importing food again. If people want food, they need to exercise their civic rights and set their government straight. By saying she would go so far as to become a prostitute to support her family, she's implicitly allowing the war to continue. I have nothing to say to someone like that."

Jörg could feel Bernadette's anger and sympathy for Diana seeping out from the edges of her words. Just like Lila, whose homeland had been stolen in the partition, someone from Belgium would always resent a German. Yet Bernadette still retained a degree of sympathy for the other woman as a member of the same generation. It could even be said that it was *because* she understood Diana's feelings and the position she was in that her tone was so harsh. Jörg could tell that Bernadette's heart swayed back and forth between sympathy for commoners like Diana and animosity toward those who had trampled her homeland and massacred her people.

"You both have your own situations to deal with," Jörg said. "I understand what you mean about responsibilities on the home front. It's like how America is profiting by exporting weapons and supplies; we're all sucking the lifeblood from one another. Still, don't you think it's wrong to impose that on the next generation? The children of today could very well grow up to be wiser than us and find a way to avoid war. Yet they'll be first to die from the food shortages."

"I really don't think the next generation is going to be any wiser than we are."

"Why do you think that?"

"Fools raise fools."

"Not all adults are fools, and some children raised by fools might resent their parents and strive to be better."

"That's something I've never seen before. The way I see it, you're plenty foolish yourself."

"I just don't want to look back once the war is over and make excuses about not being able to do anything."

"That's your pride talking. Though I understand the part about wanting to do something to ease your conscience."

"I'm fine with that," Jörg said. "I have the freedom to run away when things get difficult. No one would blame me if I did."

Bernadette shrugged, her gaze wandering around the ground at her feet for a little while.

"For example," he continued, "how about this? If I promise to buy your freedom, will you help me with something?"

"Be serious. It would cost a fortune to get me out of here. I told you how this place works, didn't I?"

"You did, but I have no intention of making you my mistress. After I pay the madame for your freedom, you can go anywhere, do anything you want. Live a free life. All I want in return is the information you have on procuring food. You said there's someone in Kleinerbrunn running an underground food trade. I want you to introduce me to them."

"You're really serious about this, aren't you?"

"I am. As long as you have proof. What do you know?"

Bernadette lowered her gaze again. "I have some relatives like you. They're part German and live over there now. We kept in regular contact before the war, but I can't get through to them anymore."

"If we used a carrier pigeon, we could even reach them from Paris."

"Why a carrier pigeon?"

"Camille talked about them, remember? She said there are a lot in France. You'll be able to use them to communicate with your relatives in Germany. Birds can only carry simple messages, though, and if anyone finds out, they'll think you're a spy."

"I'm no spy. Tell anyone that, and I'll kill you."

"I know. I'm not interested in your secrets, your thoughts, or your beliefs. I just want to know how to get food."

"And you're going to pay all that money to buy my freedom just for information? Sorry, but that's hard to believe."

"It's because it's so much money that you'll want to do whatever you can to help me, right? You won't be doing it for Diana, but for your own sake, to secure a patron and finally get out of this place. I'm telling you I can create that path for you. How about it?"

"...In that case, I'm in," answered Bernadette. "I'll tell you what I know, but that's it. Okay?"

"Sure."

A languid smile spread across Bernadette's face as she rested her chin on the back of her hand. "Once I leave the brothel, I won't dream of the Eiffel Tower anymore. I'll be able to get the peace of mind I need without venting my frustrations there."

"I guess so. I'll tell Diana what happened."

"No, don't mention any of this to her. I don't want her to feel like she owes me anything."

"But she'll miss you if you suddenly stop showing up at the tower."

"That's fine. The things we see there are just dreams. They don't actually exist. You really surprised me when you showed up here, even if I did tell you the address."

"I promised you I would. Back there."

"It's like you're some sort of monster."

A faint smirk crossed Jörg's lips, and he stood up from his chair.

"You're leaving?" Bernadette asked. "Without doing anything?"

"Would you prefer I did?"

Bernadette looked over at the bottle on the table. "There's still champagne left."

"Do you want to take a bath?"

"Yes."

"Go ahead, then. I'll rest the night here. I want to learn more about Kleinerbrunn."

"You'll be charged extra."

"Don't worry. I'll pay, however much it is."

2

Bernadette poured two bottles of champagne into the full bathtub, then removed her clothes and slowly slid in. She stretched out her body in the warm water, running her hands from her shoulders down to her fingertips with a look of pleasure. The dim lights in the room accentuated her curves, and her skin shimmered in the darkness. Her sensual body writhed in the sweet-smelling steam rising from the water.

Jörg sat on the edge of the bed, watching Bernadette. He could feel the ancient blood stirring in the depths of his soul. *Drain this woman for sustenance*, the blood commanded him, as if to say that was far more important than the joys of the flesh. Jörg ignored its demands. He forced himself to think about the refreshing breeze and woodland smells of his hometown to hold the monster's power at bay.

Bernadette got out of the bathtub, wrapped herself in a soft towel, and wiped every last drop of water off her body. Once she was done, Jörg told her to put on her clothes.

"You're really not going to do anything?" she asked. "You paid for me."

"I didn't come here today to buy your body; what I want to buy is food. I'd like to talk with you about that."

Bernadette climbed naked onto the bed, crawled over the comforter, and leaned in close to Jörg. She put her face close to his, then ran her lips down his neck. Jörg repositioned himself and kissed Bernadette's throat and cheeks in response. But that was as far as he went.

"I want you to think of me as a comrade," he told her.

"What's a comrade?"

"Someone who isn't just wrapped up in this war, but who actively resists it, even if they can only do it in their own modest way. I'd like for the two of us to have that sort of a relationship. Of course, once you're free from this brothel, it's your own choice as an individual whether you want more from me. And if I still find myself thinking about you, we'll meet again. It'll be much more romantic than sleeping together because it's your job."

"You really are a strange one. You're not a normal man."

"The war destroyed my heart. Both my body and soul aren't what they once were."

Jörg could feel Bernadette's fingers around him. She started to squeeze him harder, and he let out a moan.

"I know there are more important connections in this world beyond the physical," Bernadette said, "but you're the first customer to ever say that here. It's not fair."

"How is it unfair?"

"If we sleep together now, then I can forget the whole night as if it were a dream. But if we don't do anything, I'll never be able to forget you. I'll obsess over a hopeless fantasy and keep waiting for it to come true. Don't do something so cruel. Sleep with me and leave."

"You'd really prefer that?"

Bernadette nodded.

Jörg put his hand on hers, then pressed himself close to her soft body.

The more passionately Bernadette responded, the more strongly Jörg felt that he couldn't allow himself to get anything more than physical pleasure from her. He would get his sustenance elsewhere. *That's right*, he thought. *I can get it from the madame.* The madame was a woman who ran a traditional brothel and, even now, had managed to keep the place thriving. She must be overflowing with vitality. Taking a little from her surely wouldn't affect her in any way.

Once they had finished and Jörg was lying next to Bernadette, he circled back to the subject of the food procurement.

"Kleinerbrunn is in the Pfalz region," she told him. "Do you know it?"

"It's a fair way west, closer to the French border than to Berlin."

"It's an enclave of Bavaria, so their beliefs and attitudes are different from the rest of Prussia. They don't blindly follow the orders of the German government, even during the war, and lie about their harvests whenever they can. When the government asks for donations of pots and pans, they say they don't have any more to give. Lately, the mayor has been imploring them to buy war bonds, but nobody does."

"Sounds promising."

Bernadette smiled amusedly. "That attitude is why they have food reserves that don't show up in records. They sell part of their food stores to rich people from the cities at prices that are dozens of times higher than market value. Don't criticize them for it, though. Farming villages where all the men have been taken by the war don't really have any prospects once it ends. They have to keep farming, even though their husbands and sons will never return. Can you even imagine how cruel that is? What else can they do but find someone willing to buy from them for even a little more money so they can plan for a stable life after the war?"

"I get it. I don't intend to criticize them in the least."

"So the question is: Where do we get the money to buy the food at such high prices? There's no way Diana could pay for it all by herself. Say you temporarily loan her the money— How and when do you plan to have her pay you back? It'll be an astronomical amount by the end of the war."

"I have an idea. We'll work it out somehow."

"You seem awfully relaxed about it."

"I have something lined up. To start with, I'd like you to tell your relatives that I'll be going to Kleinerbrunn. It would look suspicious if I suddenly showed up, so I'll need you to write me a letter of introduction."

"Whatever you need."

"Thank you."

"Is there anything I should keep in mind when writing the letter?" Bernadette asked.

"Don't mention anything about my age or what I look like. With this type of work, I might need to go in disguise. I may not look like this when I go there."

"Okay. I'll watch out for that when I write it."

Dawn broke as they were still sorting out the finer details of the plan, and soon after, Jörg left the room.

He walked downstairs and settled his bill with the madame. As she walked him to the front door, he gripped her hand in both of his and theatrically declared, “Bernadette was absolutely wonderful. I really took a liking to her.”

“Thank you. That’s wonderful to hear.”

“I’ll be back. Soon.”

“We’ll be looking forward to it. I’ll let the girl know.”

Jörg felt a rich sustenance flow from the madame’s hands into his body. His energy and strength recovered immediately, leaving him feeling as refreshed as if he’d just woken up from a long sleep.

As if he’d just lost one more piece of his humanity.

Once he returned to Xandra’s inn, Jörg stopped by the Count’s room and knocked on the door. A voice bade him to enter, so he stepped inside to find the Count reading in a chair, as always.

After greeting him, Jörg said, “I’d like to borrow some money so I can buy Bernadette’s freedom.”

The Count closed his book, an exasperated look on his face. “That good, was she? Just one time, and you fall head over heels?”

“No, it’s not that. I promised her I would free her from the brothel in exchange for information about the black market.”

“That’s hardly a fair deal. You come out far worse in that arrangement.”

“Actually, I’m going to need even more than that. It’s going to cost a lot just to buy the food.”

“I have money, but I cannot lend you an unlimited amount.”

“No, I know. You and I are both immortal, though, so I can pay you back over hundreds of years.”

The Count set his book down and steepled his fingers together in front of him. “You seem to be losing all restraint.”

“You think so?”

“I’ll lend you the money—and don’t worry about interest. If I lent it to you like you asked, the interest alone would be phenomenal. However, I have no intention of making money off you, so we’ll ignore it.”

“Thank you.”

"Do you have a contact for this black market food trade?"

"Yes. Bernadette told me about someone."

"Well then, it seems all that's left is to go there and come to an agreement."

"I've already arranged for that, too. If I don't need to worry about funds, then things should go smoothly."

II
Jörg's Corpus (2)

1

On August 17, 1916, Romania declared that they would join the Allies. Ten days later, they sent troops into Transylvania to fight Austria. We heard about these developments in the trenches on the Western Front.

Count Silvestri's homeland had finally joined the war effort.

What would the Count do? He'd coldly told Milos he wouldn't do anything, even looking annoyed by the mere thought of it, but would he fight to save his motherland if it came to that?

Before that question could be answered, Romania was swiftly pushed back by the Bulgarian Army, Austria's ally. This happened right at the beginning of September. After that, the Romanians clashed with a multinational army of the Central powers consisting of troops from Germany, the Ottoman Empire, and Bulgaria, which they also lost, ultimately forcing them to abandon their incursion into Transylvania.

It was evident that Romania had attacked without being sufficiently prepared. They had sent ill-equipped, barely trained soldiers to fight generals who were tried and tested in real battle. Victory had only ever been a pipe dream.

The Count must have known that the Romanian Army couldn't win. He's spent enough time wandering around the front lines and knows all about the new weapons and tactics that are being used. As much as he says that he detests the idea of helping and that he won't do anything, he still keeps up-to-date on the latest information. While it's true that the Count is tired of war, there's no doubt that his soul has retained some of his original warrior's spirit.

Recently, whenever I sense that something is about to happen on the battlefield, the muscles in my left cheek and lower eyelid start to twitch. It feels as if a small fish that lives under my skin starts flailing around.

No one notices something like that during the chaos of battle, but when the fighting dies down and soldiers have time to look around at one another's faces, I feel a sense of shame knowing others can see my affliction. To hide it, I got a bandanna from a medic, which I wrap around my head like an old-timey pirate. I pull it down a little on the left side of my face when I need to, so people can't see the twitching.

Even when I do that, no one asks about it or teases me. None of us has the extra energy to worry about or make fun of anyone else anymore.

So far, the spasms have stayed contained to just my face. Everything else is fine. I can still move my arms and legs normally. It comes from extreme stress and overwork, so if it gets worse and the spasms spread, my head could start bobbing uncontrollably, or my hands or feet could start shaking so badly that I won't be able to walk. I've seen it happen to other soldiers in my unit. My entire body goes limp thinking that I might end up the same way.

Fritz still treats me exactly the same, even with the bandanna hiding the left side of my face. He acts like he understands my situation without my having to explain it.

Like always, he sits on the ground whenever he can, drawing in his notebook.

Artists are tough. They must face reality with the same passion they devote to their art.

Maybe once Fritz draws the monsters in his notebook, they take shape and protect him from harm. If so, then he might be less an artist than a conjurer.

We're eating one day when he whispers in my ear, "You're the only one I'm going to tell this to, but I recently saw a monster in real life. In the trenches."

At first I think Fritz's tough spirit might have cracked, so I just sit there staring at him without saying anything. He's dead serious. Still holding my bread and my plate, I shrug, then stand up and take Fritz somewhere away from everyone else.

After checking to make sure there's no one around, I say, "Are you sure you weren't just seeing things because you haven't been sleeping enough?"

"I'm serious. It spoke German."

"It spoke to you?"

"Yeah. I saw you standing around talking to it, too."

"When was this?" I ask with a frown.

"A little while ago. In a corner in the trenches."

I lean in close to Fritz and lower my voice. "Did you really see it?"

"Yes."

"What did you talk about?"

"He said he found it amusing that I could see him. He also told me I would die if I stayed here, and I asked if he was the God of death, but he said no."

"What was his name?"

"He said it was Nil, monster of nothingness."

I almost click my tongue in irritation. So he hasn't just been contacting me, but other people? What game is he playing?

"Can you draw what he looked like?" I ask.

"I already have."

Fritz takes his notebook out of his pocket and quickly flips through the pages.

The moment I see the drawing he opens to, all words fail me.

Countless lines intersect on the page, creating what I can only see as chaotic scribbling devoid of any meaning. I think it might be some sort of optical illusion, so I look at it from different angles, squint, and stare, but the jumble of light and dark lines don't take on any shape. It differs from the avant-garde style as well, which purposefully bends lines and uses angles to depict people and things. No matter how I look at it, Nil's wicked grin in the darkness doesn't come to me.

"I don't see anything," I say dubiously.

"I drew him just like I saw him," Fritz responds. "Nil didn't have a shape. He was formless, radiating heat and surrounded by what looked like smoke. This is the only way I could depict him in a single drawing. Did he look different to you?"

"He looked just like a person."

"*What*?"

"When I met him here, he was a middle-aged man wearing a soldier's uniform just like you and me."

"How come we both saw him differently?"

"No idea. More importantly, though, what did you two talk about?"

"He asked me all sorts of questions. Like if I could do other things besides draw, if I wrote poems or stories, if I could sing well, and if I could make things from empty casings and bits of metal. When I told him all I can do is draw, he nodded and said people like me can see monsters. I showed him my notebook, and he reached out as if he had arms and fingers, took my pad, and started flipping through it. Once he'd finished, he closed my notebook and handed it back to me. A gentle breeze brushed my cheek, and he said, 'Thank you for showing me something wonderful.' I actually got a little excited by that."

"You shouldn't be happy that a monster complimented you."

"But he's a *real monster…*"

"They're not that rare. He's the same as all those ones you draw, isn't he?"

"Every monster I've drawn so far was one someone else already discovered and recorded in a book." Fritz's eyes take on a strange glimmer. "I was just copying them. If they didn't provide an illustration, I'd read the description and draw it based on that. None of them is a monster I've actually seen."

"I think everything else you've drawn so far has been more impressive."

"You don't understand. Something you discover with your own eyes is so much more exciting—even if it is like smoke you can't grasp the shape of. It was close enough to touch, and I talked to it. It's not about whether it makes a good picture; what matters is that I met it face-to-face. Why didn't you tell me about it earlier? It's not fair for you to become friends with a monster before me."

"He approached me out of the blue."

"What did you talk about?"

I can't tell Fritz about simulacrums, so instead I say we talked about the sorry state within Germany and the social revolution, just as Nil had told me to. But that only makes Fritz more jealous of my relationship with Nil, and he even asks me to let him join in the discussion next time Nil comes to visit me. I give him a noncommittal reply and leave it at that, but, of course, I have no intention of letting him meet Nil. The next time I see him, I'm going to warn him to stay away from Fritz.

Just then, an officer yells out a command. Sentries have spotted the enemy. I clean up my plate so I can go back to my post, then push up my bandanna to see out of my left eye and put on my steel helmet. My lower eyelid twitches violently, but right now, I don't have time to care. I pick up my rifle and lean against the side of the trench. Fritz lines up next to me.

"What the hell is that?!" the soldier at the trench periscope cries out in a frenzy. "Some kind of giant oil cans are rolling toward us. And British soldiers are marching behind them."

"What?!"

"They might be carrying some kind of explosive. Surely they can't be thinking of throwing those things into the trench..."

"Are people pulling them?"

"It doesn't seem like it. They might be pushing them from behind, but I really can't tell for sure. They just keep coming. I can see at least twenty from here. What are they going to do with them?"

Even after an artillery barrage from the German side, the drumlike constructions continue advancing without faltering in the slightest. They move slower than infantrymen, but the British troops following behind somehow seem more confident than normal. From the way the giant drums move, it seems they're some new type of vehicle—a kind of moving metal box with the front fully enclosed. I don't have a clue what's inside.

When the British Army reaches the sea of barbed wire, every soldier in the German Army lets out the same terrible cry. The metal boxes begin to roll over the wire, crushing it easily as they effortlessly make their way across no-man's-land. Posts topple, and barbed wire is buried in the mud beneath the metal boxes, creating a safe path for the trailing British soldiers. Now with an avenue of attack, the enemy troops begin to rush toward our position.

"They broke through!" someone screams. "They got past the barbed wire like it was nothing!"

The metal boxes advance over muddy ground that would sink normal vehicles or carts. From my vantage point, I can't tell what sort of machine this is they're using.

The German officers raise the cry to attack, but not a single one of the young soldiers leaps out of the trenches. They stare as if transfixed by the metal boxes, trembling with their rifles in their hands. Melee combat is terrifying enough in normal situations, so it's only natural that anyone would resist an order to engage one of those things. Soldiers sit hunched over like baby birds, while their sergeants go around kicking them and trying to spur them to action with cries of "What are you doing?!" "Hurry up and go!" and "Anyone who doesn't charge will be shot! Now move!"

I don't want to be kicked, so I run out of the trench on my own. I don't care how intimidating those metal boxes are; I'm not about to let the British into our territory. There's nothing more difficult or more horrible than hand-to-hand combat inside the trenches.

I immediately drop to the ground to avoid sniper fire, turning my head to yell behind me. "I'll take the lead. Fritz, Hendrich, cover me."

"On it!" Fritz yells, running toward a heavy machine gun, while Hendrich acknowledges with "Understood" as he picks up his rifle and takes position behind a bulletproof shield.

I wave my arm time and again, urging the others forward, before one young soldier finally musters up his courage and creeps out of the trenches. That seems to cause the others to relax a bit and, one by one, they soon emerge from behind the sandbags.

I lead the charge, the left side of my face twitching like crazy. It serves as a constant reminder of how intently my body rejects war, even as the adrenaline courses through me. Somewhere in the back of my mind I admonish myself, asking why I ran out here rather than staying in a shivering ball in the trenches. At times like this, I have to tell that part of me to shut up. That staying still would have driven me mad, so the best thing to do was turn off my brain and fight.

Exchanging fire with the British soldiers racing toward us, my small group of soldiers approaches one of the metal boxes. Up close, it's shaped like a parallelogram and much wider than I imagined, with large rivets covering its entire body. Sizewise, it's slightly taller than a grown man and probably a little over twenty-five feet long. A row of interconnected metal plates rotate from the front to the back down both sides of the metal box, and these beltlike structures are wrapped around the outside of the wheels. The whole thing probably doesn't sink into the mud because these continually keep it moving.

Two large wheels are fixed to the back of the parallelogram, making the whole thing look like a giant fish—a metal fish swimming across a sea of mud. It emits the same coarse engine sounds as a normal military vehicle and spews white smoke from its exhaust pipe, but it's incredibly slow.

The most frightening thing, though, is the muzzles of the machine guns that protrude from the side of the metal box. We immediately drop to the ground or dodge to the side, but some men react too late and are torn apart. My brothers in arms, mowed down like long stalks of wheat reaped by a farmer.

We've avoided the initial attack, but by no means are we safe. The moment we feel it's okay to stand up, a barrage of rifle fire comes at us from a different direction. An impact strikes my helmet like a hammer, and the momentum launches me backward.

For a second, I think I've died. But then I realize I can still hear the sounds around me, so I must still be breathing. The bullet must have just grazed my helmet instead of piercing it and going into my head. A stray bullet that ricocheted in my direction.

My vision swirls, and my head thunders. The pain causes my stomach to churn, and I fight back an intense urge to vomit.

Rolling over in the mud, I throw up a little bit. No blood is mixed in with the bile, meaning I haven't taken a bullet to the torso. The excruciating stress makes my stomach tremble. I press myself to the ground and hide beneath a crumpled corpse.

I stare at the scene unfolding around me from where I lie on the ground.

The metal boxes slowly change directions and continue their assault on the German soldiers, expelling horrifying numbers of empty cartridges from their hatches. Their brass-colored shine is scattered all across the battlefield, making it feel like some sort of bizarre nightmare.

Timing my attack carefully, I stand up and run toward the machine gunner's blind spot. As I vault over the debris covering no-man's-land, I pull a stick grenade free from my belt. I unscrew the cap covering the end of the handle and toss it aside, then yank on the wire that comes tumbling out with the ball, the friction causing a spark. I crank my arm backward and throw the grenade at the metal box with all my might.

It explodes brilliantly against the metal box, and I feel a surge of satisfaction. But once the white smoke clears, I see there isn't a single hole in its surface.

My fellow soldiers also begin to throw their stick grenades, as if inspired by my actions, but the enemy doesn't even flinch. The grenades that land on the top of the boxes bounce off the metal frames and explode in different directions, blowing away the bodies of soldiers caught up in the blast.

I order everyone to retreat. There's nothing we can do except target the metal boxes with our heavy artillery once we've fallen far enough back. We engage a group of British soldiers as we flee, and the fighting turns chaotic. We stab them with our bayonets, they stab us with theirs. We shoot them with our rifles, and they shoot back at us. I turn my empty rifle around and ram the butt into a soldier's stomach, then hit him across the face, creating a torrent of fresh blood. My world turns red. Amid my hazy thoughts, a voice inside my head screams wildly that I mustn't die. That I have to survive.

The metal boxes press forward incessantly, crushing everything in their path. Incapacitated soldiers are caught up in those revolving belts, but even then, the metal boxes show no signs of stopping. Inhuman screams of agony echo across the battlefield. I stand motionless, listening with the other exhausted soldiers. No one can tell if the men being ground up in the belts of those boxes were allies or enemies. Blood trickles down my head, wetting my face. At some point, my lower eyelid has stopped twitching. Either the muscles or nerves in my face have died, or my soul has been destroyed completely, leaving me no longer able to react to this reality.

An explosion causes the metal box in the lead to tilt to one side, dig into the earth, and become stuck. We cheer and run past it. It wasn't an artillery shell that demolished the ground beneath it, but a grenade. We aren't sure if someone threw their grenade perfectly through a gap in one of the revolving metal bands or if a wounded soldier pulled the string right before being run over.

We dive into a friendly trench, and the soldiers lining the dirt wall immediately start firing their rifles at the enemy. A medic dashes over to help anyone bleeding, then has any men who can't move carried away on stretchers. It isn't just my head where I've been injured, but all over my body. I was running too frantically to notice, but there are deep wounds all over my body, sustained during the melee without my realizing it.

Once my nerves settle a little, I realize I can't move at all. My injuries are worse than the ones I received when that blast from the artillery shell hurled me through the air.

I don't feel a sense of despair. Even if the pain lasts until my wounds close, the Count's magic will heal me in good time. I'll just have to pretend to be injured until then.

They load me onto a stretcher and discuss taking me to a field hospital.

"Is Fritz Ziegel okay?" I ask.

"He's gone on ahead," replies a medic.

"Where to?"

"Try looking for him where you're going," the man says. "We don't know where people get sent."

"He went to a hospital, though, right? Not heaven?"

They don't tell me anything else.

As I lie on the stretcher, my eyelids grow heavy.

I've lost too much blood and drift out of consciousness.

2

The bodies of soldiers in field hospitals are treated no differently from objects.

They're carried in, laid down, have their wounds probed unceremoniously, stitched up if needed, and any part deemed unlikely to recover is severed—arm, leg, or otherwise.

We have no dignity as human beings here, either.

Even the sharp smell of antiseptic and the stink of human waste are overpowered by an indescribably horrible, raw, sweet stench that fills the room. It's an odor that gradually seeps its way into our bodies and lingers deep in the back of our noses.

The hospitals lack more than staff; they also need additional resources and medicine. One look at the doctors and nurses is enough to make that abundantly clear.

Bodies shredded by artillery and machine-gun fire are beyond help. In wartime, hospitals are a different type of battlefield. Doctors and nurses fight valiantly against anything that might rob us of our lives, but it's a losing battle, so I don't blame them if their exhaustion makes them treat us harshly. Soldiers scream their lungs out when the pain gets too much, break out into sudden bouts of violence at times, and don't listen to the medical professionals. Most of the men spend their time in a state of hopelessness when they sense their end is near. When that happens, they tend to die either sometime that day or, at most, a few days later.

One man jumped out of bed against the nurses' protestations and ran around the room, tearing at his bandages until eventually he fell over dead. The entire time he kept screaming that he wanted to go home and repeatedly cried out a woman's name. I later learned that his wife had fallen ill and died while he'd been away fighting, which he'd found out about.

Some men beg not to be treated. Recovery means returning to the front lines, so they plead with the doctors and nurses to amputate an arm or a leg so they can go home.

Other men are vehemently opposed to surgery, convinced that being taken to the operating room will spell their doom. Trembling like children, they swear that no man who leaves for surgery ever survives and gets to go home, having believed some horrific story they'd been told.

I'm in a large room, and the man in the bed next to me has remained unconscious ever since I got here. When the nurses come in to check on me and change his bandages, I spy some sort of gray liquid oozing from a wound on his head and immediately avert my eyes. I've seen something similar on the battlefield too many times to count, but I can't stand watching such a young woman being subjected to that horrific scene—even if she is a nurse. She calmly tosses the soiled bandages and gauze into a porcelain washing pan, walks over to another bed, and carefully wipes the face of a patient with a mucus bubble coming out of his nose. She works quickly at each bed before moving onto the next one. I can't help but feel sorry for this unflappable woman when I imagine her complaining to her colleagues about it later.

Some of the soldiers who have regained their strength call for the nurses at night and flirt openly with them. I'm surprised to see anyone has the strength to fool around in a place like this, but I have to admit it makes sense. There are no other women on the front lines, and we haven't been anywhere lately where we could meet girls. If I'm being honest about it, I'm no different. I want to feel a woman's soft body so much it hurts. I don't want to just lose myself in lust, either, but spend the night talking with her. Not about the war, but about the future. About building a house, getting married, and raising kids. I remember going into town a couple of times when I was on leave and having sex with a cute brothel girl, but I've already forgotten when that was.

My wounds heal much slower than last time. I develop a fever, and an uncomfortable, itchy sensation torments every inch of my body. Still, I'm definitely healing faster than a normal person. This is when I'll need to put on an act so the doctors and nurses don't notice I'm different.

Fritz should be in the same hospital as me, so I asked a nurse to tell me where he is. She said she'd look into it, but I never heard back, probably because she's so busy that she simply forgot the request of a single patient.

So instead, I borrow a pair of crutches from someone in my room and go out to find him. I can walk without the crutches, but I don't want anyone to notice how quickly I'm healing, so I grimace and stagger as I hobble down the hall. Looking through the patient records in the nurses' office will be faster than blindly walking around peering into each room. No matter how busy the staff are, I can't imagine they wouldn't have medical records. If I could just check them, I'd know right away where I can find Fritz.

I make it to the office, where I follow some nurses who give me annoyed looks and finally get what I came for.

Fritz's room is on a different floor than mine and pretty far away. He still can't stand, but he's regained consciousness and responds coherently when I talk to him.

Apparently, he scuffled with some British soldiers who came flooding into the trench and was stabbed in the stomach during the struggle. There wasn't any major damage to his organs, and he says he should fully recover so long as he doesn't develop any sort of serious infection. Fritz finds it hard to believe that a single stab wound to the stomach could leave a human immobile. He laughs, but he still looks like he's in tremendous pain.

I ask if he's going back to the front once he recovers.

"I don't know," he murmurs. "If I'm going to get out of here, I feel like this is my chance."

"So you thought about that, too, huh?"

"No matter how many lives I had, it wouldn't be enough to fight something like that."

I'd heard the British had taken Flers during the battle the other day. The German Army lines had been pushed back considerably compared with July 1, when the fighting at the Somme started.

"Even hand grenades didn't work against those things," Fritz says.

"Yeah. But no matter how impressive a weapon is, once it shows up on the battlefield, the other side is sure to make their own. The German Army will capture a vehicle, study it, and build something much stronger than the British version. I'm positive that very soon we'll see metal boxes fighting against other metal boxes. Think how quickly airplanes went from being used for simple observation to firing machine guns. Either that, or we'll make something stronger than a stick grenade that can take those things down."

There are no limits. And no end.

I stay silent as I listen to Fritz talk. "When that British soldier jumped into our trench and our eyes met, he looked like he'd just bumped into someone on the street. He'd resolved himself to attack us, but once he saw his enemy face-to-face, he reacted just like any ordinary person would."

"I get it. I know that disjointed feeling."

"He looked so innocent. He was probably just a college kid."

"And while you were pitying him, he stabbed you?"

"No. He just kept coming straight for me with his knife, even though his expression didn't change—but it changed when he stabbed me. His eyes glazed over like he had a fever."

"Did you let him get away?"

"No, I shot him." Fritz points to the spot right between his eyebrows. He stays silent for a moment, then adds lethargically, "There are no enemies in this war."

"We have more enemies than we can count."

"In military terms, maybe...but I can't think like that anymore."

"You mean you can't hate the enemy?"

"Not quite. There are people I want to kill. But I don't want to kill everyone."

"I don't think I understand."

"Did you hate that steel box? No, you didn't. You just fought it because you didn't want to die. There was no emotion, no hatred. We're not fighting humans anymore. I think now, we're fighting war itself. War doesn't have a shape of its own, though, so it can't be stopped. It's strange. Humans started it, but we don't know how to stop it. Everyone just assumes the war will come to an end naturally while we're all running around left and right."

"...When you put it like that, I guess I'll go home, too."

"You're sure?"

"The front lines wouldn't be the same without you. Let's take Norbert's sketchbook to his family. We can't do that if we die, so we better take care of it now, while we're still alive."

"Do you think we'll be able to get discharged?"

"All it takes is a single piece of paper. We'll manage somehow."

III
The Port of Kiel

1

Jörg hadn't seen Lila since the events at the Eiffel Tower. Xandra had been acting as her guardian instead so Jörg could focus on his plan.

Once Jörg had worked out the general outline for his food distribution plan, the Count called him and Lila to his room.

"It's about time I asked what you intend to do once this war is over," the Count said to Lila.

"What do you mean?"

"Whether the Allies or the Central powers win, the power balance within Europe will change. It's still unclear whether Poland will reemerge as an independent country."

"No matter what happens to Poland, I plan to leave here one day. I don't want to become a monster."

"So you do prefer human society? Even with all the hardships it presents?"

"Yeah."

"Restoring Poland will be an extremely difficult task. It may not be possible during your lifetime."

"Right now, I'm collecting money so I can wait as long as it takes. I don't mind spying if it helps end the war."

"Hmm."

"I get why you're worried, Count," Lila said. "You're thinking this isn't the sort of work a young girl should be doing."

"No, that's not it."

"Really?"

"Devotion to one's homeland doesn't depend on age or sex. A long time ago, I also gave everything I had in the fight to seize my homeland back from my enemies. There will always be people like us, in any time, in any nation. Though all it does is add to one's concerns."

The Count rose from his chair. "Take a look at the map on the table. Let us discuss the current state of the war."

The three of them circled the table. A large map was spread across its surface, covered in different-colored markers to represent the armies of each country.

The Count asked Lila to explain the situation on the map in her own words.

As Lila spoke, she pointed at various places on the map without disturbing the markers. "Lots of big battles are happening on the west side, and an unbelievable number of soldiers died at Verdun, but the French and the Germans are still locked in a stalemate. It's the same to the east. There's no sign that either Russia or the Ottoman Empire will surrender. In the Balkan Peninsula, Serbia fought the Central powers only to be driven out of their own homeland and forced to flee with all noncombatants through Albania to Corfu. This fighting created the Macedonian front in Greece between the Allied and Central powers."

"The Macedonian front will shift at some point," the Count added, "because the Allies keep sending reinforcements. The Serbians will coordinate with them to launch an offensive. Bulgaria and Austria must be growing weary of maintaining the front. Morale is falling among the soldiers, so when it finally crumbles, the entire army will collapse. How do you think Russia will respond?"

"Russia is an incredibly stubborn country, but the landowners are driving the farmers hard, so civil unrest could break out as poverty and starvation worsen."

"If anything happens there, it will be next year. I imagine they'll be able to contain the situation this year—if only barely—but it will become untenable by the New Year. They have the harsh Russian winters to thank for that."

"So will Russia pull back from the front lines?" Jörg asked. "Will they enter into ceasefire negotiations with the Central powers?"

"Most likely."

"That should make things easier for Germany."

"There's one other point in their favor," the Count continued. "Romania misread the situation when they entered the war; it won't end with them just retreating from the fighting in Transylvania. Romania also has a rich grain belt, and with the economic blockade forcing Germany into poverty, the German Army will advance to target those lands. They'll likely occupy Romania to gain control of their farmlands."

Jörg couldn't speak. Once again, the Count's homeland was going to fall under the control of another country. They had spent hundreds of years fighting the Ottoman Empire to gain independence, only to have their lands taken by Germany now.

Yet the Count seemed unconcerned. He glanced over at Jörg and gave a slight frown.

"Even if that helps Germany prolong its fate, it won't last long. The majority of any food they obtain will be sent to the front lines, and there won't be any left over for the home front. Berlin will continue to starve. And now there's this new weapon the British have deployed on the Western Front, which will significantly impact the war going forward."

"What kind of weapon?"

"The British Army calls them 'tanks.' They resemble the chariots used in ancient wars but differ greatly in terms of construction and application. It's a war vehicle for a new era."

According to the Count, chariots seemed to be horse-drawn carts that people had ridden in and used on the battlefield. They carried a driver and an archer to increase the effectiveness of ranged attacks and improve mobility, as the archers could use large bows that were difficult to wield on horseback and heavy arrows that were hard to carry. Armor was later added to chariots to protect the riders.

Tanks, on the other hand, were fundamentally different. They were powered by an engine and protected by thick plating, built to traverse rough terrain and trenches—weapons made to push the front line back while simultaneously creating a path for soldiers. They were also equipped with machine guns and rapid-firing artillery. One thing that hadn't changed, however, was that they still needed people to control them.

While their effectiveness on the battlefield spoke for itself, they also sent German soldiers into panic and disarray when they went up against these tanks. So far, enemy forces had been unable to resist their advance.

Jörg wondered if his corpus had encountered one of them on the front lines. He didn't remember anything like that, but perhaps those memories hadn't been shared yet.

When Jörg asked the Count about it, he said, "Your corpus might have been severely injured in a battle. That could account for the delay in your shared memories. Especially if he suffered a head injury."

"Then what can I do?"

"Meet him in person and see how he is for yourself."

"How do I do that?"

"Enter his dreams. Then you won't have to worry about other people overhearing your conversation."

"Okay, I'll give it a go."

"The sooner the better."

"Understood."

"Now then," the Count continued, "as things currently stand, the German Army wants information on British tanks. Germany was actually looking into tanks previously, but the research was abandoned by rigid thinkers among the upper brass who determined that they would be decimated by artillery in actual combat. With the panic since the Somme, however, Germany's Supreme Army Command has ordered the War Ministry to head up a committee—the Abteilung 7 Verkehrswesen—to develop a tank."

"So you're saying if we get information on tanks from the British Army, we can sell it to Germany for a fortune."

"Well, you should be able to get a decent amount for it."

"But even if we do manage to get our hands on this information, how are we going to pass it along to the War Ministry?"

"I have an acquaintance in the German Army. Romania was allied with Germany until the start of the war."

"But won't you have a hard time contacting them now?"

"On the contrary. I can simply tell him that I was opposed to Romania severing relations with Germany and lost hope in the monarchy as a result of this decision. 'Romania should never have turned its back on Germany; the Battle of Transylvania is proof of that. I wish to secretly help Germany to save my motherland.' We've known each other for a long time, so he should believe that. However, he'll probably still consider the possibility that I'm reaching out as a Romanian spy, so we should approach him with caution."

"And there's no need for me to meet with an officer from the War Ministry?"

"If you go, he'll look into who you are. It wouldn't bode well if they realized there are *two* Jörg Hubers."

"So where do we start?"

"First, you'll sneak into British controlled territory and recover detailed intel on these tanks. Take a camera and get photos of the exterior and interior. Possess a British officer and use him. Do you think you can do that?"

"Sure."

"Photographs of blueprints would be even better. The British Army has used their tanks in battle, so they should already be working on improvements. If we can obtain plans for both new models and older ones, the German War Ministry will be overjoyed."

"What's the name of the company that's designing them?"

"It's an agricultural machinery company called William Foster & Co. They make tractors. That much is already known by German spies."

"If the German Army gets this information, it could make the war last longer, though," Lila commented.

"Even with a model to work from, it's no easy task making a weapon that can be used in actual warfare," the Count replied. "It will also be difficult to mass-produce them under current conditions, where supplies are so limited. By the way, what do you plan to sell to the British?"

"They must want anything they can get," Jörg said, "but we'll start with reports on the state of the army on the German side, including the numbers and capabilities of their warplanes. For the navy, we can provide information on warships and U-boats."

The Count instructed Jörg to make full use of his simulacrum's abilities in gathering information. He could go into other people, just as he had at Verdun, so by leaping between officers in the British and French armies, he should be able to secure a considerable amount of intel. But although he was a soldier, Jörg only knew about fighting on the front lines and had very little understanding of tactics and military technology—and he knew absolutely nothing about engineering. Lila was also a complete novice on the subject, so even if he possessed someone with useful information, probing their mind wasn't likely to lead to much. Without knowing which topics were valuable, he might not obtain any important information.

Casting a calm look in Jörg's direction, the Count said he could quickly get Jörg caught up to speed. That gaze seemed to express his begrudging admiration that someone as uninformed as Jörg would try his hand at espionage.

The Count also said to Lila, "If you wish to help Mr. Huber, you should review everything you know. Especially languages and geography."

Lila nodded happily, likely because she felt she was being treated as an adult, and left in high spirits to go to her room.

Now that it was just the two of them, the Count addressed Jörg sharply. "I'm sure you know this already, but these espionage activities won't bring in as much money as Lila assumes. Think about it, and you'll soon see why. Armies spend a lot of money collecting information. Improving the quality of information means increasing the number of fixed observation points, which requires a large number of people. Now try dividing the army's intelligence budget by the number of informants. There's a limit to how much they can pay each person. And the army wants to get high-quality information for as little as possible. Payments from the army won't amount to much unless you're exceptional intelligence assets."

"Right."

"Even if Lila works as hard as she can, she'll most likely earn just enough to cover her living expenses."

"Then why let her do the job as well?"

"I want her to understand human society before she goes out into it. Lila may act mature, but she's still a child. She's treating this whole idea of spying like it's a fun little excursion. There's nothing wrong with that; it's fine to let her do what she wants because she's thinking about it like a child. But *you* have to make sure you get information while still protecting her. Remember that you're the one leading this espionage mission."

"I understand."

"The War Ministry will certainly welcome information on the

tanks. But even so, that won't give you enough money to repay your debt to me."

"Why even help if you already know that?"

"Purely to amuse myself."

"That's rather blunt."

"I'm not human, so I don't see the need to help humans. One more thing: Your plan to distribute food supplies still needs work."

"What part?"

"If only a few people get food in a starving city, sooner or later, they're bound to be attacked and have their food stolen. A secret like that gets out surprisingly quickly. Nil will double over laughing at you if he's there."

Jörg's heart thumped in his chest. "I can't deny that's definitely a risk."

"It would be more effective to evacuate the people you want to help to the countryside, instead of bringing food into the city."

"Do you have any suggestions on where they could go?"

"I may, if you're able to narrow down the number of people."

"Okay. You've given me something else to think about."

2

That evening as Jörg lay in bed, he visited his original body in his dreams. A corridor linked his corpus to his simulacrum, and Jörg's monster eyes let him see the path clearly. The corridor soon gave way to a steep slope that led him to the top of a hill blanketed in green.

At the top of the hill, Jörg saw his corpus staring off into the distance. Many memories of the battlefield seemed to overlap one another here. At the bottom of the hill stood rows of crosses, too many to count. They varied in size and orientation, looking like scarecrows in a field, and leaned at all different angles as if they'd been thrust carelessly into the soil.

The sky was the same lead-gray color as ever. Sunlight found its way through cracks in the clouds, faintly illuminating their edges.

Jörg saw the expression of his other self more clearly the closer he approached, and his corpus met his gaze with a frown. Jörg raised a hand and casually called out to him.

"So you're me?" his corpus responded. "My simulacrum."

"That's right."

"What're you doing in my dreams?"

"This is the easiest way for us to meet."

"I'd prefer if we just shared memories."

"That wasn't working, so I came to check on you. Did you get a head injury recently?"

His corpus cocked his head slightly. "Yes, I did. I was hit in the helmet with a bullet. I also picked up a lot of other bad injuries and was in a field hospital for a while."

"That explains it. If we share memories, you'll see why I'm here."

Jörg focused his mind to synchronize their memories, and the corpus grimaced in pain, as if he'd been hit in the head with a hammer.

"It feels like my brain's boiling," his other self cried out in agony.

"You'll be okay," Jörg said, comforting him. "It's always like this."

Jörg also felt his body burning. His corpus's injuries were worse than he had imagined.

Eventually, the heat dissipated, and he felt the tension leave his shoulders. The multitude of feelings that had consumed his corpus on the battlefield had imprinted in Jörg's mind, and a deep sigh escaped him as he relived those horrible experiences. "The Somme must have been hell."

His corpus didn't respond and instead glared stiffly at Jörg. "What do you think you're doing, becoming a monster?"

"You saw why I did it in my memories."

"I still don't understand. So many memories are just fragments."

"Oh. Your head injury must be so bad that some things weren't shared properly."

"So explain it to me."

"It's actually pretty straightforward. I became the same thing as the Count. This body is no longer just a simulacrum; it has all the powers of a monster. Time is going to start passing differently for you and me, and even after you pass away peacefully, I'll keep living for all eternity."

Jörg seated himself in a spot where he could look down over the grassy plain and rested his hands on his knees. His corpus sat next to him.

Gazing out over the earth haphazardly littered with row of crosses, Jörg continued.

"Those metal boxes you encountered at the Somme are what the British call tanks. They're a new weapon that are being used for the first time in this war."

"'Tanks'?"

"They were a secret weapon, so the British Army told their soldiers they were water tanks to prevent people from leaking information on the project during development."

"If those things keep attacking us, the German Army is finished."

"Don't worry; they're still a work in progress. Forty-nine were made for that battle, but only thirty-two of them actually moved. And only nine made it as far as no-man's-land."

"How come their rate of operation is so bad?"

"For vehicles, their performance is still incredibly bad. They keep breaking down."

"You weren't the one on the front lines, but you talk about them like you've seen them."

"Lately, I've been doing a job that requires me to learn about them. Or, no—it's a bit strange calling it a job. No one asked me to do it. I've come up with a plan to sell information and make money so I can buy food to send to Berlin. Nil told you about the food shortages in Germany?"

"Yeah."

"I'm going to sell information on the Central powers to the Allies, and vice versa. That way I can get money from both."

"That's treason. You're a bloodsucker like the rest of them."

"I understand your criticisms, but there's no honorable way to get the money."

"Are you really half of me?"

"Why would you ask that?"

"That doesn't sound like me talking. You're not the Count or Nil in disguise?"

Jörg studied the face of his corpus. The other man's cheek twitched violently. That reaction from the battlefield was showing up even here.

"Huh. I really seem that different?" Jörg asked, lowering his voice.

"All of this just defies belief," replied his corpus. "But no matter how long this war goes on, it'll end someday. Both sides will run out of manpower. The people just need to stay strong until then."

"I can't wait that long. They said at the start of the war that it would only last a few months. It's already been more than two years—and no one has any idea when it will end."

"So then do something to end the war."

"Isn't that a job for you, since you're the one with our real body?"

"Don't put this on me."

"See, it's because you say things like that that I have to take action."

"You really think that a monster with a half-baked plan is going to change the world?!" his corpus yelled angrily. "You just want to do something to erase the guilt you feel over Lila."

"I didn't choose to become a monster lightly," Jörg responded calmly. "This power will let me unlock my full potential, but it isn't going to erase the pain I feel as an individual."

"I can't believe what a fool you are. I would never choose to do something like that."

Jörg reached out and touched his corpus's cheek, running his fingertips over the spasming muscles. Just by doing that, the twitching subsided.

A look of surprise crossed the corpus's face, and Jörg said quietly, "You don't want to remember me as a monster, do you? Once peace returns to the world, you'll likely forget about me, along with all those horrible memories of the battlefield. That's how it should be. Do it for me. But I will always remember you. Even after you've passed on to the next life, I'll still have these memories. I am eternally grateful that your soul gave birth to me. So please, forgive me for choosing this. That's all I wanted to say."

His corpus averted his gaze. "How can you throw away your humanity to *save* humanity?" he spat. "What kind of logic is that? You take yourself too seriously. I can't believe you're half of me."

"Really? I understand it now—why it was me and not you who was separated from the body of the man called Jörg Huber. It wasn't a coincidence or because of any accident; I left your body because it was what I was supposed to do. To find a way to live away from the battlefield."

Jörg stood and brushed the dry grass from his cloak.

His corpus stood as well, and turned to face him. "I have something to tell you, too. Once Fritz recovers, we plan on going home. We're not going back to the war."

"That's a wise decision."

"Considering the current state of things, we're thinking of heading to Berlin. I want to reach out to the socialists and see for myself if revolution really does have the power to change the world. If I'm satisfied by what I see, I'll work with them."

Jörg frowned. "I can't say I approve. I don't think they have the power to change the nation."

"It's not as if I completely believe in them yet, either. But you understand this feeling of wanting to do something monumental, right? That's what makes us who we are."

"Don't trust what Nil tells you," Jörg told his other self. "He's the very embodiment of nothingness. He won't stop at reducing emperors and politicians to nothing—he'll do the same to you, too."

"He's taken an interest in me. Apparently, he's interested in people who have a corpus."

"Be that as it may, don't let your guard down around him."

"...Okay. I'll be careful."

Jörg took one last look at his corpus. "Well then, I'm off. Be well."

"Are you going to show up in my dreams in the future, too?"

"Should I not?"

"I mean, you're half of me. So do whatever you want."

3

On the battlefield, Jörg had just been a regular soldier, so he hadn't had any opportunities to command troops in strategic maneuvers or use large weaponry. Everything he knew about history and politics came from the customers who visited the barbershop where he'd worked, and he knew next to nothing about foreign languages.

There were far too many gaps in his knowledge for Jörg to be an effective spy. So, under the Count's tutelage, he filled his brain with an overwhelming amount of information. Thankfully, unlike his corpus, his simulacrum could study without tiring. It seemed like the ancient blood he'd received from the Count also helped with his education.

Once Jörg had learned everything he needed, the Count led him to a British Army camp, where he used his simulacrum to sneak in and possess the body of an officer. Controlling the man from within, Jörg headed out to where the tanks were stored, camera in hand, under the pretense that he needed photographs for a strategy meeting at the Intelligence Corps headquarters.

Jörg had found out from his corpus's memories just how terrified the German soldiers had been to face these tanks in the field. He was fascinated to see the mechanics behind the fearsome weapons.

The tanks that the British called the Mark I came in male and female types. The model equipped with machine guns and rapid-firing artillery was male, while those with machine guns only was female.

He lifted the heavy hatch and climbed inside. The control room was so much more cramped than he'd imagined from the outside, and the smell of motor oil and exhaust mingled in the stagnant air. The design didn't have a partition in the interior of the tank, so the personnel shared the same space occupied by the engine. Even with the radiator and fan, the inside would instantly become a scorching hell. On top of all that, the vibrations from driving rattled the passengers, and they could die if they hit their heads awkwardly.

The driver's seat resembled that of a car, and the barrel of a machine gun stuck out through the armor in front of the driver, with belts of ammunition spread out to one side. To the right in front of the driver's seat was the steering wheel, while there were two levers on the left. Two slits at eye level provided a view to the outside. Jörg got out of the seat and walked to the side of the tank to inspect the rapid-firing gun and its housing. He trembled again upon seeing the sheer amount of ammunition packed inside that small space. Anyone who took one of those shells head-on would immediately be torn to shreds. Next, he checked the engine compartment, finally understanding how the idler wheels and drive wheels worked to move the treads on the outside of the tank. The metal bands that rotated continuously allowed the tank to cross even the roughest of terrain.

Once Jörg had finished taking pictures, he casually asked the maintenance technician some questions.

From there, he returned to Xandra's inn and quickly set about developing the film.

The Count, for his part, arranged a meeting with a lieutenant colonel by the name of Albert Kreutzer, who worked in the German intelligence branch. The plan was for Jörg to possess the lieutenant colonel after the meeting and collect information on the German Army.

While inside the lieutenant colonel's body, he could find out the names of the subordinates and informants who'd been in contact with employees at William Foster & Co., giving him some intel to provide the British. Then, leaping from one person to the next, he would eventually arrive at someone involved in designing the tanks.

Once the film had been developed and the printing paper was dry, Jörg slid the photographs into a large envelope and placed them in his bag.

His preparations for the meeting complete, the Count took him to Lieutenant Colonel Kreutzer's house in the dead of the night. They made the trip in one leap, using the same door as always.

It was his first time visiting Berlin. Just like Paris, German towns had been placed under a blackout, plunging the town into darkness. The Allies hadn't launched the same massive bombing raids as the Germans, but small planes would still drop bombs in surprise attacks, so they had to remain vigilant.

Upon reaching the house, the Count was immediately led inside.

Lieutenant Colonel Kreutzer looked to be in his late forties. The first strands of white blended into his thick head of hair. Jörg had never seen anyone of officer rank in the flesh before. He had a completely different air to him compared with the men serving on the front line. The lieutenant colonel had a broad forehead, prominent nose, sharp eyes, and thin lips. There was a certain wildness to his physique, which also managed to emit an overwhelming sense of majesty. Jörg could hardly believe they were in the same army. Kreutzer looked like someone from another reality. His vibrant skin told of a healthy diet, even while the common people suffered under rationing, and although he wore regular clothes at this hour of the night, anyone could sense the incredible dignity with which he held himself.

With Romania now part of the war, the Count was technically his enemy, yet the lieutenant colonel didn't show the slightest hint of animosity. His wife came to greet the Count as well, giving him such a warm welcome you might almost think he was family. It seemed as if they'd known each other for a long time.

When the two of them were alone in the living room, the lieutenant colonel asked the Count directly what his opinions were regarding Romania. In a frustrated tone of voice, the Count told Kreutzer that he still considered Germany his ally, having lost hope in the Romanian monarchy for its foolishness, just as he'd discussed with Jörg. It was such a convincing performance that Jörg almost let out a laugh.

"In that case, I would ask for your help with Germany's incursion into Romania," the lieutenant colonel said calmly. "All you would need to do is provide information on the current state inside the country."

"Surely that's not something you really need me to do," the Count said, deftly deflecting Kreutzer's request. "The German Army is the strongest fighting force in history. I'm certain you'll be able to take Romania quickly without anyone's help."

"And it truly won't matter to you if that happens to your homeland?"

"Considering the current state of the nation, I have no issue with German occupation. To me, all that matters is that the country called Romania does not disappear."

"There's a good chance Austria-Hungary will intervene."

"We're well-accustomed to their tactics. They've been meddling in our affairs ever since the region was called Walachia and Moldavia. But putting that aside for now, there's another matter I'm keen to discuss. I was wondering if you might be interested in information on the British Army's tanks."

"We already have intel on them. We knew about Great Britain's 'landships' even before they appeared on the battlefield. Had we known they would be so effective, however, we would have been more diligent in our efforts to develop our own terrestrial armored cruisers. It's an idea that we first explored back in 1911, three years before the Great War began."

"I didn't know you were researching them even before the Brits."

"It'll be easy enough for us to catch up. Once we capture an enemy tank, we'll dismantle it and use it as the basis to make our own. It's well within the capabilities of German engineering."

The conversation sent a chill down Jörg's spine. Germany was certainly a major industrial nation, but the people making the weapons were those on the home front. With all the able-bodied men rounded up to die en masse on the battlefield, who were they imagining would build these tanks? Even with the women currently doing those jobs, there weren't enough people available to work in the factories—not to mention the fact that everyone was starving. Ordering people living in such conditions to rapidly mass-produce a complicated new weapon was nothing short of madness.

"And when do you think you'll capture one of Great Britain's tanks?" the Count asked.

"I can't say for sure. We'll have to wait until they deploy them again."

"In that case, I believe what I've brought you will be of great service."

The Count removed the thick envelope from his bag and placed it on the table. He prompted the other man to examine it, and Lieutenant Colonel Kreutzer skeptically picked up the envelope.

His face blanched the moment he caught a glimpse of the photos inside. Quickly skimming each one, Kreutzer asked, "Where in the world did you get these?"

"I have a very hardworking man in my employ."

"What's his name?"

"He goes by the code name 'Bat.'"

"Bat, huh? A fitting name, considering the nature of your position."

The Count gave an elegant smile. "I trust the information is to your liking?"

"Of course. And you'll be rewarded accordingly."

"Thank you very much."

Lieutenant Colonel Kreutzer wasted no time taking the stack of photographs to Abteilung 7 Verkehrswesen, where they also astonished the department head. The A7V had already commissioned multiple factories to develop plans for a tank, but no one had expected to receive photographs of the actual weapon before those plans were delivered.

"If you have any other requests, just ask. I will provide whatever intel I can," Kreutzer told the A7V. He spoke with an easy confidence, despite the fact that he hadn't collected the information himself.

And so the German Army began developing tanks under the name "all-terrain armored vehicles." It was a high-priority task given the state of the war, but with contracts with companies to finalize and the official budget needing to be decided on by the government, it would be quite some time untill they had a working prototype—something Jörg realized when he possessed A7V employees and searched through their documents.

The slow pace of bureaucracy astounded him.

How could the creation of a single new weapon require this much work? He could quickly deliver intel of the highest quality, but it would all be meaningless. Soldiers were dying on the front lines while they delayed. In the end, the men on the ground would suffer the cost of the government's inefficiency.

After learning that the budget would be passed near the end of the year and that operational testing would likely begin the following spring, Jörg left the A7V and passed through the portal back to Xandra's inn.

He stopped in at the Count's room and told him everything he'd learned.

"Tank development will start in earnest near the end of the year. They're going to start by dismantling a Holt tractor to study its structure, since it could suit the technical aspects. The plans for the cooling systems and treads will likely run into obstacles, though, because they know that if it functions the same way as the tractor, it won't be able to cross no-man's-land. Apparently they're going to build the prototype by covering a wooden frame with armor."

"The war might end before Germany completes their tank."

"It's entirely possible."

The Count gave a quick nod, then said, "Well, while we keep an eye on this, let's investigate the status of the German naval fleet at the Port of Kiel. This time, you'll be collecting information to sell to the Allies. We'll sell the intel you obtained via Lieutenant Colonel Kreutzer on Germany's land forces together with the information you get on the naval fleet. I will take care of the arrangements."

"Understood."

"There's one more thing I'd like you to do in Kiel besides collect information. There's a German man named Edmund Jansen working at the port." The Count placed a large envelope on the table. "He was bought off by the British to sell information on Germany. His photograph and profile are in here. I'd like you to find him and eliminate him. The area is surrounded by water, so disposing of the body shouldn't pose a problem."

Jörg was flustered. "Hang on—I'm just trading information. I never agreed to killing anyone."

"This is a request from Lieutenant Colonel Kreutzer. We can't refuse him."

So the pictures of the tank alone hadn't been enough to gain the lieutenant colonel's trust. Apparently, the negotiations had continued unbeknownst to Jörg.

"The Englishman who was receiving the information from Jansen was already arrested by the German Army and killed after questioning. During the interrogation, they learned the names of informants inside Germany and issued orders for their assassination. If we refuse or fail this mission, the lieutenant colonel will decide I'm working for the Allies and cut off all contact."

"Wouldn't it be faster to erase the lieutenant colonel's memory? You could make it so this man never existed in the first place."

"Do you know how many people are involved in this? Are you suggesting I go around erasing the memories of them all one by one? That would still leave written records. It would be impossible to keep everything consistent; there's bound to be a loose thread somewhere. No, killing Jansen is the quickest way."

"Then why not cut ties with the lieutenant colonel? We already gave him the information on the tanks, so we don't need him anymore."

"That may be fine for you, but it would be problematic for me."

"But—"

"I'll only say this once: I don't need disobedient servants. If you insist on going against me, then return everything I've loaned you in full right now."

"That's absurd."

"There is no room for discussion on this. If some ruffian attacks Lila while you're guarding her, you'll have to subdue them without hesitation and, in some situations, you may have to kill them. What sort of a bodyguard are you if you can't kill a person?"

Jörg squeezed his fists tight. The Count was right, but Jörg was still resistant to the idea.

"You don't need to make it look good," continued the Count, "but don't let him slip away. If we lose sight of him once, then it'll be hard to find him again. So be careful."

4

A sea breeze swept through the Port of Kiel, which was likely why it was so cold despite being the start of autumn. It sat a good distance from the open ocean, so the waters themselves were calm. Small boats and barges passed over the midnight-blue water as waves broke lazily against the shore.

At the Kiel imperial naval yard, newly built ships were hidden beneath covers as repairs proceeded on warships. The cranes lining the port moved slowly, lifting steel and other cargo that humans could not.

Jörg glanced at the Count out of the corner of his eye. Lila stood next to him in her simulacrum. She shouldn't have needed to come with them, but the Count had brought her for some reason.

The Count had told Lila that they were here to collect information on the German Navy while also searching for an undercover British spy. Hearing that, Lila had eagerly taken up her first assignment without the slightest hint of suspicion.

Jörg had to make sure Lila was nowhere near him when the time came to kill Edmund Jansen. He couldn't let her witness the assassination—a fact that would only make things harder. Jörg couldn't understand why the Count had made things even more complicated than they had to be.

Jörg still wasn't sure whether he would kill the man. He'd memorized the face in the photograph and read the profile, but his path never would have crossed with Jansen's if not for Kreutzer's request. It wasn't as if they were facing each other on the battlefield, either. The idea of killing a man like that filled Jörg with revulsion.

The Jutland Peninsula stretched north from Kiel, while the Scandinavian Peninsula jutted out on the other side of the water. Islands of various sizes dotted the sea between these two landmasses, and Kiel's position provided an excellent view over the islands. The port was surrounded by Denmark, Norway, and Sweden—all of which remained neutral—so the German Navy could construct and repair their boats here without fear.

The downside to this was that intelligence agents also liked to hide out in neutral countries. Germany sent investigators there to ferret out and eliminate suspicious individuals, trying to prevent any spies from infiltrating their homeland.

According to the Count, the German Navy had engaged with the British in each nautical theater since the war first started.

A large encounter had taken place late last May at Skagerrak Strait—a conflict the British had called the Battle of Jutland. In terms of the number of casualties and sunken battle cruisers, armored cruisers, and destroyers, Great Britain had come out far worse. However, the British had possessed far more ships to start with. Even after this battle, they still had twenty-four dreadnoughts ready for immediate deployment, with pre-dreadnought battleships and battle cruisers in reserve that could engage the enemy at any time.

While Germany had sunk many British ships at the Battle of Jutland, they had lost ten ships and hadn't been able to gain control of the sea. The battle was declared a victory within Germany, but the Count said that, strategically, the Germans had lost. He'd given Jörg a pitying smile, saying that winning tactically but losing strategically spelled doom in the long run.

The end of May was also when Jörg had possessed Johann the baker at Verdun. In the intense fighting around Fort Vaux, he had witnessed the hellscape created by the shelling and flames.

Recalling the experience still made him feel cold inside.

Jörg had charged forward, hoping a bullet wouldn't hit him, as he struggled under the weight of the full tank of gas on his back and wiped away the sweat pouring down his forehead. He'd witnessed enemy soldiers burning from the fire spewed by their flamethrowers, as well as German soldiers engulfed in flames, soaked in gasoline from punctures in the tanks left by snipers' bullets. The fighting had continued in the trenches, where Johann had been stabbed by an enemy in the narrow confines. The terror Jörg had felt in that moment almost made him lose control of himself, but the Count had used his powers to call Jōrg back at the last moment. Right around the same time, the seas near the Jutland Peninsula had been shaking under gunfire, raging as they drank the blood and swallowed the lives of men.

Jörg's hometown was in inland Germany, so he'd grown up never knowing the sea. This unfamiliar port scene filled him with more unease than wonder, and he couldn't get used to the scent of salt carried on the breeze. He'd come to carry out a mission, but he didn't feel as though he belonged here.

Magic made Jörg's group invisible to anyone else, and the three of them walked around the naval port, glancing at battle-scarred ships and submarines. The vessels here were on a completely different scale from the British tanks, looking like fortresses floating on the water. As Jörg imagined them lined up on the open sea, cannons blazing, sinking one enemy ship after another—and the tremendous loss of lives and resources to the nation—a strange feeling settled over him.

"Well then," the Count said, "this is where I leave you."

"You're going already?"

"I've done my part in bringing you here. The rest is up to you two. I have attached a special mark to the back of the man you're looking for. It's buried beneath his skin, so it should appear even if he changes clothes. Look for that symbol."

"How did you do that?"

"I used a spell that attached the mark through his photograph. Assuming the magic worked, you should be able to find him easily enough. Stay for as long it takes to get useful intel, even if that means you're here for some months. If that's enough to make you want to give up, Lila, then you're not cut out to be a spy. Come back to the inn and think of something else you can do."

Lila nodded. "Got it. We'll find him quickly."

"That's a bold claim. Then I'll leave you to it."

The Count spread his cloak behind him like a pair of wings, then vanished into thin air.

A bright smile filled Lila's face. It clearly made her happy being treated like an adult.

"Let's go," she urged. "But where should we start looking for him?"

"First, let's figure out where everything is around here."

"Starting with?"

"The office. We'll look at what kind of work this military port prioritizes to try to predict which department a spy might try to approach. Though it's going to be difficult to find him if he's already got what he came for."

"I wonder if he really is disguised as a worker like we think."

"It's likely. For now, let's walk around and familiarize ourselves with the yard."

A lot of women were working in the office. They opened envelopes, corrected order slips and invoices, and managed inventory. Typewriters ejected reams of paper accompanied by metallic clicking sounds, and an incredible number of documents had been filed and crammed onto the shelves. The men in charge were tossing any paperwork that had completed the approval process into boxes.

Jörg and Lila peered in on the work, removed records from shelves, and checked their contents. They didn't actually flip through the pages, of course; the office workers would be sent into a panic if the documents started to move by themselves. Instead, Jörg and Lila simply extracted the simulacrum of each one from its physical counterpart.

They would place a finger on the spine of a bound file and slowly draw it toward them, extracting the simulacrum within. Once they had it in hand, they could examine it like a regular document to see what it contained.

They discovered that both repairing cruisers and constructing new ships was taking an incredibly long time and found records of orders from army commanders repeatedly demanding the shipyard speed the work up.

They were also building more submarines. The sheer number was enough to make anyone wonder just what exactly they intended to do with them.

Jörg stopped browsing the pages to think.

Submarines were weapons with a limited use. Building so many of them hinted at some sort of special plan.

After they finished sifting through the documents, Jörg and Lila moved to the docks.

Discharge pumps were removing seawater from ships, the colossal weight of which was supported from beneath by a row of blocks. Workers climbed up and down the scaffolding surrounding the hulls, while others on deck were in charge of inspecting and repairing the interiors.

The men lugged heavy materials and crossed the perilous scaffolding, carrying out their jobs in silence. The sound of rivets being fitted rang out nonstop, and welding sparks stung eyes.

Every so often, Jörg and Lila would hear people yelling. It wasn't an argument breaking out, however, but orders being given and received.

The sweet smell of paint and sharp tang of metal hung heavy in the air. The shipyard overflowed with energy, yet at the same time, there was a certain lethargy to it.

Jörg found it rather similar to the battlefield. Dealing with something so massive, the average worker wouldn't know what was going on where, how far the work had progressed, or even have a good idea of any details at the other end of the ship. They could only focus on the task at hand, calmly carrying out their job in an orderly fashion.

Every one of them blindly believed that their homeland would triumph, convinced it was that very belief that would bring about victory.

It was what they'd been made to believe.

Jörg and Lila didn't need to worry about food no matter how long they stayed there. Lila had left her corpus at the inn, so as long as Xandra was looking after her physical body, her simulacrum would be fine.

With the huge number of people that came and went through the shipyard, Jörg was never wanting for sustenance, either. He took a little from each laborer.

Factories provided a steady stream of construction materials, as well as deliveries of artillery shells and daily necessities for the ships. Jörg and Lila even searched all the employees involved with manufacturing and distribution, as well as the workers who brought the food and drink into the mess hall, but they still couldn't find the marked man. They only ever saw regular people.

Jörg asked Lila if she was getting bored with the job, but she said she wanted to keep going with that same glint she always had in her eyes.

"It's interesting seeing ships get built. I could watch it all day."

"We didn't come here to tour the factory, you know."

"I know. But it just sucks you in."

"So you don't care about being a spy anymore?" Jörg asked.

"No, I do."

"What's so interesting about watching them make weapons?"

A sullen look crossed Lila's face. "That's not why I like it."

"Then what is it?"

"I've never seen a vehicle this big before. It takes your breath away."

"But you've read about them."

"The real thing is completely different from a picture in a book!"

Jorg thought for a moment. "Then are you interested in planes?"

"What's a plane?"

"A vehicle that flies in the sky. They've been used on the battlefield recently, but originally they were invented because people wanted to fly like birds. Just like how the Count can soar through the sky, humans use machines to do the same."

Lila was immediately captivated. "That sounds fascinating."

"Do you want to try riding in one?"

"Yeah!"

"I don't know how to pilot one, so it would be easiest to ask a professional to give you a ride. Or you can learn to fly one yourself."

"Even someone like me could fly it?"

"Machines don't choose who can use them. The future will open up for someone who learns a skill like that. You pick things up quickly, so you should be able to fly a plane easily enough."

"Would you want to learn, Mr. Huber?"

"Sure, if I got the chance. I have nothing but time, after all."

Lila looked up at the sky. "Imagine how it would feel to fly through the air without using a simulacrum. Once the war ends, I wonder if it will become normal for women to fly planes and design machines."

"Your gender shouldn't have any impact on what you want to do. The Count said as much, didn't he?"

"Yeah. I hope that day comes as soon as possible."

5

Several days after Jörg and Lila arrived at the Kiel shipyard, a new boat arrived at the dock, and a large group of workers came down the gangplank. It seemed additional personnel had arrived. There were middle-aged men and some even older, as well as technicians who'd been away on business at other ports. The smells of their new uniforms and bags mingled with the preexisting odors that filled the facility. Even the temperature in the shipyard seemed to rise slightly.

As the new arrivals passed by them, Lila immediately reacted and pointed out one of the men.

A strange mark hovered over the back of his coveralls. It resembled the design on the back of Jörg's hand.

Taller than Jörg and more muscular, the man looked about ten years older than he was. Jörg had caught a glimpse of the man's face when he walked by conversing with a colleague. There didn't seem to be anything particularly special about him; he had the same air as everyone else working at the shipyard. His dark hair had grown a little shaggy, but with his clean-shaven face, he didn't appear slovenly. A deep scar ran down one cheek, hinting at a history as a soldier, and the swollen skin of a laceration that had scarred over peeked out from a shirtsleeve. His drooping eyebrows, sleepy eyes, and leisurely way of talking suggested a mild-mannered personality. He was fully engaged in a bawdy conversation with his coworker, wearing an easy smile that made him look like just any other person. He didn't seem to possess the sort of keen edge required of a spy whatsoever. Yet there was no mistaking it: This was the man from the photograph, Edmund Jansen.

"How did you get your information in Berlin?" Lila asked Jörg.

"I possessed someone and went around with them. When you merge with someone, you can access their thoughts."

"Okay, then I'll possess that guy and search his mind."

Jörg hurriedly tried to stop Lila, but she'd already raced over to the man.

"No. Don't be hasty," he called out.

"I've possessed people many times by now. I know how to leave safely, too, so don't worry."

Lila's shadow overlapped with Jansen's, and the figure of the young girl turned translucent. She disappeared, sucked into the man's body.

Jörg's blood froze. He hadn't intended to let Lila be the one to possess Jansen. This hadn't been part of the plan.

The man's expression didn't change after Lila possessed him. He waved good-bye to his colleague and began walking toward the office. A short while later, he stopped as if remembering something and looked around.

Jörg turned to look in the same direction and see what Jansen was looking at. It was a cruiser getting repairs. The light pouring down on the deck hazily illuminated the shape of men working there.

"Hey, you!" the man suddenly shouted.

The tone in his voice had changed completely. It was deep, almost a growl. He sounded like a different person altogether, and Jörg got a strange feeling that instantly put him on edge.

No one else was around. The man was looking straight at Jörg. There was no mistaking it—Edmund Jansen could see him. His easygoing, everyman expression had disappeared, replaced by a stern look completely devoid of emotion. It was tinged with something much darker than simple aggression that pierced Jörg's heart.

"Yeah, you," Jansen called out to him again. "Answer me."

Jörg kept his mouth shut, feeling it would be dangerous to respond without thinking things through first. The man took a step forward, then closed the distance without hesitation. He could definitely see Jörg. Vividly.

"My eyes are unique," the man said, pointing to his face. "It doesn't do me any good in the human world, though."

When Jörg still remained silent, Jansen's lips curled slightly. "Whatever. Don't answer me, then. By the way, I felt something enter me just now. Did you throw it into me?"

Jörg had thought the man hadn't noticed, but he'd sensed Lila's presence. Left with no other option but to respond, he said, "That wasn't me."

"It's fighting like mad to get out, but maybe I should just crush it."

Jörg's heart hammered deep in his chest. That was no empty threat. This man would kill if he had to.

Jörg leaped off the ground and flew at the man. When his right hand touched Jansen, he felt something within, like a person's hands banging against a wall. Lila's emotions poured into the palm of his hand. She was screaming, "*Help me! I'm so scared!*"

Jansen twisted his body to separate himself from Jörg, but Jörg closed the distance between them and swung a fist. It sank into the other man's torso, and two invisible hands grabbed hold of Jörg's arm. Jörg pulled, tearing Lila's simulacrum free from inside Jansen.

The violent motion caused Lila to shriek. She shivered as if she'd been submerged beneath the surface of a sea of ice, apparently having experienced something horrible inside the man.

Jansen seemed shocked to discover that Lila was just a girl, but he soon regained his composure, angling his body and taking on a fighting stance.

"You're no ordinary simulacrum," he said to Jörg as if scolding him. "Only a real monster could do something like that."

If this man knew about simulacrums, then he was no regular human. Not just a British conspirator, but someone much more troublesome.

Lila's eyes went wide upon hearing Jansen's words, and she looked at Jörg. He knew what she wanted to ask, but he deliberately said nothing.

Instead, he looked at the other man and said, "You're one to talk. Are you a simulacrum living and working in human society?"

"I'm a normal human."

"Don't lie. A normal person wouldn't be able to see us."

"I used to use a simulacrum. My eyes are still affected by that."

"Who gave it to you?"

"A monster of nothingness named Nil."

"What?!"

"You know Nil?"

Jörg nodded. Jansen seemed like a tough opponent, so instead of attacking him directly, Jörg would have to do more probing about Nil. "I've met Nil and know his associates. I'd rather talk calmly than fight."

"...Very well."

The man's threatening aura dissipated. He probably wanted to avoid a fight, too. He looked around and beckoned Jörg to follow him. "Let's go somewhere there's no people."

If someone saw him talking to himself, they might think the man had lost his mind. Changing locations was the smart choice.

Leaning against the wall in the shadow of a warehouse, Edmund pulled a pack of cigarettes from his coat pocket. He put one in his mouth, lit a match, and touched it to the tip of the cigarette. Inhaling deeply, he savored the taste before exhaling the smoke. "I'm going to pretend I'm talking to myself, so play along. No one should come around here at this time."

"Okay."

"Why are you here?"

"I'm searching for British spies."

"You mean me?"

"Not just you," Jörg lied.

Edmund didn't appear to doubt him. "What did you come to find out?"

"Anything the British will pay for."

"Where are you from?"

"Germany."

"Which makes you a traitor, just like me."

"More or less."

"In that case, I can tell you there's nothing else for you to do here. A terrifyingly skilled agent has already stolen all the information."

"Who was it? Where are they from?"

"He's a man British intelligence trusts more than anyone else for intel on the German Navy. If you came here for information, you're too late. You would've had to come at least four months ago, before the Battle of Jutland. Otherwise, it's pointless."

Jörg felt frustrated. Surely the Count had known something that important. Which meant there must be some sort of ulterior motive hidden behind his orders to collect information on the German Navy and the Count's insistence on bringing Lila along. But what?

"Great Britain wanted to know how badly damaged the German Navy was after that battle," Edmund continued. "The guy I told you about didn't just come here; he got intel from ten German shipyards, then sent everything to the British. He went to Bremen, Rostock, Danzig—"

"Who is he?"

"A pure-born German, just like me. I can't tell you his name, though. He's a shipyard technician who used to be in the navy until, one day, he was accused of insulting the imperial family, and a military court demoted him for it. He's despised the German Navy ever since. He offered his services to the British embassy in The Hague and told them he wanted to work as a spy, so the Secret Intelligence Service hired him and pay him well. He's a technician, so he sees things with an expert's eye and can sketch details of warships from just a quick glance. He's the best of the best. That guy alone keeps the Brits happy. I'm just a scavenger, sending stuff here and there to confirm details."

"I saw the construction orders in the office. They're increasing the number of submarines being built. Is the German Navy planning to go back to unrestricted submarine warfare?"

"Probably." Edmund flicked his lit cigarette away. "I can't stay here chatting. It'll draw the inspector's attention."

"Will you be in port for a while?"

"Until I get my hands on everything I can. With the losses they suffered at Jutland, the German Navy probably won't be able to strike in numbers again. Great Britain already has countermeasures for submarines, so the tactics they've used before won't work again. The end is in sight."

Edmund raised a hand and waved, then started heading back toward the dock.

Lila was still hugging Jörg tightly. She'd calmed down considerably since earlier, but her body was still stiff with tension.

Jörg crouched down and looked her in the eyes.

"I saw something I can never forget," Lila said softly. "In that man's body. What do I do?"

Jörg raised a finger to his lips. "If it's scary, then it's best you don't talk about it now. You can tell me about it in your own time when you feel up to it."

"But—"

"It's okay. We're invisible, and the people here can't see us. You can find somewhere to rest or return to the inn ahead of me."

"I think I'll do that. I want to go home."

"Then when you get back, have Xandra give you some medicine and go right to bed. I'll take you to the portal."

After Lila had passed through the portal created near the office, Jörg searched for Edmund again. He found him working hard at repairs, and Jörg stayed hidden in the shadows, not letting the man out of his sight until he finished work for the day.

The evening break arrived. Workers poured out of the various boats like ants emerging from sap-drained trees going back to the nest—in this case, the mess hall.

Jörg still didn't call out to him. Edmund entered the mess with the other workers, finished his meal—potato soup and a slice of rye bread—and went outside to light a cigarette. It was only then that Jörg called his name.

Edmund gave him an exasperated look. "You're still here?"

"I forgot to ask you about Nil."

"What happened to the girl?"

"She went home."

"I've never seen a spy bring their kid with them. It's pretty reckless."

"She's not my daughter."

"Then who is she?"

"The child of an acquaintance."

"Did they ask you to raise her or something?"

"Something like that."

"It's commendable, especially in times like these." Edmund took a drag of his cigarette and blinked a few times. "I once took a parent from their child."

"What?"

"I had orders from above. It wasn't my call." Edmund was silent for a while, then finally tossed his cigarette aside and murmured hoarsely, "Have you served on the front?"

"I have."

"So you know what it's like. Sometimes a man has to kill for his job."

"I do," Jörg replied. "But it's not as if you can just let yourself be killed, is it?"

"You must've killed a lot of men, then."

"As you know," Jörg said, changing the subject, "I came here with a job to do. Your British contact is gone. They were arrested, interrogated, and executed. In the process, they gave up your name."

Edmund disappointedly clicked his tongue. "I see. So that's what this is about."

"Killing you would be easy, but I'd rather let you escape."

"Why?"

"I don't want to kill anyone on the home front. I saw enough blood on the battlefield."

"Save me your kindness," Edmund spat. "A job's a job, so you should see it through. I'll fight back with everything I've got. I was getting bored anyway."

"Don't be stupid. I'm more interested in learning what Nil did to you than fighting. That's what I came to talk to you about."

"Hmph."

"Why did Nil give you a simulacrum? And why did you get rid of it? Nil wouldn't have done something like that without a reason."

"He was just toying with me to amuse himself."

"He did it for *fun*?"

"Yeah. I had shell shock and could barely move, so he offered me a body I could use as easily as my real one. A simulacrum."

Edmund looked out toward the sea. The faint glow of a lighthouse could be seen a short distance away from the dock, its beam cutting through the darkness. "When I met Nil, he told me to enjoy myself for a while in the simulacrum. While I was doing that, he entered my soulless body and entertained himself with it. He did whatever he wanted on the battlefield and enjoyed himself in town when I was given leave, then when he was done having his fun, he pulled me from my simulacrum and tossed me back into my body. By that time, I'd recovered from my shell shock, so I guess I have him to thank for that. If I hadn't rested in that simulacrum, I doubt I would have been capable of returning to a normal life after being discharged. My entire body would shake constantly. I could hardly even piss without help."

"Monsters don't just do things out of the goodness of their hearts. Did he ask for anything in return?"

"Nothing. But ever since then, it almost feels like I'm not living in my own body."

Edmund turned and walked down the moonlit jetty. He moved carefully so as not to fall into the sea, then stopped after a little way.

"Letting Nil use my body was a mistake," he said, still facing away from Jörg. "He left a freezing cold hole inside me when he left. It keeps growing and steadily eats away at my soul. I don't know how to fight it. The war already crushed my spirit, then he robbed me of any emotion I might still have. There's nothing left in my heart anymore. I can't feel hate, but I can't feel love, either."

"But why would Nil do all that—?"

"Because he's a monster. That's how he entertains himself. It's not something humans could ever understand." Edmund turned his head slightly, looking back at Jörg. "But if you kill me, I can at least die as a murderer, instead of someone consumed by nothing. Right now, I think that's the only way I can fight back against Nil."

"I can't kill you after hearing all that."

"I don't want to commit suicide, nor do I have any intention of doing so. But I think it would be a relief for my life to end here."

Killing him would be simple enough; all Jörg needed to do was drain the man of sustenance. At this distance, he'd be done in less than a minute. If he touched Edmund, it would be over in an instant.

Resolving himself to kill the man, Jörg focused his energy into his palms. He realized there was nothing he could do to help him. Jörg felt the first trickle of sustenance flowing out of Edmund, but it didn't seem as if the man noticed, because he only turned back to look at the sea.

"How did my life end up like this?" Edmund continued, speaking quietly to himself. "When I was a kid, I dreamed of becoming an architect. Designing cities, building new homes for people, renovating old ones. And just once in my life, I wanted to get a job from someone rich or from the government and brag about it to my wife and kids. Maybe build churches, or clock towers, or theaters. But instead, I ended up as a spy. I did that before the war, too. Intelligence work was wild in the days leading up to the war. It was an important job, and it made me a lot of money. I went into town lots of times with all that cash and partied like a king. It was the only way I could distract myself after killing someone."

A quiet chuckle escaped him. "Then, when the war started, I was sent off to fight. No one had a use for me anymore, or maybe some bad guys knew my face. I went off to war, and all I did was shoot my gun and destroy occupied towns. We torched and demolished buildings that would make an architecture lover like me tremble with excitement, all because they might be hiding enemy combatants. To me, doing that felt like I was denying something inside my soul— No, like I was crushing my soul entirely. I hated it so much that I even tried to prevent the fires from spreading. There are ways to set a building's surroundings on fire that will protect the structure itself from the blaze. You can counteract a spreading fire with another fire, and they'll extinguish each other instantly. But when I tried that at Leuven, the flames were so intense that nothing could stop them, and in the end, the entire town burned to the ground. Even the library was nothing but ashes by the time it was over."

Edmund heaved a tired sigh. "There was probably a point I could have turned around and come back, but I chose the wrong path."

"I know how you feel."

"I'm already an empty shell. There's nothing inside me. That's what happens when Nil possesses you. Be careful."

Edmund slowly began to turn toward Jörg. He staggered as though someone had pushed in the back, then bent double, but he still remained standing.

Jörg squeezed his hands tight. He couldn't commit to that final push.

He had suppressed all of Edmund's painful thoughts and already absorbed this much sustenance from him. Just a little more, and Edmund would be at peace. But he couldn't do it.

Just then, a giant black shape descended from the sky. Jörg instinctively stepped back. It was the exact same bat-like, dragon-like shape he'd seen in the sky from the trenches of Champagne.

The figure flew toward Edmund and wrapped its wings around his body. Edmund's legs from the knees down remained visible, and they began to twitch violently, then hung motionless. The dark form moved away from him and stood up to its full height, transforming into Count Silvestri.

Crimson painted his mouth. He wiped at it neatly with the tip of a finger, then licked all the blood smeared around his lips like someone savoring a runny egg yolk.

Two deep wounds had been carved into Edmund's neck, each one still trickling with blood. His eyes were closed, the waxy paleness of his face looking as if he'd already been dead for several days.

The Count removed a piece of silk from the pocket on his cloak, then spoke to Jörg as he wiped his hands clean. "Well done. Mission complete."

"But I couldn't finish him off."

"You did enough. No human could recover after having that much life force taken from them. It was the same as you having already done the deed."

"Then why did you come?"

"Every so often, I get the urge to hunt humans like this. It must be a command from the ancient blood."

Which meant that at some point, the same would happen to Jörg.

"What about the body?" Jörg asked somberly.

"Once we take a photo to bring back to Lieutenant Colonel Kreutzer, it will have no more use for us. We'll throw it into the sea."

"How's Lila?"

"Xandra gave her a sedative, and she's sleeping peacefully."

"She saw Jansen's memories when she possessed his body."

"Did she now?"

"Do you mind if I go to talk with her about it later?"

"Do as you please. Whether you tell her everything or leave some things out is entirely up to you."

6

After returning to Xandra's inn, Jörg went to Lila's room for the first time and waited beside her bed for her to wake up.

Monsters had also gathered here in the young girl's bedroom, floating like dragonflies by the edge of a pond. Jörg glared at the ones that came right up to her pillow, which let out growls that sounded like grinding teeth before returning to the ceiling. But even then, they didn't leave.

When he told them to go because they were just getting in the way, the monsters protested in shrill voices. Maybe they were drawn to Lila's suffering. Or maybe they'd come to draw sustenance from her.

"I'm not letting you have this girl. In the name of Vlad, voivode of Walachia, and Count Silvestri, I command you to leave."

At that, the monsters' voices changed to words he could understand.

"Noooo, that's not why we're here."

"We're friends. *Friends*."

"Friends?" Jörg looked confused. "You mean you're Lila's friends?"

"Yeah, we are."

"Ever since she came here."

"Lila's friends."

"Kind friends."

"Then let her rest. She's extremely tired. You can't do anything to help her."

The monsters lamented and complained, but they must have understood in the end because they gradually disappeared through the ceiling and walls.

Lila woke with the rising sun. When Jörg asked if she was hungry, she said she felt like porridge, so he left to go to the kitchen. He poured some oats into a pot, added milk and sugar, then turned on the stovetop. Once the porridge was ready, he scooped some into a bowl, made a cup of tea, set everything on a cart, and pushed it to Lila's room.

By the time Jörg returned, Lila had already gotten changed and was sitting in front of a small, round table.

The color had returned to her face. "You're like my personal butler, Mr. Huber," she said with a grin.

"That's fine by me." Jörg smiled and set the food on the table. "Please enjoy, Miss Lila."

"Thank you, Huber."

Lila didn't talk as she spooned food into her mouth. Jörg stood silently by her side.

Once she'd finished eating, Lila finally spoke. "There's one thing I'd like to ask you."

"Sure."

"When did you become a real monster?"

"All I've done is improve the capabilities of my simulacrum because I thought it would be more convenient for espionage."

"Don't lie to me. I've experienced something similar before, so I can tell. One time, I possessed someone and the Count did the same thing to pull me out and save me. You couldn't have done that if you weren't a monster."

"You can do it without being a monster if you know how."

"Liar. Why won't you tell me the truth? I can't trust you or work with you like this. I can't be around someone who lies to other people."

"...Fine. I'll tell you. But in exchange, I want you to tell me what you saw inside Jansen. I have to report to the Count."

"Okay. That's fair."

Lila offered Jörg a chair, then sat on the edge of the bed.

"I'll go first," he said.

"Sure."

"A little while ago, I received some of the Count's blood and turned into a monster. The sensations I felt when I was human are still strong, though, and it doesn't feel like my thoughts have caught up yet."

"I told you not to become a monster."

"I know, I'm sorry. But I needed that power. And my corpus is still alive. Once he's released from the field hospital, he said he's going to leave the army and go back home. So Jörg Huber the human hasn't disappeared from the earth. My corpus is going to live out his life as a normal person. He'll experience joy as a human, grief as a human, and one day, he'll die as a human. Nothing will change with all his human relationships, including the relationship with his family. He left for war, got injured, then went back home. That's all there is to it."

"You're saying he's the real Jörg Huber?"

"Yes."

"Then who's the Mr. Huber here? What are you?"

"I am the thing that escaped Jörg Huber's corpus. The Count would say this version of me—the me that exists purely as a spirit—is the real Jörg Huber, but he only thinks that way because he isn't bound by the limitations of the flesh."

"In other words, you believe that *this* you isn't the real you, so there's no problem if you become a monster."

"Pretty much."

"That's a completely different way to how I use simulacrums," Lila commented.

"How so?"

"My soul doesn't split in half when I use one. Wherever I go, it's the whole me. I exist as one being. To me, simulacrums are like vehicles. Changing bodies is like changing clothes."

"I see."

"Tell me why you became a monster. If it was just for espionage, then a simulacrum would have been enough."

"I wanted power. The power to do things exactly how I want."

"And simulacrums aren't powerful enough?"

"No."

"Why not just give up on the things you didn't have the power to do?"

"I didn't want to. It's that simple."

"That's like saying you were controlled by your desires. Monsters use that about humans to exploit them."

"I know. But this is what I wanted."

Jörg clasped his hands in his lap. "I know you don't like talking about war, but would you mind if I told you a little about it?"

"Okay. Go ahead."

"I fought against a lot of enemy soldiers on the battlefield, both with rifles and machine guns, but I still vividly remember the first time I stabbed someone with my knife. One thrust wasn't enough to kill him, and in the chaos of hand-to-hand combat, I blanked out and just kept stabbing over and over again. It was the first time I truly felt broken—and by that, I don't mean I was starting to lose my mind. Up until then, I'd felt like a single person, but suddenly I could feel myself starting to split apart. That was when I realized something: People aren't made up of one solid self, but all sorts of different parts that usually stay bundled together tightly. And the string holding them all together is extremely fragile. Or maybe it's more like glue coming loose. Anyway, when some sort of outside force attacks, it's easy for that string or glue to come undone. What I experienced on the battlefield was the exact moment that string unraveled. The exact moment that glue dissolved. Anyone who's experienced coming apart like that has a hard time believing any longer that a human being is made of one unified self."

Keeping his hands intertwined, Jörg clenched and unclenched his fingers. "For the longest time, I didn't know what to do with myself after coming apart. My soul no longer had that glue—that string—that would put me back together as I had been. The Count pulled one of those scattered fragments free. The me that's here now isn't the unified self of Jörg Huber, but just one of those rescued fragments. And I'm not even sure if the fragment the Count took was worth saving. After all, the Count operates on the logic of a monster, not a human. It's possible that the moment I entered this simulacrum, I became a different Jörg Huber from that man I'd been on the battlefield. No longer just one part of my body, but something else entirely. That's why this new existence needs something to live for—and I finally found it when I decided to live as a monster. My actions might seem foolish and shortsighted to you, but I'm satisfied with how things have turned out."

Lila hadn't so much as blinked as she listened to Jörg. Finally, she said, "I don't care about the other fragments. You're the only Jörg Huber I know. To me, you're the real Jörg Huber."

"Thank you."

"Of course. So now that you're a monster, you're no longer German, right? You have no country or ethnicity."

Jörg hadn't become a monster to appease Lila, but he couldn't deny that her logic made sense from a certain perspective. By the very definition of the word, the Jörg here was no longer German. That thought made him feel a little better.

"Now it's my turn," Lila continued. "When I was inside that man we met in Kiel—Mr. Jansen—I kept seeing scenes of people being murdered over and over again. I saw through his eyes, so each time I touched a new memory, I would feel myself swinging his blade and shooting his gun."

"That's what happens when you possess someone like that."

"I wouldn't have done it if I'd known… I never saw anything that scary the other times I possessed someone."

"The Count must have chosen people who were safe to probe when he was training you."

"Yeah. It never occurred to me that the Count took that into consideration. I was such a fool. I just kept thinking that when I was inside Mr. Jansen. He looked so tough on the outside, but inside he was tormented by such horrible, awful things.

"Some of the people he killed died screaming the names of family members or clutching photographs they kept in their pockets," Lila said, frowning. "After he murdered someone, Mr. Jansen would search through their clothes and belongings for any information he could steal. Once, after swiftly dispatching a man, he searched through his personal effects the same way he always did. The dead man was wearing a pendant around his neck, and Mr. Jansen flipped it open, thinking the man must have been hiding something inside. It didn't have anything he was looking for, though—just a picture of a woman with a young child in her arms. The second he set eyes on the photo, his heart began to waver violently. He must have been thinking about his own family. Or maybe about his mother. I remember feeling really dizzy, too. Because the girl in the photo looked so much like me…"

Jörg swallowed, but he didn't say anything.

Lila continued, on the verge of tears. "If both the people doing the killing and the people getting killed know it's going to create such painful memories, then why don't they stop? People say that's just how war is, but I can't accept that."

"…Then maybe you should distance yourself from this type of work. I'm sure the Count would understand if you told him you don't want to do it anymore."

Jörg finally understood why the Count had told him to take Lila: He'd predicted she would try to possess Jansen. Lila was a curious child, so he must've thought she'd try. He'd probably already known everything she would see inside the man, as well. It was truly a horrible way to educate the young girl on society—not a human method, but one belonging to monsters. Though it was undeniable that it had had a huge impact on her.

Lila drew closer to Jörg and crouched down. She reached out and gently touched his hands. "Mr. Huber, you're a far better person than that man. I really appreciate that you told me the truth. Thank you. But I still think it's such a shame you became a monster."

"I'm sorry I hid it from you all this time. I just can't sit around and do nothing about the poverty afflicting Germany. This is the only way I know to help Diana."

"I understand how you feel," Lila said. "You had to choose this, didn't you? Even though you knew it might prolong the war."

Quietly, she murmured, "I want to try working with you for a bit longer. Until I find an answer I can be happy with."

7

That afternoon, after they'd composed themselves, Jörg and Lila went to visit the Count in his room.

The first words out of the Count's mouth were directed at Lila. "Now you understand some of the dangers involved in carrying out missions like this during a war. What happened at Kiel is just scratching the surface. Keep going, and you're bound to see much worse. Do you still wish to continue?"

"Yes," the young girl replied.

"In that case, you should learn to improve your control of simulacrums so you can extract yourself unassisted. Mr. Huber may not always be around to save you."

"Understood."

"All right, then. It's a bit sudden, but your next assignment is waiting for you. The food distribution plan. You know about this, don't you, Lila?"

"Yeah."

"The time has come to put this plan into motion. I'd like for you to help, as well."

"I don't want to help Germans," Lila responded quickly.

"Of course, you're free to help or not, however you see fit. Regardless, I would like you to go there once and see it for yourself. There are many girls your age among the starving Germans."

Lila looked down at the ground in silence, and the Count continued without waiting for her to answer, addressing Jörg.

"By the way, I obtained some interesting information about Kleinerbrunn. Would you like to hear it?"

"Absolutely."

"Fabrice LeRoy is there right now."

Jörg's entire body tensed up.

The woman he'd met in Paris, Christine, had a younger brother named Hubert. Fabrice LeRoy had been on his soccer team. The two men had both deployed together, but their whereabouts were unknown since the Battle of Artois.

Apparently, Fabrice had been captured by the Germans and sent to an internment camp inside Germany, then shipped off to work in the fields, since farmers didn't have enough men. This was an officially sanctioned use of POWs under international conventions. Young Frenchmen worked diligently and were valued highly by the *Landfrauen*, the German women who oversaw the farms—so much so that, from time to time, a *Landfrau* and a POW would even develop feelings for each other.

"In villages where the army has taken all the men, the only people around to manage the fields are women, children, and the elderly," the Count explained. "They work every day from four in the morning until nine at night. In addition to tending the fields, the women have to take care of the house and raise the children, so they never get a moment's rest. It's not uncommon for some of them to die from overwork. As such, young French soldiers come and help with the farmwork. Separated from their husbands for so long, it's no surprise that some wives begin to feel their passions stir—and the young, unmarried women who hold no prejudice toward foreigners are even more excitable. After all, there isn't a man in his prime left in the area."

Jörg's eyes bulged at the scandalous nature of what the Count was telling him. And Lila was right next to him listening. This wasn't something they should be openly discussing. Once again, Jörg was reminded of just how different a monster's sensibilities were.

"That's no excuse…," he murmured.

"Does something about that bother you?" the Count asked.

"Would *you* be okay with that? Your wife, daughters, and sisters cavorting with the enemy while you were off fighting?!"

"Whether or not I approve is irrelevant. No one can deny that it's happening, and there's nothing that can be done about it. I honestly think it's quite brave of the women. These young ladies looking beyond nationality to find love during a time of war… It's quite romantic, don't you think? Even if it is nothing more than simple lust. If Germany is going to call these women unfaithful or pitiful, then they should stop the war at once."

"I guess you've got a point…"

"As it stands now, the *Landfrauen* currently rely on Fabrice for many things. He's even helping them sell their produce on the black market."

"They really trust him that much?"

"These are strong farming women who are involving themselves in underground trade. No one can blame them for their illicit activities after losing their husbands and sons to the war. Still, it can be dangerous work. Buyers from the city might be accompanied by ill-intentioned people who use violence to steal their goods, so the women bring Fabrice with them as a bodyguard. But that's not all he does. The truth is, he also meets with people from the city behind the women's backs, exchanging food for information on the state of Berlin."

"So the residents of Berlin want food so badly that they sell information to him?"

"Precisely. The French Army tasked him with this covert operation. It must have been either right after he was thrown into the internment camp or when he was sent to the farms that they ordered someone to contact him and give him this assignment."

"But how does he get the information outside Germany?"

"Carrier pigeon, most likely. It's not uncommon for people in the country to keep pigeons and turtledoves, and no one would bat an eye to see a pigeon flying over their village. The birds likely fly either to Paris or to a relay station."

"Why a relay station?"

"Considering the circumstances, Fabrice would have a very hard time trying to conceal any transmission equipment. A carrier pigeon is far less suspicious. He can release a pigeon from somewhere near the farm, and whoever receives the encoded message can then telegram each Allied nation to relay his message. It's also much faster that way."

Just then, Jörg recalled something he had seen near Christine's apartment. When he was wandering around Paris, he'd looked up to see a lone pigeon fly into the open window on the upper floor of an apartment building. Christine had called out to him just moments after that.

Jörg had no proof that Fabrice had sent it, but if Fabrice still cared for Christine, it was possible he had purposely sent a pigeon to somewhere near her house. He might have asked whoever received the pigeon to check on Christine and tell him how she was doing. Of course, this would all have to be kept secret from the military.

"We can ignore his messages if the information he's sending is unimportant," the Count said. "But right now, Fabrice is a link in the food supply chain. He's in a position where he can intentionally limit supplies to Berlin. If the Allies order him to starve the German people, he could secretly destroy food scheduled to be delivered to the city."

The Count was right. Fabrice LeRoy was a soldier, meaning he would follow any order that would bring an end to the war. He likely wouldn't hesitate to mercilessly kill Germans on the home front just as he'd done on the front lines, the same way German soldiers had slaughtered the people of Belgium. In wartime, the people of a hostile nation were viewed no differently from soldiers—the reason being that it was citizens who built weapons, manufactured the goods required for war, and educated those who would be sent to the front lines as soldiers.

"Mr. Huber, do you know Mr. LeRoy?" Lila asked.

Jörg shook his head. "Just Hubert's sister. I've only seen a picture of Fabrice."

"And he's important to her?"

"Yeah."

"Who will you protect, Diana or Hubert's sister?"

"That depends on the situation."

"Mr. LeRoy will kill you without a second thought if he decides you're the enemy. That's how war is, right?"

"I won't die. I have the Count's blood in me."

"Diana and the others are all regular humans, though. So what will you do if they get caught up in this?"

Jörg pursed his lips. He knew what he would have to do. Even if his body couldn't be harmed, if the people he was trying to help were in danger, then he'd have no choice but to take up arms.

Lila continued. "I'm not on Germany's side, but I also don't want to stand by and watch people die needlessly. I'm going to do what I think is best. And if I agree that what you're doing is right, then I'll help you. Does that suit you?"

"Of course," replied Jörg. "That makes things easier for me, too. Anyway, we should start by going to meet Diana."

IV
Each Person's Battle

1

Jörg changed his appearance again for the visit to Berlin. This time he chose a merchant, as he figured it would be helpful in their trip to Kleinerbrunn, and decided to make him middle-aged because people wouldn't trust him during negotiations if he looked too young.

"What about me?" Lila asked.

"It would be bad for you to stay as a child, so the best thing would probably be if you looked around the age of a young secretary. Your simulacrum can be either a man or a woman with masculine features. Which would be easier for you to act as?"

"Either one's fine with me."

"In that case, try out a few different looks later and choose one. Also, to play the part, I'm going to talk down to you a little bit. You won't mind?"

"Of course not, it's just acting. But no yelling or hitting."

Jörg gave her a wry smile. "I would never do that. When we're there, try not to speak too much, otherwise you'll draw their suspicions."

"Okay. So what do we do first?"

"We meet Diana in the real world and let her see that we really exist. Then we talk with her about our plan to distribute food. The best-case scenario would be if Diana can move to the countryside with her whole family, but if that's impossible, we'll have to come up with a way for them to receive the food where they are. Assuming they can't relocate, we'll need to secure a warehouse on the outskirts of the city. There are eyes everywhere in Berlin, so we'll need a place that's inconspicuous."

"How are we going to keep watch over a warehouse?"

"We'll rent the storehouse of a monastery brewery. That way, someone will always be there to keep an eye on things, and the deliveries won't catch anyone's attention."

Gentlemen in dark cloaks weren't the only people walking through Berlin's Potsdamer Platz. Many in the crowd pulled at the collars of their thin, dirty jackets as they stumbled around on unsteady legs. There was only a smattering of horse-drawn carriages in the square, likely because most had been requisitioned by the army. The number of automobiles paled in comparison to Paris, but even so, a line of large roofless cars made their way down the roads. In their windows, healthy, smiling faces chatted with female companions—a single glance of which was enough to tell that the people riding in them belonged to the upper class.

A metallic whine accompanied a streetcar as it stopped, letting off tired-looking workers holding the handrails, who stepped down onto the street. Buildings with grand awnings lined both sides of the wide avenue, while domed roofs could be seen far off in the distance. The historic stone buildings of this big city impressed both Jörg and Lila.

Jörg wore a fedora and an outfit suitable for a middle-aged gentlemen, while Lila had on a flat cap and was dressed like a boy. Her simulacrum was slender and androgynous, but with her short hair, she looked like a typical bag boy serving his boss. Such a pair wouldn't garner any undue attention wherever they went—or so they'd decided in choosing their disguises.

As Jörg and Lila waited beneath the appointed streetlight, they saw a young woman walk down the sidewalk. She looked nothing like her appearance at the Eiffel Tower. Diana as a soul was full of youthful vigor, but the woman standing before them was rail-thin with sunken cheeks and pale skin devoid of the vibrancy of life. Her eyes still shone fiercely, though, likely because the one remaining thing she could rely on was her strength of will.

Diana noticed Jörg and Lila right away and called out to them.

"Mr. Jörg Huber, I presume."

"That's correct," Jörg replied in the relaxed tone of a middle-aged man. "And you must be Ms. Diana from the Eiffel Tower."

She nodded, then continued as if embarrassed. "Um, I...was under the impression, when we met at the Eiffel Tower, that you were younger, Mr. Huber. I'm sorry for not speaking more respectfully to you during our prior meeting."

Jörg gave Diana a quick smile and waved her apology away. "There's no need to stand on ceremony. I act young when I'm just a soul. And I'm also partially to blame for behaving rather immaturely back then."

Standing next to Jörg, Lila greeted her as well. "It's nice to meet you outside of dreams, Ms. Diana. I'm Lila."

"Oh?" Diana looked stunned. "Lila, you look like a boy."

"This was less conspicuous for coming to Berlin."

"It really suits you."

"Thank you. In England, the working women wear pants, right? I think German women should do the same."

"That's a wonderful idea. Mr. Huber, what do you do for work?"

"I trade in general commodities," Jörg replied. "I'm currently based in Prague. Which is why I know a little about the logistics of food distribution."

It was a lie, but Diana seemed to buy it.

"Where shall we go to talk?" Jörg asked, changing the subject.

"Let's go to a *Mittelstandküche*, where the middle class eat. I want to show you what it's like in Berlin now."

The place Diana took them to had been either a normal dining hall up until the start of the war or a restaurant that had closed down because of it and was now being used by the government. The soot-stained brick walls showed the building's age, and even the lights hanging from the ceiling beams were incredibly dark. The inside stank of that same odor Jörg knew from the battlefield, causing Lila to scrunch up her face slightly. At the Port of Kiel, the smell of oil and paint had overpowered the stink of human bodies, but here their lungs choked on it. The heaters were off, most likely from a lack of fuel, but the press of people made the air in the room feel warm, damp, and stagnant.

Seeing Lila's reaction, Diana whispered an apology. "Sorry. The air's horrible here. Plus it's cold."

"No, it's not so bad," Jörg answered instead. "The battlefield is worse."

"No one has soap to wash themselves with anymore. All the rations for daily necessities have been used up."

Although it was a dining hall, there were no options to choose from. Everyone just picked up a spoon and one of the bowls that had been brought out from the kitchen and placed on the serving table. The meal consisted of soup with a scant few vegetables floating in it and a thin slice of hard bread. There was no ham, milk, or coffee, and you couldn't even hope for something like beer. But at least the soup was warm.

The room was crowded with people, making it hard to find someplace to sit.

When they finally settled at a table, Jörg pointed to his soup and asked, "Is this turnip?"

"Yes," replied Diana. "They're just the ones that were used to feed livestock before the war, though—nothing like the flavorsome ones we cooked with during peacetime. But the cities don't have anything else."

Jörg scooped up a piece of turnip with his spoon and put it in his mouth. The bland soup needed more salt, and he only tasted the bitterness of the turnip. Tiny bits of potato sat at the bottom of the bowl, along with one extremely thin sausage. "You still have potatoes, though, it seems. And sausages."

"The sausage is made from rats. All the pork's gone."

An image of rats feasting on soldiers' corpses in the trenches flashed through Jörg's mind, and his throat tightened reflexively. He remembered one of the men in his squad killing the vermin with his club and army shovel, then stringing them all up in a row. He'd smiled and posed for the war correspondent's camera, and Jörg and everyone else had cheered and carried on.

Diana's voice brought Jörg back to the present.

"This is for the middle class, so the food's still passable. The public *Volksküche* soup kitchens are much worse. They don't serve anything fit for human consumption."

She picked up a slice of bread. "This is made by mixing wheat and barley flour with potato flour. A ten percent mix is called *K-Brot*, and anything over twenty percent is *KK-Brot*. They call it bread, but it's dry, crumbly, and flavorless. We can't even get *K-Brot* most days, though. We get about one egg every three weeks and water down our milk to make it last longer. Since there are no more coffee beans, people also dry and roast turnips and barley and call it ersatz coffee. You can probably imagine just how fucking disgusting that tastes."

Diana looked down, probably embarrassed at having let her emotions get the better of her. "This is what the German people eat now. Refuse it, and there's nothing else to eat. If a horse collapses from starvation as it passes by, everyone rushes out of their houses with knives to carve it up. These days, that's a feast." She gestured to the soup in front of Jörg. "Don't worry if you can't eat it. I'm sure this sort of a meal is unimaginable in Prague."

"No, of course I'll eat it. I'm part German myself."

Jörg bit into the sausage without complaint. He ate the bland turnip and soaked the *K-Brot* in the soup before drinking every last drop of liquid.

Lila shook her head, reluctant to touch the food in front of her. Her simulacrum didn't need to eat. But even so, Jörg set his spoon down and said, "Food's precious these days. Please try to eat it."

"But—"

"You'll regret it later. Not trying to understand the people who lived in the same time as you."

Lila bit her lip for a while, then seemed to make up her mind, picking up her spoon and shoveling the food into her mouth. She had only ever eaten delicious meals at Xandra's inn, so even if this was the norm for Germany these days, Jörg was sure Lila hadn't wanted to try it purely out of sympathy. After practically inhaling her food, Lila's eyes went as blank as a corpse's, probably swearing to herself that she'd never come to this place again.

Diana explained to Jörg that on the days the rations were handed out, people had to line up the night before to get food.

"And at some point, I'm sure we won't get anything, even with the ration tickets. People higher up in the supply chain buy up all the food and commodities. I heard the same thing happens on the battlefield—that soldiers on the front lines starve while the generals safe at the back have luxurious meals. That's what the soldiers who've returned say."

The longer the war dragged on, the more this kind of story spread on the home front. Protests were sure to turn violent once a city reached a breaking point, and if that happened in Berlin, Diana thought it might lead to revolution.

After leaving the dining hall, Diana led Jörg and Lila to a nearby park. They went down a boulevard dyed yellow by rows of vibrant linden trees. It must have been a popular place for people to stroll during more peaceful times, but now it lay silent. Plants grew strong and lush in stark contrast to the people devoid of energy. They saw the occasional figure of a person bent over in the grass, back hunched, grabbing at something in the ground. Searching for edible plants, most likely.

"My neighbors might hear if we talk at my house," Diana said. "It's a little chilly today, but let's talk outside."

"Fine by me," Jörg responded cheerfully. "It's a nice time of year to admire the fall foliage."

As the three of them wandered around a park as large as a forest, the fallen leaves beneath their feet released a refreshing fragrance. Jörg worried that too much walking would weaken the famished Diana, but she just kept going with a determined look on her face.

Diana mumbled that there was a bench up ahead, and sure enough, when they reached the end of the winding path, they came to a fenced-in rest area. Diana sat at the end of the left side of the bench, so Jörg and Lila settled themselves on the opposite side.

"Bernadette from Paris—you know who I'm talking about, right?" Jörg asked.

"Yes."

"She helped us figure out a way to buy food from a village called Kleinerbrunn. Bringing it directly into Berlin would draw too much attention, and we're also worried about robbers, so we're going to rent the storehouse of a monastery brewery and take the food there. No one would suspect people going into a monastery. That's where you come in, Diana. I'd like you to oversee that storehouse. If word gets out that there's a stockpile of food at the monastery, people will try to sneak in and steal it. So you'll need to be careful that doesn't happen."

"I appreciate the thought, but like I said at the Eiffel Tower, I don't have any money. Food must be incredibly expensive on the black market, right?"

"Depending on what you're buying," Jörg said, "prices can be ten to twenty times those in the city."

Diana looked dumbstruck. "I could never pay that."

"There's no point haggling, either. Too many people want it, and the rich can easily pay that amount."

"Then what do you suggest I do?"

"I'm going to sell you food at ordinary prices. If even that's too much, then you can pay me later."

"When would I do that?"

"After the war ends."

"I'm not sure I'll ever be able to pay it, though."

"Honestly, I plan on starting a business once the war's over. If you want, I can offer you a job there. I can take the remaining balance out of your paycheck in installments without making things difficult for you. What do you think?"

Diana looked at him in utter disbelief. "I don't know what to say. Are you sure you're okay with that?"

"The men will return to work once the war is over. Women working now will be forced to give up their jobs and go back to being housewives. But now that they've experienced the joy of joining the workforce, they're not going to take that lying down, are they? I'm going to find women who want to keep working and give them jobs after the war. Society may criticize me and say it's underhanded, but I don't care. This is the natural progression of the world. Every industry is going to have to hire women again at some point, because the country's going to need all the hands they can get to rebuild after the war."

"I'll do it. Please, let me help. Should we post people at the storehouse around the clock?"

"As long as they're trustworthy. But too many people makes a secret hard to keep, so be careful."

"I will."

"I'd also like periodic updates on the situation in Berlin. I'll keep sending Lila to the Eiffel Tower."

"Okay."

"This is bound to be safer than working in a brothel."

"Definitely," agreed Diana.

Jörg explained how brothels operated and how the madames exploited the prostitutes, having been told all about it by Bernadette. Diana listened intently. She wasn't the type of person who could handle that line of work, and hearing everything the job entailed, she breathed a sigh of relief that it hadn't come to that.

"I can only get enough food for your family and friends, but it should help make up for when you can't get anything from the distribution center. You won't be full, but you'll be able to eat bread made from wheat, and I can arrange to have smoked meat and root vegetables delivered, too."

Diana's eyes sparkled. "We'll get to eat real bread and vegetables that aren't rotten?"

"You will."

"I'm in. I've had enough of life under the food shortages. I'll do whatever you want to go back to eating regular bread every day."

"I'm glad to hear that. It would be risky to have one person guard the storehouse, so you should post at least two guards there at all times. Is your father off fighting in the war?"

"He is. They finally drafted him just the other day."

"So the only people left around you are women?"

"The only males are boys, old men, and soldiers who were sent back from the front lines with serious injuries. Almost all the jobs are being done by women. We make the bullets and sew the uniforms in the factories as well."

"Would you leave here for the countryside? It would be easier to get you food if you were helping out on a farm."

"...I'm sorry. I have my reasons for staying in Berlin."

"I understand. In that case, let's keep talking about what you'll need to do to manage the storehouse."

2

After they had returned to Potsdamer Platz and said good-bye to Diana, Jörg asked Lila if she was tired.

"Yeah. I can't believe they can stomach that food. Adults really are strange. If I were German, I'd throw a fit if someone told me they were going to make sausages with rat meat."

"People end up getting used to things like that when their quality of life degrades just a little bit at a time. And before they realize it, they've adapted to living in horrendous conditions. It was the same on the front lines. Killing people, eating next to corpses, not washing for days—none of it made me feel anything. And once you accept that that's your life, it's hard to go back to normal."

The next day, Jörg and Lila took a steam train out to Kleinerbrunn. It was a wine region renowned even across Europe, and vineyards stretched all the way along the river. Hordes of visitors including foreign tourists had come to the area during more peaceful times to enjoy the local wine and food.

The closest station, Sylphestadt, was surrounded by complete silence, just like every other stretch of the German countryside. Stagecoaches and bicycles served as the primary methods of transportation here, and there was even a horse-drawn omnibus in front of the station. Cars were rare, and the town didn't have electricity, so there were no streetlights looming over the square as there were in Paris. There weren't any portals directly connecting to Xandra's inn, either, so Jörg and Lila had arrived by the normal means of transportation.

The train pulled up to Sylphestadt station, and Jörg and Lila disembarked. Lila was dressed as a boy again today. She'd taken a liking to the outfit, saying it was easier to move around in than a dress.

The smell of coal was dispersed by the breeze, and they filled their lungs with crisp, clean air. A line of low, gently sloping mountains overlapped one another on the other side of the station building, the tallest of which had been transformed into shadow by the afternoon sun. The thick scent of spruce and beech drifted through the air, laced with the bittersweet smell of tree sap, which permeated their nostrils. The area was much colder than the city, presumably because of the cool breeze coming off the Rhine River.

Jörg and Lila climbed into a stagecoach waiting in front of the station and soon arrived at the home of Hanna Bauer—the woman whose name Bernadette had given them. Bernadette had also told them that all the men in the house had been sent off to war, so Hanna looked after her elderly parents as well as the farmhands.

When Jörg knocked on the door, it opened a crack to reveal the face of a young man.

Fabrice LeRoy.

The sudden encounter surprised Jörg. He had assumed that Fabrice would be working in the fields at this hour, but here he was with Hanna.

"Can I help you?" Fabrice asked in German.

"A woman named Bernadette from Paris told us about this place. I believe she already contacted you." Jörg produced a letter from his coat pocket and handed it to Fabrice. "This is a letter of proof. Please give it to Hanna and ask her to verify it."

"Very well. Please wait a moment."

They didn't have to wait long. The door soon opened again, and Fabrice led Jörg and Lila into the room.

Hanna was sitting in a chair in front of a fireplace, both elbows resting on the armrests. She wore a white apron over a long cotton dress and had her hair tied back into a high bun. Wrinkles large and small ran from the corners of her eyes to her cheeks, across her dry, sunburned skin. Her arms resembled thick oak logs. She seemed exhausted, as if she'd just returned from the fields, but her eyes were as sharp as a wild beast's.

Hanna invited Jörg and Lila to sit. She didn't offer them any refreshments, apologizing for not having anything available, and Jörg told her that was quite all right.

Fabrice remained standing next to Hanna, as if to protect her in case something happened. He hadn't said anything since their first interaction. They had no idea how much German he understood, but there was a good chance he was listening in on everything they said.

"It's definitely her handwriting in this letter," Hanna said slowly, perhaps so Fabrice could understand. "Let's talk. What do you want, and how much?"

"For now, we'd like enough food to support one family and their relatives," Jörg replied. "We'll make regular purchases."

"Any plans to scale up?"

"The food situation in the city is bad, so once it gets out that we're able to trade for it, I'm sure lots of people will want us to do the same for them."

"I really wish I had a lot to sell you, but we've had an exceptionally bad year this year. We might not have anything to offer."

"How bad?"

"Harvests have been declining ever since the war started because the men and horses we need to work the fields were taken for the battlefield. It's too much land for women, children, and the elderly to farm, so if we can't plow a field by sowing time, we have no choice but to let it go fallow. There's also the fertilizer problem. The nitrogen we need to add to the fields is all being used to make gunpowder for rifles and artillery shells.

Without fertilizer, the vegetables won't grow. Simply put, the war is making *us* sacrifice food, too. This year's potato harvest was abysmal. We might not even be able to use potato flour to make food substitutes. Instead, the government will probably start mixing in turnips and straw. It's getting to the point where we can't even call it human food anymore."

"So you're saying you don't have anything to send to the cities?"

"It's hard for us to take on new customers. It's no longer a matter of money."

"Would you mind if we tried talking to other farmers?"

"Knock yourselves out," Hanna answered readily. "Even we don't know exactly what the situation's like at other farms."

"I appreciate that," Jörg replied.

Once they left Hanna's house, Lila asked, "Are we really going to visit other farmers?"

"I want to know what the situation's like in the village as a whole," Jörg said. "Even if other farmers might not be able to help us, I want to understand what's going on. Things here are worse than I thought."

"They really are."

"We also need to make a return portal somewhere in town."

"Like where?"

"A small bar would be good. It would make sense for out-of-towners to go there."

"Wouldn't a big dining hall be easier to find?"

"The way things are, the *Bierhallen* and *Lokale* are probably all closed."

"What's a *Bierhalle*?"

"A restaurant where people can go to drink beer. A *Lokal* is a smaller version of a *Bierhalle*."

They asked people on the street where they could find a bar and came across a decent-looking establishment called Erster. The sign on the door said it was closed, but the place didn't look abandoned, just that it only opened at night.

After making sure no one was around, Jörg raised his left palm toward the door. The pattern on the back of his hand instantly imprinted itself into the door panel. Now they could go back to Xandra's inn without having to take a train.

They walked around the fields, speaking to any farmers they came across. Jörg informed them that he and Lila had come from the city and were willing to pay any amount for food, but the sweat-caked women all made the same dubious expression and shook their heads. The only responses Jörg and Lila got were "Sorry," "It's for the government, so even we don't have enough food for ourselves," and "Try asking someone else."

Now that they understood the situation to some extent, Jörg suggested they turn invisible to carry out the next stage of their plan. "We'll pin down what channels Fabrice is using to sell food on the black market, then feed his contact false information so they stop buying from him. That way, we should be able to secure that food for ourselves."

"But then Mr. LeRoy won't be able to get any more information from Berlin," observed Lila. "He'll figure out it was us."

"We'll use that as an opportunity to get Fabrice away from this job."

"How?"

"I'll explain in due time."

Jörg spotted numerous pigeon coops as they walked through the village. They were constructed of nothing more than birdhouses and wire mesh, making it easy to see inside. Each structure held up to fifty pigeons. The birds hardly reacted when the two of them approached, instead focusing on basking in the sunshine.

"What strange-looking birdhouses," Lila said curiously.

"These are lofts for carrier pigeons. The part covered in wire mesh is for them to move around in, and the board sticking out from that is for them to land on. When they're being trained, pigeons are taken outside and taught to fly back to the landing board from wherever they're released."

"There sure are a lot of them."

"They raise a lot of birds, but only a few of them will be good enough to use to send messages. Not to mention, pigeons die frequently during war. No matter how many they train, it isn't enough."

"So enemy soldiers shoot them?"

"They send hawks to attack them."

"What?! The poor things..."

"That's the most efficient way, apparently. Humans are selfish. They even involve other animals in their wars."

The French prisoners were divided into groups of ten and sent to harvest the crops. It was already late in the year to dig up potatoes, and carrots would normally have already been brought in, so this was probably their last harvest for the year.

Armed German guards patrolled the fields, but they didn't seem particularly intimidating.

"Why don't they run away?" Lila asked Jörg. "There aren't that many guards, and there are no fences or walls around the village, so it would be easy to escape if they wanted to."

"They don't know the land and don't have any maps or food, so it would be almost impossible. It depends on the land, but if farmwork is easier than fighting, then it makes the most sense to wait out the end of the war here. Times may be tough, but at least they get something to eat."

"But aren't the internment camps unsanitary?"

"They are, so if a disease breaks out inside, it can wipe out people in the blink of an eye. Theoretically, international treaties protect the rights and lives of POWs, but in reality that's not the case."

The POWs didn't return to the camp once they were done with their work for the day. During harvest season, they built living quarters in the village and lived alongside the residents. They would return to the internment camps once all the fields were bare, but until then, the prisoners worked just like the Poles and Russians hired during the busy seasons before the war. POWs worked the fields here, but others elsewhere worked in factories. International treaties provided some degree of protection for the rights of prisoners, but they were allowed to be used for labor, which every country used to their advantage.

As evening began to set in, some of the prisoners headed to the pubs. They couldn't buy alcohol, but they could get a drink made from weeds that were roasted and strained. If they were lucky, a friendly villager might even sneak them some alcohol. It was in this way that relationships began to form between the farmwives and the French prisoners.

When Fabrice wasn't in Hanna's house or tending to the fields, he met with some of the women from other farms. They were a small, autonomous collective that he had organized.

"Why form another group when Ms. Hanna takes care of all the customers?" Lila asked.

"The amount of money he can make probably differs," replied Jörg.

"Then is Mr. LeRoy charging more?"

"I'm sure there are people out there who would pay outlandish prices for whatever they can't get from Hanna. Those who can afford to buy food on the black market view money differently than we do."

"Where do we go from here?"

"First, let's check out where they exchange the goods and try to find out who he's meeting with."

It wasn't long before they got their chance.

One afternoon, a young farmwife spoke to Fabrice as he was working in the field, and Fabrice called out to the German guard before leaving. The guard didn't seem put out, so this sort of thing must happen often. The woman led Fabrice to her house, where a group of fellow farmwives had gathered out front. From there, they all headed to a storehouse and began to lug heavy hemp bags outside. Based on the musty smell of earth and the size of the bags, it was clear they were filled with vegetables and grain. The women also brought out smoked sausages, which would keep for a long time.

Eventually, a cart drawn by a large horse pulled up to the farmwife's house. An impressive horse like that would have immediately been requisitioned by the army, meaning the owner must have pulled some strings in the military to make them let him keep it. The man riding on the cart wasn't a farmer, but a portly middle-aged man from the city, accompanied by a coachman steering the horse.

One by one, the women called out to the man, who bowed graciously and spoke familiarly with Fabrice. Listening in on their conversation, Jörg and Lila learned that the man was a trader named Oskar Gulke and that he came regularly to buy their food.

Oskar hopped down to the ground once the horse stopped and, with the help of the coachman, helped load the hemp bags onto the cart. Once they were finished, he removed a cloth pouch from his satchel and passed it to the young farmwife. She smiled as she took it, then walked into her house with the other women to divide the money among themselves.

Fabrice alone had stayed behind, and Oskar handed him an envelope.

"How's the situation in Berlin?" Fabrice asked in German.

"Everyone's doing their best to hang in there, but the downtown areas are beyond help. I can't even guess how high the pile of corpses will be this winter."

"What about the socialists and the communists?"

"They're starting to take more drastic action. Russian agents have joined their ranks. The government's also keeping a close eye on anyone with Slavic or Jewish roots. They don't say it publicly, but as soon as anything happens, they arrest people on the basis of their ethnicity or political beliefs."

"And the Spartacus Group?"

"Their momentum's not slowing. If they keep going like this, they might even take power."

"You're kidding."

"There's enough resentment building up in Berlin for that to happen. The details are in there."

Oskar climbed onto the cart and told the coachman to set off. There was still room in the back, so Oskar must also buy food from other farms.

Jörg and Lila followed after them.

Once he'd bought enough food from Kleinerbrunn, Oskar headed to Sylphestadt station, where he waited for a train. A freight train soon arrived, and they loaded the goods onto it. He paid the coachman, who climbed back up into the now-empty horse cart and drove it away from the station, while Oskar waited alone for the next passenger train.

3

Jörg and Lila followed Oskar back to Berlin and infiltrated his office. They searched through his documents, checking the numbers in his ledgers and, as expected, found out that he had been buying food from other farms for more than he was paying Hanna.

But even with the costs he was paying, his customers in Berlin paid far more. Oskar had connections with rich families from before the war began, and once fighting broke out, he had become a valuable supplier of food for Berlin's wealthy. He'd even been importing goods from other countries.

After going through all of Oskar's records, Jörg and Lila returned to Xandra's inn.

Jörg immediately went to the Count's room, where he requested another loan. "I'm going to purchase the supply route of a merchant named Oskar Gulke, an associate of Fabrice LeRoy, and get him to buy food from somewhere other than Kleinerbrunn."

Naturally, the Count was reading in his chair. "You're taking on more and more debt," he replied, not looking up from his book. "Are you sure you want to do that?"

"I'll pay it back over two hundred years or so."

"That's quite a long time."

"Hardly, to monsters like you and me."

"So long as you intend to pay me back, I'll lend you as much as you like. However, money alone might not be enough. How do you intent to persuade this merchant?"

"The first thing I'll do is look into the wealthy people Oskar is connected to, to see who also knows Lieutenant Colonel Kreutzer. Once I find someone who does, I will infiltrate a gathering they'll be attending and make contact with Oskar there. When I do that, I'd like to use your appearance, if you'll allow it."

"You wish to disguise yourself as me?"

"Yes. I want to be someone Kreutzer knows, and you're the best option."

"What about me?" Lila asked.

"It's okay. You should stay here and rest."

"I want to go disguised as an adult, too."

"It's a social gathering, so it'll be nothing but a bunch of boring grown-ups. A place filled with people who only know about consumption."

"Still, I'd like to experience it."

"Children shouldn't be drinking alcohol."

"I'll say I don't drink and just have water."

"She could use the simulacrum of a young lady and attend as my niece," the Count suggested.

"Are you sure?" Jörg asked the man.

"It will be a good experience for her to see just how vapid the wealthy are. Lila can collect information from the other guests while you speak with Oskar. Do you think you could do that, Lila?"

"I can do it," the young girl said with determination.

"Well then, if you're going to pass as a young lady, you'll need to learn how to conduct yourself in high society. Xandra will teach you."

The event the Count found for them was a banquet hosted by the CEO of a metalworking factory. It was a small gathering for close associates only, but it provided an opportunity to exchange information with business owners, meaning people in positions of power would be attending.

Xandra dressed as a chauffeur and drove Jörg and Lila up to the house.

"Have fun," Xandra said playfully. "And while you're there, Jörg, you might as well get all the sustenance you need."

"Yeah. Even if I drain people like this one after the other, I won't feel guilty about it."

"Watch your tone when you speak and make sure you sound like the Count."

"Naturally."

"And don't be intimidated, Lila. Try to stay cheerful."

"Okay."

It was probably because Lila had always talked so maturely, but her simulacrum as a young lady suited her perfectly. She looked ready to hold her own in a salon filled with writers and thinkers.

Disguised as the Count, Jörg stepped down from the car with an aristocratic air, then circled around to open the door for his niece. Lila was wearing a cloak and seemed to move more gracefully than usual—the result of the high heels she was wearing. She took Jörg's hand and let him help her down to the ground.

Xandra drove off to park the car as the two of them climbed the stairs to the front doors of the house.

After they were let in, Lila removed her coat and handed it to a servant, revealing the evening dress she was wearing underneath. It had a sleek silhouette without any unnecessary curves and was lavishly decorated with beads and detailed embroidery from shoulder to chest. The dress hung long enough to cover her ankles, while the short sleeves gave way to long ivory gloves which covered her arms.

In the hall, groups of men and women sat in high-backed chairs holding glasses and chatting amiably. Enough furniture filled the room to seat all the guests, with a large table in the center lined with delicacies that were easy to eat while making the rounds.

Such splendor during wartime left Jörg speechless. Lila looked upset. They could almost taste the rat sausage and turnip they'd eaten at the *Mittelstandküche* on their tongues. While the common people ate the equivalent of livestock feed, the people here were feasting no differently than they had in times of peace, dining on beautifully browned meat dishes, duck and vegetable aspic, rich soups, white bread and fragrant cheeses, and baked pastries filled with fruit and cream.

Based on the size of the room, it didn't seem they were expecting too many more guests.

Jörg spotted Lieutenant Colonel Kreutzer and walked over to greet him. Kreutzer treated Jörg as he normally would the Count and smiled kindly at Lila when Jörg introduced her as his niece. Jörg and Lila chatted with Kreutzer and his companion for a short while.

Kreutzer announced to the room that the Count was an old friend. He said nothing about the fighting in Romania. From late September to the middle of October, Germany's Ninth Army had trampled over the Romanian Army and was currently advancing toward the capital, Bucharest. The Count had already informed Jörg that it was only a matter of time before the capital fell. As an officer in the intelligence department, there was no doubt Kreutzer knew about this, but he left it unsaid, likely out of consideration for the Count's position.

Instead, he launched into a speech about the fighting at the Somme, speaking passionately of the valor with which the German Army had defended the front lines.

"The British are completely untrained," he proudly told everyone. "They just hand out guns to the common folk, which gets them nowhere. And yet, if we did the same thing, the quality of our German blood would show. We Germans approach everything seriously, hence why people improve so much under our training. Men who have only ever worked on the farms pick up new skills with only a little guidance and are soon effective soldiers. That's something other countries could never imitate."

The surrounding industry leaders and their wives oohed and aahed, their eyes glittering. Kreutzer continued his fervent speech, going on about how the German Army would scatter any enemy, however fierce, to the ends of the earth, gesturing like an actor reciting a monologue. He even made the occasional morbid joke denigrating the corpses of enemy soldiers. When Kreutzer started making fun of men blinded by explosions wandering around no-man's-land, Lila lowered her gaze, no longer able to look at the man.

Jörg wrapped an arm around her shoulders and announced to the crowd, "It seems my niece has enjoyed her drink a little too much. You must excuse us while I find her a place to rest," and led her away. He sat Lila down on a nearby couch and asked a waiter to bring some water. When the waiter returned, Jörg handed the glass to Lila, then sat down himself.

He checked to make sure they were alone, before whispering, "I understand how you feel. To a man like that, the soldiers on the front lines are no different from fleas and lice. He would crush them between his fingers and not feel any remorse."

"I know," replied Lila. "But it still makes me want to cry. I want to give everyone like that a good smack on the back of the head."

"Those aren't the words of a proper young lady. Don't forget there are eyes and ears everywhere."

"But it's so frustrating."

"I know. This war will never end so long as people like that run society. But don't worry; what he said was all just posturing. The German Army at Verdun is outnumbered. France recaptured Fort Vaux and Fort Douaumont, and the Germans have been pushed back to their position from before the Battle of Verdun."

"Really?"

"Yeah. Things aren't going well for them at the Somme, either. The standstill there shows no sign of breaking, and all the while, wave after wave of soldiers keep dying. The number of casualties there is already equal to the fighting at Verdun. Including the injured British soldiers, they say the total number across both armies is more than a million. Just the dead alone number a hundred thousand."

Lila hid her mouth behind her hands.

"The German Army can't keep this up for much longer," Jörg continued. "And if the US joins the war, the end will be in sight. There's no way they'll side with Germany. So just put up with this for a little while longer. If it gets to be too much, go back to Xandra."

"No. I know I'd regret leaving now. It makes me feel sick, but I'll listen for as long as I can."

"Okay. It's about time I made contact with Oskar. Will you be okay on your own?"

"I'll be fine. Go."

Jörg nodded and got to his feet.

He scanned the hall, spotting Oskar just as he was excusing himself from a lively conversation, wineglass in hand. Jörg approached and called out to the man, who stared at him with a searching look.

Taking a glass of wine for himself, Jörg said, "Let's chat over there," and guided Oskar toward a windowsill. The night air was cold, so they didn't go out onto the balcony.

"I was told you're a retailer," remarked Jörg. "Your job involves bringing food into Berlin, if I understand correctly."

"That's right. I do business with our host here, too."

"And you buy your goods from more than one region?"

"Naturally, we have to source food from multiple areas to fill everyone's stomachs."

"I've heard you do business with farmers in the west."

"Yes, at times."

"Would you be interested in transferring one of your routes over to me? Not for free, of course." Jörg removed a small pouch from his jacket and let Oskar feel its weight. "Given the times we find ourselves in, I have prepared a payment that won't be too cumbersome and has a favorable exchange rate."

Oskar set his glass on a table by the window, opened the pouch, and looked inside. Yet his expression remained the same, not even betraying a hint of his greed.

"What region are you after?" he asked.

"Kleinerbrunn."

"Do you really think those farms are worth all this?"

"Let's just say there's something there that's worth this much to me."

"Give me some time to consider it."

"I'm afraid I must insist on an answer now."

"That will be difficult. I have my own circumstances to think about."

Jörg cast his gaze over toward Kreutzer, who was busily chatting with some friends. "Do you know that man over there? He's an officer in the intelligence service. We've known each other for a long time and keep one another up to date on any information involving the military. In times like these, the lieutenant colonel has grown very sensitive to the intelligence activities of our enemies. He would immediately arrest and interrogate any German who has been in contact with a foreign agent. There would be no guarantee they would come out of it alive."

"I'm sure I don't know what you're talking about."

"It would be perfectly fine to conduct business with someone from France during times of peace. But we're at war. We must be careful who we choose to deal with. If the lieutenant colonel were to hear about this, he would come calling on you very quickly."

"Where did you hear such nonsense?"

"The world's a small place. There are eyes everywhere. If the lieutenant colonel were to ask around, I have no doubt people would tell him everything about your relationship with a certain French prisoner of war."

Even then, Oskar remained silent. So Jörg gave him one more push.

The moment the name Fabrice LeRoy left Jörg's lips, Oskar hurriedly said, "Fine, you can have Kleinerbrunn," closed the pouch, and tucked it away inside his coat. "I'll tell them our deal's off the next time I go."

"That won't be necessary. You only need to stop buying from them. I shall take care of the rest."

Oskar sucked in a deep breath, then practically spat out the words "This'll only work for you the one time."

"Of course. You don't have to worry about that."

"Then if you'll excuse me."

Oskar picked up his glass, as if he'd just remembered it was there, and drained it, then headed toward the exit. His imagination must be dreaming up the possible horrors that could befall him if he stayed any longer.

Jörg took a sip from his own glass as he watched Oskar walk away. Maybe it was because his nerves had finally relaxed, but the wine tasted incredibly sweet.

4

Having gotten what he wanted from Oskar, Jörg only needed to tidy up a few other loose ends.

He planned to talk to Fabrice by himself in private, not wanting Lila there in case he was forced to use stronger language than he'd needed with Oskar. She'd felt so hurt just hearing Lieutenant Colonel Kreutzer's words that Jörg wouldn't take her anywhere he might have to resort to bribery or threats of violence.

Leaving Lila to gather information at the Eiffel Tower, Jörg leaped to Kleinerbrunn alone. By now, Fabrice and the farmwives must be waiting impatiently for the next pickup. Jörg would meet Fabrice, saying he was an acquaintance of Oskar's.

Jörg took on the same middle-aged-merchant disguise he'd used the last time he was here. When he arrived at the village, he turned invisible and wandered around for a little while to observe the state of the place.

The harvest of the meager crops was quickly wrapping up, and the French POWs had started to get ready to return to their internment camp. They greeted any villagers they recognized and spent some time chatting happily with them.

The farmwives offered the prisoners a tea made from herbs, and today, the German guards were also joining them in relaxed conversation. The Frenchmen sent to the village here must have been exemplary prisoners. A sense of calm seemed to surround the place.

Fabrice visited several houses, saying his farewells to each one, promising that he'd be back the following spring when they started sowing seeds, and lamenting that he had to say good-bye. Some of the younger women he even quickly had sex with, as if it were a common occurrence.

Fabrice spent a particularly long time talking with Hanna. Unlike some of the others, she didn't treat him as a lover, but like a reliable employee, maintaining that same resolute demeanor of a general right up until the end.

"Next year will be worse," she told him. "Even with you here to help."

"You should grow something else. Something that will sell for more," Fabrice said, sounding somewhat hesitant. "Though you'll have to spend a bit at first."

"I'll think about it."

He left Hanna's house and walked toward the prisoners' living quarters, Jörg following close behind. When they eventually reached a place where no one else was around, Jörg appeared behind Fabrice.

"I'm sorry to bother you," he said in French, "but I would like to discuss purchasing some of the crops here."

Startled, Fabrice turned around and saw Jörg. He had met this merchant before, but it seemed he'd never imagined the man could speak French.

"I'm a prisoner," replied Fabrice. "I only help with the fields because the Germans ordered me to."

"I am aware. And yet, you're well acquainted with a number of farmwives here and have your own special distribution channels, do you not?"

"You should really talk to the women about that. Harvest season's over, so I'm on my way back to the camp."

"I am here at the referral of Mr. Oskar Gulke. He and I are in the same line of work. Are you sure you wish to lose that business?" Jörg asked, and Fabrice frowned slightly. "The other day, I spoke to many of the farmers around here. I didn't get anywhere, however, so I reached out to Mr. Gulke, who agreed to allow me to take over his dealings with you."

"What?!"

"As such, from now on, I will be the one buying from you. I am already aware of the prices Mr. Gulke was paying, so you won't need to worry about that."

Jörg removed a letter from his jacket pocket and handed it to Fabrice. It was addressed to him from Oskar—fake, of course.

Fabrice silently ran his eyes over the page. He seemed absorbed by his thoughts as he read. The letter purposefully omitted any mention of providing information on Berlin, and Jörg waited to see how Fabrice would react once he finished reading.

Fabrice folded the letter in half. "I'm very sorry, but I won't believe it until I hear it directly from him. If you don't mind, I'd prefer to talk about this another day."

"Aren't you about to go back to the internment camp, though?"

"The farmwives here will act in my place. Once I verify that this letter is real, you can start working with them. I won't be here to meet with you, but I'm sure the women will be eager to help."

"I don't believe Mr. Gulke will be able to meet with you. He has begun to worry that his life is in danger."

"What do you mean?"

"The two of you traded more than just food. The German intelligence branch seems to have caught wind of that arrangement, and Mr. Gulke was forced to flee. All things considered, I won't be taking over that part of his business."

Jörg took a step forward. "All I want is food. Your presence is no longer necessary."

"What are you talking about?" Fabrice asked, taking a step back. "I just help the women on the farm. That's all."

"I know everything. But I haven't yet told the intelligence branch about what you've been up to."

"Enough with the accusations."

"Shall we go to Berlin, then? Do you think you'll be able to keep up your story in front of an officer of the Abteilung III b?"

Fabrice grimaced, and Jörg pressed further. "If you don't want to be interrogated, then do what I tell you. Convince the farmwives to give me the food supply route you were involved with."

"Is that it?"

"One more thing: Go home. And don't ever work as a spy again."

"That easy enough to say, but I'm still a prisoner."

"I'll help you escape from here."

"What…?"

"Instead of going back to the internment camp, you'll run away from Kleinerbrunn. No one will blame you for it. The army has its hands full managing all the prisoners here, so honestly, they'll probably be happy to have one less person to look after. And running away from the village will bring down fewer repercussions on the guards than if you escape from the camp."

"You want me to cross the wilderness in winter without any food or equipment?"

"I can take you to Paris. Once you're there, you can do whatever you want."

Fabrice shook his head in disbelief. "I'm French. I'm your enemy."

"I experienced horrible things on the battlefield," explained Jörg. "I know how badly soldiers want to go home. You'd much rather go home than keep doing a risky job in a place like this, wouldn't you?"

"If I go home, they might send me right back to the front lines. I couldn't handle that."

"Come up with a plan so they can't do that. Go into hiding and wait for the war to end."

Fabrice turned away, his eyes burning with anger. He didn't say anything for a while, then finally growled, "Fine. I'll do it. What do I need to do first?"

"Take me to the house of the farmwife you're closest with and introduce me as the new buyer."

Fabrice nodded, then walked ahead, leading the way.

Relieved, Jörg walked after him.

The next moment, Fabrice spun around, swinging his arm violently, and struck a fierce blow to Jörg's temple. Jörg's vision swam, and he collapsed to the ground.

Fabrice bolted off.

Jörg jumped up and chased after him. He hadn't thought convincing Fabrice would be easy, so he'd half expected things to turn out this way.

Fabrice wasn't heading in the direction of the houses, but toward the forest, and he dashed into the thicket. A second later, two gunshots rang out, apparently having been fired into the air.

There's no way Fabrice had a gun concealed on him, Jörg thought skeptically as he walked up to where the man had disappeared. Nearby was an old abandoned shack. Considering the situation, the most likely scenario was that Fabrice had hidden a gun here and used it to signal his friends.

Jörg pulled a Browning M1900 from his coat pocket and ran past an oak tree with twisted branches spread wide, heading deeper into the forest. He didn't know if Fabrice was planning to try to get away from him or to shoot him. Even if the German guards had heard the gunshots, they would have a hard time figuring out where they'd come from.

Jörg gripped the pistol tighter. He had to either eliminate Fabrice or convince him to keep quiet about their conversation. Lila's worried face appeared in his mind. He'd put off making that decision until the very last moment.

Leaves crunched underfoot as Jörg crept carefully through the forest. There were no paths. This wasn't somewhere that people and carts passed through. It was close to the farmland, though, so it seemed like people came here regularly foraging for herbs and mushrooms. Signs had been notched in tree trunks using hatchets, and the ivy that would otherwise block the path had been carefully trimmed away.

Each step forward released the characteristic smell of trampled leaves. It was almost impossible to move without making a noise. The branches of the trees intertwined like a bird's nest, and the grass, which was still green despite the season, covered the ground as far as the eye could see. Jörg kept going, careful not to touch the clusters of nettles. Forests provided excellent cover for hiding, but they made it difficult to detect someone sneaking up on you. It was different from holding a gun and charging across the open ground of no-man's-land. If Jörg was being honest with himself, he wasn't confident he could drop his target in an environment like this.

Another gunshot rang out, and a piece of a nearby trunk disintegrated, as if it had been hit with a whip. Jörg ducked behind the tree and raised his gun, finger resting on the trigger. He didn't know how many people he was facing, so he couldn't predict how many shots might come his way. The magazine of a pistol carried a maximum of seven rounds, so each person out here could have that many shots—more, if they were carrying extra clips.

Even if they shot him, though, he wouldn't die. It would hurt a lot, but if Jörg couldn't find the enemy combatants, he could always let them shoot him and wait for them to show themselves.

The Count had told him he was immortal, but Jörg hadn't actually tested that yet. It was possible he hadn't inherited enough magic and could still die. He'd find out by getting shot—not that that was a method he particularly cared to test out. It was a bad joke that left his heart feeling heavy.

Jörg took a few deep breaths to settle himself, then stepped out onto the leaf litter. He heard the sounds of birds flying through the branches and small animals running across the ground. There was no sound of flowing water, so it didn't seem there were any rivers or ponds nearby. He had been away from the front for quite a while, and right now, his nerves were winning out against that rush of adrenaline he got from fighting. He'd been living far too relaxed a life lately. This tiniest droplet of fear was creating huge ripples across his heart.

Jörg heard a high-pitched, hollow sound just as something struck him in the back. He collapsed forward and groaned, an intense pain concentrating in the middle of his spine. He knew he'd been shot, but he could still move normally. Jörg staggered to his feet, only to be shot in the chest, before another bullet tore through his head and blew him backward.

Even then, Jörg remained fully conscious and aware of his

surroundings. He simply felt warm liquid spurting from his wounds. He wasn't dead.

Jörg lay on his back, still gripping his pistol. He waited for his enemy to approach to check his pulse. He didn't think they'd leave him here. Even if it wasn't Fabrice, whoever had shot him would come over to make sure he was dead.

Footsteps crunched on the leaves, drawing closer. The person didn't seem to be trying to quiet their steps, so they must be confident they had killed him. Jörg waited for his chance, keeping his eyes open. Estimating the distance separating them by sound, Jörg sprang up when the person was within range and pointed his gun at his attacker.

It wasn't Fabrice. Unexpectedly, it was a German man. A local Fabrice had coerced over to his side with money? One of the man's eyes was half-crushed, and a large scar dominated his face, indicating he'd probably been injured and sent home from the front. Jörg faced the man, who was standing there as stiff as a board, and fired, missing on purpose. The shot was just meant to scare him. He grabbed the frozen man by the arm and instantly drew in sustenance. He must have overdone it a little, though, because the man's face turned completely white, as if all the blood had been drained from his body. A sharp metallic taste filled Jörg's mouth, and it was only then he realized that by *sustenance*, the Count meant human blood. Just like the werewolf Milos, Jörg had turned into a monster that feasted on the blood of humans.

The man crumpled to the ground, and two more people came running out of the bushes, guns blazing. One was Fabrice. He'd brought a friend.

Jörg dropped the man whose blood he'd drunk and began to draw sustenance from the two others without touching them. It took a little bit of time, but it achieved the desired effect. The third man collapsed, still gripping his gun, and Fabrice fell where he stood.

As Jörg walked over to Fabrice with his gun raised, tiny objects the size of beans fell from Jörg's body. The wealth of sustenance he'd drawn from the humans had helped his wounds heal faster and push the bullets out.

Unable to move, Fabrice sat with his back to the trunk of a tree and flailed his legs, kicking at the fallen leaves. He didn't have the strength to stand but was still vividly aware of his surroundings, fear painting his eyes darker with each step Jörg took.

A plea escaped his trembling lips. "Stay back! Stop! Monster! Get away from me!"

"Calm down, Fabrice."

"No! Don't kill me."

"I have no intention of killing you. Your friends aren't dead, either. Just unconscious."

"Liar. You drained my blood. I know you did."

Jörg grimaced, the spoke to Fabrice, keeping his tone as calm as possible. "Listen to me. If you give me your supply route for the crops like I asked and then go back to Paris, I won't do anything else to you. It's that simple."

Fabrice didn't answer. He buried his head in his hands and began to shake.

Jörg walked over and crouched down in front of him. "No matter where you run, I'll follow you. You'd best answer me now."

"I didn't want to be a soldier!" Fabrice yelled. "I'd much prefer a quiet life in my hometown. I'm done with killing and spying."

"Then you should have done this sooner. You should've fled when you first began to hate the battlefield."

"That choice doesn't exist on the front. I was too focused on trying to stay alive."

"People die because other people kill them. You should have started by setting down your gun. If all the soldiers fled, then the war would be over. You always had the option to never start fighting in the first place."

"So I should have refused my duty as a soldier, like the Quakers? If I had done that, my own army would have killed me instead of the enemy. The other soldiers would've heaped abuse on me, and my commanding officer would have executed me for desertion."

"That only makes it more unbelievable that you remained in such a place," Jörg said. "Christine is anxiously waiting for you to return. So go back home. To Paris."

The slightest hint of color returned to Fabrice's pale face. "Really?"

Jörg nodded. "You used carrier pigeons to have someone living nearby tell you how Christine was doing. Didn't you?"

"Yes."

"But you could only learn so much that way. You couldn't know how she was feeling deep down. I spoke with her directly. She's waiting for you to come home."

"Will you really take me to Paris?" Fabrice asked, tears brimming in his eyes.

"If you let me take over the food trade here. That, and one more thing: Where were you sending the information you got in Kleinerbrunn?"

"Multiple locations. Paris, Rotterdam, as far as London..."

"How did you get the pigeons?"

"When I first came here to help on the farm, someone showed me where the pigeon lofts are."

"Who?"

"One of the workers who brings food and goods into the prison complex. He came with a letter that had orders from the French Army."

"I assume you used homing pigeons. Regular carrier pigeons you would have had to keep bringing back to where you were."

"That's right."

"Which loft are you using?"

"One close to the prisoners' quarters."

"Can you take me there?"

"Right now?"

"Yes."

"I can't stand. Help me up."

Jörg tucked his pistol back into his coat, exchanging it for a bottle from one of his pockets. He held it out to Fabrice. "Drink."

"Why should I trust you?"

"It's not poison. It's medicine."

There was only a tiny amount, so while it wouldn't heal Fabrice enough to let him fight, he would be able to walk.

"Don't get any ideas," Jörg warned him. "If you do anything suspicious, I'll drain your blood again."

"What about my comrades?"

"We'll leave them here. They'll wake up after a little while."

Humans lost their memories of events that happened right before they were drained of sustenance. Jörg had learned that from the Count, so he left the men where they were and started walking away. They would have already forgotten what happened here today.

Jörg found the pigeon loft where Fabrice had described it. The

Frenchman's explanation and the message containers on the birds' legs were enough to convince him that they were carrier pigeons.

After that, Jörg ordered Fabrice to lead him to the farmwife he was closest with.

He couldn't meet someone covered in blood, so Jörg used his magic to change his current appearance into one that was uninjured.

At the house, Fabrice introduced Jörg to the woman using the exact words he had been given, telling her that Jörg would be taking over future transactions and that the price would stay the same.

The sudden visit surprised the woman, but she quickly acknowledged the change and politely told Jörg that she looked forward to working with him. Such a response spoke of the strong trust between her and Fabrice.

"I appreciate all your hard work," Jörg stressed, providing the farmwife encouragement. "I'll be making regular purchases, so I hope we can build a good relationship."

"We'd welcome anyone from the city who might want to come out here and help work the fields."

"I'll ask around. I'm sure there are people who would want to leave the city for a place like this."

"Even just looking after the livestock would be a huge help. We have to do whatever we can to get more pigs."

Once the discussion was over, Jörg took Fabrice to Erster, the bar where he'd created the portal home.

He took Fabrice's hand and pushed the door open. Instead of being greeted by the dim interior of a bar and rows of bottles, the men found themselves engulfed in a deep darkness. Fabrice screamed, disoriented, but the scenery suddenly shifted and they emerged in a hallway of Xandra's inn.

Fabrice looked around him in stunned silence as Jörg led him down the hall.

"How do you feel?" Jörg asked.

"Fine."

"Good. We'll be making the next leap soon."

The two men arrived at the door leading to Paris and passed through.

They appeared in the square in front of the Eiffel Tower. Jörg released Fabrice's hand, and the Frenchman backed away, turning around. "Paris," he said through tears. "It's really Paris."

"Do you know the way to Christine's house?" Jörg asked.

"Of course. I could get there with my eyes closed."

"Excellent."

"Am I free to go?"

"Yes."

"When I see Christine, what should I tell her about you?"

"Tell her you met Pierre Arche," Jörg said, "and that he helped you out with various matters. Don't go into details. Act as if you were discharged from the army."

"Okay."

After that, Jörg turned himself invisible and followed Fabrice.

Fabrice walked purposefully up a familiar hill, where he stopped in front of a building and gazed up at one of the floors. Jörg recalled his first day in Paris. That day, he'd stood in the exact same spot, looking up at the exact same building.

Eventually, Fabrice lowered his gaze and saw a woman walking down the street.

When she realized who it was, Christine started running toward him.

Fabrice also broke out into a run.

The two of them hugged each other tightly in the middle of the sidewalk.

Watching them, Jörg breathed a relived sigh, then turned and walked away.

5

After returning to Xandra's inn, Jörg changed from the middle-aged merchant back to his regular appearance and went in search of the Count, but he couldn't find him in the lounge or in his room. Jörg checked the dining room and the courtyard but didn't see him there, either. As he was pondering what to do—since he couldn't just keep wandering around opening doors to other rooms willy-nilly—he ran into Lila in a hallway.

She screamed when she saw him. "Mr. Huber, why are you covered in blood?!"

"Oh, I was shot a bit."

"A *bit*...?"

"It doesn't hurt anymore."

"You should get some medicine from Xandra."

"I'm fine."

"No. That's the worst way to think about this. Do you know why?" Lila asked, looking as if she was on the verge of tears. "If you start thinking that anything can happen to you because you won't die, then even your soul will turn into that of a monster… I don't want you to become like that."

Lila grabbed Jörg's hand and started walking toward Xandra's medical office. She led him straight to a room on the first floor of the west wing, knocked on the door, announced that she was coming in, and promptly turned the handle.

The door opened to a dispensary. There were no patients in the room, just rows of labeled brown bottles on a large oak table.

Xandra, in a white lab coat, was measuring powder onto the top of a balancing scale. The Count stood beside her, helping her work. He wasn't wearing his cloak and had the sleeves of his buttoned shirt rolled up to the elbows as he poured liquid from one bottle to another. After filling the bottle, he corked it and gave it a quick shake to mix the liquid, then placed it in a wooden crate. Several crates had already been filled with clear bottles containing powder wrapped in paper. The Count seemed to be enjoying himself. He looked for all the world like a perfumer mixing essential oils.

"What are you making, Xandra?" Lila asked curiously.

"Medicine for the battlefield. Milos is coming to buy some."

"Why is the Count helping?"

"Because he needs a lot."

"This isn't enough?"

"No. The Serbian Army has moved from Corfu to mainland Greece, maneuvering to eventually try to take back their capital. It's not just the French and British armies that are on the Macedonian front anymore; a Russian brigade and the Italian troops who were stationed in Albania have also joined them. They helped protect the Serbian Army while they recaptured Monastir, and now the Serbians have their sights set on the capital, Belgrade. It's going to turn into a big battle. But why are you here?"

"Could you give Mr. Huber some medicine?"

The Count stopped pouring and glanced up at Jörg. "You look as if you've been put through the wringer again."

"I let them shoot me so I could shoot back, is all. I absorbed some of their sustenance, so my wounds healed."

"I can see that. You don't need medicine for something like this."

"Stop talking like it's nothing and help him!" Lila shouted. "I can't stand seeing Mr. Huber like this."

"But he's fine."

"Still, do something!"

The Count sighed and took a bottle from the shelf. "I guess you could drink some medicinal alcohol, then. It'll help make you feel better."

Jörg drained the bottle he was given, then reported his encounter with Fabrice to the Count.

"Everything is in place for the delivery. All we need to do now is transport the food to the storehouse," Jörg explained. "To do that, I was thinking of finding out where Fabrice's carrier pigeons were going. Following a bird would give us an understanding of the French informant network."

"I see. That's a good idea."

"I can't follow every bird, though, and I don't know how to fly yet, so do you have any ideas that might work?"

"Let me send my familiars. That would be fastest."

"How much for each one?"

"Instead of you paying me for that, could you take my place helping Xandra fill these medicine bottles? Do that, and we'll call it even."

"Thanks, that helps a lot."

"It's not easy work, so stay focused. Lila, you should leave now. I don't want you to be exposed to these noxious fumes."

After the Count and Lila left the room, Xandra gave Jörg detailed instructions and taught him how to fill the bottles with medicine. Only Xandra could measure out each dose, so Jörg's job was to line up the bottles and put the paper seals on them once they'd been corked.

"It's a good thing you became a monster," Xandra said. "You don't want to let humans touch this stuff."

"It's that dangerous?"

"Yeah."

Once the bottles had been filled, Xandra led Jörg to another room. Apparently, she was going to examine the patients that had just arrived at the inn. In a corner of the room sat a cart jam-packed with bottles of medicine, which Xandra told Jörg to push.

"The patients' appearances might shock you at first, but try not to let it worry you," Xandra said as she opened the door to the adjoining room.

Jörg stopped cold the moment he set foot inside.

The scene in front of his eyes reminded Jörg of the wards in the field hospital. Curtains partitioned off a startling number of patient beds, with the room seeming to stretch on endlessly. Jörg couldn't even see the opposite wall. An acrid smell and the scent of herbs wafted through the air.

Xandra pulled back one of the curtains and beckoned Jörg over. She pointed to the patient sitting on the bed, and Jörg swallowed back the saliva that had coated his mouth. Sitting cross-legged on top of the blanket, reading a newspaper held in handlike protrusions, was something that looked like a mound of mud or a lump cut from an old oak tree. Waves rippled slowly across the surface of its body. It was alive.

Xandra took one of the bottles from the cart and uncorked it. She tilted it carefully, sprinkling a little bit of the powdered medicine over the body of the strange creature, which let out a high-pitched noise. It seemed to be happy.

"What is that?" Jörg asked.

"A human who's turning into a monster," replied Xandra.

"That's a *person*?!"

"These people grew disgusted with the world and fled here. Once they start living at this inn, they gradually turn into monsters. However, it's quite tough for a human to make the transition, so I help with medicine, removing or reducing their pain and helping them change into whatever form they want to become. I also help those who become monsters and later decide that they want to look human again."

"You can do that?"

"Yes. The appearance of a living being is transient."

"Monsters can take all sorts of different forms, but why is that?"

"Because people's reasons for becoming a monster differ. They might do it to protect themselves from bad people, to punish evildoers, to become the most beautiful thing they can imagine, to make it easier for them to get food, or to become something that can fly, run through the fields, or swim through water. There are more reasons in this world than we can imagine."

"I see."

"We also have people who just want to stay here for a little while, then use the inn to run away to a foreign country. In other words, people who are seeking asylum. We sell medicine to them, too: things to relieve their fatigue or heal their injuries."

"Times sure are tough for everyone..."

"These days, it's the people on the outside who are more like monsters. Each war meeting, politicians and generals make decisions that send hundreds of thousands of people to their deaths. The people who come here refuse to live in that world. Don't you find that honorable in a way?"

"Becoming a monster even it means abandoning what you believe in?"

"They abandon their old human form so they *don't* lose their humanity. You did exactly the same thing."

"I can't argue with that, but it's crazy to think that this many people are willing to live their lives as monsters..."

"Becoming a monster doesn't mean giving up on the world—just that you believe in a new world. That idea in and of itself isn't rare."

The monster sitting on the bed showed Jörg the newspaper and tapped the paper with its finger. The sounds it made didn't form words, but it seemed it was trying to tell him something.

Xandra interpreted for him. "He's telling you this article is interesting and that you should read it."

"What's it about?"

"A certain poet wrote an article criticizing the war. Since the fighting started, he's contributed close to twenty articles."

The newspaper wasn't German, but a German-language newspaper published in Zurich called the *Neue Zürcher Zeitung*.

"He declared his opposition to the war as soon as it broke out, so naturally, he faced some fierce criticism from his fellow Germans. All the newspapers and magazines stopped publishing his articles, and everyone accused him of being a traitor. By now, the only place that will publish his work is this paper from neutral Switzerland."

The monster continued to speak passionately.

Although its words sounded like gibberish to Jörg, Xandra told him what they meant.

I saw fire and death burn across the earth,
Thousands of innocents suffer, die, and decay.

It was then that I swore off war in my heart.
Swore off a blind god who forces people to suffer senselessly.

"He wrote that in September 1914, just after the war started. The poem isn't particularly outspoken against the Great War, but he phrased it in a way that was so natural his fellow countrymen labeled him a traitor."

"Did he fight on the front lines?"

"No, never. He worked at the German Prisoners of War Relief Agency in Bern. But he continued submitting articles to newspapers, even after working so hard it seemed he would collapse."

Jörg took the newspaper the monster offered him and looked down at the page.

So there were people like this. No—there are still *people like this.*

The monster let out another happy cry.

Xandra and Jörg moved from bed to bed, treating patients. The doctor examined each person undergoing their transformation, monitoring the changes in their bodies and selecting medicines that she sprinkled on them. Each patient let out a cry of joy when the medicine was applied. Some were changing from humans to monsters, and others were reverting to human form, but they all seemed to be bursting with excitement.

The sheer variety of monsters and people amazed Jörg.

"Have you always been a monster?" he asked Xandra. "Or…"

"It's a long story."

"I'd love to hear it."

"Okay then, once we've finished with the medicine, let's take a break."

After they had treated the last of what seemed like an endless number of patients, Xandra and Jörg started heading back the way they'd come.

The monsters slept, filling the room with an almost chilling silence. The only sound was that of the cart's wheels on the floor, which echoed around them like distant thunder.

When they got back to the dispensary, Xandra grabbed two bottles of apple cider from the corner of the room and handed one to Jörg. He removed the cap, took a swig, and let the sweetness and stimulation of the bubbles revitalize his weary soul.

"When I was a child," Xandra said, "I lived in the Crimean Peninsula for three years in a room beneath a British military hospital. There were lots of other poor kids in the same situation. More than two hundred and sixty people lived there, including the mothers."

"Why were you all there?"

"Back then, soldiers took their families with them when they went off to war. Wives raised children and looked after their husbands, all while watching the war unfold."

"When was this?"

"From 1853 until 1856."

"But that's more than sixty years ago."

"That's right. Though I'm still quite young compared with the Count, right?" Xandra chuckled. "The Crimean War was a territorial conflict between the Russian and Ottoman Empires. Russia wanted a warm-water port and land with more temperate weather, so they stormed into Ottoman territory and attacked. That was the first time Moldavia and Walachia became principalities of the Russian Army."

"The Count's homeland…"

"Yeah. Walachia had been under the heel of the Ottoman Empire for so long, and now they found themselves occupied by Russia, who had repelled the Ottomans. The Russian Army proclaimed that they had come to liberate Moldavia and Walachia from Ottoman rule, but the only thing that ended up changing was who ruled, and the people didn't believe any of their promises. The Count, however, saw this as the incident that would stir the Balkan Peninsula to action and came to Crimea to gather information. That was when I first met him."

"So you were originally from Great Britain? You have a Romanian name, so I assumed you were from there, too, like the Count."

"Correct. I adopted this name once I started working with the Count."

"How did that come about?"

"Let's not get ahead of ourselves. At the time, the European powers were on the side of the Ottoman Empire. Great Britain, France, and Italy—or the Kingdom of Sardinia as it was called then—opposed Russia encroaching into Europe and moved to help the Ottomans. The armies met on the Crimean Peninsula, and my father was sent there to fight, so my mother and I went with him. I was ten at the time."

To hear Xandra tell it, military hospitals in those days had been unimaginably unsanitary. The hospitals were constructed on top of ground filled with waste and acted as hotbeds for contagion. Outbreaks of cholera, dysentery, and other infectious diseases occurred frequently, with illness being soldiers' cause of death a whopping 80 percent of the time.

"Then one day, a group of nurses arrived at our hospital. The head nurse who led them was a brilliant woman with a tremendous work ethic, and she efficiently commanded the group of nurses, even as she herself made rounds in the wards in her black nursing uniform. Apparently, she had a powerful patron back home, and she used that connection to mobilize British politicians, efficiently improving conditions and increasing the quality of care, which left the idiotic administrator at the hospital dumbstruck. She spearheaded extensive renovations of those unsanitary hospital facilities and sterilized everything. On top of that, she also worked with a French chef to come up with a way to provide proper meals for patients in wards, who had only been receiving gruel and soup with bits of boiled meat in it. She collected statistics on an extensive range of issues, then took her data and thrust it upon government officials back home, demanding additional support. Her incredible management skills turned those stubborn men pale. The presence of such an amazing woman made a deep impression on my young self."

However, Xandra's father ended up dead in the fighting in Crimea, and her mother succumbed to disease. Xandra came down with the same affliction. Then, one day, as she was on death's door, a man wandering through the hospital in a sweeping black cloak appeared before her.

That man was Count Silvestri.

When the Count noticed Xandra looking at him, he calmly said, "The fact that you are able to see me indicates that more than half your humanity is already lost. Having witnessed this horrible reality, your soul wishes to escape from human society."

"I have nowhere to go," Xandra said. "My mom and dad are both dead. Do you think I could come with you?"

"I do not have the means to take in an orphan."

"But I'm the only one who can see you, so you're like my guardian angel."

A deep chuckle emanated from the Count. "Come with me only if it matters not to you whether you become a monster. Live with me, and you will slowly transform into one, body and soul."

"I'm fine with that. I want to be a doctor in the world of monsters. It's still hard for women to become doctors in the human world, see? The head nurse here is a genius, but everyone talks about her like she's the exception. They say regular women don't do the things she does."

"You say some interesting things, child. I've taken a liking to you. Very well, I shall take you with me."

And so, Xandra went to the Count's manor and devoted herself to studying medicines that worked on both humans and monsters. Upon reaching adulthood, she told the Count that she wanted some of his blood, which he gave her.

Jörg stared at Xandra, wide-eyed. "So you have this ancient blood, too?"

"I do."

"I thought the Count hardly ever gave people his blood."

"He doesn't give it to the people who truly matter to him. I'm sure you're already aware that he didn't give it to his wife."

"Yes."

"The Count only gives it to people he wants to use. He gave it to me because he wanted someone close by who could make medicines. Powerful medicine is incredibly useful if you want to manipulate people into doing what you want—something that he knows from personal experience can be used as a surprisingly effective bargaining chip. He gave you his blood so you'll guard Lila, right? The Count promised a dear friend of his that he would protect her, but he doesn't want to do it himself. He just wants to live a carefree life."

"That's true..."

"We're just his pawns. But we're the ones who chose to trade that for what we wanted. He thinks of us as tools, and it doesn't cause any problems if we feel otherwise. It's a mutually beneficial situation. We may be instruments to help him achieve what he wants, but we're not his slaves. We can go wherever we want, do whatever we like. He doesn't control that part of us. I'm happy I got my wish. Are you?"

When they left the Crimean Peninsula, the Count told Xandra more about the head nurse she so idolized—including how cruelly she treated her fellow nurses to help her achieve her ideals, the extraordinary demands she made of the well-meaning people of her homeland who supported her, and how she hounded them to the point of collapse for that support.

"And yet, someday she will create a bright hope for humanity's future, a light as blinding as the sun called the foundation of modern nursing," the Count said gleefully. "That's what keeps her going, even though she and others might collapse. I wholeheartedly admire those sorts of people who continue pushing forward, even in the face of destruction. Become an exceptional doctor in the world of monsters, Xandra. I have high hopes for everything you do."

Jörg silently gripped his bottle of apple cider. The Count's words sounded exactly like those of the ancient blood.

Xandra continued her story. "Russia and the Ottoman Empire stopped fighting and signed the Treaty of Paris, which ended the Crimean War. The Count's home of Walachia won its independence from Ottoman rule, and five years later, united with Moldavia to form Romania. The Count must surely have been relieved. His years of work had finally paid off."

"Do you ever regret inheriting his blood?"

"Why would I? I enjoy every day of my life. I was made to be a monster. Do you?"

"I'm still not sure."

"That time when you're unsure might be when it's the most fun. Humans change easily. Do you think you could help me fill prescriptions and make the rounds again sometime?"

"I'd be happy to. By the way, the people who come to the inn to become monsters… Where do they go from here?"

"Some never leave, and some go back out into the world. Monsters can live anywhere."

"I wonder if they all find happiness."

"I hope they do, whatever form it might take."

6

The Count released the carrier pigeons in Kleinerbrunn one at a time, sending a familiar after each one. The birds all set out in different directions, supporting what Fabrice had told them.

One pigeon flew to Rotterdam and landed at the port office. It was received by a live-in worker who told them his name was Hubert Duran.

"That's Christine's brother!" Jörg exclaimed. "Fabrice must have known, right? Or maybe he was in the dark the whole time."

"It's common practice for the person managing the information not to identify themselves. If they chose people from among the survivors at Artois, there's a good chance of them both ending up in the same role. Perhaps Hubert took this job because he was injured badly enough to keep him off the front lines but didn't want to be discharged."

"That makes sense."

The Netherlands was a neutral country bordering Germany. They took in a lot of Belgian refugees, so it wouldn't have been hard for Hubert to blend in there.

"It's an ideal relay point for the French Army," the Count continued. "But the Dutch are facing food shortages just like Germany. Hubert can't be having an easy time."

The Netherlands had tried to maintain good relationships with both Great Britain and Germany prior to the war. However, it sat in the middle of a shipping lane to Germany, meaning that it was also affected by the Allied blockade. Imports into the Netherlands had been delayed, and while the situation wasn't as dire as in Germany, the Dutch were still struggling to gather enough food.

Jörg decided to take on Fabrice's appearance again when meeting with Hubert. That way, he would be able to meet the man without raising his suspicions.

"Will you take me with you this time?" Lila asked, but Jörg shook his head.

"I can't think of anyone you could look like that would make sense."

"What if I transformed into his sister?"

"You would have an extremely hard time disguising yourself as a family member. He'd see through it very quickly."

"Lila," the Count called out, "Hubert will be much harder to convince than Fabrice. He takes a lot of pride in his mission. Leave this conversation to Mr. Huber."

"But what if something like last time happens?"

"He is not so weak that you need to worry about him."

"That's not what I mean. I'm worried *because* he's gotten stronger."

"I'm a monster now, though," Jörg interjected, "so you don't have to worry about anything like that."

"I don't want anyone who has abandoned their humanity protecting me," retorted Lila. "Having a monster's body and having a monster's heart are two different things. I want you to always keep your human heart, Mr. Huber. If you don't, then I can't be your friend anymore..."

The same complex mixture of emotions crossed the faces of Jörg and the Count. People who were monsters in body and soul; people with a human heart in a monster's body; people with a monster's heart in a human body—both men has met people who fit all of those descriptions. It wasn't that one was right and the others wrong; people were the way they were because of their circumstances. It was hard to get Lila to understand such a complex sentiment.

The Count gave a short sigh. "Then hide yourself and go with Mr. Huber. But make sure you stay quiet and just watch. Do not so much as speak to Hubert. And if Mr. Huber's life is in danger as it was the other day, come and get me immediately. Like a carrier pigeon."

"Okay."

"Is that acceptable to you, Jörg?"

"Yes," he replied. "The most important thing is that Lila stays safe. Now, let's get started."

The gently meandering Nieuwe Maas river divided the land between north and south, with ships utilizing the canals spread throughout the city to transport cargo all across Rotterdam. The buildings lining the banks supported roofs with a distinctive sharp curve, and their windows and doors faced out onto the river.

The layout of the city was so different from what Jörg knew that it impressed upon him the fact that he really was in a new country. The buildings' reflections shimmered in the surface of the water like a heat haze, and waterbirds soared in the air above them. Bare trees lined both sides of the canals, acting as a shield against the cold wind that blew across the water. At the base of the trees, wagtails hopped about, their long tails bobbing up and down, while Eurasian blue tits chirped from the branches before darting off.

The people walking along the riverbank, on the other hand, looked pale. Hunched over with hats pulled low over their eyes, they glanced at the French-looking Jörg showing only the faintest hint of interest.

They couldn't see Lila next to him in her simulacrum, so Jörg walked in silence. Talking to her would make it look as if he was talking to himself, so he kept his mouth closed. The Schiedamseweg stretched east-west through the city, and Jörg's quick steps carried him down the long street where he stopped in front of a building. It was an old structure that contained a number of office spaces, and after taking the stairs to the top floor, Jörg knocked on the door of the port office.

No one answered. Yet physical objects meant very little to a monster. Jörg stepped through the door and into the room, soon followed by Lila's simulacrum.

A man sat working at a desk in the back of the room. From the movement of his hands and the sounds he was making, Jörg could tell he was sending a telegram.

"It's been a while, Hubert," Jörg called out to the man's back. "Do you remember me?"

Hubert stopped what he was doing and the upper half of his body snapped around toward Jörg as he turned to look at him.

The man's appearance caught Jörg completely off guard. He thought for a moment that the lower half of Hubert's face had been torn clean off, but when he got a better look, Jörg realized that the man had large scars on both cheeks running down to his lips. It was a wound from an explosion.

In contrast with his pale face, Hubert's eyes were filled with a bright light. He stared intently at Jörg before saying "Fabrice" in a hoarse voice from deep within his throat. Hearing him speak, Jörg could tell that the man's injuries extended beyond his face and might even include a crushed larynx.

"Do you have a moment?" Jörg asked, before moving to Hubert's side.

Hubert remained sitting, looking up at Jörg. "How did you get in here? The door should have been locked."

"I asked a friend of yours to let me in."

By *friend*, Jörg was referring to a fellow French intelligence operative who worked here with Hubert collecting and managing information. When he named the man, Hubert gave an understanding nod, then asked Fabrice if he had been assigned the same job.

"I just came by to check up on you," Jörg replied. "Though I might be doing the same kind of work in the future."

"I haven't seen you since Artois. Have you been on the front this whole time?"

"No, I was injured and sent back soon after. You?"

"I stuck it out at Artois until the third battle, when this happened. Take a look."

Hubert rapped his knuckles against his right thigh. "Lost everything below the knee. I won't be playing any more soccer."

"...I'm so sorry."

"Don't worry about it. I have more interesting things to keep me occupied." Hubert returned his gaze to the desk. "You know what I do here, right?"

"You collect information from French intelligence operatives and wire it back to France."

"That's right. It's the perfect job for someone like me, since I can't move around much anymore. I sit at this desk all day looking through the information, then send the important details back to France. The fellow I work with takes care of the pigeons."

"I heard that food's hard to come by here. How are you holding up?"

"As you might expect, we can't buy anything decent. We pick at the canned foods the intelligence bureau brings in to avoid starving. You didn't happen to bring anything to eat with you, did you?"

"A little. I left it by the door."

"Thanks. Any little bit helps."

"Do you not go outside much?"

"I don't speak the language, and with this body, well..." Hubert gave a sad smile. "They only speak Dutch and English here. They're hard languages to learn in the first place, and the way my throat is, I just can't make the sounds."

"Don't you get bored?"

"Not really. I read a lot of books in my spare time. So long as my eyes and arms work, I can do this job. And I have to admit, I really enjoy it. It means that, even with my injuries, I can still keep fighting in my own way."

Hubert turned back to his desk and started explaining the telegram system to Jörg. He spoke emphatically, talking about it like an engineer describing an invention.

Jörg listened without interrupting, nodding along in agreement, then changed the topic when there was a brief lull in the conversation.

"Say, Hubert. Would you go back to Paris with me?"

"Why?"

"Leave the menial tasks like this to someone else and live a peaceful life at home. Christine is waiting for you."

Hubert looked hurt. "What do you mean *menial*?"

"Anyone can do this. It's just tapping out signals."

"It gives me purpose!" Hubert's eyes shone with a fierce intensity. "This is *my* battlefield!"

"You should be thinking about your sister, not the war. Even if you leave, the war will be over soon. The Central powers are losing."

"I want to take down Germany with my own two hands. It's their fault I'm like this."

"That's true of everyone who was sent to fight."

"Easy for you to say. You don't look like came away with any serious injuries."

"I don't care if you say stuff like that around me, but don't say it to anyone else. Even if you can't see them, every soldier has deep scars in their soul."

"I know that. But even now, I still wish I had my legs," Hubert said, averting his gaze. "No matter how little there is or how hard life becomes, when I'm here sending out these messages, I feel fulfilled. It's the same feeling you get running across the battlefield with a gun. I wouldn't get this in Paris, would I? Everyone would pity me, and I'd be miserable every day. If that's my other option, then I'd rather work here and starve."

"You don't need to make war your whole life, though."

"What do you mean by that?"

"Take a break, Hubert. You've done enough. You don't need to do any more."

"Have you lost your sense of pride? Where's your will to fight for the motherland?"

"Any normal person comes to their senses after a couple days on the front. They start wondering how they ended up there… Right? But saying it out loud would be like denying who they are, so they stay silent until they're discharged."

Hubert shook his head and turned his back to Jörg. "Get out of here. I want to keep working."

"I'll say it one more time: Come to Paris with me."

"You can ask as many times as you want; you'll still go to Paris alone."

"I'm not going back empty-handed. What would I say to Christine?"

"All I want you to tell her from me is that I'm still serving my country proudly."

Jörg suddenly remembered something the Count had once told him. Jörg's corpus had also refused the Count's advice to flee the battlefield. The Count had said that he could do nothing so long as his corpus was resolute. That a human will with a strength that bordered on faith would deter any magic.

Jörg slowly approached Hubert and rested a hand on his shoulder. "I'll leave for today. But I'll be back."

"No matter how many times you come back, my answer will be the same."

"I'll be coming simply as your friend. You won't mind that, will you?"

Hubert nodded wordlessly. It seemed like he couldn't bring himself to reject Fabrice completely. Jörg felt a slight sense of relief.

"Take care of yourself. It sounds a bit ridiculous to say that, though, when there are so few supplies."

"Don't worry about it. I'm going to forget everything we talked about today."

After leaving the office, Jörg took a deep breath, filling his lungs with the cold open air. He'd wanted to take Hubert home as soon as possible, but the man was so stubborn. His personality was completely different from that of Fabrice. It would be almost impossible to convince Hubert to go with him.

Still, it would be irresponsible to leave him there. Hubert was actively relaying information from spies, and their enemies would want to destroy transmission centers to disrupt the Allies' plans.

If he destroyed the communications equipment, Hubert would lose his job and Jörg would probably be able to take him back to Paris. However, that might also break the man's spirit.

Jörg walked up a gentle slope and stopped in the middle of a bridge over a canal. He gripped the railing with both hands and gazed off into the distance.

"He's a very difficult man," Lila's simulacrum said, still concealing her presence.

"Some men in the military are like him. They need something to feel pride in to make up for the tremendous loss they've suffered."

"It's the war's fault that his body is like that, but he doesn't hate war itself."

"That's the worst thing about adults. Not like I'm one to talk, though."

As Jörg stared down at the gently undulating water, dark spots on the surface began to coalesce into a shape.

He quickly backed away from the railing and steeled himself.

A shadow rose from the water until it reached the height of the bridge. The sky turned a shade of yellow. Small boats rocked by the cold sea breeze, workers unloading goods, and disheartened people walking along the river all stopped moving. Pigeons flying from the trees to the eaves of houses froze in flight, creating an eerie scene in the sky.

It was as if time and space had come to a complete stop.

Jörg was reminded of a similar experience he'd had.

The same thing happened the night I met that man in Paris!

The shadow on the water's surface took on human form, then flew over Jörg's head to stand atop the bridge. It was Nil. Today, he was wearing the same winter clothing as the townspeople.

Nil turned to face Jörg, a smile on his face. "It's been a while. Since our parting in front of the Grand-Guignol."

"You've met with my corpus. I have his memories."

"Then our little talk will be quick. Why don't you stop wasting your time here and go help your corpus?"

"And how exactly am I wasting my time?"

"Leave Hubert alone. There's nothing you can do for him."

"That's none of your business."

"You might think you just spoke with the real Hubert, but you'd be wrong."

"*What*?"

"He didn't just lose his leg; he lost his hearing, too. The real him wouldn't have heard a word you said."

Jörg's expression tensed up, and Nil pointed toward his ear. "The first thing soldiers lose on the front is their hearing. Artillery bombardments, explosions, incessant gunfire—constant exposure to all that makes you deaf. As I'm sure you're well aware."

"So you possessed him, and I talked with you."

"I simply conveyed what was in his heart. Though I did help him organize his thoughts a little."

"In that case, I want to get Hubert out of there even more."

"He looked very happy, didn't he? To be able to help society, even with his injuries. Hubert believes his work will help decide the war. People with something to believe in really are quite formidable."

Nil took a step toward Jörg. "I didn't think you'd become a real monster. I've had to change my opinion of you."

"What do you mean by that?"

"Inheriting ancient blood takes real guts. But it seems you don't know how to use it."

"I have no intention of following its commands. Even the Count stopped me."

Nil narrowed his eyes. "What a waste of potential. With that blood, you should help the revolution in Germany."

Jörg took a step back, sensing danger in the air, but Nil maintained the same distance between them.

Jörg moved Lila behind him, and Nil responded with amusement. "I remember seeing that girl behind you before. I'd hate to see anything happen to her."

"You're not laying a hand on her."

"My familiars aren't picky about who they hunt. I can't guarantee her safety."

Jörg quickly scanned the area. He didn't see any monsters aside from Nil and couldn't predict where they might be.

"You're immortal," Nil said, "so even if you get bitten, it won't matter. But what about the girl? Who's to say that what happens to her simulacrum won't affect her corpus?"

Jörg picked up Lila and bolted. He charged toward the border separating reality from this enclosed space. The moment he made contact with the barrier, he felt a heavy physical force, then tumbled out into the real world. He'd hit the barrier with so much momentum that it sent him into a forward roll over the paving stones.

Time went back to normal.

The pedestrians continued walking, and the workers returned to the holds of their ships. A northerly breeze rustled the leaves of the trees. The pigeons resumed their flapping.

Jörg's body throbbed with pain, but he clenched his teeth and got to his feet. He was glad he'd become a monster. A normal simulacrum probably wouldn't have been able to break through a barrier that strong.

Lila looked stunned, but Jörg patted her on the shoulder. "Don't worry. I'll protect you. Let's quickly go back to the portal home."

"He'll follow right behind us."

"Then we better hurry."

As they sprinted down the bank of the canal, Jörg told Lila, "I'm almost sure he'll be waiting for us in front of the portal. I'll distract him while you go through."

"No. We go together."

"Situations like these are why you have a bodyguard. Please do what I ask."

"Fine. But when I get to the inn, I'm going to bring the Count back. You can't beat this guy by yourself."

"I'd appreciate the help. If you don't make it in time, though, I'm trusting you to take care of Berlin. Keep the food deliveries going."

"That's your job! Don't just pass it off onto me! Make sure you come back!"

Violent splashing sounds were accompanied by an overpowering rotting stench coming from the canal. Jörg glanced toward it. There was some sort of invisible creature running on top of the water, keeping pace with them. White waves formed long, clear streaks on the surface. The trees lining both banks swayed one at a time, and a number of branches made a dry tearing noise before being blown away.

Jörg and Lila ran for the portal home with all their might. They had created it on the door of a small general store near Hubert's office. Coming out onto a wide street, they sprinted past a horse cart and saw the store right in front of them. But just as they were about to dive through the door, something knocked into Jörg from the side, sending him flying and separating him from Lila.

Out of the corner of his eye, he saw her turn and reach out a hand for him, but Jörg shouted, telling her to go. That stench like a rotting swamp assaulted his senses. He looked around, searching desperately for his assailant, but he couldn't see anything.

However, based on the movement of the air, he could tell the monster was heading straight for Lila.

Jörg jumped at it. Trusting his instincts, he grabbed the space in front of him and felt something furry like a wild animal. Holding it firmly in both hands, Jörg hurled the monster to the side, and an unsettling, piercing cry that sounded like nothing of this earth echoed through the street. Jörg stepped forward and, with his fist clenched, delivered a backhanded strike that luckily collided with his opponent.

"Go!" Jörg yelled again, and as he did, Lila opened the door and leaped through to the other side.

His relief lasted only an instant, however, before Jörg was stabbed in the chest, and he slumped to his knees. Something had sunk its teeth into him. It was only then that he realized there was more than one attacker. That unbearable pain pierced his body again and again, as warm liquid seeped from his wounds and pooled by his feet. He tried desperately to struggle, but could no longer move.

"Caught you," Nil whispered in his ear. "Now, let's go back. The divine go to heaven, the wicked go to hell, and humans return to humanity."

7

Upon returning to Xandra's inn, Lila sprinted down the hall, up the stairs, and into the Count's private quarters.

The Count was relaxing on his bed. Small furry balls in brown, gold, and white were clustered around him. They were surely a type of monster, but their mewling cries made them sound like a litter of kittens.

The Count sat up, but before he could speak, Lila yelled at him.

"You have to help Mr. Huber! Please!"

"What happened?"

"That thing we met in Paris was in Rotterdam. I escaped thanks to Mr. Huber, but he's fighting it all by himself. Hurry and help him!"

"Did it seem he could handle it by himself?"

"Not at all! "What is that thing? It's not like anything I've seen before!"

"You should let him be."

"What?!"

"I thought you hated Mr. Huber. In which case, there's no need for me to save him, is there?"

"What are you talking about? That was ages ago!"

"But he's German. I thought you said you don't want to help Germans."

Lila grimaced. "I do still hate Germans. But Mr. Huber and Ms. Diana are different. They're my friends!"

"Oh, really?"

"Yeah. With real friends, it doesn't matter what country you come from!"

The Count shooed the furry balls off the bed, then stepped down to the floor.

"Well then, show me the way."

By the time Lila had taken the Count to Rotterdam, the canal was empty. Both Jörg and Nil were nowhere to be seen.

There were no irregularities with the portal home, either.

Considering the circumstances, there was no doubt in their minds that Nil had taken Jörg with him.

The Count crouched down on the street and ran a finger over the surface of the paving stones. When he lifted it up again, the pad was stained with a red liquid.

"Jörg's blood."

Lila paled. "He's hurt?"

"He's a monster. He might feel pain, but he won't die. Even so, based on the amount of blood, he won't be moving for a while. Do you have any idea where Nil might have taken him?"

"How should I know?!"

"He didn't use any particular words or mention a specific place?"

Lila pressed her hands to her temples. "I don't remember. I was too focused on getting away."

"Then our only option is to follow the blood."

"How do we do that?"

"Even if the body of an immortal is completely torn apart, it will attempt to return to its original shape. The same goes for their blood. Mr. Huber's blood will lead us to him."

The Count held a palm over the blood-soaked stone. A strange pattern appeared at his feet, absorbed all the blood, then stopped in midair. The Count swung his arm, clutching the pattern in his palm. When he opened his hand again, it had coalesced into a crystal of deep crimson.

"We'll use this to find his precise location. For now, however, let's return to the inn."

Once they were back at Xandra's inn, the Count placed the crimson crystal inside a glass jar, which he set down on the desk in his room. He cast some locating spells around it, then explained to Lila that it would take some time to pinpoint Jörg's whereabouts.

"Nil can use incredibly powerful magic. He might have cast spells around Mr. Huber to prevent us from finding him. If so, then it will be difficult to locate him."

"Is there any other way?"

"We could find Nil and try to get the information out of him, but that would be a last resort. Even if we found him, I doubt he'd tell us the truth."

The Count sighed. "The issue we face now is what to do about the delays Jörg's disappearance will bring about… The starvation in Berlin needs to be dealt with urgently. Everything is already in place, but it won't happen if someone doesn't take the lead."

"I'll do it."

"Are you sure you can?"

"Teach me how. I met Ms. Diana in Berlin, and I was disguised as an adult then, so I'm pretty sure she'll trust me. I'll keep going to the Eiffel Tower to exchange information, as well as taking care of Mr. Huber's jobs in his stead."

"You'll need help. You can't carry the supplies all by yourself."

"The monsters here at the inn can help me."

"Sending monsters to a monastery storehouse? What a bold idea."

"Plenty of the monsters here were human first, so they shouldn't be scared of a monastery."

"Hmm. You have a point there."

"How can I convince them to help me, though?"

"It will all depend on how sincere you are."

"I'll try my best. First, I need to get everyone together somewhere."

"That won't be necessary. Curious monsters have already gathered around while we've been talking. You still can't see them, can you?"

"Uh-uh."

"I can make it so they'll be visible to you. You've already talked to several of the less frightening monsters, correct?"

"Yeah."

"I'll make it so you can talk to all of the monsters today. Are you brave enough to try some of Xandra's medicine?"

"Of course."

The Count removed a bottle from a shelf and passed it to Lila. "This isn't a tonic you drink, but eye medicine. Put a drop in each eye."

Lila did as instructed, wiping the liquid that overflowed from her eyes with her sleeve. She blinked repeatedly, and after a few moments, her vision came into focus.

As soon as she could see the monsters, Lila let out a scream.

"Wha—?! There are *this* many of them?!"

Monsters filled the room. They were crammed together so tightly that she couldn't see the rug, and those without a place to stand floated in the air or clung to the ceiling.

"The monsters you have seen up until now are only the slightest fraction. Most of them aren't even at the inn right now. The world is filled with monsters."

"How am I supposed to ask them for help?"

"Simply talk to them like normal."

Lila looked around at all the monsters. "Uh, I'm looking for some help carrying cargo on a regular basis. Anyone who knows how to drive a cart or automobile is especially welcome. The job is transporting food from west Germany to a monastery storehouse in Berlin. As for the payment, you can work that out with the Count."

"Now, wait a minute," the Count said with a wry smile. "You're just going to offload that on me?"

"I don't know what any of them want."

"Then I'm sure you won't mind if I decide on the payment myself."

"That's fine."

"Then that is what I shall do. Now, if you're going to have these monsters transport the goods, the best time to do that would be the middle of the night. Go to Kleinerbrunn in the evening and make your way to the destination from there. Even if it seems slightly eerie, no one will complain if it happens under the cover of darkness. Is that all right with everyone?"

They let out a roar that could shake treetops, and about sixteen monsters of all shapes and sizes came up to Lila. Some were adorable and as small as tiny birds, while others had massive bodies like boars or bears. Though they had different forms, their eyes all shone bright with the same curiosity.

"Thank you all for your help!" Lila said in a powerful voice.

The monsters seemed to settle on a good deal with the Count, and they worked hard, diligently following Lila's instructions.

Anyone who caught a glimpse of their "night procession" likely froze to the spot, staring in fright at the throng of strange shadows.

Lila had adopted the visage of the merchant she used in Berlin and donned a man's clothes. She drove the car in the lead herself, flying down the road at full speed, with the wagons loaded with goods following behind. They weren't pulled by regular horses, however, but monsters that resembled stallions with fiery manes. These black monsters flickered like flames and ran at the same speed as a car, powerfully pulling their cargo along the muddy, pebble-ridden country roads. The cavalcade stretched out in a line, and no monster driving a cart looked the same as any other. Monsters also rode in the backs, their lively eyes scanning the horizon for any unfamiliar monsters or bandits who might attack the convoy.

They traveled so fast that they might as well have been flying in the sky. The monsters' boisterous cries and excited squeals overlapped with the roar of the wind. The cacophony sounded lively and free, like a huge group of humans all playing music together, or a crowd drunk on wine and beer celebrating the harvest festival late into the night, merrily singing and dancing.

That wholly bizarre sight caused every beast near the road to shrink away, hold their breath, and wait patiently for the procession to pass. In nearby homes, sensitive infants began to wail at the noise the group was making, but assuming it to be regular nighttime crying, their parents failed to check outside.

The caravan arrived at the monastery in northeastern Berlin before sunrise. From there, Lila handled things on her own. She had already spoken with the monks, who were early risers, agreeing to pay monthly for the storehouse and telling them she would share a little of the food with them if they wanted. Two monsters stayed behind to guard the supplies—a fact that Lila kept from the monks. If any members of the monastery gave in to temptation and tried to take some of the food, they would meet with a nasty surprise and be scared off.

The Count had taught Lila that prayers and wards against evil spirits didn't work on monsters. She figured the supplies should be fine with the measures she'd put in place, but when Diana sent over her own people to guard the storehouse, their security would be fully complete.

Lila drew a diagram on a door for easy travel to the storehouse. Now she and the Count could get here instantly from Xandra's inn.

With everything in place at the storehouse, Lila went to the Eiffel Tower to tell Diana how to access the food and that if anything ever felt off, to contact her immediately by carrier pigeon. They had a bird they'd trained to fly directly to Xandra's inn.

Lila didn't say anything about Jörg. She'd planned to explain that he was off on another job if Diana asked, but she didn't. Her immense joy at having secured food likely caused her to forget about everything else.

Lila also asked the souls around the Eiffel Tower if anyone wanted to work on a farm, either temporarily or more long-term. They would look after livestock during the winter and plow and sow seeds in the fields during the spring. She proposed the idea that instead of relying on prisoner labor, they could work the fields themselves to increase crop yields that little bit more.

All of them had their own day jobs, so the souls showed some reluctance, but Lila explained that they could use the time they spent chatting here.

"We've created a way to transfer the time we spend dreaming to time in the real world. If you work in your dreams, the fields will be plowed and livestock raised in real life."

"What in the world? That sounds like sorcery."

"That's one way to think about it. But anything looks like magic if you don't know how it works. You'll still get tired like normal from working in your dreams, but everyone will be able to share the rewards."

Hanja squealed excitedly. "Count me in! It sounds like fun. Where are the fields?"

"Romania."

The land had belonged to the Count many years ago. He had long since transferred the rights to someone else, but had recently leased a portion of the arable land to grow food, intending to have simulacrums work the same fields his servants once had. The Count had said that good money could be made these days by selling food, so he wanted to give it a go. He'd never mentioned doing it to help Lila or anyone else, but that was just the way he did things.

The Count needed people to operate the simulacrums. He had suggested that using the people of the Eiffel Tower would be easiest, so Lila has raised this idea to everyone. She didn't think any explanation would help them understand the complicated way it worked, so she'd simply described it as everyone working in their dreams.

"I'll do it, too," Bernadette said. "I'm going to quit the brothel soon, so I'll have plenty of time."

"Thank you so much!"

"Me, too." Diana raised a hand. "I want there to be as much food as possible. I'll do anything that needs doing."

Volunteers called out one after the next. These women knew the ration system wasn't working, so they offered to help so that people might have even the slightest bit more to eat.

Within the span of a few minutes, everyone there had pledged to help Lila in some way.

The land the Count had rented in Romania was a wide basin between two low hills. The rolling expanse had a river winding through it, which provided an abundance of water, and the rough ridges of the Carpathian Mountains towered far off on the horizon. Beech groves covered the foothills, attesting to the ideal growing conditions. There were no homes nearby, just a few farmhouses where the simulacrums that cultivated the fields lived, their burgundy-and-orange roofs contrasting with the surrounding greenery to draw the eye.

It should have been the middle of winter, but spring covered the land. Presumably because it was all a dream.

The women from the Eiffel Tower were captivated by the view before them.

"We're really allowed to use this land?"

"And plough the fields?"

"No one's going to say anything if we grow wheat and vegetables here?"

Color filled their faces, and their hearts leaped at this new responsibility. They might not understand the magic at work here, but the women knew that growing crops, harvesting them, eating what they wanted, and selling whatever they had left as they saw fit were luxuries that were almost unheard of in wartime.

There was already some harvested produce in the storehouse, though it wasn't much, and fully-grown crops in one part of the field. Harvesting that would be their first job.

The Count walked up beside Lila, and together they looked out across the land.

"You could call this *firma de aur*—golden farmland. In the dream world, it will always be sometime between spring and fall here to make their work easier. However, time will still follow that of the real world to ensure that harvests align with the seasons. Cherries won't grow in the middle of winter, for example. You'll have to watch out for that."

"This is incredible!"

"Depending on how it's used, it has the potential to become even more incredible. Though, well, try using it as a normal farm first."

"What about livestock?"

"You can raise them here. Would you like me to get you some?"

"Yes, please."

Some of the farming simulacrums had already appeared in a corner of the field. Their facial features and builds could pass for either male or female. They were all being used by women, but it seemed simulacrums adopted gender-neutral forms.

The Count looked over toward them and called out to a simulacrum walking nearby. "Oh, Camille. You came, too?"

A smile rose on the simulacrum's well-defined face. It was an artificial expression, but it wasn't sarcastic or off-putting. "I had time."

"You don't need to work the fields here. Why not do some sculpting, since you can't do it in the hospital?"

"Kneading clay, sowing seeds; it's all same to me. Right now, farming seems more interesting."

Camille fixed her gaze on Lila. "You're quite capable, aren't you? Though I still think you're a bit of a strange child."

"I appreciate that," the young girl replied.

"The hospital is tedious, so I'm delighted you made a place like this. I'm getting on in years out in the real world. I'm over fifty, already an old woman. But I can still keep working happily here. I'll remember this for a long time. Thank you."

"I'm the one who should be thanking you," Lila said. "You all came to help when I needed it."

With a casual wave, Camille told Lila she'd see her later, then headed toward the fields.

Lila looked up at the Count. "All we want to be satisfied is decent bread and a place to sleep. Why is it so hard to make such a simple wish come true in the real world?"

"Who knows?" the Count replied. "Humans always seem to have a particularly hard time obtaining the things that matter most to them."

"We're going to change that. No matter how long it takes," Lila declared, rolling up the sleeves of her farmer's clothes and tying her hair behind her head. "Even if it takes centuries, we're going to build a world where no one is ever told they don't exist, that they shouldn't think, or that they'll always be under the thumb of someone."

8

Two years earlier. 1914. The start of the Great War.

At the end of July, the first battle began between Serbia and Austria-Hungary. On a national scale, Austria had power that Serbia could never hope to match, so everyone assumed the fighting would end quickly. However, Russia came to Serbia's aid, forcing Austria into a much more grueling campaign than it had anticipated. Serbia formed an alliance with Montenegro and prepared to meet the Austrian assault head-on.

After the assassination of the archduke and his wife, Austria couldn't go home empty-handed. Serbia had even blatantly ignored their ultimatum. The country's honor was at stake, so they had no other choice but to win.

Serbia also couldn't back down. If Austria succeeded in their plans for trialism, Serbia would become a vassal state and its culture and people would be assimilated. Their Slavic pride was on the line, so they had to find a way to resist somehow.

The Austrian Army deployed the navy's shallow-draft gunboats with the goal of using the waterways from the Drina River to the Danube to invade the Serbian capital of Belgrade. The allied army of Serbia and Montenegro mobilized in opposition. Belgrade had been occupied during the summer, but the Serbian and Montenegrin armies had won it back in a counteroffensive. After it fell again in December, a fierce assault by the allied nations drove the Austrian Army out once again.

Serbia had only managed to hold out for this long due to the constant influx of new weapons, with the Balkan Peninsula becoming a huge consumer of weaponry manufactured in other countries. Frustrated Austrian soldiers began killing any Serbian combatants they captured during the fighting. They would line them up on the side of a railroad track, make them kneel, and blindfold them before shooting them in groups.

The tracks rusted with the blood of Serbian soldiers.

But even then, Serbia wouldn't give in to Austria.

At the start of the following year—1915—Germany saw a short reprieve in the fighting on the Western Front and dispatched troops to help Austria, having formed an alliance with Bulgaria, Serbia's longtime enemy. The Germans had aligned themselves with Bulgaria on the condition that they split up the territory after the war, which also strengthened their bond with the Ottoman Empire, so they set out to crush the Serbian Army in one fell swoop.

The multinational force composed primarily of Austrian, German, and Bulgarian troops continued their attacks in October of the same year, pushing the allied Serbian forces farther back. The first to fall was Montenegro. By January of the following year, Montenegro pulled out of its alliance with Serbia and surrendered to the German Army after enemy forces pushed their soldiers back almost to the capital of Cetinje.

Wounded and bleeding, the Serbian Army devised a plan to transport refugees and their exiled government across Albania in the dead of winter and settle in Corfu.

As a soldier in the Serbian Army, Milos Krasić experienced all of this, from the first battles with Austria to the final retreat. He hunkered down in trenches and fired his rifle, reverting to his werewolf form at night to feast on Austrian soldiers.

Yet no matter how savage Milos's acts as a monster were, they paled in comparison to the cruelty he witnessed during the Great War. At this point in time, humans had become far more vicious than monsters. He never left the front, despite knowing that he could not decide the outcome of the war by himself. Milos believed that fighting alongside humans for his homeland would someday make him truly human again. It was a notion that couldn't be further from the truth for all the people who'd lost their humanity in the war. Unlike all the human soldiers who slowly lost their minds the more they fought, Milos gained a better understanding of the human mind. His heart swelled with pride at the thought that he wasn't just a monster or a wolf.

But even to Milos, that trek across Albania was a cruel, harsh journey.

The plains had been covered in a deep layer of snow. The group of Serbian soldiers and refugees stretched on for so long that he had no clue where to find the front, which crept slowly toward its goal like a long black snake on the verge of death. Cold and malnutrition sparked a wave of typhus fever, causing people to drop like flies as they crossed the plains. There wasn't even time to bury them. Everyone looked to the horizon with lifeless eyes.

No one could carry any heavy load across such a distance. Partway across the plains, people began discarding their belongings. They marched on single-mindedly, some relying on nothing but a single cane. Demoralized soldiers deserted, and many of those who stayed succumbed to cold and hunger. People keeled over where they sat every time the column stopped to rest, leaving a horrific number of corpses in their wake. The living sat beside the dead, staving off hunger by chewing on tree bark or roots. Yet still, their pursuers showed no mercy toward the tragic group. Fighting would frequently break out with enemy soldiers, resulting in even more death.

Among these people who wandered like ghosts, hobbling on his own cane, similarly tormented by hunger and fatigue, was Milos. He continued to march, not giving up, his gaze fixed on a single general who glowed like a star at midday.

Colonel Dragutin Dimitrijević.

This man had assassinated the king and queen during the May Coup to pull back the veil of despotism and establish himself in a command position within the military. Rumors said he had also been involved in the plan to assassinate the Austrian archduke and his wife. However, in spite of his violent past, as a human, Colonel Dimitrijević shone above all others in Milos's eyes. The colonel was compassionate, deeply patriotic, and never judged the value of another human being based on their status or position. His one failing was that he tried to involve himself in bureaucracy far too much for a military man, but he could be trusted with any task on the battlefield. In fact, the only thing barely holding this disastrous march together was the colonel's pinpoint counterattacks against the enemy.

The colonel also used a cane, staggering on it as he pressed forward. His ox-strong body carried Milos's and everyone else's hopes upon its back. He was the most reliable person among them, but he had suffered injury and illness many times throughout his life, and the migration across Albania would surely take a huge toll on his body. Even without the attacks by enemy soldiers, the arduous trip could prove lethal to the colonel. Yet he persevered, resolutely leading them.

When the group successfully reached the port and refugees began to climb into boats arranged by the British and French forces, who had rushed to their aid, one of the men serving under the colonel urged him to hurry aboard.

The colonel shook his head, his ever-somber expression never wavering. "I shall not move until everyone is on board. I'll hold off the enemy until the very end."

"Please, sir, listen to reason," the soldier said. "We must get the most important people on the ships first."

"Nothing is more important to a country than its people. The military exists to protect them. You all should be the ones going ahead of me."

Milos stepped forward and addressed the colonel. "In that case, we shall also stay behind to protect you, sir."

"You'll die if you stay with me."

"None of us shall die. We will board the last ship with you, sir."

Having made up their minds to remain behind, the soldiers formed ranks, and the colonel went down the line, shaking the hand of each man and clapping him on the shoulder. All the men looked thin and feeble, like beasts with tattered fur, but their eyes shone brightly above strange smiles.

They had to fight. So the Slavic people would not be forgotten.

Milos and the other soldiers checked their equipment and gripped their rifles tight.

Everyone would board the ships. They wouldn't lose a single man.

Their final stand a success, Milos and the other guards eventually boarded a boat. Accompanied by Colonel Dimitrijević, of course.

Milos lay down in the hold of the ship, curled up into a ball, and immediately fell fast asleep. His fellow soldiers similarly threw themselves to the floor, collapsing into a sleep so deep that it seemed unlikely they would ever open their eyes again.

In his dreams, Milos saw visions from his childhood. He saw his days of running through sun-drenched mountains, though he couldn't tell if he was a human or an animal. His foster father lifted him up high in the sky, smiling at him and saying, "Grow up to be big and strong, Milos. Become a man who will traverse mountains, cross valleys, and ford rivers. Everything in nature is your domain. Never give in. Protect your honor with your life."

France protected Corfu while Serbia's exiled government and army slowly regained their strength.

Milos, who knew little of the world outside Serbia, took in the warmth and abundance of this land on the Mediterranean Sea.

As the season changed, a refreshing, sweet scent began to fill the fields and farms.

The island's residents told him it was the smell of orange flowers.

They gave off a pleasing fragrance that evoked the sweet tanginess of the fruit.

The groves of olive trees surprised him, too, with small, cream-colored flowers in full bloom.

His body and heart began to soften and relax.

But it was just a moment of peace before the next battle.

As France and Great Britain defended Serbia, they continued to send troops to support the Macedonian front.

The Allies couldn't let the Central powers seize any more of the Balkan Peninsula and planned to break through their line at Greece. The refreshed Serbian Army joined them there, with their exiled government moving to Salonika.

Another battle broke out. The role of the Serbian Army was limited to fighting smaller skirmishes, but Milos and the other soldiers felt their progress shaping the path that would help decide the fate of the Great War.

Colonel Dimitrijević joined general headquarters to assist in commanding the battle. He would admit anyone to his private quarters who could provide him with vital information, regardless of rank, so Milos would visit him from time to time.

He never stopped treating everyone with generosity and fairness.

Milos often saw the shadow of his adoptive father in the colonel and always served him with the greatest respect.

It was the middle of December 1916 when Jörg fought Nil's familiars in Rotterdam and was taken away somewhere.

At the same time, Milos was fighting on the Macedonian front. One day, the commanders there suddenly began receiving orders that they were being removed from their posts.

It wasn't just the generals who were discharged, either. Rumors circulated that lower-ranked officers and people who had been working with the Serbian Army were also being arrested and imprisoned. Some had apparently even been exiled to the French colonies in northern Africa and sent to the prisons for commissioned officers in Salonika.

No one knew what was happening. Nothing about the situation made sense.

Yes, the Macedonian front was locked in a stalemate, but it wasn't because the Allied powers and the Serbian Army were pushed back by the enemy Bulgarian troops. The strength of the Allied armies grew by the day, and there were whispers around the camp that the next attack might break through the line. All this is to say that they weren't replacing incompetent officers, but gradually removing exceptional officers whose absence would prove problematic.

A few days later, the distressed soldiers received even more shocking news.

The exiled Serbian government had arrested Colonel Dragutin Dimitrijević, who had been commanding the battle from general headquarters. Moreover, he had been charged with high treason and masterminding the assassination of King Alexander of Serbia.

Milos visited his commanding officer and asked to be allowed to investigate the matter, which was swiftly approved. Milos had been using his powers as a werewolf to do the jobs that humans couldn't, making him perfect for a situation like this.

After leaving the front lines, he first checked on the men who'd been arrested and was shocked to find that everyone had some connection to Colonel Dimitrijević.

Everything immediately clicked into place for Milos.

The arrested men were victims of a power struggle that had been building within the government for years, with the crown and the establishment on one side and the supporters of the movement for Greater Serbia on the other. The sweeping moves enacted by the ruling parties hinted at ceasefire negotiations going on between Austria and the Allies.

Austrian emperor Franz Joseph I passed away in late November, so these negotiations were an act of his successor, the more moderate Charles I. Uncomfortable at the length of the war, he must have entered into secret peace talks with the Allies behind Germany's back. If so, then Serbia's revival was drawing near. The established faction's greatest obstacles to rebuilding the country were the people of the Great Serbia movement who had assassinated Austria's archduke and triggered the Great War in the first place. The members of the exiled government must be planning to settle Serbia's debts at Salonika before returning home in triumph.

As Milos found evidence to corroborate his theory, preparations for the trial of the arrested men proceeded steadily. The establishment didn't show even the slightest inclination to pardon Colonel Dimitrijević and other officers. Of those who had been arrested, the exiled government planned to execute the men who had played key roles in the plot—six officers and one activist in total. To that end, they had begun assembling people who would provide false testimony.

The more he investigated the matter, the more Milos realized just how bad the situation was for the colonel's group. Had only Colonel Dimitrijević been arrrested, the officers on the outside could revolt against the exiled government and perhaps even pull off a coup d'état, thereby freeing the colonel. However, the exiled government had preempted that possibility, arresting any officer they feared might be capable of such an act and throwing them in prison with the colonel. The mass movement and arrest of commanders in December was a tactic to prevent insurrection before it happened.

Now no one inside the army could use their influence to help the colonel. A handful of rational thinkers were urging France and Great Britain to appeal for the colonel's release. Distrusting the actions of the exiled Serbian government, France and Great Britain pursued formal diplomatic channels to persuade them to reconsider, but the establishment would hear nothing of it.

The following spring, Milos visited Colonel Dimitrijević.

A colorful array of wildflowers adorned the path leading up to the prison, and for a moment, they seemed to mask all the uneasiness Milos felt.

They stood out like symbols of truth and freedom.

Bright-yellow rapeseed blossoms blanketed the hill. Chamomile bloomed on the edge of the path, and poppies grew tall, supporting what looked like red bonnets. Arugula flowers opened into white crosses, and small green fruits hung from nettle. The first leaves of olive and plane trees fluttered. Orange flowers would bloom soon and release their characteristic sweet fragrance.

As Milos breathed in, the vibrant scent of life filling the air seemed to pierce the despair lurking deep within his chest. But he couldn't stay here savoring it.

He had to find a way to meet with Colonel Dimitrijević in secret and come up with a plan to break him out of prison.

For a monster like Milos, sneaking into a prison was easy. Once inside, he could simply put the guards to sleep. The powdered medicine he'd bought from Xandra proved very useful at times like this.

The medicine could not, however, sway the mind of a human being harboring a belief bordering on faith. If the colonel didn't agree to escape, then Milos had no way to get him out.

Milos crept silently down the prison's dim, damp halls. He found the colonel's cell and used his monstrous abilities to pass through the locked door.

Colonel Dimitrijević sat in a ratty chair, arms crossed as he dozed. His decrepit appearance made him look much older than forty, and his hulking frame—which had earned him the nickname Apis, or "Holy Bull"—was now thin and frail. The color had drained from his skin, leaving behind spots. Milos wanted to cry out in grief. This was what had become of the stubborn-headed hero who had stood against the great powers of Europe for his country, never retreating a single step in battle?

Sensing a presence, the colonel slowly looked up. His eyes had lost their usual fierceness. Upon seeing Milos, however, a glimmer of light returned to his murky pupils. His cheeks lifted in his usual amiable smile. "Milos, you're here. Or am I hallucinating?"

"I am no hallucination, colonel," Milos said, kneeling down in front of him. "I came for you. Let's get you out of here. All the necessary preparations are in place. I only need your confirmation, sir."

"Can you take the others, too?"

"For now I'm here for just you, sir. I can't escort a large group by myself."

"Then I cannot go. I stand at the helm. If those below me are not yet free, then I cannot leave here."

It was the exact sentiment the colonel had expressed during their retreat across Albania. At the time, the colonel and his brigade had continued fighting the Central forces to the very end, shielding both the refugees and his own army. Milos had been a part of that force. As the boats for Corfu left the port, the colonel hadn't even tried to board a ship until the very last moment, but continued fighting off their pursuers.

Milos recalled those hardships they'd faced together as he stared at the colonel's body, weakened by a lengthy imprisonment.

Once they had settled at Corfu and the army had reorganized under France's protection, Colonel Dimitrijević had also won victories alongside his fellow officers on the Macedonian front.

Milos couldn't believe that the exiled Serbian government was trying to execute such a great man as a traitor. The colonel had known about the assassination plot that sparked the Great War, but his conscience had gotten the best of him at the last minute and he'd tried to stop it. In the end, it had been too late and he'd ended up watching it all unfold before him. It was true that he hadn't thought through the political ramifications, but the colonel had never acted for his own self-interest or desires. Everything he did was for his country, all his choices were to prevent the Slavic people from falling under Austrian dominion. Only people with no experience under the boot of a larger power would sneer at that and call it foolishness. Serbia had been fighting the Ottoman Empire for a long time and opposed Austria and Hungary, and it was one of the countries in the Balkan Peninsula concerned over Russian interference.

Even though Milos recognized the colonel's error, he still couldn't bring himself to criticize the man.

"Please reconsider," Milos stressed. "Without you, the government is nothing but King Alexander's toadies. Do you think Serbia will survive if the country is left in their hands?"

"There are many other great men besides me. The government will surely be steered back on track. Don't worry. This arrest was a mistake. They will give me a fair trial."

Milos clenched his teeth. The colonel was being too optimistic again. His generosity and lack of suspicion toward other people was a double-edged sword. There were people in this world filled with incomprehensible malice, and the colonel didn't understand that those people weren't swayed by paragons of justice, but simply laughed as they walked over them.

There was no way the colonel didn't see how during these several months in captivity, they had completely trampled his dignity as a human.

"By the way," the colonel continued, "would you see if any letters have arrived for me?"

"What letters?"

"I have been writing to my family and friends since they put me in here, but I haven't received even a single letter in response. I do wonder whether they're actually sending them."

The guards must have been purposefully intercepting the colonel's letters to make sure he wasn't trying to devise some sort of ingenious plan.

"Please," the colonel said, almost as if it was a prayer. "Not being able to communicate with those who mean the most to me is the one thing that disheartens me most."

The colonel cherished his family and friends. To have that taken from him completely must be a heartache akin to torture. The guards knew this and did it on purpose to rob prisoners of their will to fight and crush their spirits.

"If any have arrived, I swear I'll bring them to you." Milos had already planned on searching the office later anyway, so it wouldn't take him out of his way at all. "Please give me a bit of time."

"Thank you. Could you tell me something of what is happening outside? I do still read the papers."

"They give you newspapers?"

The colonel gave a mischievous wink. "I have someone who trades them for cigarettes. The workers at the bottom are all good people. It's the top that's rotten."

Milos reported the current state of affairs in great detail. The fighting on the Macedonian front should be resolved in the near future. People were sick and tired of the drawn-out battle and were making real efforts to finally bring about a ceasefire.

The colonel listened somberly to it all, apparently still analyzing events to educate himself even in such low spirits—a habit from his days in headquarters. He couldn't play an active role in the plans any longer, though, which must frustrate him.

"I intend to fight to the very end," the colonel repeated. "Whether that's this trial, or whether I have to go to appeal directly to Alexander. There's no truth or evidence that we tried to overthrow the current government. This trial will expose their lies."

The colonel was far too optimistic. The government could have bought the judge, but he seemed to not have even considered the possibility. He believed that acting righteously as a human being and a citizen would always win out. However, the world wasn't like that now. Not in their homeland or anywhere else in Europe.

Colonel Dimitrijević might be putting too much of his hope in help coming from France or Great Britain. He was good with languages, could speak a handful of them, and had connections with people in other countries. He might be hoping for a final opportunity for the Allies to right the errors of the exiled government.

Magic wouldn't work on people whose beliefs bordered on faith.

Milos decided not to press it for the time being. "I should be going now. I'll come again later with information."

The colonel nodded magnanimously. "The Greek spring does feel wonderful," he said, before adding wistfully, "...I wonder if I'll live long enough to see the orange petals fall."

Milos left the question unanswered and exited the room. On his way out, he searched through the desks in the office. As predicted, he found a bundle of letters addressed to the colonel, so he returned to the cell and pushed them through the food slot.

"Thank you," a warm voice called through the gap.

Milos saluted in front of the door and left.

The trial held by the exiled Serbian government ended in a ruling to execute the seven officers, including Colonel Dimitrijević. The ruling commuted the sentences of four of the men, so in actuality, only the colonel and two other men would face execution. A car took the three men from Salonika to Mikra, where they were tied to stakes in graves that had been dug for them in the valley. They were executed as day broke on June 27.

In the moments leading up to his death, Colonel Dimitrijević faced his executioners and yelled, "If I am to die by Serbian guns for Greater Serbia, then I do not regret it, because I pray for the revitalization of Greater Serbia in the near future. Tell my friends."

Following the assassination of the archduke of Austria and his wife, Gavrilo Princip, the murderer, had been imprisoned in Theresienstadt, a prison for dissidents in the Austro-Hungarian Empire. He died from a worsening case of tuberculosis while in prison on April 28, 1918, the year after Colonel Dimitrijević's execution.

The rays of the morning sun began to shine from the eastern corner of the valley. Milos stood motionless, looking down on the basin. He'd been too late to save the colonel and had heard the distant gunfire just as he'd reached the spot where he now stood.

Count Silvestri walked up behind him, but he didn't turn around. Milos crouched in the frigid air for long time, then finally said, "A new Serbia will emerge. I will help them win on the Macedonian front, retake Belgrade, and return my motherland to its rightful standing. The exiled government will become a 'clean government' and return to the homeland. Not one of those generals who dragged us into the Great War will serve in the cabinet. Neither will any of those who opposed the establishment. The colonel, his friends—none of them remain in any important positions. The Serbian government will eliminate anyone they deem inconvenient, sidle up to the victorious nations with innocent smiles on their faces, and create a country that forbids any and all opposition."

"There's one thing I'd like to ask," the Count said. "Seeing what happened here, do you still want to be human? Do you still believe that humans are more wonderful than monsters?"

"I can't accept that *this* is how humans truly are!" Milos cried out.

The tears he'd been holding back poured forth, running down his cheeks to fall from his chin. "I didn't fight all those horrible battles to become like this lot! Don't you dare call them human!"

The Count didn't respond. He waited until Milos had wiped his tears with a sleeve, calmed his trembling body, and could talk normally again.

The Count chose his timing carefully, then said, "If you aren't doing anything after taking back Belgrade, there's something I'd like to ask of you."

"...What?"

"Do you remember that German man you helped in Paris? Jörg Huber."

"What about him?"

"Nil captured him early last winter, and he's been missing ever since. I finally discovered his whereabouts. But Nil has cast a powerful spell over him, and I can't get him back on my own. Would you help me rescue him?"

"Do it yourself. He's your servant."

"Once you got your country back, your life lost its purpose. The colonel you planned to rebuild your country with has been killed, and the men who helped him will still be in jail for decades. Those freed by the regency government won't ever have another chance to enter the political arena again. There's nothing left for you to do. That life is empty for you."

"Don't waste your breath."

"The truth is, Jörg has changed himself into a real monster."

"What?"

"He inherited my blood, just like Xandra. When he asked me to make him a monster, he said something interesting. He said he would give up his life as a human to save humans. He has a soft spot for children because of his work as a barber and couldn't bear to see them starve to death, swept up in the winds of war."

Milos didn't reply as he weighed the Count's words.

"I've come to view Jörg—the man who became a monster to save humans—as more human than real ones," the Count continued. "What situations reveal the true meaning of humanity? Are you trying to become like the men who killed your enemies, killed your fellow countrymen, and feign ignorance as they forge a new era? Or are you like Jörg, who will abandon even himself to save other people?"

"Don't confuse things. Jörg's situation has nothing to do with me."

"I wonder about that. I think it's extremely relevant. Of course, I don't expect you to agree to help for free. I'll offer you half off Xandra's medicine for a limited time. The Macedonian front is still active. You could use all the medicine you can get."

"It's still too expensive at half price. Make it ninety percent off."

"How greedy. You'll make Xandra cry."

"Then no deal."

"How about seventy?"

"Eighty. I won't take any less."

"If you insist. Well then, it seems we have a deal."

The early morning sun brightened the world around them, and the wind brought with it the scent of orange blossoms—the final fragrance they made just before falling.

"What a lovely smell," the Count said calmly. "I hope this era puts an end to the ethnic pride that caused all this conflict. Which people are greater, which are lesser, who has control over whom. It's all so senseless."

V
The November Revolution

1

Jörg's mind melted into a burning pain, and the world around him went dark. He felt his body being lifted and carried away, but he couldn't guess where to.

That foul stench faded, and when Nil's presence disappeared, he felt something warm encase him. It had a familiar feel to it, but he still couldn't see anything. Gradually, the pain faded.

He couldn't see an exit, and although he wanted to escape, something resisted him.

A long time passed before light finally pierced the darkness.

Jörg found himself in a dimly lit room, gazing at sunlight filtering through a window. He appeared to be lying down in a bedroom. A sudden sensation overcame him, as if his head had been grabbed and shaken. Jörg worried that someone might be attacking him, but there was no pain in his body. His vision just seemed to sway.

"You slept for quite a long time," a voice said. The shape of a large man entered Jörg's unsteady view of the world. The shaking finally subsided, and the figure solidified in the center of his vision.

Jörg gasped. The person standing in front him was the Serbian werewolf, Milos. He wasn't wearing his military uniform like before, but the clothes of the migrant workers Jörg often saw in Germany.

"Why are you here?" Jörg asked.

"I've been watching you this whole time for the Count. On the condition that Xandra sell me her medicine at a discount."

"How long have I been here?"

"Two years."

"Two years?!"

"You've been asleep for two years."

"I was unconscious?"

"It would be more accurate to say you've been trapped by Nil's magic. It's still affecting you."

"Is that why I can't move?"

"You can't move. But your body can."

"What does that mean?"

"Pay close attention to your surroundings when the world moves. You'll see what I mean."

Jörg's eyeline suddenly rose, and Milos vanished from sight. His surroundings no longer shook, but Jörg couldn't choose where he looked, and his line of sight would shift suddenly. He could only focus on whatever was directly in front of him. It felt like he was sitting in the passenger seat of a car and letting the driver choose the destination. Seeing the way his vision moved, Jörg finally understood.

He was inside someone else's body.

Trapped... In other words, Nil had probably forced him inside another person. It was like when Edmund Jansen had almost trapped Lila. Maybe Nil had even used the same magic. The height of his eyeline didn't feel strange, so Jörg figured that whoever this was must be about as tall as he was.

He didn't recognize the surroundings. The person Jörg was inhabiting moved toward the window to look outside, and Jörg realized he was in Berlin—the city he'd visited so many times to collect information and buy food. He was positive.

Milos stood next to him but stayed silent. It seemed as though this person Jörg was in couldn't see Milos.

"Are you invisible?" he asked.

"Yeah," the other man replied. "Right now, I only want to talk to you."

"Who is this person?"

"He's you."

"What?"

"Right now, you're inside your corpus. You could even say you've returned to your old body. It was pretty cruel of Nil. He trapped you inside there, but you and the corpus don't share the same mind."

Jörg cursed. "Where's Nil now?"

"I don't know. The Count is looking for him but hasn't had any luck so far. Xandra made some medicine to separate you from your corpus. I've been feeding it to you these past two years when your corpus was asleep, but I've yet to see any results."

"How in the world? And Berlin is—"

"Doing fine, thanks to Lila's skillful handling of the food supply. It's hard to believe she's just a child. She kept in contact with women from all over to keep food production and transportation going."

"*Production*? I only asked her to look after the transportation."

"She's managing something much larger now. She's borrowing a parcel of land from the Count's old dominion to grow food. It lets her increase the amount she has, even if only a little."

"That's a great idea!" Jörg exclaimed. "It's so much better for her than spying!"

"I agree. She's seems much happier, too."

"By the way, how involved is my corpus in Berlin's revolution?"

"The organization has tasked him with minor jobs: printing flyers on mimeographs, distributing them, communicating with other revolutionaries in Russia, that sort of thing… But he's really committed. When he speaks in public, the authorities practically come charging toward him, and lately he's started using some more extreme language."

Jörg let out a groan. "That doesn't sound anything like me."

"The Count thinks the ancient blood has influenced your corpus, too."

"That's what Nil wanted. I was trying to keep it in check."

"Vlad was someone who never stopped fighting the people who enslaved his homeland. If that fervor has tied itself to the German revolution, your corpus won't stop until the German government falls."

"Either way, I need to get out of here as soon as possible."

"Yes, that would be for the best. Keep taking the medicine and try to control your corpus from within. Now that you're awake, you should be able to control it a little."

2

Jörg's corpus eventually changed clothes, drank some water, slung a faded bag over one shoulder, and left the room. Milos followed, remaining invisible.

Jörg felt the cold air hit him as his corpus left the apartment. Nil had attacked him at the start of winter, so he must have slept for pretty much exactly two years. Since he'd woken up in the same season, the attack felt more like yesterday than two years ago. In the Berlin of today, a raw stench rose from every surface and permeated the air. It didn't come from any one specific place, but from the roads and inside every house. To Jörg, it smelled like wounded souls, corrupted ideals, and a dying country.

When had Germany become like this? The moment the war began? Or had it already been like this before any fighting started? Perhaps he and everyone else had pretended not to notice the rot surfacing so long ago. He felt as if he could turn over any of the cobblestones at his feet and expose a ground packed tight with the flesh and blood of a decaying country.

"Between when you lost consciousness in the winter of 1916 and now, over six hundred thousand people have died of starvation in Germany alone," Milos told him. "If you add up all the deaths since the start of the war, it's got to be over seven hundred thousand."

"Nil said the same thing. This war really did create all those victims."

"There were strikes throughout Germany this past January. They happened all at once, across roughly twenty cities. More than half a million workers took part in Berlin alone."

"And what happened?"

"They failed. The government came down hard on them. The leaders were all arrested, tried, and jailed. Do you have any idea how many strikes and protests there have been in Germany alone since the war began? Yet none of them have succeeded. The German government has no intention of changing. And what do you think will happen if it keeps on like this? The people will demand that the government itself change. By that, I mean revolution."

Jörg's corpus had been walking for twenty minutes. He'd only had some water to drink, so he must be exhausted and hungry. Water was probably the only thing in that room, so he must have gone outside to try to find some food, hoping there would be something around town. The army should have set up some portable kitchens.

"Where's my corpus going?" Jörg asked.

"To an acquaintance's house. They're going to share some food with him."

"Will they have anything there?"

"A thin slice of bread and weak soup. Maybe a potato if he's lucky."

"What about meat?"

"Things like that are all gone. But at least there's still something."

"What about the rations?"

"Practically nonexistent."

"Do you think I'll get hungry, too? I can't take sustenance from the people of Berlin. I'd feel awful."

"You have your medicine, so you'll be all right."

His corpus walked on heavy legs to a run-down general store. Acting like a customer, he chatted with the clerk before being shown into the basement. There Jörg saw food in bags and boxes, though he had no clue how it had gotten there. The earthy smell of vegetables and the sour scent of rye bread hung faintly in the cool air.

The clerk who'd brought Jörg's corpus here removed a thin slice of bread from a wooden box and placed it on plate. He filled a copper stein with water and slid it over. Jörg's corpus thanked him and sipped the water while nibbling at the rye bread. It was much staler and tougher than what Jörg knew; no one could swallow this poor substitute for bread without water. Soup probably would make it easier to consume, but there was nothing like that around, and he didn't see any cheese or sausage to eat with it. That wasn't surprising, though, considering there wasn't even enough fuel to warm up the room or the bread. Jörg was grateful just to have drinking water. His corpus licked a finger and carefully mopped up every last crumb on the plate. Words failed Jörg. His corpus was as desperate as a stray dog rummaging through garbage, and Jörg couldn't help but commiserate with him.

"I mentioned this earlier, but Lila has been handling the food supply for you. Do you know a woman named Diana?" asked Milos.

"Yes."

"Lila sends the shipments to Diana, and this is one of the places Diana supplies. She's a socialist."

"Oh!" Jörg cried out. It all made sense. Diana had asked about the French socialists at the Eiffel Tower because she was part of the socialist movement. That was also why she'd framed her question like she had to the French people there.

Milos's face contorted into a frown. "What is it?"

"Nothing. I was just thinking of how oblivious I can be sometimes."

"Germany is in a very precarious position right now. People are still fighting on the front lines, but soldiers continue to surrender, and their line keeps getting pushed backward. America finally declared that it would join the war, too. And it wasn't just empty words; they actually sent weapons and troops."

"That's a huge relief to the Allies."

"These four years have worn Europe down, but America is still fresh. The German Army made it as far as the Marne but were pushed back and suffered heavy losses at Amiens. Great Britain and France are now using tanks and infantry much more effectively than they did at the Somme."

"What have the Germans been doing? Their work on the tanks must have progressed."

"They finished a tank called the A7V and deployed it, but it didn't do much. The technologies behind it were still incomplete, and infantry tactics have advanced further."

"But hand grenades don't work on them."

"The German Army's using anti-tank rifles and bundled grenades now."

"Bundled grenades?!"

"The grenades you used had a handle, right?"

"Right."

"These have just one handle, but six grenades are bundled together at the top. The idea is that one throw provides the explosive power of six grenades. But even with ideas like that, Germany is still being pushed back. And it doesn't have anything anyway, because all imports have been stopped. All while the Allies tap the inexhaustible manufacturing of the USA and the Far East."

Wars are fought with resources. You can't win without a supply of goods, but Germany still steadfastly refused to see reason.

"Lieutenant Colonel Kreutzer from the intelligence bureau should have been involved in the development of the A7V."

"I heard about him. The Count says they dismissed him over a dispute with his superiors. Apparently, he was really upset over how long development was taking. He was the one who delivered the information on British tanks directly to the War Ministry, so he was probably frustrated that his work wasn't being utilized more efficiently. After he was relieved of his post, they sent him to the front, where I heard he died in the fighting at Amiens."

So the lieutenant colonel, who had so arrogantly mocked the death of enemy soldiers at that banquet, had been tossed onto the front lines to die a pointless death? It was a fittingly ironic end for the man.

"I feel bad for him," Jörg mumbled. "Not out of sympathy, but because he must have wanted to see a German tank crush enemy soldiers."

"The Count also acted quite cruelly," Milos said. "He probably expected something like that might happen but still sold the information to Kreutzer anyway. They'd known each other for a long time, but in the end, the colonel was just someone to manipulate and deceive."

Just hearing about it exasperated Jörg.

"A major revolution happened in Russia, where the czar was ousted and eventually executed," Milos continued. "The monarchy fell, making way for a republic aimed at founding a socialist nation. Russia then entered into an armistice with Germany and other nations in December of last year, and while there has been some fighting since then, they finally signed a peace treaty in March. Germany can now focus everything on the Western Front, but like I said earlier, it's all too little, too late. Bulgaria surrendered at the end of September and signed the Salonika Agreement, and we retook Belgrade on November 1. The Ottomans and the Allies signed an armistice at the end of October. And since the start of November, Germans around the country have continued to rebel."

"What?!"

"It all started with a mutiny at the port of Wilhelmshaven, which spread to the Port of Kiel and struck a chord in the hearts of regular people across the country. I'm sure you already know this, but Germany wanted to get rid of all the socialists, so they arrested protesters whenever people took to the streets and sent them to the front lines as punishment. But the people they arrested continued to spread socialist ideas on the front."

"And that was enough to convert the soldiers?"

"Most people only half listened to their ideas, of course. But with outspoken and active socialists in their group, people could rebel and blame it on the socialists.

"Anyway, every army was a mess internally. In the German Navy right now, seamen only get one moldy potato per man per day. All while the officers eat normal meals and even drink alcohol. In conditions like those, it would be stranger if people didn't revolt. And still, the admirals were planning to send eighty thousand marines out to a decisive battle. That's no different from sending them to their deaths."

"I see. I didn't realize things had gotten so bad…"

"Russia is hoping for a socialist revolution in Germany, too. But if that happens, all of Germany could fall into a state of complete chaos. Who knows what might happen then?"

"How are things in Serbia? What happened after you took back Belgrade?"

"Things have calmed, and there's no threat of revolution. Because Serbia persecuted and killed Colonel Dimitrijević and his followers. Do you remember that? They claimed the colonel was involved in the plot to assassinate the archduke and his wife."

"Is that what they accused him of?"

"No. The establishment gave a different reason to purge the colonel and his group. I'm sure they wanted to put the assassination behind them so they could proceed with peace talks with Austria. The assassin died in prison in April. Serbia will once again be able to wield its might and return to the international stage."

"That's tragic… But I don't feel bad for them. If they hadn't killed the archduke and his wife, we would have never been sent off to fight. Even if the colonel and the others involved did it to avoid oppression under trialism, considering everything that happened afterward and the horrific number of lives lost, I can't forgive their decision. They might have loved their homeland with all their hearts and gathered faithful people to their cause, but in the end, all it did was wreck Europe. The horrors committed in the name of humanity and people's lofty ambitions sends a chill down my spine."

Milos's expression clouded over slightly before he softly murmured, "...If you didn't know the Count, I'd beat you to a pulp for what you just said. Germany is a powerful nation. It could never understand the suffering of the Serbian people."

"If you hate it so much, then why did you help me?"

"I made a deal with the Count. I told you earlier that if I helped you, Xandra would sell me medicine at an eighty-percent discount."

"You're the worst."

"As we say in Serbia, you can't have both a goat and money."

"But, Milos, there's no end to human folly. They talk about justice and love, but deep down they only want personal gain. The economy drove this war more than any ethnic movement. How much wealth and how many resources do you think crossed borders globally while the people holding the reins sat far removed from the horrors of war? Why do you want to become something so foolish? You're a werewolf—something far greater than a human."

"You sound just like the Count. I guess you two really do have the same blood running through your veins."

"If I offended you, I apologize."

"No, don't worry about it."

Milos didn't say anything for a while, then finally broke the silence. "When I was a baby, a hajduk leader took me in. The hajduks were honorable vagabonds working toward independence when Serbia was still under Ottoman rule. They attacked Ottoman caravans and stole their goods, then gave what they stole to the Serbian people. When I came of age, I joined the hajduks and eagerly started attacking merchants."

"As a human, or...?"

"A werewolf. The hajduk leader used me in that capacity. I operated as a beast obedient to the Serbian people and transformed into the demonic wolf to tear out the throats of Ottoman merchants and soldiers when they needed me to. They treated me as one of them, which I appreciated. Can you understand that? Monsters don't see me as a monster.

I was raised by humans, and all the monsters treated me as if humans had somehow contaminated me. But humans don't see me as a human, either, because I change into a werewolf. I live as neither a human nor a monster. What would you do if it was you? Favor your birth, or honor those who raised you?"

"I don't know. I chose to become a monster."

"Yes, precisely, you choose whether to be a human or a monster, but society sees you differently. The more the hajduks looked after me, the more I wanted to be a human at heart. Then one day, we were caught in a sudden thunderstorm, and we ran into an old church at the edge of a forest. The chapel was neat and tidy, but we couldn't find a priest anywhere. We were honorable robbers, but they must have thought we were bandits, so maybe the priests got scared and hid in a back room. There were so many candles burning on both sides of the chapel that the inside was bathed in a golden light. The building was made from simple stone, but scores of icons hung on the walls, those saints and the virgin mother looking down on us as though questioning our purity. My fellow hajduks faced the statues of the Pantocrator at the front of the chapel. They bent their ring and pinkie fingers, drew the sign of the cross with their other three fingers, and bowed their heads. Then they sat on the pews and wiped themselves dry, lit votive candles, knelt, and prayed in whatever way they wished. I was a monster, so I'd hardly ever had the chance to see the inside of a church, and I watched with rapt fascination. The gold paint on the icons' backgrounds glittered like the sun, and I felt real warmth coming from it. Oh, how it calmed me—and a moment later I heard a voice call down to me from the ceiling."

"What did you hear?"

"God's voice."

"God spoke to a monster?"

"Yes. I'm certain I heard it. It said, 'Milos, continue fighting for yourself, keep living, and do not stop searching for what it means to be human. Do that, and one day you will transform from a monster into a real human being…'"

"That all sounds pretty dubious."

"Think of it like a delusion. I was the only one who heard it. That God of course was not the same God humans believe in. It was a strange experience, but the words shook me to my core. I would have doubted them had a human said them to me, but they'd come from God. So I had no choice but to believe them."

Milos's expression softened slightly. "The true God is likely a being that would even bestow His mercy upon a monster. The sum of my actions may lead me to a path that would make me a real human. I pondered that idea and realized it holds equally true for any person."

"What do you mean by that?"

"What does it mean to be human? Maybe if you're not constantly asking yourself that question, it's all too easy to turn into something inhuman. But persistently asking yourself that will just keep someone barely human. And humans refusing to ask themselves that question is what brought about this senseless war. You started as a human, so you may not understand what I mean."

Jörg had been listening in stunned silence, but he answered immediately. "No, I understand. I understand completely."

He had tried to abandon his humanity on the battlefield. Had he not, he could never have kept on living. The people who kept fighting were those who couldn't give up on themselves—humans who weren't human.

At that moment, the owner of the general store started speaking to Jörg's corpus. "We move on Berlin tomorrow. You'll head for the Reichstag. Some will go to the palace, but the emperor retreated to Spa in Belgium and isn't back yet. If the government is going to respond, then the Reichstag is the best bet."

"Don't tell me I'm going in unarmed. The military police will have cannons and rifles."

"Members of the Spartacus Group have guns. As do the soldiers who joined us. That should protect the people to some degree."

"Then I'll take a hunting rifle. I can use bird shot."

"Do as you see fit. But the police are more likely to target and arrest you if you're armed. Leave your gun at home if you want to avoid that."

"Understood."

The owner handed Jörg's corpus a pouch, saying it contained two days' worth of food. There was no way that tiny bag could hold anywhere near that amount, but he thanked the clerk and stuffed it into his satchel.

3

When Jörg's corpus returned to his apartment complex, he found a familiar man standing out front. Fritz Ziegel. A shoulder bag lay draped across his coat.

Fritz turned to him and waved. "Sorry for showing up so suddenly."

Jörg's corpus let out a cry of joy. "How did you find this place?!"

"Someone told me where to go."

"Who?"

"Nil."

"You still talk with him?"

"He just shows up on his own." Fritz opened his bag to show what was inside. "I only have two. Take one."

A pungent, sour-tinged scent wafted up. Jörg's corpus drank back his saliva. "Apples. Real apples."

"They have them if you go to the right places."

"They must have cost an arm and a leg."

"You can say that again. I learned that the apples also come from the Far East. Have you ever heard of a country called Japan?"

"The German Army fought with them at Tsingtao, right? They're a small country, but they sent ships all the way into the Mediterranean when the British asked."

"That's right. They've gone into full-scale production since the start of the war and are sending a lot of things over. It's been an economic boon to their whole country."

"Like America."

"Maybe. But if you're going to get anything, food would be better than booze now, right?"

"Thank you. I could cry."

Jörg's corpus walked up the aged stairs ahead of Fritz. Upon returning to his room and unlocking the door, he motioned his friend in first and then shut the door behind them.

Fritz set his bag down on the table and gently removed the apples. "I couldn't get much else, just a carrot and some parsley stems."

"It's plenty. Over here it's hard to get anything except turnips. People have turned parks and apartment courtyards into farms, but they don't produce very much."

"The city has different soil than the country. That's not surprising."

The apples were sour but tasted as sweet as honey to the two men. As Jörg's corpus savored his apple intensely, he asked Fritz, "What did Nil say about me?"

"He said you're walking a very human path...whatever that means."

"Did he tell you what I'm doing?"

"He did. That's why I'm here. The government is not going to show the socialists any leniency. I figured that if you were in danger, then I'd come get you and we could escape together."

"They can oppress us as much as they want—it's pointless. The harder life becomes, the more workers join the movement. Because socialism considers how to deliver wealth to the poor."

"And how do you plan to make that happen?"

"The capitalism that created our modern society makes it seem like anyone can acquire wealth if they work hard. They tell you to work and get money, and so long as you don't stray from that path, you'll be rich someday. But that never happens. The rich want to reduce labor costs to increase profits, so they try to keep worker wages low. As industry develops under this model, the wealth disparity between workers and the rich grows. The overall wealth in society increases, though, so at some point all that wealth accumulates at one end. In other words, the economic cycle becomes divided between society's upper class, where the capitalists are, and its lower class, where the workers are. Wealth doesn't move from the upper to the lower classes but just circulates among the upper class. On the other side, the money in the lower class circulates among the lower class and no one can move up. The people work hard in the hopes of breaking into the upper class, but even a lifetime of work in the lower classes can't earn enough money. That's the system that emerges. All that wealth and the divided economy needs to be stirred from top to bottom again to redistribute wealth. That is the ideal socialist society."

"It's a wonderful story, but can it actually work in the real world?"

"There's only one way to know. But the movement is still in its infancy. The Russian Revolution just happened, and no one knows how its economy will react. I'm not giving up hope, though."

The corpus's eyes shone brightly. "We're staging a big protest in Berlin tomorrow. The chief executive at Kiel resigned on the fourth, and the workers and soldiers' council seized control of the city. That fire has started to spread across Germany, and it won't be stopped."

"Do you think I could join?"

"You want to come?"

"I want to check out the protests for myself and draw what I see when I get home. It's actually one of the reasons why I came here."

This stunned Jörg's corpus so much that his hand holding the apple stopped moving. "You're going to draw something besides monsters?"

"Ever since I went home, my mind has been filled with everything I experienced in war. The monsters are gone. All I can picture are our dead friends and the faces of the soldiers I killed. So I've started drawing people recently."

"Really?!"

"It comes and goes. I'm sure I'll stop wanting to draw people someday and will go back to monsters." Fritz laughed at himself and devoured the apple, core and all.

"Who's going to lead the protest?"

"The Spartacus Group. Tomorrow's protests were Liebknecht's idea. They're looking to mobilize people at factories and barracks, too. And citizens from all over Berlin will be there. Isn't that incredible?! The *Obleute*[1] are advocating for groups of elite soldiers to lead an armed revolt. Their creed is 'All or nothing,' and they insist that nothing can be achieved without meticulous planning. But that's not necessarily true."

Fritz muttered, "That's a little too extreme."

"I think Liebknecht is more grounded and realistic than the Stewards. If the people themselves don't act, then the revolution will never succeed."

"Emotionally, yes."

"Let's get to bed early tonight so that we're ready for tomorrow. Sorry to cut this short after you came all the way out here."

"Don't worry. We can catch up after the protest."

"Thank you, I appreciate it."

---

1 (*Obleute* here refers to Revolutionäre Obleute, the Revolutionary Stewards, an organization of leaders from metalworker associations around Berlin. *Obleute* translates into English as "representatives.")

* * *

That evening, after Jörg's corpus and Fritz went to bed early, Milos said to Jörg:

"Wait for me in your corpus's dreams. I'm going to bring Lila."

With that, Milos left for Xandra's inn.

Jörg entered his corpus's mind and searched for a corridor. He would just borrow a dream as a place to meet Lila's simulacrum. He planned on talking with her there without his corpus realizing it.

At the end of the corridor sat the kind of plaza commonly found throughout Germany. The square was surrounded by buildings housing things like a long-established restaurant, a bar with a flashy sign, a café, a distillery, a general store, a lawyer's office, and a clinic, while a tram pulled up to the station in the center. As Jörg stood waiting, a horse-drawn carriage drew near, and Lila stepped down from the passenger compartment.

He hadn't seen her in years, and though she still looked like a child on the outside, something about her seemed more grown up. He wasn't sure what to say to her but eventually muttered, "Hey, long time no see," which sounded like an extremely stupid thing to say.

Frowning in disappointment, Lila said, "You've been away for two years, and that's all you can think of?"

"Sorry."

They stood silently apart for a while longer before bursting into fits of laughter, steadfastly shaking hands, and finally embracing like family.

Lila said through tears, "So Xandra's medicine finally worked. You're almost free."

"It's all thanks to you." Jörg sniffled. "You saved the food supplies to Berlin. Thank you."

"I was only able to do it because you laid the foundation, Mr. Huber. We just put your plan into action. Our only issue was volume."

"You don't have anywhere close to enough, though, do you?"

"Either way, it's better than nothing. No one can get rations anymore, and Diana said this is our last hope."

Jörg sighed in relief. "I'm glad it's helping, even if just a little. I didn't have hopes for anything bigger."

"We're growing food now, too. We realized that buying food wasn't enough and that we also needed to produce it. Right now we're considering how we should rebuild things after the war. Once it ends, a whole lot of soldiers are going to go back to their towns, right? Men with injured bodies and minds won't be able to start working right away. So we need to keep focusing on women doing the work."

"I'm sorry you have so much additional work. And it was my plan."

"It doesn't matter anymore who came up with it. Everyone just wants to be able to eat like they used to."

"How is Milos involved?"

"He helps a little with analyzing military information. The Count is there, too, so everything's completely safe. Milos said he has lots of free time now that Serbia is free."

"He told me a bit about that."

"Mr. Huber, you should be more concerned about tomorrow's protest than about us. Berliners' frustration is at a breaking point, and if they clash with the police or military guard, it's going to become a riot."

Lila removed a bottle of medicine from her bag. "I hope this will be the final push that lets you escape your corpus."

Jörg took the bottle, removed the cap, and drank the entire thing. The pit of his stomach burned as if he had just downed some hard liquor, but he didn't feel himself separate any further from his corpus.

His spirits sank, but Lila comforted him.

"Nil used complicated magic, so you won't get out easily. We have to be patient."

"What am I going to do if I can never get out?"

"Then you should just go back to being a regular person."

"Wouldn't you have a problem if I went back to being a regular German again?"

"My insistence on that has disappeared. Like a lingering snow that has melted." Lila continued brightly. "Watch out for your corpus. He might be your body, but you can't control him, so he could do anything."

"Yeah."

"It's hard to imagine that Nil won't try anything tomorrow. Milos and I are going to turn invisible and keep an eye on you. If anything happens, we'll be there to help you this time."

4

The next morning, people all around Berlin headed toward the city center, wave after wave assembling together. The workers first arrived at their factories and called roll under the instructions of the workers' unions before abandoning their posts and marching through the town as one. Other people came directly from outside of town. They worked their way to the city center, the net of their siege slowly tightening.

The protestors formed a massive river, filling the streets and squares. People packed the streets tightly enough to hide the gaps in the sidewalks. Signs reading PEACE, BREAD, AND FREEDOM waved in the throng. The words dripped with the obvious anger of people who had families taken by war, health robbed by food shortages, and loved ones stolen from them by starvation and disease.

The crowd spilt into two groups toward their destinations. One group headed for the Berlin Palace still void of its emperor, while the other struck out for the Reichstag.

Armed members of the Spartacus Group led each body. Some soldiers in the German Army had not stood with the government, but joined the protesters instead. They marched with their rifles, ready to fire immediately in case of emergency.

The guards around the palace and the Reichstag erected barriers and waited behind them for the crowd to arrive. If the protestors turned violent, these men would bear the brunt of their assault. They had strict orders to prevent the crowd from entering the buildings.

The guards frowned through steaming breath as they watched the wave of oncoming masses. If ordered to, their job required them to turn their guns and cannons on the people.

A heightened energy seemed to propel the crowd today. This was the first time the authority of the emperor had shown signs of crumbling since the founding of the nation. The guards might be crushed along with it… The thought tormented their nerves.

They secretly envied the turncoat soldiers hidden among the crowd. The guards couldn't turn against the nation so easily. A guard's duty is to protect the country, a duty that sometimes calls on them to fire on their own citizens. But the outcome seemed uncertain today.

Jörg's corpus carried a hunting rifle in front of him as he marched with Fritz at the head of the crowd. Fritz observed everything with a careful eye. Another armed group had joined them on the way. Rebel soldiers.

Jörg remained trapped, but he could feel himself gradually disassociating from his corpus's body. The magic joining them had weakened slightly. Jörg tried to interfere with his corpus's movements. He could, though the change was minimal. Xandra's medicine was certainly working. Milos and Lila followed behind him in support, their bodies invisible to the world.

With flushed cheeks, Fritz watched the people's expressions and movements. The tightly packed throng filled the air around him with hot steam and stink, but he didn't seem affected.

A dry cracking sound came from in front of them. From their time on the battlefield, Jörg's corpus and Fritz recognized it as the report of a gun.

Someone had fired off a round somewhere, but the tension didn't seem to spread, and they saw no wave of people trying to flee in their direction. It was most likely someone shooting their gun into the air. The people in the back continued to push forward. Even the sound of gunfire wouldn't stop them.

Jörg's corpus spoke to Fritz. "If any shooting breaks out, get out of here immediately. Go back to my apartment and wait for me there."

"Okay."

"If I don't make it back, then get out of Berlin as fast as you can. You have to make a record of this."

"Of course. Just you wait and see. I'm going to create something incredible."

They turned left in front of a long-abandoned butcher and continued their march forward.

At the same time, the advancing crowd of protesters and the guards in front of the Reichstag were about to begin their showdown.

The police on foot and horseback in the front row issued final orders to the mass of people and tried to intimidate them. Guards yelled at the crowd to advance no farther, to disperse immediately, and to return to work, but the masses kept marching.

"Peace! Freedom! Bread!" they chanted as they pressed upon the guards. "Stop the war!" "The politicians must resign!" "Get rid of the kaiser!"

Spurred on by the intensity of the crowd, the members of the Spartacus Group in the front waved their weapons and yelled "We demand that Wilhelm II step down!" "Dissolve the government!" "The republic is the future!" "Build the Bavarian Soviet Republic!" "Long live the Bavarian Soviet Republic!"

The throng wedged between the police and pushed them back in two directions. The horses beneath the officers began to fret and back away. In previous protests, the mounted police had chased demonstrators away and mercilessly trampled them as they fled, but that intensity was gone today. Realizing they couldn't withstand the crowd, they decided to open a path for the surging protesters.

The masses moved toward the barricade like a wave crashing inside a compact harbor.

Dismayed, the guards pointing their rifles at the throng cast their eyes around, seeking the tacit order of the commander standing behind them. Sweat dripped down the commander's back in the frigid air.

If the police weren't going to stop them, then he and the guards would face the group head-on. The people leading the masses carried rifles. They weren't all socialists. The group contained large numbers of army deserters. If either side shot, the bullets would certainly hit their marks, and even one shot killing someone on either side would doom the day. The protest would become a riot. Once that happened, there was no going back. The commander couldn't see the end of the masses. His soldiers stared intently at him as if clinging to his presence. Asking him for orders, questioning him about what to do.

Trembling, the commander inhaled deeply. Freezing air rushed into his lungs, but it didn't calm his nerves, and his body burned. Giving himself over to that heat, he declared, "All soldiers, lower your weapons. Stand down."

For a moment, the soldiers stirred. But they all soon followed the order, draping their rifles over their shoulders and moving away from the barricade.

"It's the tide of the times," the commander told himself. "At a time like this, there's nothing we can do."

The crowd rushed past the guards and occupied the area in front of the Reichstag. No one could predict what they would do next or where their enthusiasm would lead them. Prince Maximilian of Baden—Max von Baden—observed the developments with a growl. The situation couldn't be saved. The German Empire was over. If the crowd entered the plenary chambers, disaster would follow. Anything could happen.

Max phoned the German Supreme Army Command in Spa, Belgium. He called to recommend a formal declaration of abdication from Kaiser Wilhelm II, who was residing there. Some voices within the Reichstag had already been calling for him to step down for a while. Now was the time to decide.

But the kaiser gave only a vague reply, not actually responding to Max's request. Max couldn't fathom how the man still didn't understand the current situation. Chief of Staff Hindenburg was still in Germany, but Deputy General Ludendorff, by now essentially leading the war effort, had already fled to Sweden on October 27. That same day, the German government expressed its desire to end the war in final negotiations with US President Wilson, and on October 28 preparations began for a transition to a parliamentary monarchy. The kaiser should have already been back at the royal palace in Berlin to provide instruction to the people, but he lingered in Spa, deaf to Berlin's requests. Germany's only route out of this war was for the government to decide things independently and work it out on their own.

Before noon, without having received approval from the kaiser, Max declared the abdication of Wilhelm II to the Reichstag. With that, the Majority Social Democratic Party of Germany demanded that Max resign as chancellor. He agreed and stepped down from his position, with Friedrich Ebert of the MSDP inheriting the role.

Ebert had studied under Rosa Luxemburg, even working alongside Karl Liebknecht for a time. He later broke off ties with them when they formed the Spartacus Group. Two of his sons died fighting in the war, and the youngest son returned home seriously injured. He immediately accepted Max's nomination as temporary chancellor.

Meanwhile, at two that afternoon, Philipp Scheidemann, a member of the same party as Ebert, received a piece of disturbing news from his assistant during lunch. Liebknecht planned to declare Germany a free socialist republic without waiting to hear a statement from the German government.

Afraid that Liebknecht would steal the right to govern from

underneath them, Scheidemann rushed to the window, threw it open, looked down at the crowd, and shouted:

"The Hohenzollerns have abdicated! Long live the *German Republic*!"

After he finished speaking, Scheidemann calmly returned to his lunch.

How dare they try to create a socialist state. Now Germany is officially a republic.

Two hours later, at four p.m., Liebknecht of the Spartacus Group stood on the palace balcony and announced the Free Socialist Republic of Germany. As this announcement came after Scheidemann's, it naturally could not be enforced.

As temporary chancellor, a furious Ebert slammed a fist on his table, raging at Scheidemann's unauthorized actions. Ebert was factoring in the continuation of the monarchy—that is to say, the kaiser still officially reigned, and they planned to transition to a political system with a constitutional assembly.

But Scheidemann's actions prevented Germany from following the same path as postrevolutionary Russia. It ensured that Germany would not have a new kaiser and would not move toward socialism, but would engage in the journey toward becoming a republic.

The following day, Wilhelm II fled for the Netherlands. After the war, the Netherlands refused to surrender him to the Allies, allowing him to escape retribution for his sins in the Great War.

5

Assembled in front of the Reichstag, the people at the head of the protest heard Scheidemann's proclamation and at first couldn't believe the news. The kaiser had abdicated, and Germany would be a republic. The war was over—was that what he had just said?

The people rejoiced. Scheidemann's voice hadn't reached everyone, so when those at the back were informed of what he had said, they finally understood.

After all their efforts and repeated protests, their moment had finally arrived.

The group swayed more fiercely than when they first assembled. The wave no longer needed to push forward anymore and so boiled up on the spot.

The police and guards were no longer their enemies. They were fellow citizens celebrating the end of the war. Completely stunned at first, the guards and police first grimaced, but as they watched the feverishly celebratory crowd, their tension began to slowly fade until they looked wholly relieved. Some, however, cried bitter tears, knowing that Germany had lost the war.

Jörg's corpus and Fritz were caught up in the revelry around them. There were no food and drinks to celebrate with, but the two men slapped the backs and shoulders of everyone around them as if it were the middle of the harvest festival. "Hey, the war is over!" "Are you serious?" "It's true—the war is over!" "Unbelievable!" "What a dream!"

Beside the two men, Lila said, "When the end comes, it happens so quickly."

"It does." Milos looked around as if blinded. "These Germans will probably keep celebrating for a while. But the harshness of reality will return."

"Even when Great Britain lifts the blockade, imports won't arrive immediately. Germany will continue to go hungry."

"Are you going to stand back and just watch?"

"Of course not. We'll keep working our fields, and the people will survive somehow. Would you like to come with us, Mr. Milos?"

"Me?"

"With the war over, the men have nothing to do. So come help us on the farm. We don't care where our workers are from or whether they are men or women. We welcome anyone who wants a slow, relaxing life."

"You've started speaking like the Count."

"You think so?"

"He must have affected you. But I'll pass, thank you."

"Why?"

"I want to plow Serbian land. I'll wield a hoe instead of a gun. The time has finally come when I can do that."

Lila's face brightened, and she thrust her hand out toward Milos. With a smile on his face, Milos extended his own hand and shook hers firmly.

Watching from inside his corpus, Jörg felt his entire self relax.

As he gazed around the crowd, he noticed something strange in the air.

The people were avoiding a little patch of ground. A man stood in the center, surrounded by what looked like a void. No one could touch it.

Shock erupted in Jörg when he saw the man's face. He should have been in Rotterdam, but Hubert Duran was standing right there, staring ahead blankly. It looked as if even he didn't know why he was here in Germany. He craned his neck toward Jörg, seemingly realizing that someone was looking at him. That was when his expression cracked. The smile rising on his face told Jörg that Nil had been hidden deep within and had now surfaced.

Hubert—no, Nil—turn around to face him, raised a hand, and spoke directly into Jörg's mind.

"Congratulations. Germany has taken the first step toward a new era."

"Why did you bring Hubert here?" Jörg asked.

"He's always been curious about what's happening in Berlin. He said he wanted to see the moment the German Empire fell. So I granted his wish."

"Still, how dare you bring him to such a dangerous place."

"He didn't have a simulacrum, so I had no choice but to bring his real body."

"I doubt you did all this out of the kindness of your heart. What are you after?"

Instead of answering, Nil exited Hubert's body.

Hubert lurched like a marionette with its strings cut. He was conscious but looked around with fresh eyes that seemed even more confused. He must have experienced his time under Nil's control as some sort of dream. Now himself again, he wasn't sure where he was. He was deaf. And he probably didn't speak much German. He most certainly couldn't hear the screams and words the crowd yelled.

A frightened Hubert started to run but bumped into an invisible wall and bounced backward.

Jörg looked up and scanned the surrounding area.

At some point the space around them had sewn itself shut. Hubert, Jörg, and the others were trapped in this space, separated from the crowd. The Berliners stopped still as if frozen, laughing as though about to burst.

Nil stepped back, took on human form, moved next to Fritz, and patted him on the shoulder. He kept watch on Jörg's corpus out of the corner of his eye as he leaned over and whispered something into Fritz's ear. His words reached Jörg loud and clear.

"That Frenchman there is the one who killed your friend Norbert Kerner. Now's your chance to get your revenge."

Jörg yelled at Fritz, forgetting that his voice couldn't reach him.

"Don't listen to him, Fritz. Where's the proof? Don't let him convince you."

His corpus seemed to sense Nil's presence. But Nil's words might have enchanted him, too, because he stared intently at Hubert.

"He's certainly French," the corpus said.

Jörg and his corpus shared memories, so he would remember the photograph Christine had shown him in Paris.

"Any Frenchman here now could only be a spy. He's here to give German secrets to foreign nations."

Jörg tried to stop his corpus as he stepped forward. His legs froze. Looking practically paralyzed, his corpus stood in astonishment at the bizarre events occurring inside his own body.

Jörg continued to resist with all his might. He was glad to have detached even this much from his corpus.

He pleaded with his corpus from within.

"The war is over. Germans and the French don't have any more reason to kill each other. Don't let Fritz kill him. If you're really his friend, stop him!"

Fritz shook with excitement. "He really killed him?" he asked Nil. "It was really him?"

"That's right. No doubt about it."

Fritz stepped resolutely forward toward Hubert.

Just then, Milos appeared in human form and stood in front of Fritz, his arms spread wide.

Fritz frowned at him suspiciously. "Move aside."

"Don't believe anything Nil says. Do you know that man? You can't remember the face of every single soldier on the battlefield."

"...No, but I remember that guy."

"Nil put that memory in you. He's trying to change you from a soldier to a murderer."

"Why would he do that?"

"Because he's playing with you. That's how he is."

"Nil has no reason to lie."

"He has scores of reasons. He's a monster. He enjoys tricking humans and causing destruction. You should know who you're dealing with."

"And who are you?"

"I'm someone who helped your best friend."

Fritz turned to look at Jörg's corpus. Jörg stifled his corpus's movements, but to his friend, his corpus must appear as immobile as someone in the depths of shell shock. Fritz ran over to check that everything was okay with him.

Just then, Jörg's corpus slipped free of Jörg's control and spoke hoarsely. "Don't worry about me. Do something about him."

The words stunned Jörg. Regardless of how deeply his corpus carried his grudges during the war, Jörg couldn't believe what half of his soul had just said. Jörg struggled harder to silence his corpus, but the man slipped free again and said, "I'd do it if I were you. Hurry up, take care of him!"

"No!" Jörg yelled again. *"Look at him—that Frenchman. Shelling scarred his face, and he's missing a leg. He can't even hear anymore. Our army did that to him. That was war, and we didn't have a choice. We hurt their comrades like they hurt ours, and we hurt ourselves as well. It's the same with him. He may be from a different country, but he's a soldier like us. He suffered the same hardships we did. They destroyed other people's bodies and ruined their lives, but they suffered the same things themselves. And you still want to take the life of our comrade in suffering."*

But Jörg's speech must have not reached them, because his corpus joined Nil in trying to stir Fritz to action. "Don't think about him. It's what you want that counts."

Jörg was horrified. They were halves of the same soul—but his corpus didn't even try to listen to a word he said. Maybe this was what it was like for the ancient blood to control a human. This ancient blood that never showed mercy to an enemy resonated with Fritz to extract revenge.

Just then, Nil removed a Dreyse M1907 from his coat and pressed it into Fritz's hands.

"A pause in the fighting doesn't mean the end of the war," Nil continued. "People can't detach from their feelings that easily. Decades can pass, but the mental wounds of war don't heal, and their souls will continue to erode. Those who fought on the battlefield, those who suffered on the home front, those waiting for relatives to return home—they'll all continue to curse the war their entire lives. If you want revenge, now's the time. Shoot him with this gun before you lose sight of him."

Jörg pleaded wildly:

"You had to kill each other on the front lines. I've also killed enemy soldiers who left their families behind in their hometown. Which is precisely

why we must not kill each other after the war. There's no reason why you should be the only one who gets revenge. Come on, Fritz. You're not your normal self now. You're not all here."

In the next instant, Milos moved like a flash, grabbed Fritz's wrist, and twisted. He slipped behind him and pushed him face down, pinning him to the ground with a knee. Fritz struggled like a massive fish out of water, spitting insults. Just seeing how violently Fritz struggled made Jörg realize how important a friend Norbert had been to him, speaking to a pain that burned Jörg's chest. That resigned Fritz who so calmly talked about his memories with Norbert was nowhere to be seen. Beyond respecting Norbert as an artist, he must have relished a sense of friendly competition and hoped to compete as rivals after leaving the army. That opportunity had been lost forever. And a Frenchman had stolen it from him. Hubert might not have been the one who shot Norbert, but a French soldier certainly had.

Jörg thrashed wildly inside his corpus. He couldn't stay in there anymore. He had to find some way out…

An unbearable sensation like all of his skin tearing away tormented Jörg as he almost broke free from his corpus. Pain assaulted the entirety of his body as it slowly ripped apart. And then Jörg tumbled out of his corpus.

The assault of breaking through Nil's magic agonized Jörg's corpus as well. Jörg pushed his dizzy, wavering corpus down to the sidewalk, gripping the man's chest with both hands.

"Why? Why would you believe anything Nil says?"

Jörg's corpus stared up in wide-eyed disbelief, mouth agape. He obviously hadn't understood the situation.

Jörg continued. "All of Europe is connected. Once you start talking about revenge along ethnic lines, it never ends. Creating a pristine world requires denouncing the transgressions of every single ethnic group throughout time and could lead to the elimination of every last one. That's different from enacting justice in the name of God. It does absolutely nothing except help bring forth irreplaceable nothingness."

"So then what do we do with these feelings?" his corpus screamed. "I don't need your empty talk of justice. I just want to be rid of these feelings. Is that not human? Or is that too much to ask?"

"But can you imagine what's waiting for you once you've done that? Nothing but hell."

Fritz kept resisting with all his might, but Milos exhibited extraordinary strength. Fritz eventually lowered his head like a feverish patient dropping off to sleep and began to weep loudly. The gun tumbled from his hand to the ground.

Nil snorted and shrugged as if disappointed, then reached out and scooped the gun up. "And here I thought I was going to see something entertaining. You are all so cowardly."

Just then, Jörg heard a voice he knew well rumbling in his ears. "Enough. I would ask you to stop treating these humans as your playthings."

Breaking through that invisible barrier, the Count descended through the closed-off space. He glanced over at Jörg's group quickly before glaring at Nil. "You've lost, Nil. Not every human is going to do as you say. Be satisfied this time that the revolution has succeeded."

"I'll decide whether I'm satisfied or not."

"Leave now, and I won't do anything. Get out of here."

"Let me ask you one thing."

"What?"

"Why did you let Jörg here become a monster? Why let him inherit blood that you wouldn't even give to your dear wife?"

"Purely out of boredom. I wanted to see what someone who would give up his life as a human to save humans would do."

"...You don't need to hide your true intentions from me, Count. You're a monster, but you can't completely forget your human heart. You actually wanted more creatures like you, didn't you? If so, then go ahead. That's more or less what I want from you. For you to reign supreme, slowly increasing the ranks of those who inherit your blood, creating more bats to feast on human sustenance. Romania as it stands now has no meaning to you anymore. The empire created by that immortal blood is the real Walachia, the dominion of your voivode Vlad!"

The Count laughed. "I would not welcome that. I simply want to live a slow, relaxing life."

"Have you forgotten Vlad's dying wish?"

"Don't talk to me about that. You never served him directly. You don't understand his noble thoughts enough to make light of them. He was not someone who would turn himself into a monster to gain an empire. He loved the land and the people of Walachia as a human being. I merely inherited his passion. Which has been satisfied now that Romania has gained its independence. The one thing I regret not having done yet is finding the spirit that tricked Elyne and tearing it apart. I'm starting to wonder if that might have been you. You're the one searching for someone who will always be by your side, which would be why you pulled me into the world of monsters, is it not?"

Nil didn't answer, instead smiling faintly and narrowing his eyes. "I don't believe you. You have so much power and magic, but all you really want is to die as a human being."

"But what about you? Why involve yourself so deeply in human affairs? Do you really love humans that much?"

"I simply roam the lands in search of absolute nothingness. You do know what nothing is, don't you? The absence of God. 'For I have damaged that which God hath made, and yearn for it to return to nothing like myself. And when all has been wiped away, then I, too, shall vanish with them.' I'm simply searching to taste every last drop of that moment of bliss. The history of humanity is an endless cycle of form creating nothing, and nothing giving birth to form. Watching from afar, there is nothing more entertaining than this."

"Don't bore me. Living peacefully, eating good food, and enjoying your time as you see fit does more than enough to drive the world. That life is radically more beneficial than war."

"But war is fun, is it not?"

"That is not something a monster should say."

The instant the Count swished the hem of his cloak, a fierce gale tore through the enclosed space. Jörg and everyone else planted their feet firmly into the ground to prevent being blown away.

The Count spoke to Nil. "You shall sleep for a while. This ancient blood demands it."

Nil bared his teeth in a playful laugh. The Count readied himself for a fight. They seemed poised to pounce upon each other at any instant, but Nil suddenly looked down at his feet as the color drained from his face.

Something like black smoke spouted from the paving stones, wrapping itself around Nil's feet. In the next second it crawled up his legs, writhing around his body like a tangle of snakes.

Jörg observed the black smoke. He realized that it wasn't smoke, but actually sharply defined souls. An endless stream of monsters muttered nonsensical words, screaming as they twisted themselves around Nil. Jörg had seen them before. They were the same nameless monsters he had seen at Xandra's inn. They completely paralyzed Nil in accordance with orders from the Count, pinning Nil in place with a force like a steel net.

With Nil wholly immobile, the Count rose into the air and changed into that giant black shape Jörg had seen at the Port of Kiel. The instant he covered Nil, a terrible scream pierced the air, and the black cloud dispersed.

The swarm of monsters had devoured Nil in an instant. The Count joined in and began absorbing magical power from him. Nil fought back. The monsters glomming onto Nil screamed as if struck by lightning and jumped away. Some lost arms or legs in the attack. Some were torn to pieces. The ones still clinging to him burned and smoked. The Count held Nil by the scruff of his collar; Nil winced in pain. A pitch-black liquid dripped from his palms.

"Let go of me," Nil whimpered hoarsely. "I'm a monster. No matter what you do, I won't die."

The Count gripped harder. The liquid sprouting from Nil's palms intensified. "You might not die, but I can put you to sleep. A sleep that lasts decades. Until humanity heals."

"You're too late." Nil smiled. "This war *started before it even began*. Do you understand me? The most trivial of incidents fueled fires that had been simmering across Europe for decades, sometimes centuries. Do you really think a break in the fighting can extinguish those fires? This war was nothing more than a preliminary skirmish. Someday a truly great war will sweep the land."

"I won't let that happen."

"That body once fought against the Ottoman Empire. I assume you don't regret that. Things like that will repeat again and again. This is Europe's fate."

"Even so, I'll stop this disaster you seek."

"How interesting. See you again in a few decades. Until then, I'll sleep as you requested."

Nil's head fell backward, his knees buckled, and he crumbled on the spot. It looked as if the force animating his body had been suddenly whisked away. The thing that had been Nil couldn't retain its human form and dissipated into smoke.

Hubert trembled, hiding behind Milos. Jörg didn't know if he'd seen this gruesome sight or not. But Hubert at least would have sensed that something out of the ordinary had just occurred.

Once Nil had turned to smoke, the monsters eating away at him quietly disappeared. Only the Count remained. He hunched over, crouched down, and picked something up off the ground. He held some small black ball between his thumb and middle finger, raising it up as if examining it in the sunlight.

Milos addressed the Count. "He shrank down quite small."

Jörg asked, "So that's Nil's true form?"

"This is his core that no one can consume. Oh, my stomach feels heavy." The Count let out an unnerving groan. "I shouldn't take sustenance from monsters. I feel wretched. Like I want to vomit. I need to hurry back to Xandra's inn and get some medicine."

"This is the first time I've seen a monster consume their own kind."

"It happens frequently in emergencies. I didn't feel like doing it all by myself, so I asked for help."

"Why did those monsters attack Nil?"

"They are all beings that can no longer exist in the human world for one reason or another. I'm sure they have their reasons to despise someone like Nil."

Jörg released his corpus and stood.

His corpus stared hard at him. "When did you arrive back inside me?"

"It's a long story… But I didn't choose to be there."

"How dare you interfere with Fritz's vengeance."

"You needed to think clearly. You wanted a socialist revolution, not personal revenge."

"But if I can't help my best friend, what good is revolution?"

"That head injury you picked up during the war must have changed you. That doesn't sound like something I would say at all."

"What would you know about it?" Jörg's corpus squeezed his hands. "You fled the front the first chance you got, so you know nothing. Up until two years ago, I was always fighting on the verge of death. I even fought British tanks."

Jörg glanced down at Fritz pressed against the ground. He was still crying. He hadn't seemed to notice Jörg yet. Perhaps Fritz couldn't see him.

Just then Lila walked up and thrust something out toward Jörg's corpus. She had picked a sprig of white lilacs. Indicating toward Fritz with her eyes, she said. "Give them to him."

Caught completely off guard, Jörg's corpus couldn't speak for a moment, then asked briskly, "What are they? Some magic flowers that will heal his soul?"

"Nothing like that, but he needs them to return to reality. You received some once, too."

A mix of emotions passed over his face. He was remembering the day the Count had given him the lilacs. Ever since that day a shell blew him out of the trench, Jörg had been living two strange, distinct lives. Two lives that shared memories. They were completely separate right now, but that day had altered the boundary between them.

Taking the flowers, Jörg's corpus gave a curt "Thank you" before facing Fritz and offering the flowers. "Can you stand?" he asked.

"No," Fritz answered through his sobs. "I don't have the strength."

"Stand up, even if it's hard. The war is over. We can go back to our regular lives."

Jörg watched the two men apprehensively, and the Count called out to everyone to head back to the inn. "It's so oppressive here. The enthusiasm of these people celebrating their victory is overbearing. I feel like I might faint."

Milos asked, "What about the Frenchman?"

"Let's take him back to Paris through the inn. His sister is waiting for him. After that, he can choose his own path."

"And Nil?"

"We can throw him in the nearest river."

"Wouldn't it be better to seal him away with magic?"

"It wouldn't make a difference. He's not someone who can be sealed away. Nothing is an undying presence that exists in every era. After a few decades, this black sphere will naturally resurrect itself."

"So humanity must deal with him forever, always subject to his mischief?"

"Precisely. That's how monsters are."

6

November 11, 1918. Inside a freight car the French military had established as their headquarters in the forests of Compiègne outside of Paris, Germany signed an armistice agreement with the Allied powers. This concluded the Great War. The railway carriage had been the dining hall of the French marshal.

The armistice came into effect at eleven a.m. Central European Time. When the hour struck, the sound of gunfire stopped across the continent.

The following day, the Austro-Hungarian Empire also transitioned to a republic. The Austrian emperor Karl I relinquished his rights of dominion over Austria and Hungary, the two countries split, and each became responsible for their own fates as republics.

Over the little more than the four years and three months that the war lasted, the Allied and Central powers mobilized a total of approximately sixty-five million soldiers, with 8.02 million dying either in the fields or in hospitals. That number doesn't include all those who went missing, people who lost their lives during the revolutions each country experienced, everyday citizens slaughtered by invading armies, or all those who died of starvation.

Lila's homeland of Poland declared independence in November of the same year, with Józef Piłsudski inaugurating the Second Polish Republic as its head of state. The Polish people rejoiced at the long-awaited reemergence of their motherland, and many returned home from their scattered locations.

One hundred twenty-three years had passed since Russia, Prussia, and Austria had partitioned their homeland.

In the lounge of Xandra's inn, Lila looked satisfactorily through her cashbook and said, "Considering my age and the short amount of time I was working, I think I've saved up quite a lot of money, don't you? I can use it to live in Poland."

The Count lay on a bed that had been brought into the lounge. He had been in a bad state ever since taking sustenance from Nil in Berlin and had slept most of the day through. Xandra continued to give him medicine, but it didn't quell his queasiness, and his face still writhed in agony.

A new idea occurred to Jörg. He wondered if perhaps the Count's relaxed lifestyle wasn't just an attempt to suppress the power of the ancient blood, but a result of him feeding off bad monsters to remove them from human society. Each feeding weakened him, and he would need Xandra's medicine to recover.

He wanted to ask the Count about this directly, but he kept quiet because he knew the Count would evade the question. His tendency to not clearly convey his true thoughts was both a good and alienating quality.

His head resting on a pillow, the Count looked at Lila. "The adults will return from around the world and rebuild Poland piece by piece. You'd best leave it to them for the moment. I'd like to know what you plan to do once you go back."

Lila set down her pen, closed the cashbook, and looked up from her desk. "Honestly, I'm not sure of the best way for me to live my life. I don't even really know how old I am."

"I can use my magic to make you any age you want. If you want to go to school, I can make you look the right age for that. Once you have your papers in order, come see me, and I'll fulfill my duties as your guardian."

"Thank you. If I can, I'd like to become a teacher and help young kids learn."

"Oh, really?"

"I believe that education will stop us from creating mindless or monstrous people. By that I mean improper education makes it easy for people to become fools or monsters. I want to fight against that."

"It's a dream for the future."

"Or I could become an editor at a publishing house for children's books. I want to make a lot of books for children. Adults will read them, too, right? I met people from all sorts of countries at the Eiffel Tower, and they taught me so much. I want to create books that people in other countries can read."

"That's a much better job than being a spy. If you ever need anything, you're welcome here anytime. I'd be happy to give you advice."

"Thank you. But I don't think I'll be coming back often."

"What about the farmland in Romania?"

"I plan on keeping it. I'm going to manage it and sell the harvests. If possible, I'd like to use magic to ensure that normal people can't find their way inside. If war ever breaks out again, I'd like the people to use it like they just did."

"Then it would be better to buy the land outright."

"Can I?"

"It was originally my land. I know the owner well. It would be easy to arrange."

"Thank you so much!"

"'Deep in a mist-covered valley, a man protects the *firma de aur* for all eternity. His name is Count George Silvestri. We are the only ones who know this secret.' How does that sound?"

"Perfect."

"You know, if you are going back to Poland, you might want to consider using a new name."

"Why?"

"Just Lila might not be enough. You need a name for your life in Poland. How would you feel about me giving you a new one? To celebrate your new life."

"I'd love it. Please."

Lying on his bed, the Count raised his right hand. Wiggling his fingertips as though trying to grab hold of something, he muttered, "Angelika Kowalska. That is your new name. Use it well."

"Thank you."

The Count next looked to Jörg. "Jörg, what do you plan to do now?"

"I'm going to go with Lila to protect her. I'm her bodyguard, after all."

"You still haven't repaid your debt to me."

"I'll transfer money to your bank account every month, so please let me leave the inn."

Lila chimed in from beside him. "Mr. Huber, don't put too much on yourself."

Jörg asked, "Do you not want me as your bodyguard?"

"I want to live my own life and not depend on anyone. So I don't want to tie anyone to me."

"But it's my job. It always has been."

"You're going to start a company, right? You'll be really busy. You can just come check in on me when you have the time."

"Would I get in the way if I went with you?"

"That's not what I mean. What I want to say is that I want you as just a regular friend. What do you think?"

"I'm German, though. Can you be friends with a German?"

"Yes. I'm not scared of them anymore."

Just then the air swirled, and barely comprehensible words filled the room.

"That's the pack of monsters in the room," the Count said. "They're staying hidden so as to not surprise Lila, but they're all saying good-bye."

The voices sounded tearful, perhaps because they were sad to see Lila leave. So they were telling the truth earlier when they called her their friend.

The monsters' voices climbed to a feverish pitch. And with that, their now-clear words resonated inside Jörg's head.

"Good-bye, good-bye, little human girl."
"Once you leave this inn—"
"Your eyes will most likely—"
"Never see us again."
"What you call monsters—"
"Are just illusions living in your dreams."
"But that doesn't matter."
"Go and live as a human."
"Live as a true human, for the rest of your days."

"We'll meet again someday," Lila said to the monsters. "I'll never forget you."

She then turned to Jörg and said through a smile, "Mr. Huber, would you please cut my hair?"

"Sorry?"

"I would like a barber to cut my hair. Before I leave this inn."

"You'd let me do it?"

"Of course. I'm sorry to have made you wait so long. It would be my pleasure."

The memory of the day Lila refused his offer of a haircut rose vividly in Jörg's mind. Two years had passed since then. Their relationship had certainly improved, but honestly, a considerable chasm still lay between them.

That was fine.

Because even if that gap never fills, humans can walk the same path together. They can still look toward the same future.

Jörg nodded and smiled wide. "Thank you. I shall give you the most perfect haircut. I promise."

VI
Burning the Future Away

1

Most of the following words are records of disasters.

Those who wish to avert their eyes and block their ears should simply skip past and remain silent.

*

After the Great War, Germany's political situation kept the country in chaos.

The socialists and communists, who took such pride in having achieved freedom and peace though revolution.

The weary soldiers, returned from the front bearing the shame of having lost the war.

A deep chasm formed between these two sides.

The soldiers continually complained to the people of the fatherland.

"We were still winning in the field. The kaiser only abdicated because of the socialist revolution back home. That's why Germany lost."

The soldiers on the front lines couldn't see the entire picture that the generals did. They assumed that victory in their particular theater equated with German advancement. Germany was winning in their minds, so they believed they could have overcome the Allies had they only pressed on further. That disappointment and frustration morphed into hatred for the socialists and communists at home.

The German government, which feared that the country would move to the left after the war, used the anger of these returned soldiers. It created the Freikorps and encouraged them to join. The Freikorps were groups of private citizens charged with ensuring the safety of the homeland, but in reality they existed solely to rid Germany of socialists. Those returned soldiers clung to their military pride and so readily joined to satisfy their senses of self-worth.

However, discontent plagued the Spartacus Group, too, now rebranded as the Spartacus League. While the revolution had brought about the end of the war, Germany didn't move to a socialist state like Russia had done. The Spartacus League felt a sense of urgency for their mission, so they continued protesting after the war in order to push the socialist revolution even further.

Karl Liebknecht supported the protests, but Rosa Luxemburg fiercely opposed them. She had always been a vocal advocate that a true socialist state could not be achieved with an organization at the helm and that the people of the nation standing up for themselves was the nature of revolution. The frantic pace of events worried her, and she feared for the future of socialism in Germany.

In fact, contrary to the hopes of the socialists, the German people did not continue the revolution. Unlike Russia, Germany provided farmers with a strong social network, lessening the need for forceful rebellion. Food scarcities continued in the cities, but as the economy slowly recovered and people could live somewhat regular lives, most people simply wished to return to their prewar quality of life. They cared not a whit for major societal revolution.

So the German government treated the Spartacus League's protests as a rebel uprising and ordered the Freikorps to get rid of socialists.

Scheidemann, who had declared *"Long live the German Republic!"* from the balcony of the Reichstag during the November Revolution, worked with the financial officer of the Social Democrat Party's Division Fourteen to formulate a secret plot for the assassination of Liebknecht and Luxemburg, even placing a bounty on their heads.

Whoever kills or captures Liebknecht and Luxemburg shall receive 100,000 marks.

January 5, 1919. The Spartacus League held a huge protest in Berlin, which turned into an uprising that eventually ended on the twelfth. Three days later at nine p.m., Liebknecht and Luxemburg were suddenly arrested at a hideout in Mannheim by soldiers under the command of an army lieutenant and city councilmen, after which they were escorted to the citizens' council headquarters. They were placed in the Eden Hotel for a while before being taken to separate locations. On the way they were both beaten repeatedly with rifle stocks, receiving wounds harsh enough to fracture skulls.

Liebknecht was shot near a pond in Tiergarten Park, his corpse later brought to a mortuary as a John Doe.

Luxemburg was shot in the head during transport. Her body was taken to Tiergarten Park, the same park where they killed Liebknecht, and tossed from the Lichtenstein Bridge into the dark waters of the canal.

The men of the Freikorps cheered at the dull thud and spray of white foam, then returned to the road to continue the hunt.

2

A short while after the body of Rosa Luxemburg, skull shattered, brain blown apart, sank to the bottom of the canal, a giant black shape swooped near the Lichtenstein Bridge.

With large wings that made it look like a massive bat or dragon, it flew down into the canal from the clear sky, extracted Luxemburg's soul, and carried it carefully away from the bottom of the river.

Appearing almost groggy from sleep, she stared up at the person holding her. An elegant-looking man with long black hair pulled neatly behind his head, he stared straight at her with eyes as green as conifers. The Polish Luxemburg knew such features well. Unlike her assassins, this man handled her with care that let her know he was no enemy.

"Who are you?"

"You can simply call me Count," the man replied. "I've been watching you for a long time. But always from a distance."

"Always?"

"Yes. Even when you were imprisoned."

"I don't remember ever meeting you."

"Every day, a bird would visit you between the iron bars of your window. That was me."

"Really?" Her eyes grew wide. "You talk like this is some sort of dream."

"You can think of it that way."

Still in the Count's arms, Luxemburg turned to face the water.

When she did, the Count said, "Forget about those remains resting down there. That is just an empty shell."

"But it's my body."

"Who you are is right here in this spirit."

"Why did you rescue me?"

"You gave your entire life for your ideals. I like people like that."

She laughed lightly. "I fought for reality, not an ideal. I simply wanted everyone to eat good bread and sleep soundly in warm beds, as equals. Would you set me down? This is kind of embarrassing."

"If that's what you wish."

"Please."

Still holding Luxemburg, the Count stooped over. Her toes scraped the water. The surface felt hard, like glass. She stepped down and stood on the water without sinking into the canal.

Looking around, she saw a young man leading Liebknecht along the opposite bank. From his awkward gait, it was obvious that he had just turned into a soul. The young man guiding Liebknecht wore a black cloak like the Count's. A wind crossed the canal and rippled its hem. The young man released Liebknecht's hand and said, "You're on your own from here. Someone important is waiting for you over there."

Liebknecht smiled and replied, "Thank you, Jörg."

"You're welcome."

"If only our party had more people like you. Then I might still be alive."

"It's a flattering sentiment, but I'm just a monster."

The souls of Luxemburg and Liebknecht joined hands in the middle of the canal.

They thanked the Count and Jörg, then looked toward the sky. Rays of sparkling light penetrated the clear, cold sky to coat the land.

"Let's go." Liebknecht gazed contentedly up into the light. "Progress was our purpose in life. Spartacus was our passion and our spirit. That is the same as our soul, our core, the will of the proletariat, and action. That will never change."

"Do you think paradise really exists up there?"

"I don't know. But the only way to find out is to keep going."

As the two souls began to pull away from the earth and ascend into the sky, the Count said to Jörg, "I don't know if they'll arrive there uninterrupted. I just pray that nothing interferes with their ascension. The masses might try to pull them back down."

Jörg asked, "What if they can't make it to heaven?"

"Then they'll most likely stay somewhere between heaven and earth. Like us."

"You mean, somewhere that's neither heaven nor earth."

"It's more comfortable than people assume."

"To think that people who lived their lives with such integrity would end up like this. Humanity really is beyond saving."

The Count smirked. "The socialism they preached is truly a respectable idea. But the majority of socialists around the world are not the ideal humans those two imagine. Most socialists boast about how they achieved enlightenment through socialism. So anyone who is not enlightened is wrong and incapable of proper thought. See? To people like that, the masses and the workers are still *the unenlightened* in need of their guidance. It's such an arrogant fantasy. Do you think the masses would follow such elitism? Enlightened or not, every human has an inherent worth that cannot be infringed upon by anyone else. The justice that the majority of socialists believed in didn't fail on principle. But they prattled on about peace and equality while disdaining most average people. The burden those two were made to carry for that reality was just too cruel."

Jörg squinted as he looked skyward. "How many more times will humanity have to repeat its mistakes before it can finally reach true happiness?"

"I don't know. Maybe never," the Count bluntly said, then continued, "Poland will start fighting the Soviet Union soon."

"What?"

"Józef Piłsudski desperately wants Poland to return as a major power someday. He's going to actively amass a large army to take back Poland's former territory to the east—meaning Belarus and western Ukraine. The war will certainly affect Ukrainians and Jewish people in the region. The Polish people once had their language and culture stolen from them by Germany and Russia. And now they might do the exact same thing to Ukrainians and Jewish people."

"What would Lila say about that? Poland may believe that their actions are rightful, but it will start another war."

"Foolishness or justice, that it not for me to say. I've heard that Piłsudski is a great man. All we can do is hope that he listens to his conscience."

3

After the protest in Berlin, Jörg's corpus let Fritz stay in his room at the apartment. Still trapped in the depths of depression, Fritz never left the room. He did nothing day in and day out, sleeping most of the hours away. When night arrived, he would eat a slice of bread, have some water, briefly browse the newspaper, and then head back to bed. Even cats didn't sleep as much as him.

Fritz still felt an overwhelming shame over losing control in front of Hubert. He would mutter that he didn't know why he had acted like that. Even when Jörg's corpus told him that it was all Nil's doing so he shouldn't let it get to him, Fritz whined bitterly that he could have prevented it if he had had more control over himself.

Even so, every day he seemed a little more like his former self. He kept the lilac sprig from Lila in a cup on the table. The white flower still bloomed wide, its sweet fragrance filling the room. Fritz gazed at it every day. Jörg's corpus wasn't sure what about it helped him, but the lilac seemed to soothe Fritz's mind. Or perhaps the flower's beauty helped Fritz pull himself together.

Jörg's corpus couldn't forget Lila's face when she had handed him the flower.

He didn't regret the act of going off to war. Not the days he'd spent fighting, nor even how it had brought about food shortages in his homeland.

However, he felt that if he had to apologize to anyone for one thing involving his complicity in the war, it was for crushing the children's futures, regardless of ethnicity or race.

But Lila's eyes held no accusation toward anyone.

She hadn't tried to preach any worldview like a proselytizer.

It touched somewhere deep inside him.

In a certain way, he felt burdened by a load heavier than shame.

She wouldn't allow him to run away or even die. She simply wanted him to rebuild society as a human being. Or at least that was what her eyes seemed to say.

Jörg's corpus waited patiently for Fritz to recover. Everyone who went to fight shared the same feelings of failure and futility. A tiny trigger had caused that man—a man who tried to preserve his mind by drawing—to lose all control of himself. That itself was nothing to be ashamed of.

Protests still happened occasionally in Berlin, and Jörg's corpus would join them. The socialists were fully committed, and when he heard their speeches at the gatherings and helped with the protests, he truly believed they could change the country—but he sensed a grim social trend spreading throughout society.

It had the air of a losing battle. He was overcome with a concrete sensation of imminent danger, though he could not specify what.

During the January protest, Jörg's corpus felt a new ominousness in the air. He could clearly feel the darkness surrounding the returned soldiers in the Freikorps because he had been a soldier once, too.

The Freikorps' mentality differed radically from that of the riot police or the officers and guards. They acted on base hatred. While such intensity made sense on the battlefield, releasing it in everyday life was equivalent to setting off a bomb in the city. Such a thing should never happen because it harms everyone. However, they didn't even try to hide their anger. They wouldn't refrain from taking it out on anyone they viewed as an enemy. Even if they directed their malice toward only specific individuals at first, at some point they would bear their fangs at everyone.

Liebknecht and Luxemburg were murdered on the fifteenth, and the news of their arrest flashed across all of Berlin. Jörg's corpus searched his apartment and ordered Fritz to go back to his town.

Seeing his friend in such an unusual state seemed to bring Fritz back to reality, because he somberly asked, "What's happened?"

"The Freikorps have started an open hunt for socialists. They killed

Liebknecht and Luxemburg and have begun arresting members of the Spartacus League."

"So now the German government has ordered them to get rid of socialists?"

"I hate to say, but the German revolution is over. You need to leave."

"You aren't coming with me?"

"There are still some people I want to check on. I'll leave as soon as I know they're safe. Write me once things have settled down. I'll write, too."

"It'll be dangerous by yourself. We should go together."

"I could have a tail already. And two people would stand out more."

"You don't need to worry about others when your life is in danger."

"Exactly. I agree. But several of my comrades came back from the front with injuries that make it hard for them to get around. They might be too slow to get away on their own. I want to help them while there's still time."

"Why do you have to do all that? They'll find their own way out. You might just end up getting in the way."

Jörg's corpus looked over to the table. The flower Lila had given him still bloomed fully. It was a strange flower. It was real, but it never seemed to wilt.

"I feel that way every time I think of the girl who gave me that flower," he continued forlornly. "We were just pawns to be used and discarded in the war. The lowest-ranking soldiers in every country were all like that. We only fought because we didn't want to die, but now that we're home we don't need to live that way."

Thinking of his other self, the person who had taught him that, made him sentimental. He had rejected that idea fiercely then. Because that was all he could do at the time. But the beauty of this flower caused those words to seep deep into his soul.

He continued. "If I leave the city now without doing anything, then I wouldn't feel like a human being anymore. Regardless of what I did on the battlefield, I don't want to throw away my pride at being human. Abandoning my comrades because I'm scared of the Freikorps makes me nothing but a coward. So I have to do what I can to help them, and when I'm satisfied, I'll leave straightaway."

Fritz gripped his hand. "No. If that's how you feel, then I really can't leave you here."

"It'll be okay. And don't worry about me. I'll be fine."

"But—"

Just then, a voice spoke up in the room as though to cut in on their conversation. "Excuse me for interrupting."

The two men turned toward the voice and saw the monster Jörg standing there…dressed in a long cape like Count Silvestri. Today he was showing himself to Fritz, who looked back and forth comparing the two. Fritz let out a wild yelp, sounding like a dog that had been rudely woken up from where it napped beneath a ray of sunlight.

Jörg's corpus set a hand on Fritz's shoulder and spoke slowly. "Calm down. There's nothing to be scared of. He's another me."

"I didn't know you had a twin brother."

"I don't. He's half of my soul. The human called Jörg Huber is the combination of me and this guy. We exist apart from each other and have our own distinct personalities."

"I don't understand this at all."

"Don't think too hard about it and just think of this guy as another me. He has the same name. You don't have to try to differentiate between us."

He turned back to Jörg and asked, "Why are you here?"

Jörg said, "If you have the time to argue, then come with me. I'll take you out of here so you can escape to another country. We'll need to make a stop at a certain inn on the way, though."

"What are you after?"

"I can't leave my corpus to face danger, can I? I've seen the cruelty of the Freikorps with my own eyes. You could never face such mania head-on. You're better off fleeing to a safer country. Fritz, you can make a name for yourself in the art world in a country with freedom. You'll be a big success."

Jörg then turned to his corpus and winked through a smile.

"You could be a stylist in the fashion world or for movies. If such glamorous work isn't for you, then why not own your own chic hair salon? Live a carefree life doing what you want."

"You don't get to decide our lives for us."

"Germany lost the war and still chose violence. It's going to continue to be savage. Once they're done hunting the socialists, they'll find other targets soon enough. Any society that learns to eliminate outsiders with force is destined to use violence to crush its own people. There's no point in staying in a country like that. You were probably just thinking about going somewhere else inside Germany, but going abroad is the better option."

"Can you guarantee that wherever you take us to will always be just and peaceful?"

"Has a country like that ever existed? At the moment, however, there are plenty of places better than Germany."

Jörg pointed at the door. A strange design covered the door panel. Countless geometric shapes, lines, and letters filled a circle.

"If you're worried about your friends, I can go speak with them. But first I'd like you two to go through this door."

"I sincerely appreciate your kindness." Fritz eyed Jörg dubiously. "But nothing in life comes free."

"I want one of your paintings when you become a successful artist. Once I find a painting of yours that I like, then you give it to me for free."

"Deal. I'll tell the people I work with that if a man named Jörg Huber ever shows up at the gallery, I promised him that he could have one painting of his choosing for free. It will be effective even after my death."

"Wonderful. I look forward to the day."

Jörg opened the door to reveal not the hallway of the apartment building, but a pitch-black expanse. The sight of it alone terrified Fritz. "I don't know about this. I have to get a lot of things from my house, and I need to tell my family where I'm going."

"As I said, we'll be stopping by an inn first. Feel free to use it as a base until you decide your final destination."

"But—"

Jörg's corpus pulled Fritz forward by the arms. "It's pointless worrying about what's on the other side. Let's just jump on through."

And the two men plunged into a darkness that might contain even the slightest bit of hope.

June 28, 1919. The armistice signed between Germany and the Allied powers at the Palace of Versailles in France placed excessively harsh conditions on the unstable postwar Germany, even receiving some international criticism. Notably, payment of reparations placed Germany in an excruciating position.

However, the more hardline factions within the Allied nations considered the restrictions lenient.

In January 1923, France's president, Alexandre Millerand, accused a workforce-strapped Germany of failing to meet the terms of the treaty because it did not supply enough coal and so, along with Belgium, invaded and occupied the Ruhr region. Instead of dispiriting the Germans, this event fueled a surge of nationalistic honor inside Germany.

Six years later, amid a period of unprecedented economic instability at the start of the global depression, the German people voiced fierce opposition and resistance to the content of the Treaty of Versailles. Moving to utilize all the boiling anger, Hitler and the National Socialist German Workers' Party—the Nazi Party—slowly grew in power, creating slogans about restoring pride in the fatherland to agitate the people into abandoning the treaty and restoring their economy. The majority of the German people welcomed their rise. The social forces capable of halting their impact had mostly been eliminated from within Germany since the end of the Great War.

As soon as one war ends, the next one begins.

September 1, 1939. Nazi Germany invaded Poland, with the Soviet Union invading sixteen days later on the seventeenth.

The two countries divided Poland and occupied their respective territories.

Lila's homeland had yet again lost its peace and freedom.

And then, May 10, 1940.

Just like in the Great War, Nazi Germany invaded Belgium.

On the afternoon of the sixteenth, the German Army left the town of Leuven intact and shelled just the university library, which had been restored following its destruction in the previous war. On the morning of the seventeenth, German bombers dropped explosives on the southern side of the library. It burned for two straight days, tumbling to ruin just as it had during the 1914 invasion.

The root of this second tragedy was the outcome of one misunderstanding.

After the Great War, Germany paid reparations to completely restore the library it had burned in the last invasion—both the building and the collection. However, part of its construction included plans for a monument in front of the new building—one seemingly designed to trample on Germany and Belgium's efforts and struggles to restore their relationship. On it, the American architect and designer of the new library, a Francophile named Whitney Warren, proposed the following inscription:

Furore Teutonico Diruta, Dono Americano Restituta (Destroyed by German fury, rebuilt by American donations)

The dean of Leuven University deemed this inscription inappropriate for congenial postwar relations between Belgium and Germany and refused to allow it. However, Warren opposed the dean and repeatedly protested, and this commotion reached German ears. Warren's proposal was ultimately rejected, and though Warren capitulated, the monument was approved for use in a war memorial in Dinant recognizing the large number of Belgians who had lost their lives in the 1914 German invasion.

Three years earlier, at the war memorial's inauguration ceremony, the German government learned of the inscription and sent a message to the Ministry of Foreign Affairs denouncing it as slander against the German Army and demanding it be removed. The German Army later reduced the monument to rubble when they invaded Belgium again in 1940.

However, some of the German soldiers marching on Leuven mistakenly believed that the inscription was engraved on the library as originally planned and not at Dinant, so they destroyed the library.

And like an act of hatred calling for another, or a monster whispering lies into a soldier's ears with a wicked smile, the tragedy of more than twenty years ago repeated itself. The library restored through hard and earnest work was once again burned to ashes by the German Army.

The German soldiers were watching the Leuven library burn before their very eyes, feeling as if a burden was being lifted from their souls, when a sudden scream rang out from overhead that made them freeze.

A giant black shape appeared in one corner of the gray sky. A monster with wings like a dragon or bat emitted an angry shriek that sounded like metal rubbing against metal. The monster flew in circles over the soldiers' heads, looking upset enough to attack at any moment. They covered their ears as they crouched low, shivering, and for a long time the creature seemed uninterested in flying away.

Between the sharp, ear-shattering screams, some soldiers clearly heard a person speaking.

"Those who know no justice or have no knowledge shall be forever cursed."

The shape finally disappeared off into the distance.

Yet the soldiers lay trembling on the ground.

The entire experience was altogether too bizarre, so the German Army service record for that day contains not a single mention of this strange event.

5

In the courtyard of Xandra's inn, the rays of a spring sun shone down through the December day as lilacs bloomed fully. A vibrant green carpeted the ground, while butterflies and honeybees danced around the flowers.

The Count watched this scene from his window before turning back to his room, sitting in a chair by the fireplace, and leaning into the backrest. The courtyard stayed in constant spring and his room was warm, while a bitter cold assaulted the area around the inn.

Nazi Germany's invasion of Poland catalyzed the start of Europe's second great war, which was really a continuation of the previous one. Those last twenty years had been nothing more than a long respite from the fighting.

Milos still fought in Eastern Europe. In 1918, at the end of Europe's Great War, Serbia, Croatia, and Slovenia came together to form the Kingdom of Yugoslavia. But in April 1941, Nazi Germany and its allies invaded. The kingdom was again divided into occupied territories, with one region controlled by the Independent State of Croatia, which was a puppet state of Germany and Italy; one region controlled by Italy; one region controlled by the Kingdom of Hungary; and one region controlled by the Kingdom of Bulgaria. The sundered region of the kingdom once called Serbia fell under the control of Nazi Germany. Milos yet again began fighting Germans to win back his homeland. He seemed destined to never stop fighting. Who knew if that day would ever come.

Someone rapped on the door, and Xandra entered. She looked worked half to death.

Recently, people had been fleeing here in numbers that put the last war to shame. Xandra had her hands full dealing with it all. The majority of arrivals were refugees. Anyone looking at their shattered expressions and the fear on their faces from the massacres and persecution would understand the horrors going on in the larger world without ever setting foot outside, grumbled Xandra.

The door inside the inn that Jörg had used to let his corpus and his friend flee overseas remained. The refugees flocked to the inn to use it.

Jörg still acted as Lila's bodyguard while running his trade business—having hired Diana and the other working women right away, as promised—involving himself even further with humans. He told anyone looking to flee Europe about the door and led them to it.

People leaped through portals to the inn and then traveled to their land of refuge. He only told them about the door and left the rest to them. So while Xandra managed the traffic, she did no more beyond selling healing elixirs to those who wanted them. The refugees who visited the inn could finally relax. They thanked Xandra profusely and passed through a new door filled with hope, even though they could imagine the hardships that waited for them at the destination.

For the Count, the whole thing resembled scenery viewed from a moving train. It meant little to him, and he stayed out of it. He paid attention to only one thing: Lila.

As Xandra threw herself into a chair looking as if she'd finally found a moment to rest, the Count muttered, "Lila hasn't come back. And it's been a while since the Nazis took over Poland."

"This is precisely when Jörg will be protecting her," Xandra continued. "No one is as upset and troubled by Germany's invasion of Poland as he is. I'm sure he and Lila are working tirelessly to liberate Poland. Lila's a grown-up now, so she must be connected with some very devoted people."

"I wonder if she ever became a teacher. Or do you think she's doing something else?"

"Knowing her, whatever she's doing, she's giving it her all. She speaks up if something bothers her, and she's all smiles when she's enjoying herself, all while sharing good meals with people from other countries."

"And Nazis despise people like that."

Xandra leaned back in her chair with a smile. "If you're so worried, why not go to Poland and check up on her?"

"It's not that I haven't considered it."

"We could always make some more people like us. Like Nil said, you can make a kingdom of the undead to oppose humanity."

"A wretched idea. And far too complicated."

"Then trust in Jörg and Lila and wait."

The Count stared intently at the fire burning in the fireplace. "...Honestly, I'd be lying to say I never considered that. If every human became immortal, then the reasons behind all this senseless killing and war would disappear completely. Murder and war lose all meaning in a world where no one ever dies. But humans are mysterious creatures. If they became immortal, then they might become more malicious than real monsters now. So I have to be careful about what I do."

"What a pain to consider."

"Indeed."

The Count looked away from the flames and back to Xandra. "What do you imagine Nil is up to?"

"It's a good era for him. He's most certainly enjoying the nothing that this world keeps creating. He must be gallivanting around, enjoying good food and cigars with foolish government officials, idiotic generals, and people who happily keep creating new weapons, all while walking hand in hand with Death."

"...If so, then I'll have to face him someday." The Count stood from his chair. "It's a shame that I must, but it's my duty."

6

Unofficial rumors of a strange figure flying over the Leuven library spread through the home front. They reached the ears of Fritz Ziegel in the USA through his friend in Germany.

Fritz was working at ports and in factories but continued drawing. Feeling that the strange figure of Leuven was the same thing he saw during the Great War, he picked up his colored pencils and began drawing in his Brooklyn apartment, adding in some essential elements.

He hadn't drawn a monster for a long time. Remembering the days on the front lines when he would draw frantically whenever he had the chance, Fritz ran his pen across the paper as if something compelled him.

Soldiers with hollow eyes huddled low in trenches. A black creature dancing in the gray sky. Burning structures bent and twisted and the forms of people covering their eyes as they screamed. He called this collage-like drawing *The Razing of Freedom and Spirit*, signed his name, and dated it. It was the first of Fritz's drawings to incorporate both humans and monsters.

Had he stayed and created this drawing in Germany, it certainly would have elicited scorn and political consequences. The works of famous painters dealing with such topics were subjected to a variety of insults by Nazis supporters. They would say things like "It doesn't depict the bravery of our soldiers" or "It's too depressing" or "It doesn't convey the pride in being German."

Still a nameless artist in the USA, Fritz hid everything he'd created since the outbreak of the second great war in his closet.

The US joined Europe's second great war in 1941, and Fritz and Jörg spent every day on edge, since people viewed German Americans as potential enemies of the state.

Jörg was the one who had suggested Fritz keep his drawings in his closet. He was in the US, too, working as a barber, and stayed highly attuned to public sentiment. Works critical of war were becoming hard to display even in America right now. It was always that way during wartime. Criticizing war was simply not allowed. Even with pieces that had no ulterior motive, simply depicting war in a negative light was reason enough for the government to condemn the work as detrimental to public sentiment and for the masses to criticize the creators.

Jörg advised and supported Fritz, telling him that someday he would be able to paint freely and that he simply had to wait for the time when he could display his work publicly.

In September 1945, Europe's second great war came to a close with another German defeat. And so, this war came to be known as World War II, ending with an inconceivable twice as many military casualties as WWI and an estimated twenty-six to thirty-four million civilian casualties. For the missing, the total is still unknown. The evil within humans that people came to know during WWI evolved into a more terrible manifestation of cruelty and foolishness.

The works Fritz created during the war were extremely dark and raw, but after the war, one art dealer fascinated by the spark hiding within such darkness bought some and began advertising them with captivating descriptions. They stimulated the sensibilities of the younger generations and gained a sort of cult status among certain circles. Many people came to art galleries in large cities to see Fritz's paintings, which became quite popular, critiqued, and even complied into a book. Such fleeting popularity never lasts long, but his growing reputation allowed his work to reach the generation that needed to see it most.

1964, winter.

Manhattan, New York City.

Fritz's paintings were hanging in an art gallery on Houston Street, when a man walked in and stopped before a certain piece. He didn't move from that spot for quite some time, but he eventually called the gallery owner over and said that he wanted this painting.

The owner was overjoyed and immediately ordered his assistant to pack the painting up. This picture had been hanging for a long while, and while many people admired it, this man was the first person to ever express a desire to own it.

The man asked the owner if the artist was still alive. When the owner respectfully inquired whether the man knew the artist, he replied that his name was Jörg Huber.

The owner stood in disbelief and looked at the man again. "I didn't think the day would come when I would actually meet the man called Jörg Huber. While he was still alive, Mr. Ziegel said that if a man of that name ever said he wanted a painting, to let him have just one for free. To tell the truth, Mr. Ziegel had a dear friend named Jörg Huber. Unfortunately, Mr. Huber passed away just recently. What a strange coincidence that a man with that exact name would appear directly after."

"Where and how did this Mr. Huber die?"

"He succumbed to old age, sleeping in his bed at home. Apparently, it was a peaceful death. Mr. Ziegel left us right at the end of last year.

Their families gave them proper burials. I had the pleasure of knowing both men for almost a decade, and they were always gentlemen. Their company was always a gift."

The man named Jörg solemnly closed his eyes for a moment, then quickly composed himself. "Did Mr. Ziegel create many paintings?"

"He didn't make many tableaux, but he left a lot of pen drawings. His drawings of monsters were used for things like the covers of horror novels. Honestly, his popularity derived from the cult following arising from those. I'm sure the government would have made life dangerous for him had he remained in Germany. I'm so glad he found his way to America before the war started."

"I actually know the place this drawing was based off."

"Really? Just from the scenery?"

"It's from the trenches in Champagne. I remember it well," Jörg said, tenderly stroking the frame. "How are things these days?"

"Well, African Americans have been fighting for their civil rights, and that movement seems to be in its final stages. Socialist revolutions are active in Central and South America, and the fighting in Vietnam doesn't seem likely to settle soon. Every country has spilled their fair share of blood. It would be wonderful to find a proper end to it all, but, well, that seems unlikely. I really don't know how important any of the movements actually are, but the people involved must have their reasons if they're willing to risk their lives. There are people in every age who must act against injustice, even when they know the government will massacre them."

A wry smile rose on Jörg's face as he asked, "And when you were young, did you fight anywhere?"

The owner shook his head no. The answer made it difficult to tell if he meant that he hadn't or that he wouldn't talk about it.

Jörg thanked the gallery owner and accepted his picture. He tucked it under an arm as if he were hugging an old friend or comforting the corpse of a soldier who had endured the same hardships as him—then left the gallery.

Walking east away from the store, he stopped in surprise, seeing a familiar figure at the intersection on Chrystie Street. The Count. They hadn't seen each other in decades.

The man in the long black cloak hadn't changed in the least. But today he wore a thin bal-collar overcoat well suited for New York City. He wore a black jacket with black slacks beneath it, complemented by a white shirt and crimson tie that gave him an elegant and composed air.

As he approached, the Count suddenly asked, "Did you find the picture you wanted?" It was as if he already knew why Jörg had come to New York City. Like always, he was quick to see how the future would unfold.

"Yes," Jörg answered. "Since we're both here, how about we have a coffee in that café over there?"

"Sounds wonderful."

Upon entering the café, the Count grimaced at the bright light pouring in through the large windows.

"Would you prefer somewhere less bright?"

"Does the light not bother you?"

"Sunlight doesn't trouble me yet. But in a couple hundred more years it might. Let's go to the back."

"I'd appreciate it."

They ordered coffees from the waiter, and before their drinks arrived, Jörg opened the package and showed the Count the picture.

The Count admired it, adding, "*The Razing of Freedom and Spirit*?"

"That's right."

"Are you sure it's appropriate that you own it? Don't you think something like this should be out in human society? It looks like the war in Vietnam won't end anytime soon but will continue to wreak its horrors."

"This is archived in a famous art book. And the artists who saw it when they were young started to create paintings with similar themes in their own unique styles. The value of this image will carry on into the next generation. So I figured it was time that I acquired it."

"I see."

"I'll take good care of it." Jörg ran a loving finger over the picture. "It will always remind me of someone I'll never meet again."

The Count sipped his coffee and continued. "How is Lila—sorry, Angelika?"

"She's already in her late fifties, but as tough and spritely as ever."

"How did she do during the war?"

"She resisted society in her way. With her personality, she was never going to suffer in silence."

"She joined the resistance against Germany?"

"Yes. Too many times what she did made me break into a cold sweat. I helped a little, too."

"She even survived the Warsaw Uprising. It wasn't just soldiers; a lot of civilians were executed then, too."

"True. At the time I couldn't say anything to her, having been born and raised in Germany. For a long time I felt like I couldn't show myself in front of her. I thought about turning myself invisible to protect her that way, but she wouldn't have it. She told me that was the worst way possible to avoid issues and that I shouldn't look away from reality, regardless of whether I was directly involved or not. Because what happened there could happen anywhere in the world."

"That sounds like something she would say."

"It really does. She always called me her friend and said that people and nations are different."

"I see..."

"She finally let me conceal myself once she got married. I couldn't be around her all the time with a husband in the house."

"That was a good idea. Bodyguards should stay hidden."

Jörg smiled. "Back then, Xandra's inn was a kind of safehouse to Lila. That place let her rest her soul, and it's the reason why she was able to go back to the human world. Fritz was saved through his art, while Lila was saved through her life at the inn. It was the same for me. With a place that provides sanctuary and rest, people can someday return to the real world. But when Lila returned to human society, she felt frustrated right from the start."

"How do you mean, frustrated?"

"Without a simulacrum, she couldn't move around instantly, and everything took a lot of time. She would often complain that her body felt heavy. But that heaviness was also a kind of proof that she was human, so it made her happy, too."

Jörg's gaze flickered through the window to the bright world outside, then continued.

"And in a couple of decades Lila is going to be called peacefully up to heaven. That's so soon. And with that, my job as her bodyguard will also end."

"What's she doing now?"

"She was a teacher during the war, but now she's working as an editor at a children's book publisher. The libraries in Warsaw have a lot of books she edited. She even got her pilot's license. She can probably fly better than I can now."

"What do you plan on doing once she has passed? That's actually why I'm here."

"Are you going to ask me to come back to Xandra's inn?"

"If you'd like."

"I can't go back there."

"Why not?"

"There are still things I want to do."

"Like what?"

"Lila once told me, 'The winds of war don't distinguish between adults and children. They turn everyone into monsters.' And she's right. It can happen easily at any time in human society. So I want to be someone who intervenes to stop that. I want to point out the narrow-mindedness of foolish societies and move people out of the path of those horrible winds. Only a monster can do that, right? Only someone who will live until the end of time."

"That's not a monster's responsibility. That's a fantasy."

"What are monsters but a fantasy? It's just like books and fairy tales. At least from the perspective of those who stay near people."

"But humans will at some point cause their own extinction. It's practically fated. Their meaningless existence is beyond saving. And only a fool would spend their time on something like that."

"I have nothing but time. I'm not going to rush anything; kind of like solving a difficult puzzle."

The Count looked seriously at Jörg. "If that's your ultimate answer to the ancient blood you inherited, it's a sad way to live."

"I'm enjoying myself, so don't worry about me. I think it's a passion-filled life worthy of this ancient blood."

The Count said nothing for a while. He looked as if he was trying to remember the most important word in the world and had grown frustrated at his failure. But he eventually said nothing more than "We should get going" and stood up from his chair.

The two walked away from the table and left the café. The Count said, "Feel free to contact me about anything. You're welcome at the inn anytime."

"Thank you. I appreciate that."

"And the door for refugees. Would you like us to keep it?"

"Please. I have a feeling the world will still need it for a while."

"Understood."

The Count waved and turned, spreading out his wings like a giant dragon or bat, and soared off into the sky. The mass of people crossing the busy Manhattan streets didn't see him. Only Jörg saw him fly away.

Jörg squinted, eyes still on the sky.

The Count flew as beautifully as ever. Strong enough to overcome anything.

The black figure soon melted into the gray clouds. The border between sky and ground was a place where neither God nor human would ever wander.

Jörg turned his gaze back to the ground.

He readjusted his hold on Fritz's drawing and briskly stepped forward, toward the future and its infinite possibilities.

Postscript

Lila and the Winds of War is a fantasy novel featuring monsters, and a work of fiction. Characters, groups, places, and other story elements are in no way related to any real-life counterparts.

The sections depicting historical events were written based on a large number of research materials; however, this work is not intended to serve as a textbook or thesis and includes scenes in which fictional or unbelievable plot developments occur to align with the plot.

Documents pertaining to WWI can be found in Japanese, English, German, French, and a wide variety of other languages. Countries outside of Japan are particularly rich sources of information, with many pictures and videos on the subject. The following page lists some of the sources I used. If this book interests you enough to go and read about the historical facts, then that would make me incredibly happy, for there is no greater joy for an author.

Any errors are the sole responsibility of the author, Sayuri Ueda, not the result of any of the authors of the works cited. Additionally, any words or phrases that may be considered improper or unsuitable regarding human rights from a modern perspective are intended to reflect the historical setting and are used as they would have been at the time.

List of Primary Sources

Yamanoue, Shotaro. *World War I: The Forgotten Battles*. Kodansha Gakujutsu Bunko, 2010.

Willmott, H. P. *World War I.* Edited by Makoto Iokibe and Haruo Tohmatsu. Translated by Masahiro Yamazaki. Sogensha, 2014.

Miyake, Tatsuru. "World War I in Diary Entries from a Catholic Farming Village in Bayern." *Memoirs of the Institute of Humanities Meiji University*, no. 63 (2008): 185–229. https://m-repo.lib.meiji.ac.jp/dspace/bitstream/10291/11963/1/jinbunkagakukiyo_63_185.pdf.

Miyake, Tatsuru. "Village Priests in World War I: A Chronicle (1917–1918) Catholic Village Society in the Franconian Region of the Kingdom of Bavaria." *Sundai Historical Association*, no. 133 (2008): 91–124. https://m-repo.lib.meiji.ac.jp/dspace/bitstream/10291/12859/1/sundaishigaku_133_91.pdf.

Lecture Series: Thinking About World War I[1]

Fujihara, Tatsushi. *The Turnip Winter: Starvation and the People in World War I Germany*. Jimbun Shoin, 2011.

Ootsuru, Atsushi. *Prisoners of War: Working in the Gap Between World War I and All-Out War*. Jimbun Shoin, 2013.

1 This series has 12 volumes in all, and those not included here were also very informative.

Koumoto, Mari. *Conflicting Forms: Art and World War I*. Jimbun Shoin, 2013.

Hayashida, Toshiko. *Fighting and Non-Fighting Women: Gender and Sexuality in World War I*. Jimbun Shoin, 2013.

Koseki, Takashi. *Conscription and Conscientious Objection: Great Britain's Experiences in World War I*. Jimbun Shoin, 2010.

World War I: Modern Perspectives (4 volumes)

Fujihara, Tatsushi, Takashi Koseki, Akeo Okada, and Shinichi Yamamuro, eds. *Vol. 1: World War*. Iwanami Shoten, 2014

Fujihara, Tatsushi, Takashi Koseki, Akeo Okada, and Shinichi Yamamuro, eds. *Vol. 2: All-Out War*. Iwanami Shoten, 2014

Fujihara, Tatsushi, Takashi Koseki, Akeo Okada, and Shinichi Yamamuro, eds. *Vol. 3: Psychological Transformations*. Iwanami Shoten, 2014.

Fujihara, Tatsushi, Takashi Koseki, Akeo Okada, and Shinichi Yamamuro, eds. *Vol. 4: Legacy*. Iwanami Shoten, 2014.

Becker, Jean-Jacques, and Gerd Krumeich. *La Grande Guerre: Une histoire franco-allemande*. Translated by Hisaki Kenmochi and Akiyoshi Nishiyama. Iwanami Shoten, 2012.

Hoshikawa, Takeshi, ed. *Illustrated Explanation of the Strategies, Tactics, and Weaponry of World War I*. 2 vols. Gakken Visual History Series. Gakken, 2008.

Shiraishi, Hikaru. *Visual Encyclopedia of Small Firearms Used in World War I, 1914–1918*. Ikaros Publications, 2017.

Chamberlain, Peter and Chris Ellis. *Tanks of the World: 1915–1945*. Edited by Artbox. Dainippon Kaiga, 1996.

Saiki, Nobuo. *The History of German Tank Development*. Kojinsha, 1999.

Walther, Peter. *The First World War in Colour*. Taschen, 2014.

Richter, Oliver. and Jochen Vollert. *Grabenkrieg: German Trench Warfare*. (2 volumes). Tankograd Publishing, 2012.

Richter, Oliver. and Jochen Vollert. *Sturmtruppen: The Kaiser's Elite Stormtroopers*. Tankograd Publishing, 2010.

Miyake, Tatsuru. *The German Navy's Sweltering Summer: Seamen and Naval Officers in 1917*. Yamakawa Shuppansha, 2001.

Mino, Masahiro. and Masao Koshimizu. *The Deadly Struggle for the Sea: A History of Naval Battles in World War I*. Shinkigensha, 2001.

Ikeda, Norizane. *A Military History of Propaganda*. Chuokoron-Shinsha, 2015.

Jeffery, Keith. *MI6: The History of the Secret Intelligence Service, 1909--1949*. (2 volumes). Translated by Shouko Takayama. Chikumashobo, 2013.

Schivelbusch, Wolfgang. *Die Bibliothek von Löwen. Eine Episode aus der Zeit der Weltkriege.*[2] Translated by Yoshinori Fukumoto. Hosei University Press, 1992.

Shiba, Nobuhiro. *An Illustrated History of the Balkans*. Kawade Shobo Shinsha, 2015.

MacKenzie, David. *Apis, the Congenial Conspirator: The Life of Colonel Dragutin T. Dimitrijević*. Translated by Nobuhiro Shiba, Shingo Minamizuka, Isao Koshimura, and Masako Nagaba. Heibonsha, 1992.

Takahashi, Yasuyuki. *The Greek Orthodox Church*. Kodansha Gakujutsu Bunko, 1980.

Castellan, Georges. *Storia dei Balcani*. Translated by Tadashi Hagiwara. Que sais-je? Bunko. Hakusuisha, 1993.

Stoicescu, Nicolae. *Vlad Țepeș, Prince of Walachia*. Translated by Shirou Suzuki and Manabu Suzuki. Chuokoron-Shinsha, 1988.

Bandou, Hiroshi. *Polish People and Europe During the 19th and 20th Centuries*. Aoki Shoten, 1996.

Frölich, Paul. *Rosa Luxemburg*. Translated by Narihiko Itou. Ochanomizu Shobo, 1998.

Kautsky, Luise, ed. *Rosa Luxemburg Letters*. Translated by Hiroshi Kawaguchi and Keiko Matsui. Iwanami Shoten, 1932.

Onozuka, Tomoji, ed. *Reexamining the Causes of World War I: International Labor Allocation and Crowd Mentality*. Iwanami Shoten, 2014.

Kodama, Kazuko. *Florence Nightingale*. Shimizu Shoin, 2015.

Araki, Eiko. *Reevaluating World War I from the Perspective of Florence Nightingale's Descendants—Nurses*. Iwanami Shoten, 2014.

Tokunaga, Satoshi. "Florence Nightengale and the Establishment of Modern Nursing: The Inherent Contradictions Between Science and Christian Beliefs." *Bulletin of Japanese Red Cross Kyushu International College of Nursing*, no. 12 (2013). https://jrckicn.repo.nii.ac.jp/?action

2 Löwen and Leuven refer to the same city. I used Leuven in this book.

=pages_view_main&active_action=repository_view_main_item_detail&item_id=310&item_no=1&page_id=13&block_id=17.

Boudard, Alphonse. *L'Âge d'or des maisons closes*. Translated by Harumi Yoshida. Kawade Shobo Shinsha, 1993.

Kashima, Shigeru. *The Brothels of Paris: Maisons Closes*. Kadokawa Sofia Bunko, 2013.

Kashima, Shigeru. *The Brothels of Paris: Champs-Élysées*. Kadokawa Sofia Bunko, 2013.

Hisako, Kuroiwa. *Carrier Pigeons: Another Form of Information Technology*. Bungeishunju, 2000.

Yoshida, Kazuaki. *War and Carrier Pigeons: 1870–1945*. Shakai Hyoron Sha, 2011.

Monestier, Martin. *Les animaux-soldats: Hhistoire militaire des animaux des origines àa nos jours*. Translated by Harumi Yoshida and Teruko Hanawa. Harashobo, 1998.

Fukui, Norihiko. *Belle Époque Culture at the End of the Century*. Yamakawa Shuppansha, 1999.

Miyago, Toshio, ed. supervisor. *Fashion in 1900s Paris: Department Store Catalogs During the Belle Époque*. Art Digest, 2007.

The poem that appears in the story is an excerpt from the Bhagavad Gita recorded in *The Complete Works of Hermann Hesse: Volume 16, Complete Collection of Poetry*. Edited and translated by Hermann Hesse-Freundeskreis / Forschungsgruppe Japan. Rinsen Book Co., 2007.

Analysis

Hiroko Ooya (Literary Critic)

When an author is deciding what to write and what they want to convey, they sometimes choose a genre completely at odds with their theme. Like using a murder mystery to depict human affection, for example, or when authors address modern social issues through the lens of historical fiction. These approaches are not particularly rare.

For this reason, Sayuri Ueda chose to merge these two seemingly incompatible ideas—fantasy and extremely realistic descriptions of war. Naturally, she chose fantasy for a reason.

But what were her reasons? That's what I'd like to unravel by following the story.

The setting is Europe in the midst of World War I. During that long period of seemingly endless fighting, an explosion erupts near a young German soldier named Jörg in Champagne on the Western Front. He thinks he's about to die when a mysterious man saves him.

Wearing a stylish cape that is wholly out of place in a war zone, this refined gentleman is well-dressed, calm, and dignified. The next time Jörg opens his eyes, he finds himself in a clean, comfortable inn, where the man—Count George Silvestri—tells him a shocking story.

Jörg learns that the Count is a monster that has been alive for four hundred sixty years and that he has brought only half of Jörg's soul to this inn. The Jörg there now is in a simulacrum the Count created, while his corpus and the other half of his soul are still in the trenches of Champagne. The two bodies share memories through their dreams. And now that Jörg is in a simulacrum, he can leap into the bodies of other people and travel anywhere in the world via a door with a pattern on it. The Count assigns Jörg in his simulacrum to protect a young girl named Lila.

Being thrust suddenly from realistic depictions of a battlefield to a fantasy world might confuse some readers, but this is where the first reason the author chose fantasy becomes apparent.

Why give Jörg half a soul? Jörg, who has grown sick of war, asks the Count to bring his corpus to the inn. But the Count refuses, saying, "Your corpus in Champagne worries more about what's going to happen to his fellow soldiers than his own safety, and he would never desert them."

Jörg's corpus has rid himself of the half of him that detests war and faces the fighting with new enthusiasm. He views the fight for his homeland in a fresh light. Fantasy enables the reader to briefly confront the complexities of the human mind.

The book depicts several aspects of humanity's multifaceted nature. Strength and weakness, truth and lies, compassion and selfishness. These forces intermingle to create human beings, and we learn how environments and experiences can easily alter that balance. The way the book depicts the differences between times of war and peace is particularly striking.

Just as there are many human emotions, there is more than one way to see the world. For example, Lila, the girl whom Jörg is tasked with protecting, treats him with a cold indifference due to her homeland of Poland having been invaded and destroyed by the Germans. Lila is referring to the Third Partition of Poland from over one hundred years earlier, and she doesn't care in the least that Jörg was in no way involved in the event. Had they met as simply two people, they might have been friends, but she holds the unreasonable belief that their histories and nationalities make them enemies.

War is a cruel, absurd environment that distorts reason and morals. People are robbed of their most basic human rights, their pride as human beings, and their perspectives of right and wrong. Those ideas aren't thrust upon people authoritatively by governments, but imprint themselves naturally among the citizens who don't doubt their truth. War turns people into monsters. Crossing borders in his simulacrum and observing Europe under the war, Jörg learns the truth of that—for both enemy and ally.

Here, we encounter the second reason for making this a work of fantasy. The reader witnesses various people with Jörg as he travels around Europe in his simulacrum: people starving on the home front; generals who see soldiers as nothing but disposable commodities; women crossing dangerous bridges to get food. He meets people in the socialist movement who seek revolution and an end to the war, as well as people who have found a purpose in life through the war. And among all these people, he discovers the earnestness of these souls hoping to find a shred of human decency.

Jörg thinks of any way that he can break through this mess and bring an end to the war—even if doing so requires that he abandon his life as a human and become a real monster.

Now we come to the third reason: why monsters exist in the novel. The Count, who has lived for over four hundred years, and all the immortal monsters that appear in the book, have all experienced war in the past. In fact, it may be more accurate to say that the experience of war is what made them monsters. Their motives differ, but otherwise they're the same as Jörg. That is to say, they serve as proof that humans have been waging an endless cycle of war for hundreds of years.

Readers know the harsh truth that World War I wasn't the first war, nor the last. As the reader comes to see the people's elation at the end of the war in 1918, they naturally feel pained, knowing that these same characters will get swept up in the next world war only twenty years later.

Why do humans keep fighting wars? Is there no way to stop it?

This is the final—and most important—point of the book as a work of fantasy.

There might not be any way to rid Earth of war. But within that reality, it might be possible for humans to retain their humanity. So long as we remember to act as humans, we can rise again after we're hurt. So then what is it that makes us hold on to our humanity?

This plea is hidden in the author's skillful depiction of monsters. When I reached the end of the book, I was shaking. The monsters in the book are a metaphor—although for what, it's not my place to say here. It's something that should be experienced while reading the book. Once you understand what those immortal monsters represent, Jörg running the length of Europe to save people and his actions imbuing Lila and a vast many others with hope will take on a new meaning. That's when you'll realize there's a monster beside you, too. Then you'll agree wholeheartedly with the reason this story used fantasy and what Sayuri Ueda wants to say.

This is a story of will.

A work that conveys why Sayuri Ueda chooses to write fiction.

This book serves as a strong testament to the idea that war is more cruelly real than any novel and conveys that reality precisely because it is a work of fiction. Certain truths can be told only through fiction. *That* is the power of story.